The Intrepid Miss LaRoque

Betty J. Vaughn

TotalRecall Publications, Inc.
1103 Middlecreek
Friendswood, Texas 77546
281-992-3131   281-482-5390 Fax
www.totalrecallpress.com

All rights reserved. Except as permitted under the United States Copyright Act of 1976, No part of this publication may be reproduced, stored in a retrieval system, or transmitted in any form or by any means electronic or mechanical or by photocopying, recording, or otherwise without prior permission of the publisher. Exclusive worldwide content publication / distribution by TotalRecall Publications, Inc.

Copyright © 2016 by: Betty J. Vaughn
All rights reserved

ISBN: 978-1-59095-710-3
UPC: 6-43977-26028-4

Library of Congress Control Number: 2016948017

Printed in the United States of America with simultaneous printings in Australia, Canada, and United Kingdom.

FIRST EDITION
1   2   3   4   5   6   7   8   9   10

This is a work of fiction. The characters, names, events, views, and subject matter of this book are either the author's imagination or are used fictitiously. Any similarity or resemblance to any real people, real situations or actual events is purely coincidental and not intended to portray any person, place, or event in a false, disparaging or negative light.

The scanning, uploading and distribution of this book via the Internet or via any other means without the permission of the publisher is illegal and punishable by law. Please purchase only authorized electronic editions, and do not participate in or encourage electronic piracy of copyrighted materials. Your support of the author's rights is appreciated.

With thanks to the people who continue to make my writing possible and my life rich: my daughter Joanna Meredith and her children, my sister Helen Brumbaugh who reads and offers critique, my uncle Dr. Lonnie Blizzard who provides me constant encouragement, and last but not least, Marty Atwater---a prince among men, and my love.

About the Book

With the war ending, Cissy LaRoque no longer needs to spy but that will not stop her from finding a new career where she can prove her worth beyond serving as some man's appendage. Provoked and titillated by a man she cannot have but craves, she puts aside romance and enters the world of business. Wildly successful, she is happy in what she has achieved and frustrated by what she has given up.

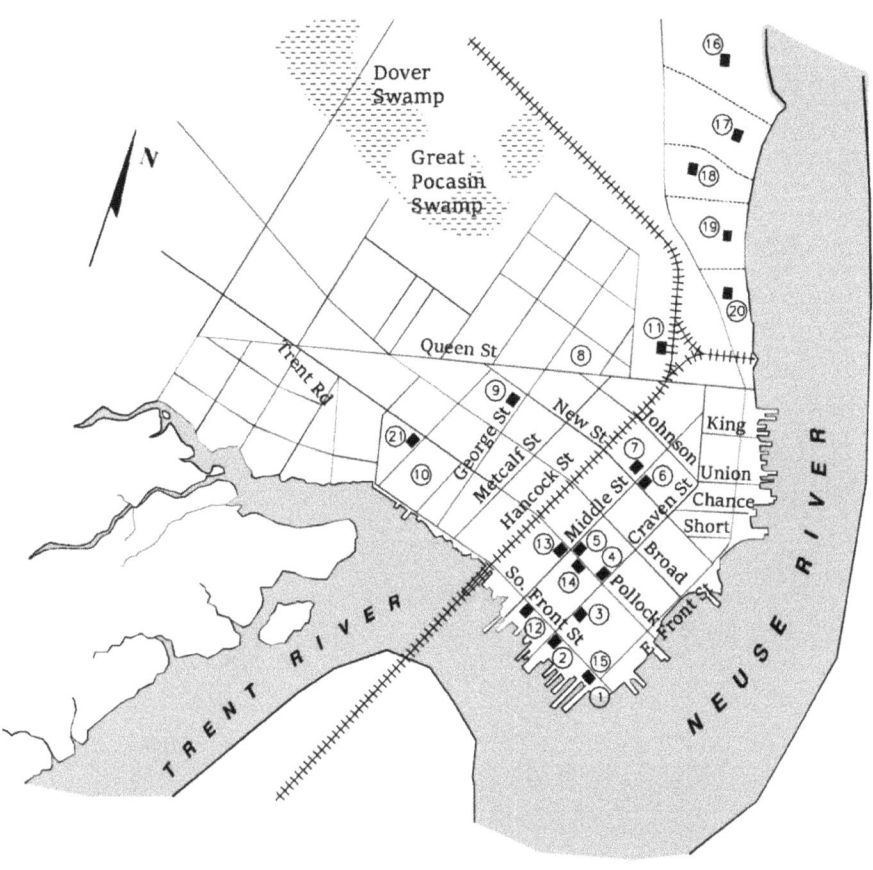

NEW BERNE, NC
1860's

LEGEND

① Union Point
② Harvey Mansion
③ Isaac Taylor House
④ City Hall/Post Office
⑤ Christ Episcopal Church
⑥ First Presbyterian Church
⑦ New Berne Academy
⑧ Cedar Grove Cemetary
⑨ John Wright Stanly House
⑩ Tryon Palace Grounds

⑪ Railroad Station
⑫ Gaston House Hotel
⑬ Ryan Madison's Office
⑭ John Harvey's Office
⑮ Laroque Office and Warehouses
⑯ Laroque House
⑰ Evangeline's House
⑱ Carline Framingham's House
⑲ Ryan Madison's House
⑳ Logan Gwaltney's House
㉑ Jones House (JAIL)

LENIOR COUNTY, NC
1860's

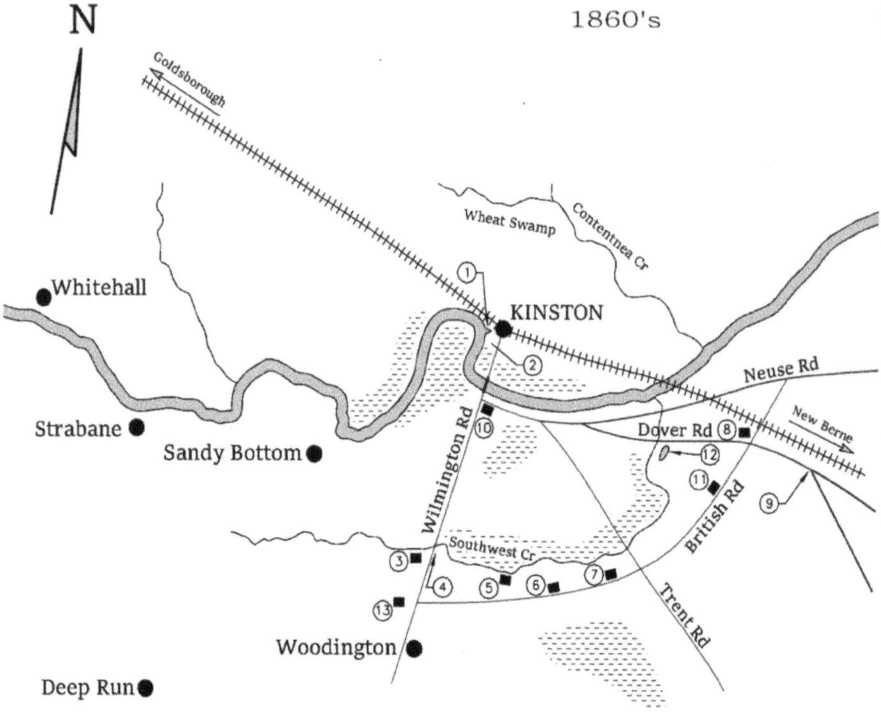

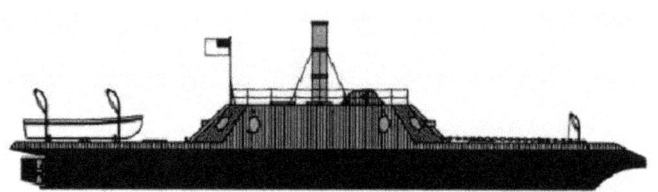

LEGEND

① Ram Neuse (Cat's Hole)
② Sugar Hill
③ Waller House
④ Battle at Southwest Creek
⑤ Penny's House
⑥ John Bartlett's House
⑦ Fitz Kennedy's House
⑧ Cobb House
⑨ Wise Fork
⑩ Harriett's Chapel (1st Battle of Kinston)
⑪ Noble's House
⑫ Mill Pond
⑬ Williams' House

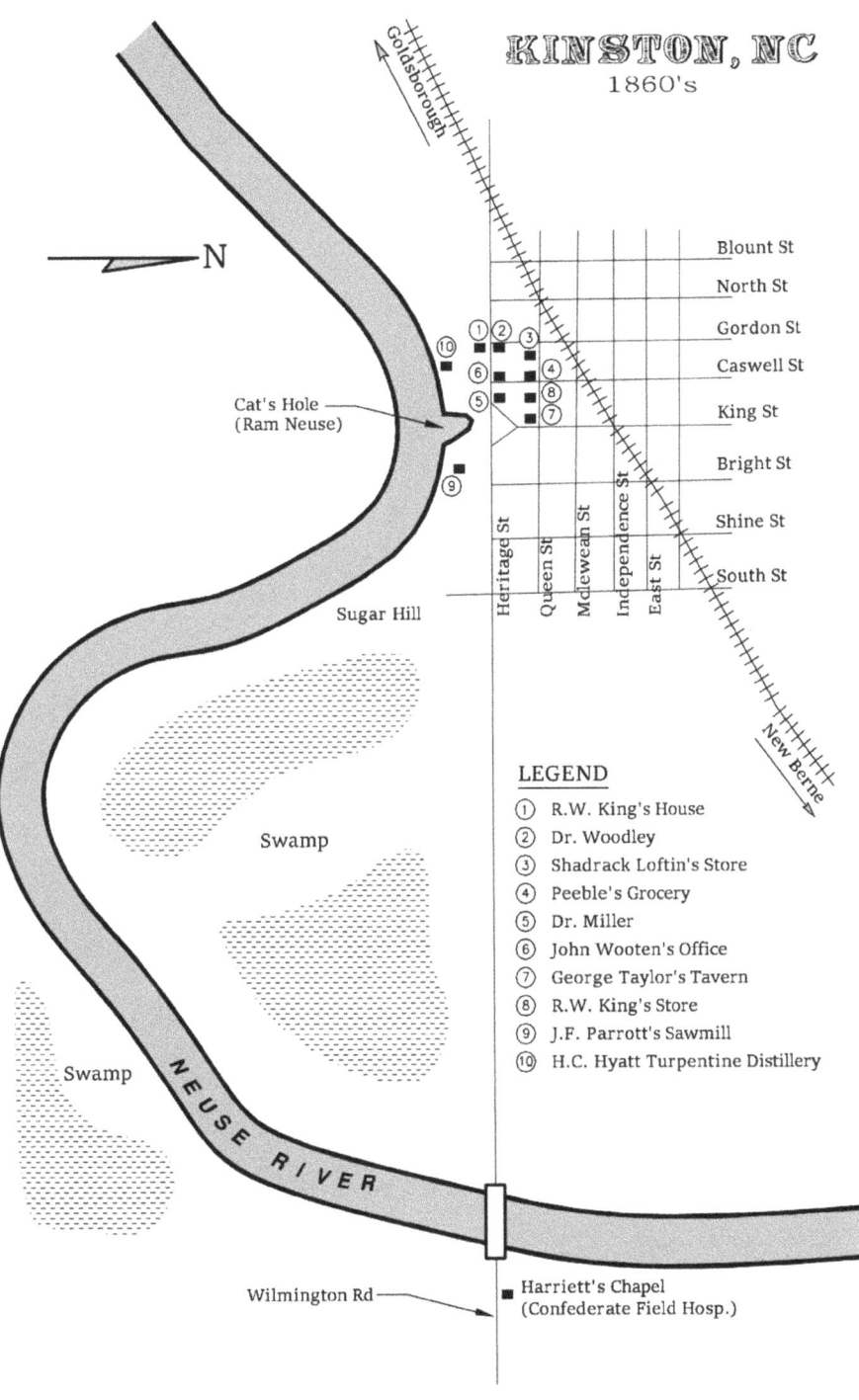

WILMINGTON, NC
1860's

LEGEND
1. Bellamy Mansion - Union headquarters
2. Wright House
3. St. James Episcopal Church
4. Laroque House
5. Laroque Office/Warehouse
6. Confederate Headquarters
7. Thalian Hall
8. Wilmington - Weldon RR
9. RR Depot
10. Jailhouse
11. Wilkins Drug Store
12. Dorsey's Tavern
13. Catholic Church
14. Seaman's Hospital
15. Dudley Mansion
16. Clarendon House Hotel

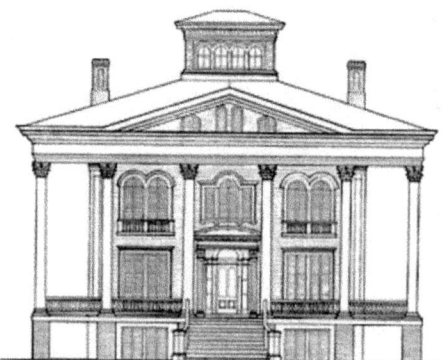

BELLAMY MANSION

Chapter 1

"What on Earth do you mean? Why would she have left the ship? That's impossible!"

Evangeline LaRoque watched helplessly as her husband stared at her in stunned disbelief. His daughter, Cecily had pleaded a headache and left for her cabin long before The *Gray Ghost*, bound for Nassau, had sailed from Wilmington harbor. They were already well down the river and to the point where they must prepare to run the gauntlet of Union gunboats that were blocking the mouth of the Cape Fear, when Evangeline went to her stepdaughter's cabin to check on her. Both the impetuous young woman and her valise had vanished.

Graham clenched his jaw and turned to study the shoreline as they entered the inlet for a run past Fort Holmes on Smith's Island. Fortunate in timing, it was the dark of the moon, optimum for running the blockade. They had waited for a couple of hours in the small harbor at Smithville for the signal that Union gunboats were at New Inlet to the north and east of the small town, thus indicating escape by Old Inlet in the southwest. Already they were steaming past the island defenses at Fort Fisher and Fort Buchanan prepared for the run into the open sea. While Frying Pan Shoals extended from Smith's Island like the handle of a skillet and would slow any pursuers forced to skirt the dangerous shallows, the shoals would not buy any dithering time from the shelling of a determined gunboat. For a moment Graham watched the reeds that painted a waving black ribbon along the edge of the lighter water before wheeling around. He headed for the pilothouse at a gallop leaving Evangeline standing at the railing with Andy, their two-year old son clutched to her breast. She tugged her shawl around him, enveloping them in shared warmth. The chill wind of early Monday night, January 11, 1865, tugged at her hair and caused her to shiver. Vaguely she wondered if it were the cold or fear that made her quake.

Evangeline listened to her husband's retreating steps and prayed. Soon she would have to seek the safety of their cabin in case the ship were to come under fire, but for long minutes she stood with eyes closed asking God to watch over Cissy wherever she might be and to guide them safely through the Union fleet that hounded the shores off Cape Fear. Evangeline suspected that, despite the danger inherent in a return to the Wilmington wartime base for Graham's fleet of blockade-runners, his worry for his daughter would force him to turn the ship around.

Graham had planned to reach the safety of his offices in Nassau and shift the focus of his shipping line there before embarking for Europe. The immense fortune those ships had earned him rested in gold deposits in Parisian banks. A wealthy man prior to the war, he was now rich beyond his wildest dreams. He did not intend to face Union imprisonment, nor expose his family to the rigors of an enemy occupation. Paris, his money, and distant family drew him to France where he intended to stay until things were resolved. Then, he would return to his home in New Berne, which he had abandoned not long after Union occupation of the town.

The previous night his informers had warned him that another Union attack on Fort Fisher was eminent. Although the November 1864 attack on the huge earthen-works fort had been repelled, the large armada already in Beaufort to the north made another assault a likely Union success. Such a defeat would spell doom for any ships still in Wilmington, would herald the fall of the town itself, and thus be the catalyst for the unavoidable collapse of the Confederacy. Graham wanted his family safely away when that happened.

His other ships had been in Nassau since November, well away from enemy clutches. He would have left with his family then if it had not been for a severe case of croup that had kept Andy bedridden with fever.

Evangeline turned from the railing when she saw the faint white of the distant breakers of the Atlantic. It was time to go below deck. With her head down to cautiously edge around the ropes that lay in treacherous coils at her feet, she had gone only a few paces, when she felt arms encircle her. Looking up, she saw the glint of gathering tears in Graham's eyes. She looked at her husband, her unspoken question apparent on her face. He answered by shaking his head.

"It's too late. Captain Wilkinson says the tide and wind would force him to turn at sea. And that's too risky with Union ships lying just to the north. We have no choice but to trust him and go on to Nassau. He knows his business." Graham choked back a sob, "Oh, my God, what possessed Cissy to go back? Why now of all times? She knows the danger."

"She's worried about Logan, darling. She hasn't heard from him in over a month, not since the Yankees took Plymouth in late October. Although you ordered her to stop couriering information to Logan, I suspect she has continued to spy for him. The cook thinks she gets letters from him through the vendors in the market and probably sends him messages the same way." Evangeline also suspected that Cissy's long ago trip to France with her late mother had been so unpleasant and traumatic for the young child, that it colored her adult decision to avoid a repeat trip there.

His voice cold and accusing, Graham stormed, "I warned her after the debacle in New Berne, when that damned Frenchman kidnapped and nearly raped her, I would brook no further such ventures. And you chose not to tell me? What were you thinking?"

"Please, save your wrath, Graham. I don't deserve chastisement. He kidnapped me, too, if you will remember, and me pregnant with Andy. I'd done no spying." Evangeline controlled her temper before continuing, "I just found out last night what she has been up to when I was finalizing things with the household staff. With the flurry of leaving, I had no time to tell you. With you gone until an hour before we left, when was I to bring it up? Besides, with Cissy and the rest of us leaving, it seemed a moot point anyway." Taking a deep breath to collect her composure, she continued, "I'm sorry. I didn't mean to snap at you anymore than you did at me. We are both worried sick for her. In a way, I understand why she slipped away. She has been working with Logan since New Berne was first taken. She loves Logan. They're engaged. If she can help him---if he needs her, she wants to be there for him. If it were us and we were in their shoes, I would do no less. She also told me that she was not excited about returning to France. I think the memories are painful for her. We have no choice but to rely on her good judgment to do nothing foolish. Frankly, I'm proud of her and I trust her. She'll not be stupid."

"But, she's just a woman."

Evangeline smiled, "I'm going to overlook that remark."

"I don't mean to disparage. I cannot bear to think of the dangers to a woman alone with no man to protect her."

Evangeline chuckled, "She a better shot, better on horseback, smarter, and braver than most any man I know. Except for my husband, of course. She is nearly twenty-one years old, a woman who knows her own mind, and she intends to follow it. I'm no happier and no less worried than you, but this is her decision and we must accept it.

***

Twenty five miles away, Cissy snuggled into the feather mattress of her bed and blessed the small household staff of maid, cook and butler that had stayed behind to watch the house during her family's time abroad. Until she could learn what had happened to Logan and whether or not he needed her, the servants would see to her comfort and safety. She had confided in the Irish housemaid, Annie, to expect her return. Annie had insured that a hot supper and a warm bed awaited her. She could trust the woman as the two of them had developed a mutual rapport. Both were engaged to soldiers at the front and both couriered information whenever they gleaned anything of use while reading to or writing letters for the occasional Union prisoners in the hospital. It still chaffed that they were not allowed to nurse the soldiers in any real way for fear that they would be exposed to unseemly sights for young virgins. With so much sickness and death, it seemed silly to her to maintain rigid adherence to the old norms in the midst of a rapidly changing world.

She refused to dwell on the anguish that she had caused her parents who would have discovered her absence by now. She blocked any thought of how much she would miss them and her half-brother Andy. And she absolutely would not consider what would happen if and when Wilmington fell. After all, she reminded herself, she had survived for months in Union occupied New Berne before leaving to join her father in Wilmington. Fluffing her pillow, she turned onto her side and slid into sleep.

She awakened refreshed of body, but troubled in spirit. Guilt at what she had done and the worry she had caused her family spread like a wildfire through her veins. For one mad moment she thought of following them to Nassau on the next ship. The stern voice of reality scotched that idea at its birth. The odds were great that no more Confederate ships were leaving the port of Wilmington, nor were any of her father's still there. Cissy bit her lip in concentration but found no way to undo the rashness of her actions.

She tossed back the covers and gritted her teeth against the chill of another cold morning. Once more Annie O'Neal had failed to stir the embers in the hearth and lay on fresh coal. She hurriedly donned her robe before dashing to the bucket that was kept by the fireplace. Cissy hastened to add the warmth-giving black lumps and some kindling to the still glowing embers. Jabbing with the poker to fuel the embers with oxygen, she soon had a crackling blaze. Annie walked in singing an Irish ballad just as she returned the poker to the stand.

"I declare, Annie, you are one no-account maid, and if you weren't my friend, I would purely fire you."

"Oh, stop yer grumbling. A little cold is good for the body; gets you moving." Annie grinned impudently, "If I was lighting this fire for ye, ye never would have learned to do a coal fire on ye own. Times are changing, Missy. We have ourselves a war right here on our doorstep. 'Tis no telling what skills be needed before all be done. You might consider me as something of a tutor for learning the basic things yer fancy upbringing didn't teach ye. Ah, 'tis lucky ye be to have a good Irish country girl like me."

"You were not employed to teach me skills," Cissy snapped, but her smile and a soft chuckle betrayed any sting in her retort. It was useless chastising the cheerful Annie anyway.

Cissy continued, "Papa says the Yankees are going to take Fort Fisher for sure any day now. If they do, Wilmington's goose is cooked. I don't know whether to try to get to New Berne, or if we should just stay here. It's a mess trying to travel with the railroads being used to haul soldiers. There are no boats to take and if there were, they'd be shot out of the water. I don't relish taking a buggy through the countryside with so many Bushwhackers and contrabands running around. I could go alone on horseback but then I'd have to worry about somebody shooting me to get the horse. Mercy, what a mess we're in. I can't imagine what possessed me to think I should stay behind."

"Same thing that possessed me to stay, I suspect. We both want to be here for our men when they come home. Least ways, I sure do." Annie grinned, "I promise I'll start the fire tomorrow if we can find any wood. That's the last of the coal. Rufus says he's going to get us some firewood if he can find it. Otherwise, we're going to get mighty chilly. Sure is a shame there's no peat here for burning. It does make a lovely, warm fire."

The girls continued to commiserate about all of the things that were running short or had long since vanished. The boom of cannon fire at Fort Fisher promised greater deprivation ahead. For most of the war, thanks to Graham LaRoque's blockade-runners, his household had not suffered the privations that plagued much of the South. The last few months had brought a gradual shift as fewer and fewer ships managed to get through. Were Fort Fisher to fall, they all knew the final cork would plop into place, plugging the only remaining port for the South's vital lifeline to supplies of every kind. The very thought of no more coal to keep at bay the cold chill from winter waters and windswept town caused Cissy to shiver. Sighing at the thought of more challenges to confront and survive, she shrugged her shoulders with resolve. The only choice was to learn how to make do and do without. Annie would have to teach her how to light a wood fire and keep it going...assuming Rufus could find any wood to burn. Firewood was becoming scare, too, in a land where the armies of both sides plundered even pasture fence rails and sheds for their campfires.

On Friday morning, after pulling on a woolen day dress Cissy joined Annie in the upstairs hall and they descended the steps to find Rufus standing in the front foyer. They could tell from his expression that the news he carried was not going to be welcome. For a moment all Cissy wanted to do was to turn on her heel, march back to her room, crawl into bed, and forget that the last four years had ever happened. Each day just seemed to bring more misery and loss. She was thoroughly sick of war and all that it entailed.

Rufus wasted no time telling her that finding coal or firewood was impossible. The only recourse that he could offer was to chop down the rear picket fence and use it to keep warm until he could find some other alternative. Cissy wearily nodded her head in agreement. If they were careful and only used it to heat the stove in the kitchen for cooking, they would have several days of fuel. The idea of a warm bedroom was now an absurdity. The thought of a hot tub bath had just become an unaffordable luxury. Cissy spent the remainder of the day in the kitchen knitting socks and rolling bandages for the soldiers. Annie sat with her and the two of them fretted over what they should do. Cissy was all for leaving, provided Rufus would go along for male protection. Annie was equally determined to stay. Rufus kept out of their way hoping to just manage for another day.

The distant cannons awakened the household the following morning to the answering cacophony of rattling windows and dishes. Cissy wasted no time dressing in the chill of her room before hurrying down to the kitchen. Annie was already at the table staring morosely into a cup of coffee. She glanced up when Cissy entered and forgetting that she was the servant, nodded in the direction of the coffee pot. Cissy snorted and walked over to the stove where she grabbed a pad to hold the pot. She poured herself a cup and joined her maid at the table.

"Looks like they're bound and determined to take Fort Fisher. Even from nearly twenty miles away it's a fearsome noise. I can't begin to imagine what it must be like for our poor boys."

Annie looked up and just shook her head. "More bad news. Ye'd better enjoy that cup of coffee as cook says there'll not be another."

Cissy looked at the tall black woman in amazement. "Are you sure, Reesie?"

"That I am. And if the Yankees descend on us like a swarm of locust, there ain't gonna be much else neither."

Cissy finished her coffee in silence. Mulling over the difficulties ahead, the uncertainties, she made up her mind to go to her father's offices on Chandler's Wharf and see what might still be in the warehouse there that they could use. Rising from the table she walked over to the sink and deposited her cup in the washbasin. Turning around she said, "I'm going to Papa's office. You get our shawls and bonnets, Annie. You're coming with me. If there is anything we can use, we're bringing it back here. Tell Rufus he needs to drive us. I don't intend to just sit around here and wait for those damned Bluebellies to land on me like a duck on a Junebug. I intend to figure this out the best I can so we come through this in one piece and without starving to death. It's bad enough to be cold, but to devil with being hungry, too."

Reesie chuckled, then remarked, "Well, you better figure out how to steal some firewood or we're going to be eating raw food provided we can get any. That fence we tearing down ain't going to last long."

"I'll do what I can, Reesie. Please ask Rufus to hitch up the buggy. And do hurry. I don't know how long we have before the Yankees take Wilmington."

Cissy gathered her wrap, the spare keys to her father's offices and warehouse from the desk in his study, and a large wicker basket from Reesie. She was waiting on the front stoop when Rufus pulled to the front of the house. Calling for Annie to hurry, she clambered into the seat of the carriage and pulled the lap robe over her knees. The warm brick Rufus had wrapped in an old scrap of carpet made a welcome rest for her feet. She was so thankful that her father had hired the man when he first moved to Wilmington. She suspected Reesie was even more grateful, as more often than not, she spent the night in his apartment over the stable. After those nights, Reesie sang while she made breakfast and Rufus would walk into the kitchen with a twinkle in his eye. The rest of the household pretended ignorance of the arrangement.

Annie clambered in beside her and they headed toward the river. Annie bounced and chattered with excitement as they rode, happy to escape the confines of the house. The carriage rattled over the cobbled streets laid down from stones used as ships' ballast from vessels that for decades had sailed empty into port and then left with holds filled with turpentine, pitch, tobacco, rice and cotton from the Carolinas. One bump on the cobbles was sufficient to launch both girls into the air. They giggled as they struggled to right themselves.

Passing the Wright mansion, Cissy acknowledged the jaunty wave of an Englishman from where he lolled against a pillar on the porch. Employed by the Liverpool house of Alexander Collie and Company, most of the young Englishmen that resided there had taken themselves to the safety of their homeland, but Collin Farnsworth had remained. He and his fellow compatriots prior to their decampment had thrown a number of lavish balls to which Cissy had been invited. Despite his disappointment that Cissy had not responded to his flirtations, the irrepressible Collin continued in cheerful pursuit of Wilmington debutants. He seemed to be in no hurry to return to England.

The carriage made the turn from Market Street onto Water Street. Cissy found her father's offices shuttered and locked. Sorting through the keys, she tried each in the stout door but none seem to work. Frustrated she went back through and tried again. This time the last key turned the lock. She walked into the dark office followed by the others and immediately opened shutters to let in light. Giving each of them a section of the offices and warehouse to search and sending them off, she then began her own systematic quest for anything useful.

Cissy looked up at a distant squeal of pleasure from Annie signaling she had found something. She smiled to herself and wondered what it might be as she continue her own search. She was almost ready to abandon the offices and join the others when she remembered the small storeroom in the rear. Hurrying there she flung open the door and peered in. It was so dark that she could make out only vague shapes. Returning to the front office she found a lamp and lit it. In the storeroom once more, she held the lamp high and looked around before setting it on the floor in the far corner where she would be unlikely to knock it over. She began at the rear and searched the shelves against the back wall that were lined with boxes. The dusty records she found there were of no use to her. Continuing to the right side wall, she found more boxes. She lifted the lid of one of the larger boxes. Then Cissy's own cry of joy rang out. The lead lined box held bags of coffee and tea that her father kept for use in the office. Other boxes were filled with the tea biscuits, sugar and cinnamon he loved. The whiskey soaked fruitcake that Reesie had made for him to keep at the office rested beside the box of coffee. It was still wrapped and un-sliced. She salivated at the very thought of its moist richness.

She continued going through the boxes but found nothing else of any use. Hauling her treasures from the cupboard, she carried them to the front office where she stacked them near the door. As she bent to push them into place, Annie heaved into view muttering as she came.

"Ah, the Blessed Mother and Holy Saints preserve me. This is not half heavy. I can do naught but drag it. There be another couple of bags in the warehouse even larger than this one. Rufus will have to fetch those and put them all in the carriage."

Cissy beamed at her when she saw that Annie had found a large bag of coal. At least they had bought a few days more of cooked food and warmth. She could only pray that Rufus had succeeded in finding something they might use. When he too emerged from the doorway that led to the warehouse, he was carrying a large box and grinning from ear to ear.

"Salted herring. It ain't my favorite but it's food. There are some more boxes of food down there: flour, a rasher of bacon, a side of ham, and such I have to go back for. There are also some barrels that can be broken up and used for firewood. I don't think we are going to do this in one trip though."

"Wonderful. I'm thrilled that we cannot. Let's load what we can and we'll come back for the rest this afternoon. Perhaps, we should use the wagon for the next trip."

They worked the rest of the afternoon hauling things to the house on the corner of Water and Orange Streets that had been her home for the last two years. Dusty and tired from the labor, Cissy and Annie sat at the kitchen table sipping a cup of sweetened coffee. Despite Annie's efforts to engage her in conversation, Cissy merely nodded and continued to enjoy the coffee. With supplies in hand, she must now deal with new worries and the ever-present quandary of whether or not she should try to return to New Berne.

After the defeat of New Berne in March of 1862, she had learned just exactly what occupation by the enemy brought with it. Unlike many fellow townsmen, she had been lucky to have the friendship of the soldiers that occupied her stepmother's former home. Even were she to reach their New Berne home, would it still be standing, occupied by Union forces, or worse yet: dangerous and destructive squatters? With the railroad cut, the roads muddy from winter rains, and patrolled by roaming bands of thieves and worse, the route home was no more appealing.

After a restless night that brought no answer to the questions that buzzed in her mind like bees around a hive, she arose still weary. The frigid bedroom added urgency to dressing and grooming for church. She would have liked to remain at home that morning. But, need to be among her fellow townsmen and to hear what was happening at Fort Fisher provided the spur to venture forth. Annie was waiting for her when she entered the kitchen. A Catholic as well, she too was dressed for mass.

The faces they met as they stood in the churchyard following service were all grim. The only news of any importance was that Fort Fisher still held. Speculation ran that it would only be a matter of time before it was lost and the enemy marched on Wilmington. They all looked like people awaiting the gallows, praying for divine intervention but facing the reality of doom. Some of them were saying their 'farewells' with plans to leave for the country as soon as they finished packing. Others staunchly swore they were staying, determined no Yankees would drive them from their homes. Yet, uncertainty would flicker in those same faces with each jolt of cannon burst. Were the town shelled, it would be a matter of life and death to wait there for some fatal shot to rain down upon them, destroying the homes they treasured and the families they could not live without. A few left the churchyard, less resolute than when they arrived. Fear was infectious and spreading rapidly.

The walk home was somber. Both girls were terrified of staying and terrorized by the thought of what leaving might bring. Sniffing the air, they could detect the faint smell of cordite carried by wind from the battle some twenty miles away.

Annie looked up at the sky and muttered, "I wish that cannonading would stop. It makes me nervous."

Cissy snorted, "Be glad it hasn't. When the firing stops, it means they're coming this way. As long as I hear that distant gunfire, I know our boys are holding out."

Chapter 2

Logan Gwaltney touched the package of letters in his breast pocket for luck. It helped to keep it near as a reminder that once the war was ended they would wed. He considered the bundle of letters from Cissy his sacred talisman. At the moment he needed one. He reminded himself that as a spy, loosely attached to General Branch's command, he did not have to be in the thick of the fight. Yet, he had chosen to be there to fight regardless of the risk. He needed to be there to defend the city where the LaRoques now resided. For more than a week, soldiers assigned the task of defending vital Fort Fisher had been bombarded by fierce fire from the determined ships that rode the waves just off shore. Winter chill, lack of food, and the misery of sure defeat had sapped them of most of the final reserves of strength needed to resist the might of besieging Union forces.

Cursing, he rolled to his right away from a sudden hail of bullets that peppered the sand and threw grit into his eyes. Logan cursed the rifle he held, as it was useless against the cannons that rocked the earth as he lay digging his fingers into the cold, damp sand. Logan cursed the years of war that had left him battle-weary, infested by lice, and dressed in tatters. He cursed the misery of near-starvation, exposure to cold and rain by day and night, and the sight of his friends blown to fragments before his eyes. Were it not for the dream of marrying the woman he loved, building a home filled with children, and a return to life without war, he could not have endured. For one brief moment he pictured Cissy, his friend in childhood and now the woman he was determined to marry, sitting in church praying for the soldiers that were fighting against over-whelming odds to prevent Wilmington's capture by the enemy, praying for him especially---or so he hoped. Was Sunday an auspicious day for killing and dying he wondered? Shaking his head to clear it of negative and distracting thoughts, he squinted at the line of sand dunes along the shore. It was time.

Logan loaded his rifle and aimed at the wall of blue infantry that surged up from the beachhead in front of him. He did not see them as men like him with families and loved ones, but only as a deadly menace that must be stopped. He did not take time to regret the killing that he delivered. He knew he would later if he lived. For the moment, his focus was on loading, firing, reloading, and trying to stay alive long enough to repeat it all. A sudden barrage of heavy artillery made the ground under him heave with shockwaves. For several minutes, he was deafened from the impact of the repercussions. He did not hear the call to retreat, only sensed that suddenly he was in the forefront of the line and his fellow Confederates were pulling back. Crouching he turned and ran, zigzagging from right to left to make a more difficult target. Tumbling over the first revetment, he paused in the relative safety of the depression to get his orientation and determine what to do next. None of the options looked good. Rising again he ran for his life, wondering every second if he would be hit by the bullets that filled the air around him like deadly drops of fiery rain.

A high-pitched scream announcing the arc of a cannonball filled the air. Immediately Logan dropped to his belly and clapped his arms over his head. It landed some distance to his left blasting everything nearby with fragments of hot iron. A sudden stinging in his left thigh made him twist around to see how badly he was hit. It looked to be a minor wound where a fragment had sheared through his pants leg and grazed the flesh. He was bleeding but not alarmingly so. Logan pulled the scarf from around his neck and used it to bind his wound.

Taking another deep breath and ignoring the dull throb of pain that had begun in his leg, he resumed the crouching run toward the outer barrier of earthen embankments where his fellow Rebels were already congregating to make another stand against the invaders.

Captain Robert Chapman gathered his men around him as they looked at the fallen left flank of the fort. "It's no use men. We drove them back three times. This fourth assault has stamped paid to this fight. If we hang around here we're going to end up in a Yankee prison for the rest of the war. Let's get down to those boats and get across the river while we still can."

Logan joined the rest of the company as they ran down to the shore. Tying his boots around his neck by the laces he waded into the frigid water. It had reached his waist by the time he got to the boat. His teeth were chattering like castanets. Shivering so badly he could barely control his movements, he laid his rifle in the bottom and then heaved himself over the gunnels. The rest of the men followed suit until they were all in the boats and ready to push off for the far shore. Again Captain Chapman's voice rang out, "Stay put boys. Lets see what that battery of ours that just started up can do against those Bluebellies. We may need to go back."

Logan groaned with misery, his own curses joining those of the men in his boat. Union batteries were firing shells around the small flotilla. While none of the boats were hit, the water that splashed over them when the shells hit the water did nothing to improve their mood. Fishing in his watch pocket with numb fingers, he squinted to read the time. Shit, he swore. It was almost ten o'clock. Apparently, Chapman at last was giving up as he took that moment to order them to row across to Battery Lamb. The men put their backs into it, eager to get off the water. Little relief was waiting for them. After thirty wet miserable minutes hanging around in the battery, they were again ordered to move out. Above weary heads, thousands of exploding rockets from the captured fort created a brilliant panoply of color against the velvety darkness of the night sky. Logan looked up in awe at the sight as he picked up his rifle and began to walk, his wet, nearly frozen shoes squishing with each step.

Marching down the road to Wilmington, he was grateful for movement as it helped to alleviate some of the chill. Four miles later, they halted and built fires to dry their clothes and bedrolls. It was late when he had chewed his bite of hardtack and settled down to sleep. He slept deeply despite the frigid night. Sheer exhaustion from a long day of combat and frayed nerves insured it. He awoke Monday morning to the thin light of dawn. His leg had begun a steady throbbing and his stomach rumbled with hunger. There was no point in searching his knap sack as it was empty of even crumbs. Rolling up his blanket, he joined the other bleary eyed men around him as they began trudging along the road into Wilmington. By mid-afternoon they were all thirsty and hungry. More than one soldier muttered curses in silent fury at the intoxicated officers that had allowed all of their rations to fall into the hands of the enemy.

Logan noticed a ramshackle farmhouse on the edge of the woods. A column of smoke rose from its chimney to drift in the air. The scent of burning wood and frying meat assailed his nostrils and made his mouth water. "Any of you boys got any money. Let's take up a collection and see if we can buy something to eat from that house over yonder. If I don't get something, I'm going to purely die of starvation right here in my tracks."

With the thirty Confederate dollars he collected, Logan and two others set out. They were able to buy enough cornpone and fried fatback that each of the small company had a bite to eat. After the sparse meal, the company walked on until dark when once again they built fires and made camp. After a quiet discussion it became apparent that there was no more money to buy food. A glum mood settled over the men, their silence broken by an occasional rumble of hunger from an empty belly.

"Dagnabbit," Robert Watson, an enlisted man who had been reassigned to the navy, swore softly. "It don't have to just be money. Ain't we got something else we can trade with somebody?"

Another spoke up, "I got an extra pair of britches if you think that'll help?"

Logan stood up, "Any of the rest of you got anything, add it in. All we can do is try. Let's have it and a couple of us will walk down the road to that cabin we passed and see what we can get."

Once more he returned with food. Soon bacon was frying in a pan and rice boiling over the fire. When the bacon was crispy, the fat was poured into the rice. When the rice was done, the bacon was crumbled in and stirred around. The men gathered around the fire with their pans waiting for a serving. It wasn't much, but to the hungry men it was a feast. That done they threw more limbs on the fire, and gathered as near as they could to its warmth without singeing their clothes and blankets.

Logan's friend Laird commented, "It's colder than a witch's tit out here."

"Yeah, it'd freeze the balls off'n a brass monkey," Watson declared.

Jethro, another naval man, piped up, "I'm so cold your girlfriend couldn't warm me up."

"Hell, she couldn't warm me up neither." Laird snorted derisively, "Wrote me she's done and married somebody else."

"Now that was *cold*," Logan said. The men all laughed with sympathy. Laird wasn't the first of them to hear such news from the girl they'd left behind. Logan touched his letters from Cissy for reassurance before he drifted into sleep.

They moved out at dawn and walked with renewed vigor. By eleven they would be in Wilmington where they could find food and lodging. Mile after mile, they looked down the road eagerly anticipating the first glimpse of the city's church spires and the awaited relief from the misery of the past few days.

Logan was lucky in Wilmington. He managed to get a new pair of cardboard-soled shoes and a new uniform from the supply officer. After a bath and a meal, he fell into his bunk and slept like the dead. Not even dreams interrupted the next twelve hours of oblivion. When he awakened, he knew that his time in Wilmington was short and he had not yet seen Cissy. He did not wait for breakfast. There was no time. He hoped there would be a bite of something to spare at the LaRoque's. If not, he would have no choice but to march on an empty stomach. He had done it more times than he could count, so one more day of gnawing hunger was just that and no more. At least he could see Cissy free of the pestiferous lice and filth that had plagued him for weeks.

With a slight hitch in his step from the wound that was still bothering him, but with a heart filled with joyous anticipation, he walked down the street whistling. It was a beautiful day. Even the sun seemed to smile on him. When he turned onto Orange Street the sun ducked behind a cloud bringing momentary shadow. As though it had touched his heart as well, he paused. He thought of the girl that had jilted his friend Jared and wondered if the same fate awaited him just ahead. He considered the fact that she and her family might have well fled on her father's ships to safer quarters. And looking down at his shabby attire and emaciated frame, he wondered if he was even worthy of someone like her. He had nothing that he could offer beyond his current unprepossessing self. He knew not whether his home in Craven County had survived the war and even if it had, what would be left to begin a life with a new wife? His Confederate notes were worthless. His land lay fallow, lost to the weeds, and with no money or slaves left to begin again, of little use. He had no trade. He had never expected to need one. Logan squared his shoulders and hobbled the remaining yards to the LaRoque house, trying his best to ignore the nagging pain in his leg. He felt his thigh and was alarmed at the tenderness and heat in the wounded flesh. Perhaps he should have seen a doctor, but then he reminded himself, what time did they have for something as insignificant as a flesh wound when they were faced with the agony of dying men and the desperate rush to salvage those whose wounds would leave them maimed but alive.

Pulling himself up by the iron railing, Logan ascended the arced brick steps onto the landing. Standing in front of the paneled door, he took a deep breath and raised the knocker allowing it to fall heavily. He could hear its echoes in the cavernous entryway beyond the wooden barrier of the solid walnut door. As he stood there waiting he pulled his collar up against the chill, catching a glimpse of himself in the side windows as he did so. Had he been a vain man, he would have groaned at the change four years of war had brought. He was too thin, dressed in ill fitting and poorly made clothes, and unkempt looking at best. Disgusted at himself and ashamed for a beauty like Cissy to see him, he had half turned away from the door when it opened.

Not recognizing the bearded soldier that had started a slow descent down the steps, Annie's voice halted him in mid-step. "Was there something ye be a needing, mister?"

Logan turned to the lilting Irish voice and cried, "My word, Annie. Are you not knowing me now?"

"Excuse me, sir. 'Tis a right idiot I be. For sure, ye're Miss Cissy's own Mr. Logan. She is going to be so relieved to see ye."

"She's still here then? Somehow I thought the family would have left by now."

"The others did but she sneaked away to wait for news of ye. Fool that she was. What could we do one way or another anyhow? And now, we be stuck not knowing where to go nor how to do it."

"That is a worry." Logan shook his head in sorrowful awareness that he could offer no assurances. "Is Miss Cissy in this morning? I have only a moment to tarry and would dearly love to see her."

"No, 'tis sad I am to tell ye. She left about twenty minutes past and probably won't be back for some time. She be purely bound to get away from here. I've tried to tell her there be no way. No trains are going to take us civilians. The boats are no option. And we be scared to death to risk the roads on our own. I don't know what she thinks she can stir up running around town looking for help. Those as can go are long since gone."

"I can't wait. I could get shot for desertion as it is. Tell her I'm surviving even if a mite worse for wear." Logan paused, "She needs to stay now and take her chances. The Yankees are only a few hours away from taking the town. Y'all are better off to just hide what's valuable and hunker down."

"Holy Mary Mother of God, what a woeful mess. I sometimes wish I'd stayed in Ireland."

"Annie, before I go, do you think maybe you could rustle up a bite of something to eat. I am just nigh onto starving."

"We got lucky and found some things in Mr. LaRoque's storerooms down by the wharf. Otherwise, ye'd have to be a termite to find anything to eat around here. Come on back to the kitchen and I'll have Reesie fix ye right up."

"My fiance, Seamus O'Sullivan, would you be a knowing him? He was at Fort Fisher, but I've not seen him. I was hoping he would make a wee visit before leaving again."

Logan could see she was near tears and regretted he could only shake his head. "I'm sorry, Annie girl. I don't know the man. If he was lucky the Yankees captured him. At least he will be out of the shooting and get something to eat. Try not to worry. I'm breaking rules to be here. If he is still in

Wilmington, he might not have been able to slip away to see you."

Logan followed Annie into the kitchen where Reesie soon had a cup of hot coffee in his cold hands. As he sat there warming them, Reesie busied herself putting together bacon biscuits he could carry with him. Annie's questions about the battle for Fort Fisher, met with brief answers. He was simply too exhausted by war to even want to talk about it. When he left, disappointed at not seeing Cissy, he could only pause on the sidewalk and lift a weary hand to the two servants who watched his departure. At the same moment both Annie and Reesie spotted the bloody handkerchief knotted around his thigh and his limping gait as he left.

Calling out, Annie queried, "Are ye hurt, Logan?"

Waving his hand dismissively, he plodded on with dogged resignation. It would be at least an hour before he could catch up with the tail end of the Confederate column that was hastily decamping inland. He only hoped that he would not be missed and labeled a deserter. And the only reward for his troubles had been bacon biscuits, not the kiss he had anticipated from seeing his sweetheart.

Logan glanced at his pocket watch. It was already eight o'clock. Gritting his teeth against disappointment and the dull throb in his leg, he marched west. Each step grew increasingly painful causing him to worry that the wound might be more serious than he thought initially. Shrugging off the gloom that he had allowed to catch up with him, he shrugged his shoulders to ease his backpack and forced another weary step to follow the last. He had walked about three miles when he saw the tail end of the straggly gray column trudging down the road yards in front of him. With no greeting of any kind, he silently merged with other grim faced men as they left another defeat behind, another survival under fire, to venture forth into whatever might lay ahead. He knew as well as they that the prospects for the South were beyond dismal.

At ten that morning, the men crossed the Northeast Cape Fear River, and after a thirty-minute halt, they were ordered to continue on to Goldsboro with the anticipating of catching the train there. On arrival at their destination, the weary column grimaced in collective misery at the empty tracks in Goldsboro. They were too late. With no other recourse, the men resumed marching down the deserted railroad tracks, this time bound for the railroad station in the hamlet of Burgaw. After twenty-seven agonizing miles, it was four in the morning when they were at last allowed to rest. Too tired to make camp, the men dropped to the ground where they stood and slept until the call to rise a mere three hours later. Much groaning and cursing from the men did nothing to change orders and the brief rest had not done much to relieve bone deep fatigue and cold stiffened joints. Starvation rations of a little cornbread and bacon added little fuel. And, any spare body fat for energy had long since disappeared. Even so, a train arrived at nine and they boarded it for the short ride to Magnolia. In Magnolia they waited for another train that would take them back to Goldsboro. It was three in the morning when they arrived. Most had slept on the train, too exhausted to wonder at the futility of the circuitous route that served only to bring them back to Goldsboro.

Awakened at six, Logan joined the other men as they ate unappetizing mush. No one even grumbled or cared. Marched to the courthouse, they camped there in pouring rain. It continued through the night and greeted them on Saturday morning. Logan didn't mind the cold rain. The chill cooled his fevered brow and helped with the throbbing in his leg that was growing steadily worse. He thought of going to the hospital tent and having the surgeons look at it. The lethargy of fear, despondency, and exhaustion held him captive.

The men waited all that rainy Saturday. At nightfall, they

marched back to the station and again crawled onto the train. The destination was Greensboro. None of them really cared. The only thing waiting for them was more misery and the chance of death. They were not to be disappointed in their hopelessness. Arrival in Greensboro on the Sabbath meant they could buy nothing to ease their hunger, or their thirst for a dram of whiskey to brighten the mood. Logan didn't care. The pain in his leg had become consuming. He was in fitful slumber when the train left the station that night bound for Richmond. Unlike his fellow soldiers, he slept most of that following Monday and had only just blearily awakened when his friend Laird announced that they were in Richmond. It was midnight. Logan forced himself to fall into step with the others as they left the train, only to stand in the rain for an accursed thirty minutes.

"Sons of bitches!" Laird growled, "The consarned officers have gone off and left us to fend for ourselves. Damned if I intend to stand here all night while they tuck themselves into nice warm beds."

On all sides, men grumbled, but no one moved. Thirty minutes later the mutinous troops were at last ordered to seek shelter in the train sheds for the remainder of the night. Logan fished for his pocket watch when they were out of the rain and ordered to bed down in the uncomfortable shed. It was after three in the morning and he was so weary, so very weary. He collapsed just inside the door, too weak and miserable to go further. The place he claimed would have to do.

He did not awaken at dawn when Laird and another of his buddies picked him up and laid him on a stretcher. His companions realized he was too ill to continue on to Drewry's Bluff. His only hope lay in the treatment available at Chimborazo Hospital perched on a hill above Richmond. Laird watched the ambulance wagon wend its way from the station certain that he would not see his friend again in this world.

Logan could not have said what aroused him to consciousness. He did not know if it were the pincers of pain that tore at his hot flesh or the ominous words that somehow sank into his oblivion and brought him to awareness. He hated the words he heard from the sawbones that saw only his wounded leg and knew no way to deal with it other than amputation. Despite a throat so parched he could make only the faintest of whispers, he ordered, "No, Doc. Don't take my leg. I don't give a damned if it kills me, I don't intend to live a cripple."

The doctor had heard it all before. Past weary and frustrated by his own helplessness in the face of so much agony and death, he quietly responded, "I know, son. I can't say as I blame you for feeling the way you do, but if I don't take that leg the gangrene is going to kill you. You really don't want to die, now do you?"

"I'm not going home just a piece of a man. I don't want my girl pitying me and marrying me out of obligation. I just can't do it. And, without her loving me the way I do her, I don't want to live," Logan stubbornly insisted.

"If she loves you, one leg less won't change you as a man. She'll be there for you; and if she isn't, a leg isn't the only problem. Now, you let me try to save that life of yours. You're too young not to have a chance to at least die an old man like me." The doctor squeezed Logan's shoulder trying to convey the urgency of the operation, and in that one caress, the need to choose life.

When Logan did not respond, he took the decision from him. The doctor handed Logan a jug of moonshine whiskey and ordered him to drink. Welcoming the offer of relief the strong drink would bring, Logan drank greedily. Watching Logan slide into drunkenness, the doctor nodded at the waiting orderly, indicating that it was time. "Pour some whiskey on his leg, man, then pour some more in him. I want him out cold. I would to God I had some opiate to help with the pain, but it's not forthcoming and we can't wait."

Logan tossed his head fretfully when the orderly poured more whiskey in his mouth. Succumbing to the futility of his efforts, he at last resigned himself to the unavoidable and drank until he slid into a stupor, knowing that his dreams of a future were ended. He would never return to Cissy and expose himself to her revulsion and horror at his mutilated body.

Hating his own revulsion at what he had to do in order to save the man's life, the doctor waited until Logan was firmly held by the strong arms of the kind black man that had worked with him for the last three years.

Chapter 3

Cissy watched the rain run in rivulets down the windowpanes as she stared morosely at the dripping gray trees that arched in a stark frame around her bedroom window. Clenching her fist, she cursed herself for being a fool. She should have stayed with her parents on the boat bound for Nassau. It would have at least been warm and sunny and there would have been food, lots of food. The thought was enough to remind her that once again they were without firewood except that which was fed ever more sparingly into the stove in the kitchen, and food was running short. She tugged the cumbersome quilt around her shoulders against the bone-piercing chill of the room.

Like a fresh scab, Cissy picked at the memory of February 22, when Mayor John Dawson had turned over the city to General Alfred Terry. With Yankees swarming the streets like blue-clad pestilence, the usually mild Rufus had stood like a human barrier against the front door each time she tried to leave. She might be the chatelaine of the household now that the rest of the family had gone, but she held no power against the united front of her three servants who were determined that the four of them would remain safely tucked away from the enemy's line of sight.

Again she sighed in disgust. It was ridiculous to stay locked inside when locks would not keep out a determined enemy. It was ridiculous to stay locked inside when they were freezing to death. It was ridiculous to stay locked inside slowly starving to death. She had had enough. The sudden emergence of the sun became a spur. Raising the window, she looked out and down. There was no convenient trellis liked the one she had once climbed, but there was a big soft azalea bush not too far below. Not bothering to question her decision, she whirled around to her bed and ripped off the top sheet. Tying it to the leg of the heavy chest by the window, she dropped it out to see how far it would reach. It wasn't as close as she might have liked, but it would have to do. Cissy was leaving. She wasted no time putting on her petticoats and then added another to help cushion the blow were she to slip. She then snatched from the wardrobe a warm cloak with a hood and a serviceable day dress, appropriate for staying cloistered but not one she would normally wear out. But this was not normal. She did not want to ruin a nice frock tumbling into a bush and she didn't want to look like the daughter of a prosperous blockade-runner. Walking to the window she studied the sheet that was now draped out the window. She considered it for several seconds, before hauling it back in and tying intermittent knots, thinking that would make it easier to cling to. Cursing the convention that demanded women wear cumbersome skirts, she gingerly crawled out the window gripping the sheet for all she was worth. There was no way that she wanted to end up with a broken limb.

Releasing her hold on the final knot, she fell into the azalea and tumbled to the ground in an ignominious heap of petticoats. For one dazed moment she just lay there collecting herself. Then she grinned. Freedom. Oh, how wonderful it felt. Struggling to her feet, she brushed away the leaves that had lodged in her hair and gingerly tested her limbs. Nothing seemed to be broken and nothing hurt. Repositioning the hood over her hair and plucking up her skirts, she made a mad dash for the street. She did not stop there. It felt wonderful to be out of the house, at last able to satisfy a gnawing curiosity as to what had happened to the town since Yankee occupation.

Avoiding mud and the errant dog that barked in warning, Cissy hurried toward Market Street and the main commercial district. She had brought no money, but that mattered little. She just wanted to be among a wider circle of people than the days of isolation had allowed. She wanted to breathe the slightly fetid air from the river marshes that lined the banks of the harbor, relish the sense of a new beginning that had been forced upon them, and see what changes war had wrought.

With her head down she plowed forward and right into the blue-clad arms of a man, one who let out a sudden whoosh of air at the impact. Looking up to apologize, the words died in her throat at the sight of the dancing blue eyes that stared back at her.

The man chuckled, "I must say, you keep turning up like a bad penny."

"I could say the same for you, Colonel Madison," she snapped out, shocked but at the same time aware of a small thrill that skittered along her spine. "Well, well. It wasn't enough for you to be in on the capture of New Berne. You just had to mosey on down here and mess with Wilmington, too."

Ryan Madison repressed a smile. He had enjoyed his encounters with the saucy minx prior to her departure from the occupied town of New Berne. Apparently she had changed little. "I'm sure you realize that I serve at the discretion of my superior officers, hence my arrival in your adopted city. Putting that aside, tell me: are you on another of your little spying missions, or did your departure from New Berne spell the end of your fledgling career."

"I have no idea what you mean by that remark." Picking up her skirt, she prepared to step around him.

"Not so hasty, Miss LaRoque. Need I remind you of the perils to unescorted women in a town full of soldiers?" Taking her elbow, he turned her back in the direction from which she had come. "I am escorting you home. I strongly advise you to stay there unless you have someone to accompany you."

Cissy didn't hesitate at the lie that sprang to her lips. "It's impossible. The servants are all ill and there's no food in the house. I was forced to leave and find something to keep us all from starving. Now if you will just release me I'll go about my business."

Not to be sidetracked, Ryan asked, "Your parents...?"

"They left just before the occupation, so it's only me and our servants."

"I'm surprised that you didn't accompany them." Ryan noted the blush that spread across her checks at his words.

"Well, I..." Flustered she stammered. Squaring her shoulders, she declared, "It is none of your concern why I stayed behind."

"Quite so, however, it is my *concern* that you arrive home unmolested."

"Why should you care? I have told you I need to purchase supplies." Cissy was far from ready to return to the boredom of the house.

"I will see to it that you have supplies. It will be far easier for me to procure something than it would be for you. Unfortunately, there is little to be had in local markets at the moment."

"Now, I do wonder why that should be," she blurted sarcastically.

"No doubt, it has something to do with us damned Yankees *messing* with Wilmington."

"No doubt." Cissy pointed her nose in the air, pulled her arm from his grasp, and marched down the street toward her home. Ryan strolled behind perversely whistling *Yankee Doodle*. His heart was the lightest it had been in the months since the ending of his love affair with another beautiful southern woman.

He had admired the fiery Cissy LaRoque from the first time he met her when she had climbed a trellis to spy on him and his men who were discussing military strategy, and had the misfortune to get caught. When she stopped at the gate of a handsome Italianate house with a bed sheet dangling from one of the second story windows, Ryan laughed until tears ran down his cheeks.

"Miss LaRoque, I truly had hoped you had reformed since last I saw you."

Not acknowledging the reference, she stated, "I'm home. You can go now."

Ryan chuckled, "Yes, I do believe this is where you came from judging by the rather telling exterior decor." Taking her elbow, he opened the gate and walked her to the door. "Not to worry, I will return with some supplies. Now you go on in and behave yourself." He waited on the street until her knock brought someone to open the door for her. It was then that he noticed she had no purse to carry a key and thus no money for shopping. Nonetheless, he would return with food if for no other reason than the fact her audacious spunk lifted his spirits.

Walking into the foyer with a fierce scowl on her face, she glared at the three anxious servants waiting for her. "Don't say a word."

Three sets of silently raised eyebrows greeted her remark before each of them turned and walked toward the kitchen. Muttering under her breath, she followed them. She knew that unless she offered some kind of explanation, it was going to be a chilly household until she did.

Glaring at them, she stared into each of their faces before beginning. "I'm going crazy just sitting in this house day after day. I'm cold, miserable, hungry, and bored. I felt as though I would scream if I didn't get away for just a few minutes."

Rufus tut-tut-ed.

Annie announced: "Ye're daft in the head to go out there all by yerself. Ye be lucky ye weren't assaulted."

Reesie listened with her eyebrows raised and her arms crossed before she calmly replied. "I know exactly what you mean, Miss Cissy. We all do. It ain't that you went out that's so bad, it's that we worried not knowing if you was safe out there. You like a wild animal that ain't meant to be caged, but you need to remember we're family here. We got to trust one another with our feelings and we need to work together, elsewise how we going to make it through the rest of this here war. We work out something so we ain't so cooped up. None of us like that."

"I'm sorry. I know you're right to be annoyed with me. I just never stopped to think that finding me gone would be so upsetting for you." Cissy smiled, "One good thing though, we are going to get some food. I ran into that Yankee colonel that was living in Miss Evangeline's house in New Berne and he is going to bring us some things we need."

"I do love a silver lining in these clouds." Annie grinned, her anger forgotten as her own stomach was rebelling at the near starvation diet. "I sure do hope he be coming soon. My stomach has done nothing but growl for days."

Rufus loathed to relent, nodded his head, "That sure gonna be a blessing."

Cissy left them in the kitchen anticipating a better supper than what they had endured of late. She also was determined to get the sheet out of the window before the colonel returned. Any more ribbing from him would just be too much to endure for one day, food or no food. A sparse midday meal had long come and gone before she heard the anticipated knock at the door.

Racing to answer before the others could do so she swung the door wide to face Colonel Madison who stood with both arms full of bundles. Cissy was so thrilled by the sight of the proffered food that she could have gladly kissed the man. His greeting quickly squelched any such thought.

"I see you have completed airing your bed linens. You know I always thought you southerners were too reserved a lot to allow your neighbors and passing strangers to view the sheets that hold nubile young women at night. Or is that some custom you have for attracting suitors? If so, perhaps, I might be interested." It was obvious by his grin that he anticipated her reaction.

"Colonel Madison, as I live and breath, that is the most insulting remark you could have come up with." Cissy's eyes snapped fire. She refused to acknowledge the breathless, exhilarated feeling he inspired in her. For a moment she wondered why Logan did not make her pulse race the way this man did. She blinked and shook her head to chase the thought away.

"Well, surely you don't want me to think you are using your bed sheets for a ladder so you can escape to meet some smitten, secret-telling Yankee? I believe you were becoming rather adept at that particular enterprise prior to your departure from your fair hometown. Of course, I can't blame my men too much. Had I been blessed with your attentions, I might have unwittingly spilled the beans myself," he teased.

"I have absolutely no idea what you are referring to, Colonel Madison."

"Ah, perhaps my suspicions are unfounded. In that case, I apologize with all due sincerity. Now, do permit me to come in and deposit this load. It's becoming heavy," Ryan smiled winningly as he awaited her response.

Somewhat mollified, although she knew he was enjoying needling her, she gestured as she replied, "Forgive my manners. Come in, please. I *am* grateful for your help."

As she led him to the kitchen, she could not help but ponder the handsome man behind her. The sky blue eyes, broad shoulders and slim hips of this man were too attractive for her peace of mind. Infuriated at her disloyal thoughts, she could not resist flinging a biting comment over her shoulder. "For medicine and food I suppose you Yankees *are* a bit useful. Of course, that wouldn't have been a problem if you had never come here."

"Let's not argue the war, shall we? And do call me Ryan. We have been acquainted long enough that is surely permissible." Ryan's chuckle was tinged with sadness. Judging from her stiff back, hunger outweighed pride. He could do no more to help than offer a small supply of food that would last only a few days. He would try to bring more, but with departure back to New Berne and the anticipated inland battles imminent, his assistance would be brief in time.

When they entered the kitchen, Ryan placed the bundles on the table and turned to meet the thunderstruck Annie. Recovering herself, she gave a saucy grin, "Ah, Joseph, Mary, and Jesus. If ye be what the Yankees look like, I think I might fancy one meself. The name be Annie O'Neal and 'tis pleased I am to be meeting ye. Would ye be married now? If not, I wouldn't object to having a go at ye."

"Annie, this is Colonel Madison. Colonel these are my servants, Reesie and Rufus." When Cissy turned to Ryan after making the introductions, she was amused to note the blush that suffused his checks. "I hope Annie's effusive appreciation has not embarrassed you, Colonel?"

Ryan winked at Annie before looking pointedly at Cissy, "Now why would any gentleman object to an offer from such a comely lass? However, my heart is taken, Annie. I confess I am totally smitten by a young lady I have met in your fair Southland. She doesn't yet grant me her affection, but I still hope." For a moment Ryan regretted throwing that particular red herring into the conversational mix. Both regret and pain for what he had lost was reflected in his face, giving lie to the levity of his words. While he was more than a little attracted to Cissy, after her departure from New Berne he had been wounded near Kinston and nursed to health by a local woman with whom he had fallen desperately in love. Although his love for Penny Kennedy was a futile thing, it was impossible for him to put her from his mind. Flirtation was one thing, an available heart quite another, yet that had not stopped him from making a comment that he knew Cissy would interpret as a greater interest.

Reesie was watching his face and could not help but puzzle at the source of that raw pain. Her heart went out to him, making her want to offer consolation, yet sensing that his pride would be offended were she to voice it. He was a good actor, but not enough so to hide all emotion were one watching closely as she had been.

Annie snickered at Cissy's obvious discomfort and pointedly ignored the warning glance shot her way. "Why, Colonel, Cissy told us she be knowing ye from New Berne, but I had no idea ye be her beau. Ye both must excuse me for flirting."

"Annie, you well know I am engaged to Logan. Colonel Madison was never my beau," Cissy snapped with vexation.

Reesie shook her head at the two girls and moved to sort through the things on the table. With a calm voice, she invited, "I know it ain't my place to mention it, but I'm sure that Miss Cissy was thinking on having you join her for supper as a thank you for all this. I can fix a fine meal from these things you've brought us. We were plumb near starving around here. Least we can do is feed you something home-cooked."

Forced into extending an invitation, Cissy made herself smile, "Yes, please do stay. It is the least I can offer in repayment."

Ryan very much wanted this respite from war and feeling like the enemy. While he might still be the enemy, for a few hours he could escape into a normal world. He beamed with gratitude when he bowed to Cissy. "I accept with great pleasure. I have yet to enjoy the much-reputed southern hospitality. Not that I fault any of you, mind you, under current circumstances. However it would be good to have a few moments of quiet civility among friends, if I may presume as much."

Annie wasted no time responding, "Anybody that keeps me from becoming a wee bag of bones be welcome here. Why don't ye take off that coat and tell us about what all is going on. We've been so penned up, we don't get much news."

"Annie, unfortunately for you southerners, the news is grim and getting more so," Ryan stated as he struggled from his topcoat and gave it to Reesie. He then followed Annie and Cissy to the parlor where he seated himself by a weak fire that was struggling to stay alive. He gestured to the fire and asked, "May I add a bit more firewood for you?"

"We have little so we are burning it with great care. Annie, would you have Rufus bring a little more wood here. This room is as cold as a tomb." Cissy's blush told Ryan just how much she hated this poverty and want that the war forced on her and her fellow citizens. While Rebel passions might heat the heart, it did little to warm bones or feed bellies.

Overly aware of him and the effect he had on her nerve endings, Cissy shifted nervously on the edge of the divan as she cast about for a topic of conversation. Ryan saved her the trouble.

"It seems you have a tendency to jump from the frying pan to the fire: first, the capture of New Berne and now here. I can only surmise your father, due to his shipping interests, has prudently decamped with Mrs. LaRoque to a safer port. What challenges my understanding is why they would have left you here." He lifted his eyebrows in inquiry.

Again Cissy blushed.

Intuitively he knew, "Ah, so you managed to avoid their plans for you. You do have a knack for landing in trouble."

"My reasons for staying are none of your concern, sir." Cissy stuck her nose in the air as she said it, eliciting a chuckle from the man standing across from her.

"Of course not. It is mere idle interest on my part and due to previous acquaintance some concern that you might not have reformed your former spying activities. There is no point at this juncture. Your armies are starving, as are the South's citizens. With the loss of Wilmington, Lee cannot feed his troops and cannot provide the war materiel needed to wage battle. He will fall. That leaves only Gen. Johnston. With this push towards the interior, the Union will ultimately defeat him as well. It would be prudent of you to keep as low a profile as possible until you can be reunited with your parents under peaceful circumstances. I don't mean to antagonize you, but to warn you as a friend."

Cissy cried, "I am so tired of it all. I don't care anymore if we win or lose. I just want it ended so we can go back to living again. I hate it. I hate being cold. I hate being frightened. I hate being hungry. There's no fun left in life...just the need to survive and face another dismal day."

"Trust me, there's no joy in army life either. If I had known what it would mean, I suspect I would have decamped to Europe and found another way to serve my country. Do you think any soldier enjoys watching his friends blown to bits by cannon, shot dead, or wounded and left to die. You cannot image the stench of a battlefield. Not to mention the screams of dying horses and mules that are innocent victims of the whole mess."

"So, why don't you all just go home and leave us alone?" Tears sprang unbidden into her eyes and rolled silently down her checks.

"It's not so simple. There are those who believe the Union is worth preserving and to that end, this must be resolved. Whether or not this was the wisest way to resolve it, men will argue about for decades to come."

Ryan had not meant to do so, but her woebegone expression drew him. He sat by her side and drew her into the protective circle of his arms. He felt her body yield as he pulled her close, her soft curves awakening feelings he thought long buried. The golden halo of her hair was irresistible. Not thinking, he pressed a kiss onto the crown of her head, while he soothed her as one would a baby with soft cooing sounds.

Hoping to distract her, he remarked, "Your step-mother was with child when I last saw her in New Berne. I hope she is well and that you have a healthy new sibling."

Cissy sat up and smiled, "I do. His name is Andrew but we call him Andy. He is adorable and I miss him so much. Hopefully, if the war is really ending as you say, they will come home soon. I confess at this point I wish I had not fooled my parents and had gone with them."

"You just cannot help it can you?" Ryan lifted his eyes from the inviting nearness of her lips and chuckled before continuing, "So, how *did* you fool them?"

"I slipped off the ship just before it sailed. They didn't realize I was gone until it was too late to turn back or my father would have insisted on returning for me."

"And your reason for staying..."

"I thought I could help my fiancé by learning things after you Yankees took over. I knew we would lose Ft. Fisher. I think we all did."

Ryan pushed back the spark of jealousy caused by her mention of a fiancé. He had wanted her badly when he first met the audacious little spy in New Berne. Had it not been for his frustrated love affair with Penny Kennedy, he knew in his heart he would have chased her until she was his. Refusing to let his thoughts go there, he remarked, "As I said, you just cannot help it. You need to keep your nose out of Yankee business this time. I won't be here to help you if you land in hot water."

"Don't worry. I've had enough of the whole mess. I just want it done with now."

"Good girl."

Enjoying her nearness and trying not to think of how long it had been since he held a woman he desired in the circle of his arms, Ryan was reluctant to stand when Annie returned to announce dinner. The smells emanating from the kitchen assured him that it would be a good one, but he felt an even greater hunger for the soothing balm this feisty, difficult young woman brought his heart. Her spirit and zest challenged him, fired his passion, and lifted his spirit. For a moment, he wished his heart were free of the pain and loss of another.

Feeling her stomach growl in response to the promised feast, Cissy had no such compunction about leaping to her feet. Her excitement evident, she announced without thinking about her pride, "Wonderful. I am so hungry I could eat a tough old rooster at this point."

The meal was every bit as delicious as the aromas had promised. None left the table hungry. For the inhabitants of the house it was a momentary respite from weeks of scant and unappealing food. For Ryan there was simple joy in sitting at a dinner table enjoying good food and the company of Cissy and her irreverent Irish servant/friend. He was amused by Annie's none to subtle attempts at flirtation, however, she held no charm for him that could allay the simple attraction of her mistress, nor the woman who had broken his heart two years previously with her rejection.

Cissy walked him to the door at the end of the evening and thanked him for the food. She surprised him and herself as well when she leaned forward and gave him a chaste kiss on the lips. Blushing at her temerity, she ducked her head in embarrassment, wondering why it did not seem nearly daring enough to satisfy her.

"Thank you, Cissy. That was the nicest thing that has happened to me in months." Ryan smiled, "Remember, no more climbing out windows, spying, or otherwise risking that pretty neck of yours. I might not be around to save you next time."

"Even if you are a Yankee, I hope you keep safe."

"Goodnight, Cissy. I suspect we're leaving tomorrow. If I can I will either drop off some more food, or I'll ask one of my men to do it for me before we depart." He reached for her then and pulled her close. Gently he kissed her lips and when she began to respond he felt his body stir with answering need. He forced himself to step back.

Cissy stood in the door watching him walk away. Sensing her eyes on his back, he turned at the corner and blew her a kiss before vanishing into the dark shadows that lined the street. She was standing where he had left her, her hand pressed to the lips he had just claimed. Despite the fear of an uncertain future promised by coming days of battle, he felt a sense of elation. Perhaps, she was not as immune to him as she wanted to be. Unfortunately, he wasn't immune either.

Chapter 4

A persistent buzzing in his ear, a throbbing ache in his leg, and the shrieks and moans from nearby beds convinced him he had died and gone to hell. Where else but there could such misery exist, he wondered. His eyes would not open, or if they were, then there was only darkness around him. He couldn't be sure. Maybe that was the way it was in hell, too. A crawling sensation on his face added to the torment. Weakly he lifted his hand and brushed at the annoyance only to have it return within seconds. Next he reached for his aching leg in the hope that he could rub it and ease the pain. His groping hand found nothing where his leg should have been. Shocked, his eyes opened a slit. The world spun in a dizzy circle before coming to a wobbly rest. Then he remembered. He was not dead...just damned well wanted to be. Feeling eyes on him he shifted his gaze to his left and met the gaunt face of another man sitting on the edge of a cot watching him.

"Damned flies'll drive a mortal out of his mind if this war hain't already done it." The man swatted at one that landed on his bare arm but nothing but a nub lifted at the effort. "Name's Nemus. Been a wondering if you was gonna wake up?"

"Where is this?"

"Chimborazo they call it. Hell of a name for a shithole ain't?"

Logan was too weak to respond. Sick with fever, weak with loss of blood, and despairing of heart, he could only pray to be overtaken once more by unconsciousness. At least then he could forget the physical torments and the fact that now he was only a piece of a man. If God were merciful, he would have died. He much preferred that to living a life as a cripple, unworthy of claiming the love of a beautiful, vibrant woman like Cissy. Mayhap he might still die. The way he felt, it seemed likely. For a moment the thought brought a fleeting smile to his lips before he slipped back into sleep. He had no way of reckoning how long he had slept, only that he awakened to the dark of night feeling as parched as a fish in a dried out river bed. His feeble croaking at last aroused the garrulous man beside him enough that he moved from his cot to hold a glass of water to Logan's lips. Logan tried to transmit his gratitude with his eyes, as he had no energy to do more.

"Shore am glad you're stirring even if you are as weak as a newborn kitten. Doc said he had about give up on you when you took such a high fever. Said if you come around, you'd probably make it. Looks like you ain't going to be doing no more fighting though. Our boys are about played out anyway, best as I can hear."

Logan blinked in reply before closing his eyes and sinking into fitful sleep, one that brought corpses marching like silent sentinels across the blackness of his eyelids. Their empty sockets seemed to be looking at him in accusation for having lived. He wanted to tell them that he would have preferred to be walking beside them with both legs under him than to face the empty future that he envisioned. He watched their jaws gape in a toothy rictus as they laughed at him. In the throes of the dream, he swung his arms to smash at them and drive them away. His cries demanding they stop tormenting him aroused Nemus who lay slumbering in the next bed.

"Dammit, man. Wake up before you rouse the whole damned hospital. I don't know what you're adreaming, but it must be pure tee awful."

"No more than living."

"Count your blessings, Johnny boy. You coulda been kilt.

Least you ain't laying out there in the dirt with buzzards pecking on you."

Logan didn't answer. Over the coming days he kept his distance from fellow patients and the harried and overworked staff. His doctor harangued him for making no effort to eat, get out of bed, and participate in his own recovery. He didn't care. Until he could decide if it was worth the effort, he intended to just lie where he was. Some small inner voice tried to tell him that it wasn't all over, that he could still have a good life, and that if his girl loved him the loss of a leg would not matter. But, it damned well did matter to him. And despite his best efforts to simply die, his young body betrayed him in the effort. He grew stronger by the day and more and more restless. To be bedridden was a constant misery, but the thought of trying to get around with only one leg was terrifying.

His doctor took the decision out of his hands. He walked in early one Monday while Logan was listlessly picking at his meager breakfast. With a grim look of determination on his face, he wheeled a converted chair in front of Logan and glared at him. "You're coming out of that damned bed, if it takes me and half of Lee's army to haul your sorry ass up. Now, heave yourself over here into this damned thing, or get ready to be shoved in it. I don't much give a hoot which it is, but you are moving out of that bed for the rest of the morning."

Logan's fixed stare was as sharp as any cavalry saber. For long moments the two men glared at one another, neither willing to cede the point. Tired of the stand off, the doctor nodded his head at two male nurses.

"Shit. I wish you'd all just leave me the hell alone, dammit all." Logan sat up in the bed and swung his stump over to the edge. Using his good leg he managed to stand up and swivel enough to fall into the waiting chair. "Hope the hell you're satisfied," he snarled.

Not answering, the doctor wheeled him over to a window.

The day was gray and gloomy, certainly nothing to inspire an elevated mood. "Stay here until your dinner arrives, then you can get back in bed. After laying around so long, you'll be ready to stretch out by then."

Logan shrugged his shoulders in dismissal as he stared out the filthy window. The dull throbbing ache in his leg didn't help his disposition any. The thoughts that nudged into his brain were as pestiferous as the flies. He did not want to think about Cissy. It hurt too much to imagine how she would flinch at the sight of his new deformity. He knew he couldn't face her, couldn't deal with that kind of pain. All that long morning he pondered his future and how he had to go about reordering his life, one that did not include the woman he loved and had promised to marry. He had listened as other soldiers spoke of going to California or Texas when the war ended. It had not appealed to him then, with land and a woman to wed waiting for him. Now the idea drew him. He would sell his land in New Berne and go west. That was the least he could do for her, give her the freedom to find a whole man and not one she pitied.

Over the coming days he grew stronger and spent increasing hours blindly staring out the window. He thought of writing Cissy and telling her the engagement was off. But that meant offering some kind of explanation. That defeated him. What was he to say? That he was too much of a coward to face her? That he considered his life finished for all real purposes? That he could not stand to look into her eyes and feel her revulsion for his maimed body? The more he worried it around in his head, the more certain he was that simply moving on with no word was the best approach. He just didn't know if he had the energy to move on. Hell, he didn't know if he had the energy to face another day. Furthermore, he didn't even want to.

The doctor walked in the following morning and snatched the covers from Logan as he lay in bed refusing his meals. The doctor stood glowering in heavy silence before barking, "Dammit, boy. I can save you from a wound. I could maybe save you from someone else. But, there's not a damned thing I can do to save you from yourself. Only you can do that. Now, just get on about it, or get the hell out of this hospital. Too many good boys need this bed for me to waste it any longer on you."

* * * * *

Hundreds of miles south, Graham kissed his contented wife and pulled her into the circle of his arms. Their passion sated, both snuggled close despite the warm breeze wafting through the open window by their bed. He could hear the soft dry rustle of the palms as they murmured in the wind and breathed deep with near contentment. The only image that disturb this hiatus in paradise was that of Cissy's face. He could not help the involuntary snort of anger that escaped him.

Evangeline turned in his arms to face him, "What's wrong, darling? You sound provoked."

"I'm sorry sweetheart. I had hoped I could take you to France and show you my parent's home, but it's impossible now. As soon as this war is ended, we have to return to Wilmington. Every time I think of Cissy there, alone in an enemy occupied town, I cringe. God only knows what she will get herself into this time. I shudder to think she might be back to spying. The foolish girl doesn't begin to comprehend the danger of her rash actions."

"Graham, when we realized that night that Cissy was not with us, I knew the dream of going to France was finished. I am as worried as you are. We have no choice but to return the moment that we can. I just hope it will be soon. The worry has been a constant upset."

"I know. How well I know. I could ring her stubborn, willful neck. At the same time I suppose I have a perverse pride in her daring. God only knows what she will get into that stubborn head of hers next."

"Do you know what is happening with the war? I don't know if papers arrive that have news or perhaps some ship that may have word of what is going on."

"What I have heard tells me that it cannot be much longer. Wilmington has fallen. With the port there closed, the South will be getting no more imports. Without them, there is nothing to feed the effort."

"Oh, no, that means twice that Cissy must deal with being in an occupied town. I can only pray she doesn't aggravate the Yankees with any more of her spying schemes."

Graham snorted before dryly responding, "One would have hoped she had learned her lesson in New Berne. But, then, this is Cissy we are speaking of. The sooner we can return and set things in order the better I will like it. I am so damned worried about her that I cannot focus on business issues that are going to be critical once this war is finished. I would leave today if I thought I could slip in to some obscure part of the coast. Surely there is something I can do."

"Oh Graham, if you leave you must take Andy and me, too. I don't want to be left here without you. I know nobody here."

"I would not dare risk your life and my son's. It's just that I have to try to protect my daughter, foolish though she is. I will not endanger the two of you." Graham rolled over and pulled her close. He swore he would find a way to slip back into Wilmington and soon. And it would be alone. "Don't you think we could find something more pleasurable to occupy ourselves with this evening?"

He watched his wife's face in the moonlight, loving the gleam of renewed arousal that lit her eyes. She said nothing as she turned her face to his kiss. Nothing mattered to him at that moment beyond losing himself in his wife's arms. He would deal with his intransigent daughter later, for now his need for

Evangeline drowned out all other concerns.

He awakened in the night to the sound of distant thunder and for a moment thought it cannon fire before he realized he was far from the fighting at home. The hours until dawn were filled with plans and alternatives as he weighed how best to salvage his business interests, re-establish his base in New Berne, and see to his daughter's safety. Trying to avoid tossing about as he wrestled with the problems, he held himself stiff. Perhaps it was that very rigidity that caused his wife to stir and slowly open her eyes.

"You're not sleeping, darling. Are you worrying still? Surely you need to rest as there is nothing you can do for now."

"I'm trying to sift through my options for a number of things. It isn't just Cissy, although that is a priority. I must also reorganize my business affairs for the time when we can return home. I need to ascertain which ships I wish to retain and which I might want to sell and replace with more modern propulsion. I must establish new trade partners and revitalize some of the previous ones. Soon we will need to close down here and pack for our return. There is much to be done." He left unsaid that he planned to leave her to see to the packing after he had gone ahead. There was no question in his mind how she would object to that were she given time to wage a battle with him over it.

The very thought of leaving her and his son behind was painful. While he had friends in Nassau, he had enemies, too. Any man as successful as he was had those who would resent that success, and through jealousy create problems. Then there were those who had been bested at business by his acumen and were resentful of their own loss of business. Although Evangeline was past the years of debutante freshness, she was a desirable woman that turned men's heads with lust. He did not want to leave her and his son on foreign soil with him too far away to afford immediate protection. They represented his second life, a rebirth, one that was filled with far more joy and contentment than he had ever felt with his first wife, Monique. The only good thing to have come of that ill-advised marriage was his much loved and incomparable daughter. While she tried his soul at times with her impetuosity and rashness, he loved her beyond measure. In her were combined the best of both of her parents along with the worst. She carried Graham's sensitivity and Monique's verve. Monique had given her a lush body that men would crave. From his mother had come her beautiful face, turquoise eyes, and long thick hair the color of ripened wheat. She had inherited his shrewdness and courage. Graham was secretly proud of her daring even while it terrified him as a father. He could not help the smile that settled on his lips when he remembered the times her stubborn determination had landed her in some pickle. He drifted into sleep with that smile still curving his lips.

The following morning Graham sat in his office on the Nassau docks. The job of reorganizing his business for the after-war world had his total attention. When his assistant burst through the door shouting, Graham did not at first hear him. Again he shouted, "Sir. Just got a paper from New York. I think you're going to want to read this."

Graham glanced up in irritation, "What are you yammering about. You know I asked not to be disturbed for any reason this morning. It's vital that I concentrate on reorganizing my business. I cannot do it if I am constantly interrupted."

"I'm sorry, sir. I still think you would want to see this. It might have some bearing on what you are trying to do." Tentatively the man offered the New York Times for April 26, 1865, two days previous.

Graham looked at the blaring headlines: *Union, Victory, Peace: Johnston surrenders entire army at Bentonville, N.C.* "Dear God. I knew it was coming but I'm still not prepared to see it. I'm sorry I barked at you. You were right to bring this to me.

With Lee's surrender at Appomattox on April 9, this is the end of the Confederacy. It means that it's critical for me to get some kind of transition back to the states begun immediately."

As Graham lost himself in the article, his assistant left the room un-noticed. For Graham, it was both good and bad news. While he had never truly believed the South could prevail against the might of the North, his heart still lay with his homeland. With its defeat, the question would be what the ramifications of that loss would mean to the rebellious states. Would they be punished? How would the return to Union government be managed? How would it affect shippers like him who had provided blockade-runners to the Confederacy? What he could not have known as he sat there debating his options was that in two short days Lincoln would fall to an assassin's bullet and any clemency the South might have anticipated would be doomed in the aftermath.

Graham suddenly chuckled. He would not have to incur Evangeline's wrath by sneaking home without her. With the war over, they could all take one of his ships directly into Wilmington. Perhaps he should leave Nassau as the homeport, he mused, at least until he could see how things were going to shake out for the conquered south. After all, he had earned no friendship from the Union with his blockade-runners. He left his office to return to his quarters and ask Evangeline to begin packing. They were leaving as soon as he could provision the ship that sat idle in the harbor.

* * * * *

With only minor skirmishes left, for all real purposes the war had ended after four long and bloody years that left few families untouched. From foreign soil, seaports and battlefields, from hospitals and prisons, weary men made their way home. Some plodded, some limped weary mile after weary mile on legs weak from hunger and defeated of spirit, whether victor or vanquished. A few caught railroads or ships. Even fewer rode horses or mules, as so many had been killed in battle or by exhaustion and starvation. But all had one destination in mind: home...or what was left of home. Yankee or Rebel, home was the constant sustaining refrain that kept them going regardless of the obstacles.

All except, Logan. He had left the hospital in the dark of night a week before the cessation of war not knowing where he was going, only that he was going. He accepted that he was taking a bed needed by men in need of the kind of care that no one was capable of providing him. How could anyone restore his leg and his hope for the life he had anticipated? With a crudely fashioned peg strapped onto a stump that was still sore, and a crutch for support, going was far tougher than he had anticipated. The first day had found him just beyond the outskirts of Richmond where he slept in the moldy straw of a barn and forced himself to ignore the rumblings in his belly. He arose in the morning and removed the stale bread he had reserved to nibble on. It didn't offer much in the way of energy, nor did it sate his hunger, but it was the best he could manage. He strapped his peg on and stood. The pain struck with such force that he reeled into the straw, dropping like a rock.

"Ah, shit. Did I need anything else to deal with?" He looked to Heaven as if he expected an answer. Neither that nor deliverance from pain arrived within the next hour. Strapping the peg to his back in resignation, he managed to heave himself to one leg by supporting his weight on the side of an empty stall. He had never stolen in his life but at that moment he would have been tempted to steal a horse had the barn contained one. As it was, the crutch and sheer grit would have to propel him on his way. He clenched his jaw and faced a gray day, the threat of eminent rain an unwelcome greeting.

By noon he was exhausted to the point it took every ounce of resolve he could muster just to keep going. Looking down he sneered at his stump and cursed it once again. At the rate he was going, it would take him a year to walk to New Berne. And if he didn't find something to eat soon he would starve to death long before that. Pulling his coat closer around his body to ward off the chill, he paused for a moment in the road, head down, gasping. He heard the jangle of harnesses and the wheels of a wagon and knew he needed to move out of the middle of the road, but he was too spent to care.

"Whoa!" A deep voice rumbled from the wagon, "The good Lord bless you son, but you are a miserable sight."

The stranger draped his reins over the dashboard and clambered down. When he reached Logan he did not need to be told that the man had reached the end of his tether. "Here. Let me help you into the back of the wagon. Looks to me like you could use some drying out and a little food."

Logan looked up into clear blue eyes wreathed in the wrinkles of a jolly spirit. "That's a fact. I would be purely grateful."

By the time they reached the farmhouse, where the man who had introduced himself as Robert Singleton lived, Logan was nearly comatose with fatigue. His body cried out for rest, food, and comfort. And his spirit craved some bright spot to light the way to a future he could bear. Preacher Robert threw Logan's arm over his shoulder and all but carried him into the welcome warmth of the kitchen where the aroma of apple pie and roast pork caused Logan to wonder for a brief moment whether or not he had died and gone to heaven without being informed of the event. If so, he was all for being in heaven.

Mattie Singleton bustled over like a round butterball of loving concern, "Mercy me, Papa. Just look at this poor boy. How many more of our young men are out there suffering as they try to return to their families? You just plop him right here in this chair by the stove and I'll fetch him a nice cup of okra coffee. I'm the preacher's wife Mattie. What is your name, son?

I am sorry I can't offer you real coffee but we haven't seen any of that since '62. With this war done with I sure do look forward to the real thing once more. Now, don't mind me. You just set yourself right here and rest. Soon as I pour the coffee, I'll put supper on the table. You look just about plumb tee starved pure to death. Didn't they feed you boys none in the army. Course it's to be expected, I suppose, since nobody's had much to eat for the last year or so. Slim pickings for sure for us all. Papa, you go wash your hands. Now do you want sugar and milk in this coffee? Of course we don't have sugar either, but I do have some honey one of the parishioners found in that old hollow tree in the woods yonder. Mercy, I don't think you ever told me your name."

Logan looked up in awe at the non-stop flow of words from this tiny little round woman. He could not prevent the chuckle that escaped.

Robert smiled at his wife and then Logan, "Mama, this is Logan Gwaltney. Mattie here is never at a loss for words. Don't worry about trying to keep up. It's like trying to dam a river. It takes a strong one to break the flow."

Mattie flapped her apron at her husband. "You hush now, you dear old thing. You are going to give Logan just the worst impression of me. Now Logan, don't you mind us one bit. This coffee is going to have you perked up in no time. Let me just finish roasting these sweet potatoes and we'll set down to some vittles. I just don't recollect if you wanted milk and honey or not, but I'll just put them right here on the table and you fix this up just like you want it. I take it you're not from around here. I don't believe I know anyone of that last name in this area. I suspect I've met just about everybody for miles around at church or revivals. Of course, I could have missed someone. Are you married? I do hope your sweet wife is not worried to death about you. Certainly everyone is concerned about our poor southern boys trying to get home. In all charity, I am sure that Yankee feel the same way, God bless their misguided hearts. The ones that are waiting for their men to come home are the lucky ones, don't you know? All too many boys are buried in some forsaken place far from all who loved them. It just breaks my heart, it does. Papa, while I get supper on the table, would you heat up some bath water and let's see if we can get this poor stray lamb clean and his clothes, as well. I do apologize for the mention, but I don't want any lice or bedbugs in my house. Heaven forbid the like. Papa, would you get a fire going in Charles' room, too. That's our son. He's moved out now and married. Thank the good Lord he came home just a few days ago. He was sick with a terrible case of croup, but I do believe he's on the mend now. Lela...that's his wife, was thrilled to death when he just walked right down the lane and into their door, calm as you please after three years without hide nor hair of him. And him with a precious son he'd never laid eyes all. Him being born a few months after he went to war, don't you know?"

Logan sipped on the coffee and felt a trifle better. He just prayed she would soon finish the meal so he could eat, bathe and crawl into Charles' bed. The very thought made him tremble with longing. He was even grateful for the chatterbox of a woman as it kept him from having to respond. Even had he tried, he doubted she would have paused long enough to hear. Hell, she barely paused to take a breath.

Chapter 5

"Jesus, Mary and Joseph! If I don't get me a breath of the Lord's own good air, I think I'll turn up me toes. Tis enough of this imprisonment here, I tell ye. I'm for taking a walk and I'll not be gainsaid."

"Annie Brigitte O'Neal you are an idiot to leave this house when the whole town is swarming with Yankees like bees around a hive. Have you lost your sense? Don't you recall that Colonel Madison told us to just stay home and keep as low a profile as we possibly can. We don't need any trouble with the Union army. You know we are already under suspicion from our previous activities spying on them. You walk out that door and you're asking for trouble.

"Begorrah and be damned. I be leaving." Annie marched out the door and into the chill of an early April morning.

Cissy leaned against the door that still reverberated from the emphatic slam of Annie's departure and debated if she should follow her. Although she could sympathize with Annie's boredom and need for freedom, when Ryan had brought that last packet of food just prior to his departure, he had reiterated their need to stay put. Despite her rebellious nature, Cissy had taken it to heart. Intuitively she sensed that with the end upon them there was no longer anything she could do to help the confederate cause. It helped that she knew Logan had survived the battle at Fort Fisher. She had heard nothing since, but could only pray that he was unharmed. As for Annie, not having heard anything of her beau for months, Cissy understood her need to seek some information, whether good or bad, about what had become of him.

She spent the rest of the morning in the library pretending to read a book that held no interest for her. At noon she picked at the dinner Reesie had brought her on a tray. Anxious at Annie's continued absence, she threw the book she had been pretending to read onto the floor and began to pace the room. A peremptory banging at the front door shattered the quiet of the afternoon. Her heart in her throat she ventured into the foyer and peered through the sidelight to see a grim faced Union officer preparing to once again pound on the door. Stiffening her spine and dreading the worst, she opened it.

"And to what do I owe this rude intrusion, sir?" Determined to bluster her way past the impertinent man that glared at her, she pointed her nose skyward.

"Don't play the innocent with me, Miss LaRoque. You and your servant are highly suspect for your past activities. I want to talk to both you and Miss O'Neal right now."

"I find your behavior and manner rude in the extreme. I have no knowledge of what you can possibly suspect me of and I refuse to admit you into my home. Furthermore, my servant is out at the moment on an errand for me and I don't know when to expect her. Your timing is most inconvenient. Please excuse me."

His foot firmly shoved into the doorway prevented her closing the door. Pushing past her, she was nearly capsized before he grabbed her elbow to help her regain her balance. "My pardon, miss. It is not my intent to be any more offense than necessary, but these charges against you are most serious. You will answer to my questions, either here or downtown. Rest assured you would find these premises are far preferable." He extended his hand, not surprised when she ignored it. "I am Colonel Brandon McLean formerly of the 76th Pennsylvania Battalion. I have been assigned to assure the security of the area."

"Colonel McLean, do you seriously consider a helpless, nearly starved to death woman like me of some real danger to you and your precious Union army?"

McLean bit back a chuckle at her audacity, "Miss LaRoque, ladies of uncommon beauty and charm such as you have proven to be more than capable spies during this conflict. Much harm was done to our plans by information you charming ladies have elicited from gullible and lonely soldiers in an enemy land."

"I cannot answer for the actions of other ladies of our dear Southland. Please do not presume to tar us all by the same brush. If you have nothing provable against me, and surely there is nothing, then you cause us both undue stress by your uninvited presence here."

"Be that as it may, I will await the return of Miss O'Neal. Shall we adjourn to the parlor?"

Cissy turned so he could not see her biting her lip with frustration. She could only wonder what Annie might have done to cause this unexpected intrusion. Nodding her head, she motioned for him to follow her into the parlor. It was as cold as a tomb as no fire enlivened the dead ashes in the fireplace. They did not have enough wood or coal to heat the various rooms and still stoke the fire in the kitchen needed for cooking the sparse remainder of their food supplies. Had it not been for Ryan's last package, there would have been no food to cook at all, sparse or otherwise.

Despising herself for using Ryan and hoping not to create undeserved problems for him, she smiled. "Colonel Ryan Madison of New York is a good friend of mine. I am sure he would vouch for me and allay any suspicions you erroneously hold."

"Aye, I know Colonel Madison. However, I was unaware of any romantic liaison that he might have formed with you Miss LaRoque."

"You miscomprehend me, sir. I did not say there was any romantic involvement. I merely stated that we are friends."

Cissy smiled winningly. Casting demure eyes downward, she looked up at him through her lashes.

Unwilling to acknowledge the allure of the woman despite the twitch in his trousers, Brandon looked at the ceiling and drew a deep breath. "May I be seated to await Miss O'Neal? I also have some questions I must ask of you?"

Smiling pertly and sashaying over to the sofa, she swept a hand to indicate a seat beside her. "Please, do join me. It has been most tedious here for days now. I have had no company beyond my household staff and find myself quite bored." Indicating the book she had tossed to the floor earlier, she commented, "Not even Mr. Dickens can entertain me today. Perhaps, a handsome soldier and determined visitor such as yourself can offer me some small glimpse of what transpires beyond my cloistered walls?"

"I suspect that you and the rest of the South are aware that military occupation is going to mean a change of lifestyle and mindset. Despite the brilliance of your generals, the south is defeated and the army is now in charge. I am here to warn you that any attempts to gain information to pass on to the Rebels is futile at this point."

"That comes as no surprise. With the loss of the port here, the South was doomed." She tossed him a saucy grin, "I suppose that means you Yankees will be going home soon?"

"I am sorry to disabuse you of that notion. The army will continue to occupy Wilmington for some time. The South will be a conquered territory until it can be repatriated."

Cissy sat without comment trying to digest that last remark. It was a tough one to swallow and one her fellow citizens would resent as much as she. The latest outrage had occurred two days earlier and the anger over it was fresh in her mind. On April 7, Union forces under Brigadier General Joseph Hawley had entered St. James Episcopal Church with hammers and pick axes and proceeded to rip out pews and church fittings despite the vehement objections of Reverend Alfred Watson. The local citizenry was beyond incensed by the disrespect. Calmer minds among the elderly remembered that the British had done much the same during the Revolutionary War. And now, as in the earlier war, the church was again a hospital for the enemy.

After five tension fraught minutes broken only by the repeated clearing of his throat and the ticking of the mantle clock, the Colonel walked over to the window and peered down the street. The soldiers he had stationed in front of the house and at the ends of the block were the only occupants.

Cissy shifted in her seat. She was worried about Annie as it was unlike her to be gone for so long, but she dared not let the officer know of her concern. Her well-schooled manners demanded that she offer refreshments, but with only a bit of tea and coffee left from Ryan's gift she was loathed to waste it on an uninvited guest.

He returned to the sofa, crossed his left leg at his calf and leaned back. Looking at the gleaming boot, crisp uniform, and well-nourished body, she could not help comparing his attire to the sorry state of the southern soldiers that had marched past her door on their way inland. Feeling spiteful, she couldn't resist her remark, "I am aware that my hospitality is lacking. I regret that I cannot offer you refreshment. As you might imagine, our resources are strained by the war and the occupation. I have not dared to venture to market, and if I had done so, there is nothing to be had and I have nothing but useless Confederate notes with which to purchase anything. However, I would be happy to have my housekeeper fetch you a glass of water if you wish?"

"For the moment, I'm fine. Please don't disturb yourself."

Cissy fidgeted and McLean drummed his fingers on his knee. Cissy felt his eyes repeatedly studying her profile and curvaceous figure. When she caught his eye in the middle of one such perusal, he blushed like a maiden. He shifted again in his seat and pretended to study the wallpaper. He did not see the smile that curved her lips at her awareness of what he had been doing.

Perhaps if he were susceptible to her, Cissy might be able to finagle a way for Annie and her to allay his suspicions. "Excuse me, Colonel McLean, but I should have offered the reason for Annie's continued absence. You see, her fiancé has been missing since the battle at Fort Fisher and she is worried sick. I am sure she is just trying to find some word of what may have happened to him. If you have a sweetheart at home, you must believe that she would do the same."

"It is unfortunate that I am not one of the lucky ones with wife or sweetheart to dream of. I was stationed in the west prior to the outbreak of hostilities. There was a great scarcity of available women at the fort."

Persisting, Cissy added, "Then no doubt your mother and sisters are eagerly awaiting your return."

"I would that were so. My parents are long departed from this life and since I was an only child with a lack of any close relatives, I doubt that I would be greatly missed. Like your friend Madison, I plan to stay on in the South now the war has ended. I have no one to go home to and I quite like the area."

"Oh, your poor man. How very sad for you." She took the opportunity to gently pat the hand that he had been drumming on his knee. "Wilmington is lovely. New Berne is too, and once my parents have returned we will be residing there. If you wish, I could help you meet some of the people here before I return?"

He was saved the need to answer by a loud wailing that announced Annie's arrival long before she reached the door. "Ah, it seems Miss O'Leary at last returns."

Alarmed by Annie's wild sobs, Cissy rushed to open the door for her. Soldiers on either side had a firm grip on Annie's arms. She couldn't tell if it was to keep the girl on her feet or to prevent her getting away. Looking each man in the eye, she glared at them.

"How dare you manhandle my poor maid? Can you not see she is totally distraught?" Pulling Annie away from the soldiers, she wrapped her arms around her as she led her into the parlor where the uncomfortable officer waited for them. "Sit down, you poor thing and tell me what is wrong."

"Oh, me heart be broken. Me Seamus be gone." At that, Annie again wailed loudly and buried her face in Cissy's shoulder.

"You mean he's been killed? But, how do you know?"

Rather than answer, Annie again burst forth with wild crying. Cissy quietly remarked to the colonel who stood by unsure what to do, "Seamus O'Sullivan was Annie's fiancé. She has been hysterical with worry for weeks now and thus went to seek word of him. Would you be so kind as to pour a bit of brandy for Annie. You will find it on the sideboard in the dining room if we still have any."

The minute the colonel was beyond earshot, Annie whispered, "They caught me in the hospital at St. James Church trying to get information from the wounded men. Just play along with me or my jig be up." Again, Annie sobbed miserably, increasing the volume when the colonel's footsteps announced his return.

Cissy groaned inwardly to hide her anger and frustration with her maid. Did she not have the sense to realize that spying was pointless now? Coaching her face into one of sympathy for Annie's 'plight,' Cissy reached for the glass the colonel offered Annie."

"Colonel, I beg you to allow Annie time to grieve the loss of her fiancé. I am sure she meant no harm when she went to the hospital to seek information on his whereabouts. If you would be so kind as to return tomorrow, I am sure she will be more composed and able to allay any concerns you might have about her purposes today."

Colonel McLean appeared embarrassed at the woman's obvious distress and seemed relieved to have an excuse to quit the premises. He nodded and wasted no time excusing himself. Cissy noted he had cast another discretely appraising and appreciative eye over her body as he departed. She chuckled that once more she seemed to have attracted a Yankee colonel. She could not help puzzling that she would find other men, and Yankees at that, so attractive when her heart should be firmly committed to the man she was pledged to marry. Logan had been her friend since childhood; she concluded that perhaps that explained why it was still hard to picture him as her lover. She shook her head to clear the doubts from it. Of course, she loved Logan---only did she really love him the way a woman loves a man? That thought had begun to plague her.

The minute they heard the door close behind the colonel, Annie's face went from rain to sunshine. The mirth in her eyes quickly vanished at Cissy's glare.

"You blooming idiot! You know there is no point in trying to spy now. What good is it going to do at this point with the war over? All you have managed to accomplish is to renew Yankee suspicions about us. And don't think you are off the hook either. When Colonel McLean returns tomorrow, what is he going to be able to accuse you of?"

"Twas a foolish thing, for sure. Jesus, Mary, and Joseph but I be tired of just sitting around here. I truly did hope to learn something of Seamus while I was poking me nose around the Yankees."

"Your nose alright! You were busier chopping it off despite your face than accomplishing any good poking it in where you have no business being. I declare if you land me in a pickle with you, I will turn you out, friend or not, for being so stupid."

"Ah Cissy, me girl, you don't be so mean as all that. Mayhap I should take to the stage. I rather enjoyed that performance, I did. Now take heart. I'm sure by tomorrow this won't be so important. Maybe the colonel will even forget about me."

"We should be so lucky!"

They were not. At ten the next morning, the knocker on the door banged to announce the arrival of the colonel and his aide. The gravity of his face caused Cissy's heart rate to speed with alarm. Struggling to gain her composure and calm her shaking hands, she invited, "Please gentlemen, be so good as to follow me into the parlor. If you will seat yourselves, I will summon Annie."

"That will not be necessary. Miss LaRoque, let's speak plainly shall we? You and your servant have been the cause of some speculation as to the extent of your activities over the last months. With the hostilities at an end, I am sure we all realize the futility of any dealings that might bring the wrath of the government down on your heads. I cannot prove any suspicions that have been alluded to regarding you and Miss O'Neal as our men have been remarkably adept at avoiding implicating you. At this point, if you will assure me that neither of you will conduct yourselves in such a way as to warrant further attention, then I would prefer we allow this to go unremarked."

"You are most kind, sir. I am grateful that you are willing to overlook any unintended rashness on our part."

Brandon nodded before turning to his aide, "Sergeant, would you wait for me on the sidewalk, please?"

"Yes, sir."

Puzzled, Cissy searched the colonel's face wondering what more he might have to say. Again fear coiled itself around her stomach making it clench.

When the sergeant had gone, Brandon McLean gave her a warm smile. "I know this is not the most opportune of circumstances in which to strike up an acquaintance, but I would very much welcome the opportunity to call on you socially. I confess I find you a remarkable and beautiful young woman, one that I would like very much to know better."

"Colonel..."

Brandon interrupted, "Please, call me Brandon. The title only reinforces the divide this war has brought."

"Of course, Col...er...Brandon." Cissy said it with hesitation. Biting her lips, she struggled with how to reply to his intentions. If she angered him by rejection would he then turn a harsh eye in her direction, a scrutiny she deserved? If she accepted his suit would she bring the censure of her neighbors upon her? Even though the immediate ones had evacuated during the struggle at Fort Fisher, they would return and soon rumors would fly like angry wasps were she accused of consorting with the enemy.

As though he could read her thoughts, Brandon gently lifted her hand to his lips where he kissed it and then lowered their joined hands to his knee. He smiled into her eyes allowing her to read his sincerity. "I am aware of the reasons you must hesitate. I assure you that regardless of your reply I wish you only the best. I will be discreet and not cause undue attention when I call on you, if you will but permit it?"

She knew she should refuse, but something in her rejected that. She liked the man. He was good-looking, courteous, obviously cultured, and he made her insides tingle in a confusing way. Much the way Ryan Madison did, she realized. Not as much maybe, but she felt a definite attraction despite the fact both were enemy soldiers. "Colonel...Brandon, I would like that. But, it will be difficult. I do not wish to bring the animosity of others onto my family and me, regardless of what my own preferences might be."

"I will be careful and call only at night and when no one is about in the streets. Is that acceptable to you?"

Cissy stared in silent confusion fearing any personal relationship with an enemy, nice or not.

Taking her silence for acquiescence, he nodded, "Good. If I may, I will return this evening? I have some things that I think will make your life a bit easier: coffee, flour, ham, peas, sugar, sweet potatoes and some other items that are difficult for you to procure at the moment."

Cissy chuckled, "You certainly do know how to court a girl, sir. How can I possibly refuse such an offer?"

He flushed red at the implications. "I am so sorry. I mean no disrespect."

"Don't be so serious. I am only teasing. Please, do call this evening. And after dusk, please."

He left whistling. She was not so carefree. Scolding herself for being a fool, risking the wrath of her neighbors, and feeling like she was betraying Logan, she could only wonder what idiocy made her invite the attentions of another Yankee. She supposed that after years of misery and war, she just wanted to see them as men like any others and not enemies. No doubt the deciding factor was the food, she reasoned. Already she salivated at the thought.

It was bad enough that Ryan made her heart race, now she was allowing a determined Yankee officer to call on her. Perhaps she was just fickle in her emotions, a shallow flirt. Logan deserved a far warmer love than she held for him. His had been a steady friendship since childhood, like the brother she had always longed for until little Andy came along after she was already grown. Unfortunate though it was, Logan had never inspired the kind of passion that she suspected a woman should feel for the man she planned to marry. She touched her lips in memory of the kiss that Ryan had planted there. It had ignited a flame in her that she had never felt before, making her long for some unknown fulfillment of its promise.

Cissy debated telling Annie that she was off the hook and the colonel would be returning that evening as a suitor. Her stomach grew queasy at the very thought of baldly announcing that. Taking the less taxing route, she decided to say nothing until he returned and then downplay the whole visit.

By the time he arrived, darkness had wrapped the streets in shadows broken only by moonlight that sifted between the leaves of the ubiquitous Spanish moss-draped live oaks. Watching from the window of the parlor, Cissy hurried to slip out the front door and meet him on the walkway to her house.

Nervous, she rushed into conversation. "Oh good evening, Brandon. It is a lovely night isn't it? I confess after being inside all day it would be lovely to stroll about the garden. I hope you don't mind?"

"Allow me to leave this sack of a few provisions by your door, and I'll be happy to offer my arm." She bit her lip as she waited, praying that they could slip into the shadows before Annie missed her and came looking.

Two weeks later, Brandon again returned with food. They had no sooner seated themselves on the garden bench than the clatter of hooves and wheels rolling over the cobbles came to a halt at the front of the house. The sudden banging of the front door knocker sounded like thunder in Cissy's ears. She could not imagine who would be calling at this hour of the evening in an occupied town. Alarmed she raised her eyes to Brandon's.

Her panic must have been evident, as he arose smoothly. "Please see to your guests, Cissy. I'll return another time."

She watched as he slipped away in the night. Then mustering her courage, she dashed through the back door hoping she had not been missed.

Chapter 6

Logan rolled over on his bed in the sparsely furnished guest room and thanked his lucky stars that Preacher Robert and Miz Mattie were such Godly souls. They had fed him, bedded him down in a clean and soft bed, and allowed him to rest until his bodily needs urged him to rise. Judging by the light in the room, the morning was well towards noon. Reaching under the bed he found the chamber pot, used it and dressed. He was still awkward in adjusting to his lost limb and nearly lost his balance. Standing to pull on trousers was one habit he needed to lose. It was easier to do it seated on the side of the bed and then lean back to tug them up to his waist. At least, he chortled with irony, he only had need of one sock so the sole pair he owned could be rotated and he need don and tie just the one shoe.

Dressed, he mulled over the decisions he had come to when he first awakened. Once his strength returned sufficient to permit continuing, he would reach New Bern and there counsel with his attorney to affect the liquidation of all property that he now owned following his father's demise. He had no hope that it would fetch its worth, but any funds he could realize would help him begin a new life, one that would begin in San Francisco. The city had always tantalized him and it seemed as good as any for starting over.

Logan spent the next few days with the Singletons. He answered their endless questions about the battles he had endured and his vision for the South after defeat. They worried southerners would be punished by a vengeful North. Logan's own concern on that issue and his desire to escape his previous life and commitments were the spurs that drove him to go westward. The allure of the fortune to be made in the wide-open western territories added to the appeal. The prospect lifted him somewhat from the depression that had seized him when he awakened to find his leg gone. He struggled to find a decent way to break his engagement to Cissy. The firm conviction that it would be easier for the both of them if he vanished without contact settled deep down in the pit of his belly. With the certainty that he must free her to find another, he did not have the strength to fight his longing for her if they were to meet face to face. Accepting his path was that of a coward despite his underlying desire to do what was best for her, he would utilize the services of longtime family attorney, John Harvey. He could rely on him to be discreet and to do what needed to be done to sever any connections to his past in New Berne.

Despite the inconvenience of his missing leg, three days later he left the Singleton's with more optimism than when he had arrived. Days of good food and a comfortable bed had given him strength. His determination of a plan for his future increased his sense of purpose. The elderly couple had provided a hospitable respite and a much-needed opportunity for healing and reflection. It wasn't so much that he was happy at the prospects for his future as simply having made peace with a new direction that would take him beyond all that he had known, and those that he had loved and loved still. Part of him was terrified and yet another felt freed, freed of the past, old hurts, old longings, and old expectations. It was as though he had awakened with amnesia and needed to redefine who he was and what he wanted from life. And, he needed to find a way to accept his new impediment and go forward without the expected pity and accommodation that he would receive from those that knew and loved him. That was the last thing that he wanted. And, that was the one thing his pride could not accept.

It was another two weeks of walking and sometimes

catching a ride, sleeping in barns and an occasional spare room, eating sporadically or going hungry, before he reached his destination. New Berne was in the throes of spring. It was as though all of nature was in lush celebration of the war's end. Azaleas, Carolina jasmine, wisteria, daffodils, tulips, iris, dogwoods, redbuds, a late blooming forsythia all competed with the emerging green of tender new leaves and the cloud of yellow pine pollen that greeted springtime in the Carolinas. He cursed the sneeze producing pollen while his senses reeled at the beauty of the reawakening world. Logan walked down Pollock Street towards Harvey's office with the wind lifting his hair and felt as though his heart would burst at this homecoming. He was torn, captivated by his hometown in all of the glory of springtime. The sparkling blue of the rivers that joined at Union Point, the gracious old homes, the canopy of spreading branches and birdsong overhead momentarily weakened his resolve to leave. Shaking his head to remind himself of why he had chosen to go west, he continued forward.

He paused at the shiny new shingle advertising Colonel Ryan Madison, Attorney at Law. He had a vague recollection of Cissy mentioning that the officer had lived in Evangeline's house following occupation of New Berne by the Union army. Again he shook his head at an enemy officer staying on to make the South his home. Cursing under his breath, he muttered, *'If the South is so damned wonderful, why wage war against it and nearly destroy it in the process?'* Ahead he could see Harvey's offices. He had no reason to linger in front of this one.

Sitting in front of John Harvey's mahogany desk, Logan felt a bead of sweat pop out on his brow. He wanted to squirm in his seat like a miscreant child in church. It took all of his self-control to sit quietly and not react to Harvey's stern comments. If he had not felt guilty of cowardice before, the man's remarks would have brought it on full- blown. As it was, he could only agree with every censorious statement the man uttered.

"Logan Gwaltney, I have known you since you were knee-high to a grasshopper and I have never known you to be a spineless idiot. It seems to me you lost your reason as well as your leg in this dad-blamed war. How can you sit there and tell me you are selling out the land that has been in your family since New Berne was settled? That is a sad thing for me to contemplate, but even worse is to think that you plan to hightail it out of here without a by your leave to your fiancée, the woman you have eaten your heart out over since you were a lad. Don't you think Cissy LaRoque deserves more respect than that? And then there's Evangeline. She is like a mother to you. Not to mention, Graham LaRoque who's loved you like a son. This is going to hurt them all. Dammit. It hurts me for that matter."

"I am as sorry as I can be, sir. I have worried this over in my mind for weeks now and it just seems like the best solution for everyone. I appreciate how you feel. It isn't a lack of gratitude for the love I have received from so many good people that I need to leave. As for the land, it needs more to bring it back than I have funds to hand. I can't even pay the taxes on it. It's far better to sell it and realize something than to have the sheriff seize it."

John Harvey shook his head with resignation and proceeded to copy down Logan's instructions. When they had finished, he rose from his desk and walked around to Logan. Struggling to his feet and balancing on his crutch, Logan extended his hand. The attorney shook it before dropping it to pat Logan's shoulder. Clearing his throat, he said, "God speed, my boy. You remember this is still your home. If you need to, you come back to us. You know I don't feel right about this. I think it is total hooey. The LaRoques don't deserve you just clearing out this way. It's going to hurt them all, especially that fiancée of yours."

"Thank you, sir. I appreciate what you're saying. This will

all be for the best in the end, I do believe."

"God willing, my boy. God willing." The attorney shook his head with resignation as he turned back to his desk. It was moments like this that he hated the job that he had been paid to do. He hated the hurt that would come of it. Staring down at his desk he pondered how so many lives could be impacted by one lost leg. While he could understand the reluctance Logan felt at facing Cissy as a lesser man physically than he had been before the war, he did not agree with the decision to just turn tail and run. Cissy deserved better, deserved to know that Logan had survived, and deserved the option to make her own decision.

Logan entered his boyhood home for the last time. Looking around the once elegant foyer, he was saddened by the squalor that years of neglect and war had created and for a moment he regretted his decision to sell the land his ancestors had claimed from a virgin wilderness. He could only hope that if they were watching, they would understand and forgive. Shrugging his shoulders to shake off the thought, he pulled the loose brick from the back of the dining room hearth and reached into the gap to withdraw the gold coins he had sequestered there prior to leaving for war. The money, while not a huge sum, would still purchase him food, lodging, and a train ticket west. Hopefully, soon Harvey would have his land sold and additional funds would arrive to help him start a new life. He visualized Cissy as he had last seen her and held her in his arms. Logan prayed that one day she would forgive him.

*****

Cissy's thoughts were far from Logan as she dashed from the garden tryst with Brandon and through the hallway to the front door, arriving just behind Annie who had already swung it open. Both girls gaped in surprise.

Hurling herself into waiting arms, Cissy gasped, "Father,

you're home!" Without awaiting his reply, she immediately turned to her stepmother and hugged her in turn. Her baby brother protested at being caught between the two women and struggled to get down. Cissy laughed at the red-faced boy. "Andy, you little scamp. Have you forgotten your sister? I want to hug you, too."

A happily smiling Evangeline handed the boy over to Cissy who promptly sent him into gales of laughter. "Ah ha. I see you haven't outgrown being ticklish."

Graham smiled at his reunited family, greeted Annie, and then excused himself to assist with the removal of their things from the hired hack. Reesie and Rufus, having heard the commotion, rushed into the foyer just as Graham turned to go out. They followed him to the curbing, babbling their excitement and describing the ordeal they had suffered since his departure.

Shocked at the deprivations they had endured during his months away, he was doubly thankful for the goods resting in the hold of his ship in Wilmington harbor. With the registry of the boat changed to France during his final days in Nassau, the military occupation would not be so hasty to harass him or his captain, and the ship's contents should be safe from confiscation and undue taxation beyond the normal duties. With the rising sun of morning, he would take Rufus to the harbor with him and return with sufficient food to replenish the depleted larder.

Following a joyous reunion and dinner, Graham, noting Cissy's unease, confronted her as to the cause. Reluctantly she confessed that had it not been for a Yankee officer's assistance there would have been little on the table.

That night when Logan sought his bed, miles away, Cissy sat by the small fire burning in the parlor grate and tried to explain to her father why she was receiving foodstuffs from an enemy officer. Blushing furiously under his accusing glare, she shifted in her perch on the edge of the dainty chair, one she had chosen deliberately as the location cast her face in shadow. Cissy worried her lip as she stalled in her reply. She had wanted to cry for joy at their unexpected arrival, but that had quickly turned to chagrin when Graham had risen from the table and gone to the kitchen where he hefted the sack of food Brandon had left before returning to the dining room in full fury.

Taking pity on her, Evangeline murmured, "Graham, darling, surely this will wait until tomorrow. I confess that I am beyond exhausted and you must be as well. I feel certain that Cissy has done nothing more than struggle to survive in very difficult times. When we are hungry, even the enemy that is willing to help is welcomed. Certainly, had it not been for that same enemy's help in New Bern when I was pregnant and so very ill, we would not now have our beautiful son."

Graham worked his mouth as he swallowed against the gorge that rose in his throat at the thought of his hungry daughter pandering to a Yankee officer's attentions. It cost him to dampen his temper and rise. Not looking at Cissy, not even acknowledging her, he offered his elbow to his wife. "By all means, my dear. We should retire before you are overly fatigued."

Graham left the house the following morning believing all were sleeping except for the servants. He needed to visit his office and warehouse, contact the employees that he had kept on reduced retainer while his Wilmington based shipping was closed after his departure, and settle the manifest from the ship that had brought him back from Nassau. He pushed Cissy's behavior to the back of his mind until he had time to deal with it rationally. His anger was still hot but more pressing matters took precedence. He intended that his family would not starve and would not consume anymore of the Union officer's gift to Cissy. To that end, the first order of business was to arrange delivery of the foodstuffs he had brought with him on the ship.

Cissy had peeked through the edge of her drapery and watched him leave. Not wasting a moment she dressed and quickly tiptoed down the stairs avoiding the creaky treads. Once she was safely beyond the confines of the house and yard, she broke into a brisk walk. It was imperative that she find Brandon McLean to warn him not to come to her home again. What her father would do if he found Brandon on the doorstep asking for her, she dared not imagine.

In a way, she was glad to end any potential involvement with the man. It was not worth the risk for the sake of some flattery to her ego, besides she still had much to prove to herself to want the confinement of marriage or a relationship with a man, her engagement to Logan not-with-standing. Thinking back to the day she accepted his ring and promised to marry him, she realized her heart had never been in it. Perhaps, when he returned from the war she would find a way to break the engagement or at least postpone it until her mind was less unsettled. Her old need to prove her merit, and to accomplish something that made her proud and deserving of love, still nagged. She could not help but wonder how long her mother's rejection and hostility when she was a child would continue to hurt and make her feel unworthy. Had it not been for that need she would never have ventured into her brief career spying for the lost Confederacy. That period of feeling as though she were making a contribution to helping her fellow townsmen had helped to temporarily assuage the feelings of inadequacy. With the war ended, she was determined find some other way to accomplish something that she could look to with pride.

The catcalls of Union soldiers loitering in the intersection of Fifth and Dock Streets pulled her from her brooding thoughts and reminded her of her destination. Ducking her head, she increased her pace the remaining block to the Bellamy home. The elegant mansion, the most beautiful in Wilmington, was built just prior to the war by physician and planter John

Bellamy and now served as headquarters for the occupation. She could only hope that Brandon was there and free to receive her. Luck was with her. He had just emerged from an inner office and was standing in the hall when she entered. Looking up, he smiled in delighted surprise, exclaiming, "Cissy, what an unexpected pleasure. What brings you here this morning?"

"Good morning, Brandon. Do you think we could perhaps stroll on the veranda for a moment?"

Agreeing, he took her elbow and guided her outside to one of the wicker chairs that graced the tall porch on the left side of the building. "May I have someone fetch you some coffee?"

"Thank you, no. I have only a moment before I must dash home. I came to warn you that you must not come to the house again. My father has returned and absolutely forbids me any further contact with Union personnel. I am sorry, but you mustn't call on me again."

"I see." Brandon swallowed his disappointment and managed a wry grin, "Damned Yankees are such a nuisance, eh? I do understand, Cissy. I don't like it, but I suppose were I your father in similar circumstances, I would feel the same way. It is a pity, as I had hoped to come to know you much better and with even greater affection."

"Thank you for your kindness, for everything, really." Cissy stood and offered her hand.

Taking it in both of his, he bent and kissed it. "Goodbye, Cissy. Go with God and may good things always find their way to you." He squeezed her hand gently before stepping back and releasing it. He stood watching her until she disappeared around the far corner.

Her walk home was filled with sad ruminations of what war had done to alienate well-meaning people, turning them from sympathetic figures into enemies. She could have liked Brandon, maybe even fallen in love with him had they met without the impediment of wartime allegiances. Cissy slipped into the rear door of the house and was back in her room and changing into a nicer frock, when Evangeline knocked on her door to ask if she would like to come down for a late breakfast.

It was pleasant to sit with the woman, one that was far more a mother to her than her birth mother, and catch up with the time they had been apart. The exotic nature of the Nassau Evangeline described captured her imagination, while her own stories of what the last weeks had been like in Wilmington appalled her stepmother.

"I'm sorry if I have disappointed you by befriending the Yankee officer. We were so hungry and desperate for food and fuel that it just didn't matter anymore where it came from or who gave it. I know that was upsetting for my father and it makes me sad to know he is so unhappy with me."

"Cissy, your father and I were well fed and warm, safe from war in Nassau. If anything, he is angry with himself that he could not spare you the hardships that you have endured. When he thinks about it a little more, he will realize that you were just trying to make it possible for the four of you to survive. Once he talks to his staff and learns something of the recent tribulations for the people of Wilmington, he is going to regret speaking so harshly to you last night. Don't press the issue. Give him time to digest it all and soon it will be fine between the two of you."

"I hope you are right. I hate it when he is so angry with me." Cissy bit back tears. For years it had been just her and her father, bonded together by their mutual emotional dependency on one another after her mother had abandoned them. He had perforce been both mother and father and thus doubly important in her life. Somehow he must forgive her for having anything to do with their enemy; otherwise she could not stand it.

A morose Cissy spent the remainder of the day pulling weeds in the small flower garden by the house, reading and then re-reading the same pages in the novel she had begun, pacing the floor of her room, and steadfastly ignoring Annie's attempts at conversation. At last she heard the front door open announcing her father's return and imminent suppertime. She arose from her chaise-lounge, brushed her hair, and shook the wrinkles from her dress. When the tinkling bell announced the evening meal, she gathered her courage and slowly descended the stairs to the dining room where the rest of the family was already seated. Sliding into her chair, she placed her napkin on her lap and bowed her head for the blessing.

Graham cleared his throat, then paused, letting his gaze settle on each of those well-loved bowed heads around his table. "Our Father, we give thee thanks this day for the food before us to be shared as we are once again united as a family. We thank thee for allowing us to survive the hardships these last weeks have brought uniquely to those who were left behind and those of us who were away. Grant us thy healing grace and peace as we attempt to forge a new life fraught with unknown perils, remindful of the need to put the past behind us. Grant us the wisdom to find a way to tread the treacherous pathway before us in the presence of our recent enemies and find forgiveness in our hearts for the wrongs they have done us, just as we have done unto them. We ask this in Christ's name. Amen."

Cissy looked up to find her father's eyes on her. She gave a tremulous smile, daring to hope that things were once more right between them. The twinkle in his eyes as his smile answered hers sent her heart soaring. She dared not ask what had quieted his anger. She could only be grateful that it seemed to have gone.

The supper was punctuated by the sound of casual conversation between Evangeline and Graham around his day at the office. Cissy listened but refrained from entering the discourse. She was happy to relax and enjoy the ambiance of a re-united family. At the end of the meal, Graham asked her to join him in his study. Her heart gave a sudden plunge in anticipation of yet more scolding just when she thought all was forgiven.

With trepidation, she entered the study and at his gesture, closed the door behind her before she sat across from him at his desk. Seizing the initiative, she said, "Again, I am so sorry I disappointed you while you were gone. I know it was wrong of me. Please forgive me."

"Cissy, there is nothing to forgive. I was too harsh and lacking in understanding last night for all that you have been through in the weeks I was away. How can I blame you for doing all that you could to find food for yourself and our servants? Your resourcefulness, while repugnant on the face of it, at least allowed you to survive. Without the food given you by the enemy, you could all have well starved to death. Rufus told me how you went to the warehouse and found food and fuel but that had run out, too, and with nothing to buy, or to buy with, how desperate your situation had become. I ask you to forgive me for being so harsh and quick to judge."

"It's fine, Papa. I don't blame you for being angry." Smiling, Cissy rose from her seat and circled the desk to climb in his lap, as had been her habit when she was a child.

Hugging her to him, Graham sighed, "I was worried sick about you when I realized you were left behind. You cannot know the terrors I endured imagining all kinds of horrible things that could have happened. I am just so grateful to see your pretty face and to know that you are well. Now give your papa a kiss and hop off. You weight a sight more now than you did when you were five, my girl."

Standing, they returned to the parlor where Evangeline was playing the harpsichord. She looked up when they entered the room and smiled. "Come, let's sing and make happy. I am tired of so much sadness. The last four years are done. It is time to move on."

"That it is, my dear. I am glad to be back and ready to make our way to New Berne and settle into our home. I can only hope that it was not damaged during our absence."

"I want to go home, too. When do you think we can leave?" She lifted her fingers from the keyboard as she awaited his reply.

"I am not sure as I must get things organized here so my ships can return from Nassau and Europe. I intend to resume normal operations as quickly as practicable. I will retain this house and the shipping concern in Wilmington since this is the larger port. However, rebuilding the business in New Berne is an imperative. After that, we will have to see which town makes more sense for us to reside in."

"You would really consider making this our home instead of New Berne?" Evangeline was not sure she wanted to know the answer.

"This is not yet home for us. At the moment, I suspect none of us are ready to abandon New Berne and move here permanently."

"I think a solution might be to let me run the one office and stay there while you run the other. You could teach me what I need to know in the meantime and you could still go back and forth if needed. I would really like to have something to do with myself." Cissy held her breath as she awaited his reply.

Graham looked at her without comment for several long moments. "For the moment, I think we should hold any decisions of that nature in abeyance. I'm not ready to separate our family again when we have so newly reunited. Now, let's have that music."

Chapter 7

Frustrated that her father rebuffed her continuous pleas for some job in his office to occupy her days, Cissy reluctantly bided her time. Daydreams of the handsome Yankee, Colonel Madison, invaded her idle moments all too often. As she stared out her bedroom window, the hated embroidery forgotten in her lap, Ryan Madison was at that moment marrying the woman that had stolen his heart in December of 1862 when she had found him following battle near her home and saved his life. Despite despairing of the chances for a marriage between them, he had found his way back to her. Cissy was but a pleasant memory as he pledged himself to Penny Madison.

For Cissy, his memory was all too alive and became more so after her father brought home a letter from John Harvey addressed to her. At a loss as to why he would be writing to her, Graham handed it to his daughter. "This came for you today at the office. I must say I am surprised Mr. Harvey would be writing you."

Cissy rose from the wicker chair tucked into a corner of the veranda and reached for the envelope. "I cannot imagine."

Tearing it open, she quickly scanned the contents, her face growing paler by the moment. It was fortunate that the chair was touching the back of her legs as she all but fell into it. "I don't believe it, Papa."

Graham took the proffered letter, reading it twice before he responded. "Why Logan would sell his family's heritage and run off to California is a puzzle. Why he would not even write to tell you of this is a greater one. I frankly don't know what to make of it. I know the boy loves you...has for years. It just doesn't make any sense."

Meeting her father's eyes, she tried to mask the feelings of guilt engendered by her attraction to two Yankee officers that made her heart pound with far more excitement than that initiated by thoughts of Logan. In a strange way her hurt was more from the awareness that her childhood friend and fiancé had jilted her without even the courtesy of a letter, than any feelings of a forlorn lover. Her father and step-mother had both loved him like a son and must be feeling some of her own pain that he had not trusted them enough to share such a momentous decision. For a while she knew her pride would be hurt and her love for her friend a vacuum in her heart. At the same time she felt a sudden euphoric sense of freedom. Ryan immediately flashed into her mind: the sparkling blue eyes alive with humor and desire, his kindness, his witty and spirited repartee, and the rush of longing she felt each time she had seen him.

Chiding herself for her wayward thoughts, she reassured her father. "I will be fine, Papa. Please don't worry about me. I think Logan was always more my friend than anything else. Perhaps, he sensed that. I'm just sorry that he did not feel comfortable writing to us and explaining his decision. I know you and Evangeline both cared so much for him that this has to be a blow to you, too."

"Ah, Cissy. I had such hopes that the two of you would marry. I admit I longed for it and promoted it. He is a good man and would have been a loving husband to you. I now must trust that he knows what he is doing, although the reason for it is a bafflement. Perhaps when we get to New Berne, Mr. Harvey will be a bit more forthcoming as to why Logan has done this."

Lost in thought, Cissy merely nodded her head in acknowledgement as her father walked away. A sudden sadness overwhelmed her and a tear slid down one cheek as she slowly removed the ring Logan had given her when she promised she would marry him once the war was ended. Regret that she could not love him enough was juxtaposed with the suspicion that perhaps had he loved her more, he would have written her with some explanation rather than leaving it to the impersonal services of an attorney. She had never known Logan to be a coward. Intuitively she knew something was wrong in his life that he could not even face her. But the 'why' escaped her.

The following days left her little time for melancholy reflection as her father was determined to move them all back to New Berne. Ever the cautious one, Evangeline was ambivalent. She wanted to see her former home that juxtaposed the one she now shared with Graham and she longed for the face of her old retainer Beulah. But they had no way of knowing if either house still stood. Her servant and those of Graham, Toby and Bessie, who had been left behind to secure the houses, could neither read nor write; and the intermittent letters from his office there had been about business, not personal concerns. Andy, fretful with teething, factored into her decision to have Graham go ahead of them to ascertain what conditions they might expect on their return.

Cissy supported her decision but was careful to refrain from overt comment that would further anger her father. Although he had overlooked her trafficking with Yankee officers in light of the desperate plight they faced in Wilmington, he had maintained a certain distance. Harvey's letter had not helped as she suspected he questioned whether or not she had been totally loyal to Logan during their engagement. If Logan had questioned her love for him, Graham must have reasoned that could have been the rationale for decampment to California. Even so, she longed for the opportunity to help in the office in his absence and was plotting for the proper moment to broach the subject.

Luck was with her. The day before Graham was to take the train to Goldsborough, then Kinston and on to New Berne, his chief bookkeeper fell and injured his back signaling weeks in bed when he would be unable to work. Always good with numbers, Cissy pitched her case to her father. He was nearly as surprised as she when he finally agreed to allow her to fill in while Marsh Jones recovered. His general manager Zeke Smathers would handle the shipping while Robert Ridgeway would continue as the warehouse manager. Not wasting any time, Graham had Rufus bring the buggy around after an early supper and he returned to his office, Cissy in tow. There by lamplight, Graham reviewed the books with her, the combination to the safe and outstanding invoices and manifests.

"If you get into a fix and don't know which way to turn and the other two can't help, go to Robert's house and have him help you. Other than that, if neither of you can figure something out, either telegraph me if it is important enough, or save it for my return if it will keep."

"Everything seems fairly straight forward, Papa. The books are pretty self-explanatory it appears."

"Even so, just remember Robert, Marsh, and Zeke have all been here a long time and can help you when you need it. Don't be too proud and stubborn to ask, missy," Graham admonished.

"I promise." Cissy beamed happily at her father. "Thank you for giving me a chance. I won't let you down. You're going to be proud of me."

Graham kissed her on the nose, "I am already proud of you, kitten. Now let's go home. I have an early train to catch and a long day of travel."

Her father, valise in one hand and Evangeline's hand in the other, descended the next morning to find Cissy waiting at the foot of the stairs dressed for her day at the office in a plain dove gray dress with navy trim. She beamed at them as she adjusted her bonnet strings. "It is so beautiful out, I thought I would walk to the office. I want to be there when the others arrive."

"Well aren't you the early bird, Cissy." Evangeline answered Cissy's smile with one of her own. "I must say you look like a very pretty bookkeeper, darling."

Graham laughed, "Certainly prettier than Marsh. Give your papa a hug as I am leaving for the station as soon as I have a bite of breakfast."

"Have a safe trip, Papa. I hope you find things are not too badly affected by the war in New Berne."

Evangeline frowned, "As do we all, Graham. Not only am I worried for the state of our houses and Beulah, Bessie and Toby, but I am concerned for what may have happened to your warehouse and office."

"I suspect the houses may have fared better than the warehouse. According to vague reports I received, during the yellow fever epidemic a couple of years ago, a number of the waterfront warehouses were burned to try to stop the spread of the disease. The union forces seemed to think the water-logged basements in the warehouse district were the source of the sickness."

Cissy kissed her father's cheek and turned to leave. At the door she looked back at him, "Try not to worry about the office here. You have enough to deal with when you get home to New Berne."

The coming days found Cissy working with a passion to organize paperwork so that she could make heads or tails of it. While Marsh may have been an accurate bookkeeper, his writing was often to the point of bare legibility and his filing system non-existent. Once that was accomplished, she spent any spare moments studying manifests and the various other aspects of running a shipping company. Robert and Zeke at first humored her, but as they realized that she was a determined pupil and a brilliant one, they went out of their way to teach her the particulars of Graham's business.

Evangeline and Annie gave up on Cissy keeping them company in the evening. She managed to get home in time for supper, but once done with that she went to her room for a bath and to study. The maps she carted home at night provided insight into the scope of the ports in various countries where her father conducted business, and others that might prove interesting in future. She frequently fell into exhausted sleep holding a geography book to her chest that she had studied intently in her research into goods that could be procured in the various locales and those items that a particular port might need to import due to a lack in that area.

One morning as Cissy was preparing to leave for the office, Andy sleepily fanny-bumped down the steps and held his arms up to her. Staring into his little face, Cissy was struck with guilt. "I have been a bad sister. I know you think I have forgotten all about you, Andy. I'm sorry. I'll try to get home early today so we can play. Okay?"

He nodded his head and stuck his thumb in his mouth worrying the spot where a molar was trying to come through. Drool ran from his thumb onto his chin. Cissy leaned over and wiped it on the hem of his nightdress. "I bet Mama doesn't know you are down here. Let me take you back upstairs, precious."

Evangeline called down the stairs, "No need, Cissy. I was just coming after him. I think he has been a little bit lonesome for you. For that matter, we all have."

"I'm planning to be home earlier tonight so we can visit. I guess I have been so wrapped up in learning as much as I can, that I forgot about everything else."

"I understand. I know how much you want to prove yourself to your father. Frankly, I hope you succeed beyond all expectations. He is overworked even though he will not admit it even to himself. Perhaps, when he sees how dedicated you are he will allow you to continue to share some of the load."

"I have to show more than dedication. I have to understand everything and be able to make decisions and foresee opportunities and problems. That will take time but each day seems a little clearer and easier."

In the month since her father had been gone, Cissy was beginning to assume more and more responsibilities at the office. Both Robert and Zeke frequently came to her to explain a problem and she would listen intently, ask probing questions, and then make tactful suggestions, careful to wound neither man's ego. Often they came away thinking her solution had been their idea. It did not bother her. She was gaining far more than she was giving by gaining their trust and respect. Her father had always been more than fair to his employees, earning both their trust and dedication. She saw the wisdom in his methods when she considered the men who, during the later days of war when business was so curtailed, had reduced their own wages and continued to work maintaining and repairing the office and warehouses in readiness for the day when life would return to normal.

When Marsh's wife came to the office to explain, that as she put it, her husband's leg was "still all stove up," Cissy hastened to reassure her that he would not lose his position and income. While she commiserated with his wife over the man's woes, she could not help the secret elation that welled up inside. Her job would continue uninterrupted for a few weeks longer and she did not intend to waste a minute. Even though she was returning home for a timely supper and an hour or two in the company of her family and Annie, she did not abandon her nightly studies. Even the arrival of the letter from her father asking them to return to their home in New Berne, did not faze her. Promptly she wrote to advise him that she would need to delay her return due to Marsh's continued absence. At the moment home was the office that held her enraptured each day.

Evangeline went through her days singing. Graham's letter had brought assurance that both houses and all three of their faithful servants had survived the war relatively unscathed except for thinner bodies that announced a time of limited availability of food. Graham grudgingly acknowledged that the Yankee colonel that had provided them with a pass to leave occupied New Berne to go to Wilmington, and provided a doctor and medicine for Evangeline during the difficult days of her pregnancy, had protected their homes from any vandalism. Cissy smiled secretly when Evangeline read that part of the letter to her. His face continued to haunt her mind in rare idle moments given up to daydreams.

Another month in the office raced by after Andy and Evangeline's departure. Despite Annie's protestations of loneliness since her days were spent in the house with only Rufus and Reesie for company, Cissy prolonged her hours in the office. With the lengthened daylight of late summer, night came late allowing her more time to work. After repeated arguments about her safety walking the streets at dusk with Yankee soldiers and freed blacks roaming the streets catcalling and making unsavory remarks, Cissy finally gave into Rufus and allowed him to bring the carriage to get her each evening. Secretly she felt relief. The long hours at the office and studying until late at night were beginning to take their toll.

Sunday morning, September third, dawned clear and without the normal heat and humidity that often accompanies summer in eastern North Carolina. Cissy tossed back the sheet that she had pulled up in the middle of the night and walked over to the open window. The dogwood tree below had long since lost its flowers and now formed a canopy of green leaves. A cardinal sat on a verdant branch singing in crimson splendor. It suddenly struck her that she had not taken a day to just enjoy herself since her father left for New Berne.

"Annie!" She called into the hallway.

"Ah, faith and begorrah! What're ye hollering about at this hour of me morning?" Annie's tousled head emerged from behind her door.

"Let's have a picnic. We can have Reesie make something for all of us and drive over to the lake and enjoy the beauty of the day. It has been so long since we could do that and I so have missed being by the water."

The denizens of the house on Orange Street were all imbued with a holiday excitement. Chicken was soon sizzling in the black iron skillet, late-season corn boiling in a pot, and biscuits baking in the oven. Some stewed apples and pound cake promised a sweet finish to the meal. Cissy searched a seriously depleted wine cellar to find the perfect bottle of Bordeaux to share with Annie. She suspected Reesie would find some of the strong cider favored by Rufus for the two of them to share. Soon the entire excited household was loaded in the carriage and bound for Greenfields, a popular lake once owned by Dr. Samuel Green who had built a dam and mill there on the rice plantation he had purchased in 1790.

Cissy could not help but preen a little when a man standing on the corner when they turned from Orange onto Fifteenth lifted his hat in salute and called, "Lovely, lovely, miss."

Annie harrumphed, "Well, he could have spared a glance in me direction. Tis fetching I look meself in this bonnet."

"Of course, you do, Annie," Cissy hastened to assure. She refused to allow Annie's sour expression to detract from the day.

After another mile, Annie shrugged off her pout and sat erect in the seat. "Oh what a glorious day. If the sky were any bluer I would be thinking it had been painted on up there."

"It is beautiful. I confess I have been working so hard trying to learn Papa's business that I have missed just having fun. I'm sorry I have not been a very good friend of late."

"I haven't liked it, but I know how much you want to

impress your father. Let's not think about that now that we are at the lake." Annie gave another excited bounce on the seat as she noted all of the men lolling around the shore. Refusing to think about the fate of her missing fiancé, she gave a saucy wink and wave to one of the fellows who had caught her eye with his blatant stare.

"Careful, Annie. Those men are going to think you girls are fast women if you keep winking and waving." Reesie frowned disapprovingly in her direction.

"Oh, pooh. I'm just having fun."

"It ain't going to be fun, if they think you girls are good-time women. Now you behave yourself."

Cissy's own attention was captured by another man, one she knew. She ignored Reesie's chiding of Annie, pondering what she would say should Brandon notice her. Hoping to avoid an awkward meeting she turned her head away and started a spirited litany of praise for the lake and weather that obviously had lured so many of the local citizens to enjoy the day. Reesie had turned her attention to Rufus to direct him to a likely spot for a picnic. Annie was still ogling the handsome man that had captured her interest. Cissy, realizing no one was listening, allowed the spew of words to trail off.

As soon as Rufus stopped the carriage, Reesie bustled about spreading the blanket and unpacking the basket. Annie wasted no time moving slightly apart from the others, face turned toward the group of men...even knowing they were probably Yankee soldiers. Left to her own devices, Cissy walked a short distance along the lake where she was hidden by the trees and shrubbery and out of sight of the direction where she had last seen Brandon. Ten minutes later, the hesitant touch on her elbow was enough for her to know that he had found her even before she turned to face him.

A slow smile began in his eyes and then spread across his face. "What an unexpected pleasure to see you here today. I thought that day at the Bellamy house I would never lay eyes on your lovely face again."

"Thank you for the pretty compliment, Brandon." Cissy paused, "I would like to explain about that."

"There is no need to explain. As I said before, I can understand your father's objections."

"He may have softened a bit. It is too soon to say." Looking up, Cissy met his eyes, "I really like you for a friend. I think you are a nice man even if our politics are at polar extremes. This is just too soon for most southerners to be happy about having soldiers from the north continuing to occupy us and impose military law. Maybe someday it will not rankle so. I hope so. I am sick of war and everything it has cost us and continues to cost us."

"That I agree with wholeheartedly. No one with any humanity likes war. It comes to us and we find ourselves caught up in it with the best of intentions and high ideals, but the process itself is anything but."

They continued to walk away from the others as they ambled along the shore of the lake. Brandon kept his hand on her elbow as he guided her along. "Cissy, one of my men tells me that you are regularly seen at your father's shipping offices. Can you tell me what is happening with you?"

"My father and the rest of the family have returned to New Berne so he can assess the damage there and re-establish his business. I was to go, too, however his bookkeeper was injured the day before they left and I persuaded my father to let me take his place until he recovers."

Brandon watched her eyes light with pride as she explained, "You love it don't you?"

"Yes! I love every minute, problems and all. I finally feel as though I can do something besides knit and embroider, both of which I do poorly to say the least."

"I see."

"I think it is very good for me. I was feeling so cooped up and bored that it feels good to have a real purpose to occupy my day."

"I thought perhaps that fiancé you mentioned might have claimed your hand in marriage by now?" He was watching closely as he said it. Holding his breath, he awaited her response. He did not miss the sudden flush that reddened her face, nor the turn of her head to the side as though studying the azalea bush along the path. Several minutes elapsed and he was preparing his apology for impertinence when she spoke.

"Oh, that. We found we do not suit after all. He has left for California and a whole new life."

"Then his departure is indeed my good fortune, if I may dare so hope?"

Chapter 8

Marcel Lambert, an unrepentant reprobate, murderer, thief, and scoundrel, scion of a distinguished and titled French family, fingered the lucky pack of cards in his vest pocket. The bullet lodged there was a constant reminder of how close he had come to death at the hands of Logan Gwaltney. The fact that Logan's bullet had prevented him from raping that stubborn bitch, Cissy LaRoque, was of no consequence to him other than frustration that he had not succeeded in conquering her. When the bullet hit, he had fallen face forward. Momentarily stunned and then clever enough to feign death, he had remained still until they rode away leaving his supposed corpse to rot in the woods.

"Call." The grim voice of the man across the table from him jerked Marcel's wandering thoughts to the game at hand. His latest deck of marked cards was the best yet. His skill at slipping a needed card from his sleeve was also useful. He was steadily winning a fortune cheating anyone gullible enough to continue playing him. Soon the need to marry an heiress like the LaRoque bitch would no longer be a necessity for his financial comfort.

Laying a royal flush on the table, Marcel rose to scoop the pile of coins and bills into his hat. "Thank you for an excellent game, gentlemen. Perhaps tomorrow we might play again so you have an opportunity to recoup your losses."

"Not so fast, you fucking asshole. You can't have an ace of spades because I do; and I don't take none too kindly to being robbed by the likes of you."

Marcel eased his hand into his pocket where he kept his Derringer. As the man began to rise, Marcel fired, hitting him between the eyes. Not waiting for anyone to apprehend him, he fled from Archie Drake's grog-shop into the night. He wasted no time grabbing his things at the rooming house and fetching his horse from the stable. Raleigh had just become too hot for him.

Marcel stopped on the edge of town. While Wilmington offered the best gambling prospects with so many soldiers stationed there, the sheriff would not have forgotten that he had cheated him at cards, escaped from his jail, and then stolen a horse. New Berne might be a problem since it was there that he had abducted Cissy and her pregnant stepmother. Despite his supposed demise, were he to show up he could be in trouble. Raleigh was now closed to him. He had already tried his luck in Richmond and was decidedly unwelcome there. Drawing on his knowledge of the area, he decided he would try Fayetteville. Despite being smaller than the other towns, he was at least unknown there. That alone might not solve his problem. His eyes narrowed in concentration as he considered his options. With a gift for languages and a knack for accents, he decided he would try changing his identity.

The newly created Lord Markham Latham sat on his horse practicing an upper crust British accent. Pleased with himself he galloped off. A beard, a monocle, and a change of hair color would help with his new persona. Once he was comfortable as Markham Latham, he would test the larger towns again, perhaps Charleston and Savannah. Always in the back of his mind was revenge on Logan Gwaltney and Cissy LaRoque for thinking they could best him.

* * * * *

At that very moment, Evangeline sat in the dining room with her husband. She had just learned that the new house just past Evangeline's on land once owned by a neighbor, Caroline Framingham, belonged to a Yankee colonel and his new wife, a southerner. Evangeline sat musing before remarking to her husband, "Graham, do you happen to know who this colonel is? If it is the one who helped Cissy and me then I would so like to thank him. His doctor is the one that made it possible for me to be well enough to survive when that scoundrel, Marcel Lambert, abducted Cissy and me."

"I didn't catch the name but I will let you know as soon as I can ask around." With feelings still running strong against the Yankees that occupied the town, Graham hesitated to suggest a social call on the colonel's wife, southerner or not. Along with others in the area, he could not help but resent the quiet infiltration of former soldiers who found the local area more appealing than their homes in the north.

Evangeline smiled, "Perhaps I'll walk over to Caroline's and see who her new neighbors are."

Graham gave a non-committal 'hmm' in response.

Changing tack, she inquired, "Are things going well at the office, Graham? I confess to curiosity since you rarely mention it."

"I was more fortunate than I dared hope to find my buildings survived, not to mention our houses. However, with the ships I donated to the Mosquito Fleet all sunk during 1862, I am faced with the prospect of trying to get more built before I can do much here. I have hesitated to mention it, but I am seriously considering the need to return to Wilmington where I still have enough ships to conduct business."

"Could you perhaps divert some of them here instead?"

"I have done that according to what could be spared for this port. The fact remains, that Wilmington is now the main focus of our business. But, don't upset yourself unduly. I still have things that must be done here, so we will remain awhile longer." Graham squeezed her hand gently. He knew that the thought of leaving New Berne again so soon after arriving, and returning to Wilmington...while larger and with much more to offer...it was still not home. He could only hope in time that it would become a home to her. He was secretly excited by the chance that Wilmington offered and intended to expand the business there while keeping only a small concern in New Berne until business picked up enough to warrant a larger operation. Once that happened he would hire a manager for the New Berne office and keep only one of the houses they owned in New Berne for occasional visits.

"Have you heard how Cissy is coping with things in Wilmington? I do so hope it goes well for her while we are away."

"It's amazing. Zeke telegraphed me to say that she has taken to it like a duck to water. Seems she is working hard, studying the business, and has some really good ideas. I confess I thought she would be tired of it in a week. Instead she is increasing business by approaching potential customers to explain the advantages of using us for importing and shipping. It doesn't hurt that she is a beautiful girl, but that alone would not sell a hard-nosed businessman. She is also showing them a document she created comparing costs, speed, number of ports, and several other advantages over our competitors. I am proud of her, but I don't want her to do this any longer than necessary. Now that the war is over I hope she will find a man she can love and marry. I would love some grandbabies."

"Really, Graham? Well then perhaps the idea of becoming a father again isn't too appealing." Evangeline looked away, pretending insouciance.

"What? What did you say?"

"I said: we will have another little one to love in about six months." She could not stop the grin of pride that suffused her face with happiness.

"We will?"

Evangeline laughed at the look on his face. "Now, why do you act so surprised. You do know how it comes about."

"You make me so happy. I confess I have wanted another of our own." Graham wrapped her in his arms so tightly she squeaked. "My apologies, darling, I guess I got carried away. You are sure you are going to be all right? The pregnancy with Andy was an ordeal for you."

"I think it will be better this time. I don't have the constant nausea that I had with Andy. Thank Heavens. And there isn't a war going on to make everything more difficult." Remembering her abduction late in her pregnancy with Andy, and how close she came to not surviving, she shuddered. With a sigh she rejoiced that with Marcel Lambert dead that was one peril she would not face with this pregnancy.

"I still worry. We aren't spring chickens anymore, you know."

"Graham LaRoque, don't you dare call me old." Evangeline laughed as his face reddened.

"I didn't mean it that way. Do forgive me." A sudden sparkle lit his eyes. "Come upstairs with me and I will show you how old we aren't."

Hours later Graham held his sleeping wife in his arms and pondered what to do. He did not want to relocate his family too late in the pregnancy. That meant he would have to push up the move to Wilmington despite his earlier promise to delay that decision.

* * * * *

A couple of weeks later, Cissy had just walked up the steps after a long day at work where one shipping problem after another had demanded her attention. When she entered the door, Annie was waiting.

"Ah faith and begorrah, don't ye be looking tired now?" Annie waved an envelope in the air above Cissy's head. "Guess who just dropped a letter off for ye?"

"Annie, if you know I am tired, don't you know better than

to weary me further with childish games?"

"Ouch. I was only having a wee bit of fun. Have yer old letter then." Annie handed her the letter and flounced up the stairs not bothering to hide her pique.

Cissy walked into the parlor and sank wearily onto the divan. Turning the envelope over she slid her nail under the wax seal popping it open. Extracting the enclosed letter, a playbill for a performance by the celebrated violinist Sigesmund Thalberg fell into her lap. Cissy opened the letter and noted that it was from Brandon inviting her to the performance on Saturday evening. He had preempted her need to reply by saying he would call on her the next day at the shipping office. She tucked it into her reticule to take it with her to the office not wanting to leave it where anyone in the house could see it. While Reesie could not read, Annie could and would. Walking back into the foyer she picked up the pile of letters and bills that had been left on the foyer table and walked to the office in the rear of the house where she settled at her father's desk to read them. There were two letters from New Berne, one from her father and one from Evangeline.

Normally she would have read her father's letter first, but fearful of its contents she opted for the one from Evangeline. Evangeline's was full of news from Bessie, Tony, and Beulah, and the ordeal they had endured during the two years after the family moved to Wilmington. In retrospect it was fortunate that the Yankees had requisitioned Evangeline's house for officer's as their excess food supply had been passed secretly from Beulah to Bessie and Tony, sustaining all three of the LaRoque servants. Without Beulah as the cook for the officers during the time they occupied Evangeline's house, they would have faced starvation. The paragraph that held her attention longest was the one describing the new house and occupants just past that of Caroline Framingham, Evangeline's nearest neighbor on the right.

Cissy sat back in her chair and scolded herself for a girlish fancy. Of course, Ryan Madison had moved on with his life. He had never done more than harmlessly flirt with her and extend kindness. Nothing in his demeanor had ever suggested that he was ready to court her in earnest. Nevertheless, the hope she had held in her breast as a beacon of light was extinguished with news that he had married. Having him and his bride for neighbors was not an appealing prospect and dimmed any real desire to return to New Berne. She accepted the fantasy that she had built in her mind as just that, but her heart was still heavy. Something about Ryan had sparked an excitement in her like none other. Shrugging her shoulders, she laid Evangeline's letter aside and sat in silent contemplation. She had lost a fiancé without an opportunity to determine what had driven him away. She had lost a daydream romance that had warmed her in lonely hours. Having been rejected by her mother, the loss of a fiancé, and now, a fantasized-about-lover was even more painful. Once again she questioned her ability to find love in her life. She knew she was loved by Graham, Evangeline, Andy, and even Annie, but somehow it wasn't enough.

Leaving her father's letter unopened, Cissy strode onto the piazza that overlooked the Cape Fear River below the bluff on which the house sat. A soft breeze lifted her hair as it sighed through the trees. She took a steadying breath of the brackish air. All of her adult life she had looked for something to give her a sense of worth beyond being the daughter of a rich and respected man. The last few weeks running the shipping business in Wilmington had done much to continue what she had begun during those months when she had actively spied for the Confederacy. Closing her heart to romantic wishes, Cissy resolved to make a name for herself in her father's business, one that would bring her respect in her own right. With her spine straight and her chin up, she swore to become a woman to be reckoned with. *You must forget Ryan*, she whispered.

Brandon's pursuit of her was not without appeal. He was a good man, attractive, and pleasant to be with. While she had no long-term ambitions with him, would she be able to conduct a mild flirtation to assuage her insecurities without increasing the complications that might bring? She would accept the invitation to hear the famous violinist. It was something to do, after all, and she was young and not without the yearnings of any young woman her age. The difference was that she would keep her heart safely her own. Recalling her early romance with the cad, Nate Pearson, when she was seventeen and now the failed romance with Logan, and Ryan's marriage, she decided she had had enough of risking her emotions.

Walking back into the office, she closed the French doors behind her and picked up the letter from her father. Sitting in his large leather chair, she opened the letter and spread it out on the desk. The further she read the more alarmed she became, not at learning Evangeline was pregnant, although she did wonder that her step-mother had not mentioned it in her own letter, but at the return of the family to Wilmington. With her father in the office, she would be relegated to the house once again. After all the work to become proficient in the business, she felt an overwhelming frustration. Nothing seemed to be going right. After the difficulties of war, she had anticipated a smooth path forward into the future. Her youth and natural optimism had not considered the realities of life.

Following supper, Cissy retired early to her room supposedly to sleep. However, sleep was elusive and she did little but mull over her options until the rising sun drove her from bed, her decision made. With her father determined to base himself in Wilmington, she would ask to be allowed to return to New Berne with Annie as a companion and run the smaller office. With his shipping business closed during Union occupation, surely the staff was depleted and he could use someone with experience. She had another month, no more. During that time she would learn everything she could to prove her ability to handle the office there. With an office to run and a business to build, she would have no time to consider her neighbors, new or otherwise.

Cissy had been at work for over two hours when Brandon arrived in her office wreathed in smiles. His face lit up even brighter when she agreed to accompany him to the violin concert on Saturday.

"That's wonderful. I think we will both enjoy the music. Do let me take you for dinner at the Clarendon House Hotel first. The food is quite good. Perhaps you have been?"

"No, I confess I have not. Our meals have either been at home or in the homes of a few neighbors that we met over the course of the last couple of years." Cissy, bit her lip considering how to word the next remark. "Even though the war is over, I would not feel comfortable out in public escorted by an officer of the Occupation. Would it be possible for you not to wear your uniform Saturday night?"

"Of course. If it would make you more at ease, I am happy to wear civilian attire. Now, tell me you will dine with me prior to the concert?"

"That sounds fine, but I will meet you in the hotel lobby." Cissy was aware that to appear in a public house unescorted was more than unseemly conduct for a maiden. To meet with the enemy for an evening on the town was not an event to endear her to the local citizenry either. If challenged by one of the few acquaintances she knew in the area, she had decided to explain it as a business meeting conducted on behalf of her father. And then, she would pray they would have forgotten it by the time he arrived from New Berne.

"As a gentleman, I regret that I cannot call for you in a respectful manner at your home. I confess I am uncomfortable to have you walk unescorted in the early evening."

"I regret it, too, but it is for the best at the moment. It will still be early enough that it isn't dark and you may walk me back after the concert as I would not want to walk alone once it's night."

"Most assuredly I will escort you afterwards. Now, I must return to my duties while you occupy your pretty head with those papers stacked on your desk."

Taking her hand in his, he gave it a gentle squeeze before leaning over to press a kiss on it. "Until Saturday. The hours cannot fly swiftly enough."

"Yes, until Saturday."

Cissy spent Saturday morning churning through her wardrobe for a formal dress that was not too badly out of fashion. Staring at the choices, it dawned on her that for the first time in her life she had gone for years with nothing new to wear. The last fabric that she had for a new dress was a soft apple green silk moiré that her father had imported for her. The dress was one of her favorites and it was flattering. The cut was perhaps outmoded, but then what other lady in town had anything new? They were all in the same situation as she or even worse off. With her hair swept up and held by diamond pins and the diamond jewelry her father had gifted her on her sixteenth birthday, the dress would be more than adequate.

Walking to the full-length mirror that stood in the corner, she held the dress against her body and admired it once again. It was still fresh and new looking as there had been little occasion to wear it after they had left New Berne and the active social life she had enjoyed there in the early days of the war. She turned quickly when the door swung open. Cissy could not stop the sudden flush of guilt that turned her face a bright red.

"You might knock, Annie. I would never presume to enter your room without first doing so."

"Ah, don't be so testy." Annie walked over to finger the silk of the dress. "What a lovely fabric it is. Now then, where would ye be off to in these fine togs?"

"If you must know, I am going to hear Sigismund Thalberg at Thalian Hall tonight."

"I don't recall ye mentioning it to me. Oh dear, I need to find something suitable as well."

"No need, you are not going."

"Is that so? Your father told me to be sure to accompany ye when you go out in the evening. He would be furious with me for allowing ye to go alone. It just isn't done."

"Annie, don't scold me. I know what I'm doing."

"Aye, ye know, but no one else does apparently. If he finds out I not be doing me job, he will fire me. Then what would I do?"

"He is not going to fire you because he isn't going to find out." Cissy reluctantly acknowledged her companion's concerns, "I'm sorry, Annie. I realize I am being unfair to you. If I get into trouble, I will make sure you aren't blamed. I will be safe, really. I'll leave early while it's daylight and I'll be escorted home."

Cissy winced. She had not meant to allow that to slip.

"Jesus, Mary, and Joseph. And just who is this escort that ye be so secretive about?"

"Annie, if you must know Colonel McLean will be returning me home. Before you say anything, I realize my father would have a fit. It isn't like I am planning to marry Brandon. I'm just tired of doing nothing but working and sitting home, so I said 'yes' when he offered to take me to the concert. For goodness sakes, I haven't been to a concert and dressed up in almost three years."

"I'm bored, too. I suspect I would go out with the devil himself if he asked me. Just be careful."

"I will, I promise. Now that is out of the way, I plan to take a bath and wash my hair. Once it's dry I need you to help me pin it up and get in this dress. Try to keep Reesie from being too curious, would you? Maybe it would help if you walked with me a short distance when I leave."

"Aye, I suspect it would. And don't be worrying about Reesie. I will think of something."

Cissy hugged Annie. Pulling back she smiled, "Thank you, Annie. You are a dear. I know you are bored, so let's plan something we can do together besides going to church. Maybe, we can find that soldier that was flirting with you in the park."

"Mayhap, we could." Annie grinned, "Mayhap, I have."

"No? You sly fox! Looks as they you won't need to go out with the devil himself. So what is it that *you're* keeping secret?"

"If I tell then it be no secret..."

Ignoring Cissy's entreaty to stay and talk, Annie twirled around, "I'll tell Reesie ye be needing bath water."

"Thank you, Annie," Cissy called as the door closed.

When Annie returned to help Cissy dress, she was her usual cheerful self. Their earlier testiness was forgotten as she chattered away. When she had finished lacing Cissy's dress, she sat her at the dressing table and began pinning up her hair. Finished she stood back and exclaimed, "Walk over to the mirror and take a look at yer fine self. Ye look beautiful."

Admiring Annie's efforts, Cissy peered at herself in the mirror. "Thank you, Annie. I love how you did my hair. I could not have done it alone."

Gathering her reticule and a scarf to protect from the evening chill, Cissy prepared to slip down the stairs and out the front door. Annie shooed her along as she tiptoed down after her. "Reesie should be gone a few minutes more. I sent her to the wharf to fetch some things for tomorrow's dinner. I told her ye were not feeling so well and I would take a tray up to ye later for yer supper tonight. I guess I be eating twice...downstairs for me, and upstairs for ye. Do be quiet when ye return or she will know we have been up to no good. I will walk a ways with ye be ye wanting it?"

"No need with Reesie away. Try not to worry while I am gone. I'll be fine. I want you to know you are a true friend, Annie. I am in your debt." Cissy grinned, "When I get home, I will tell you all about the evening.

For the first time since the war, Cissy felt elegant and celebratory. The dress enhanced her curves and coloring, the knowledge giving an added sparkle to her eyes. When she walked into the hotel lobby, every head swiveled in her direction. She could only pray that it wasn't in shock at her appearing alone. Quickly stepping forward, Brandon extended his arm to escort her into the dining room. His eyes had latched onto her from the moment she arrived, so much so that he stumbled slightly on the threshold as they stepped onto the dining room's plush, patterned cream, red and gold carpet.

"Excuse me. Your beauty has me mesmerized. I have always found you lovely beyond compare but tonight you are truly dazzling. I feel so fortunate to be with you."

"Thank you, Brandon. You look very handsome yourself. I hope wearing dress attire and not a uniform was not a problem."

"Not at all. For the concert, I probably would not have worn the uniform anyway. Besides, if it makes you find me handsome, I will burn the uniform and wear nothing but this." Brandon smiled at her blush.

"You must think me horrid for saying anything about what you wear. After all, I do not know you well enough to be so presumptuous."

"Trust me, horrid is the very last adjective I would ever apply to you."

Uncomfortable at the stark emotion in his eyes, Cissy looked around at the room, relieved to note that there were only a couple of other diners, both Union officers. She noted with appreciation that it was a well-appointed room with glistening gas chandeliers spreading a warm glow on the rich decor.

Highly polished wooden sideboards held shiny silver serving pitchers and platters along one wall. On the opposite wall a bank of floor to ceiling windows were elaborately draped with gold-fringed red velvet, held back by heavy gold tassels. Each table was covered with a dazzling white tablecloth bearing a vase of red roses in the center, and set with silver, crystal, and red-rimmed china. A waiter interrupted her scrutiny when he arrived bearing a bottle of champagne and oysters on the half shell.

"I took the liberty of ordering champagne for us. I do hope you like it, if not I will gladly order something else."

"I love champagne! I haven't had any since before the war."

"Ah, forbidden subject tonight. And the oysters...?

"I grew up eating them. These look delicious."

"Then I am off to a good start. I have to confess I have already arranged our selection of dishes. I wanted to make it special for you."

"It already is." Cissy was determined to enjoy the evening, and having a handsome man spoil her was a nice part of it. Brandon talked freely about his life, his dreams, his favorite foods, and his pastimes. Enjoying the best meal since before the war and all of its deprivations, Cissy ate steadily, adding nothing to the flow of conversation except when directly questioned about something. She did not want to talk about her life and her own dreams. She was thoroughly schooled in the path men and the world in general expected a woman's life to follow. Brandon might compliment her on helping her father while he was away, but she seriously doubted he would approve if he knew what her own plans and dreams were.

Jolted from her thoughts, she looked up and met Brandon's puzzled expression, "I'm sorry. I hope I am not boring you. You seemed a thousand miles away just now."

Flustered at being caught wool gathering, she cried, "Oh, no. Please forgive me if I seem distracted. I really am fascinated by all that you have told me."

"I fear I have given you little opportunity to say a word. I suspect I may be trying a little too hard to impress you. If I am, Cissy, it is because I am very taken with you and hope that in time you will come to feel that way about me."

Cissy looked into his eyes, trying to decide how to respond to his honest declaration. Finally she blurted, "Please, I do not wish to become involved with anyone at the moment and not in the foreseeable future. There is much I want to do and prove to myself that doesn't include a romantic entanglement. You deserve someone who can return your affection. I fear that someone may never be me as I ask only for your friendship."

He looked both puzzled and a little offended when he inquired, "Does that have to do with me, or with something else?"

"Certainly there is nothing that is not admirable about you. At another time in my life, perhaps we might have been more to one another." Cissy looked down for a moment. A part of her wanted the affection that he offered her. "Brandon, I really do like you. It isn't that. For one thing, I hope to return to New Berne soon and run my father's business there."

"Doesn't he have a man in place to handle his affairs at that location?"

Cissy's face froze into an icy mask. Brandon could see his remark was unwelcome. But what woman would prefer the world of men to being a wife and mother? His experienced did not allow him to conceive of such a thing. "I mean that commerce is a little unusual for a woman, particularly in shipping. Surely, at some point you want what every woman wants?"

"And what is it that every woman wants, Brandon?" Her voice was deceptively soft.

"Why a husband, home and family, of course. I've never met a woman that wanted to be a spinster."

She could not stop the retort, "Perhaps you should broaden your experience."

She was seized with quick contrition. "I am so sorry. That was unforgivably rude. Let's just forget this whole conversation and enjoy the evening."

Brandon agreed readily, but she sensed that his ebullient mood had vanished. The silence on their walk to Thalian Hall was broken only by the wind rustling the live oak trees that swayed overhead.

The concert was a joy and eliminated the need for personal conversation. Thalberg's reputation as a virtuoso on the piano was not unwarranted. Brandon's knowledge of classical music was far superior to hers and he was pleased to be able to share it with her between numbers. When the pianist swept into Fantasy Opus 33 on Melodies from "Moise," an opera by Rossini, he leaned over and whispered, "This is his own composition. I confess it is lovely, but I find him better as a performer than a composer."

"I think it's beautiful. But then, obviously my ear is not as educated as yours. How is it you know so much about music?"

"I will tell you later."

She was so enraptured by the next piece, Beethoven's "Moonlight," that she did not realize he had taken her hand securely into his own. When the last strains of the music died away, she looked down she at their entwined fingers as they rested on his thigh. She could not decide if she wanted to tug her hand away or continue to relish the warmth it brought to have him hold it. As Thalberg began a composition by Chopin, Brandon resolved the issue by casually shifting to drape his arm around her shoulder. As he gently massaged it with his hand, Cissy relaxed more and more. He did not remove it until the end of the concert, when they rose to join others in a standing ovation.

When the audience had at last exhausted its admiration,

Brandon remarked as they descended to the street, "I confess when he retired in 1858 following an American tour, I thought to never hear him again. I am so delighted that he included Wilmington in this reprisal tour. I am told that he played here once before as well. Do you know anything about that?"

"No, I'm sorry. We lived in New Berne and I did not follow Wilmington news. Perhaps it was in the paper there and I just failed to notice."

As they walked down Third Street towards her home, Cissy commented, "I think you were going to tell me how you know so much about music."

"Ah, I will." Brandon paused before continuing. "I think possibly it began in my childhood in Philadelphia. My parents frequented the theater, and once I was of an age to behave and be attentive, they began taking me. I was immediately enthralled. So much so, that I begged my parents to take piano lessons." He laughed deprecatingly, "Sadly, I am much better as a member of the audience than as a performer."

"I would love to hear you play sometime. I am so unmusical it will sound just divine to me. Besides, I suspect you are being too modest."

"I wish that were so, nevertheless, I will be happy to play for you whenever you wish. Do you have a piano at home?"

Cissy worried her lip. She was in a quandary of her own making. His presence in her home would imply an ongoing courtship, one that her father would not welcome. And, it was a path she had sworn to avoid. Careful to make no promise, she replied, "We have a harpsichord that Evangeline plays for us, however it wasn't used while they were in Nassau towards the end of the war. She says it is badly out of tune. She is planning to have it repaired when they return from New Berne."

"I see. I suspect with Mr. LaRoque's objection to me as a suitor, I will not be playing for you anytime soon."

At her door, he pulled her to him and gently kissed her. At

first she was stiff and unyielding, but as the kiss deepened she felt herself responding. When the kiss ended, Cissy sighed as she leaned into his broad chest. She could feel him pressing soft kisses into her hair. It had been so long since she had been held and admired by a man, she was loathed to bring it to an end. However, propriety and her own resolve demanded that she do so.

Brandon was the first to speak. His voice was husky with emotion when he whispered against her ear, "Cissy, I am falling in love with you. I know you don't feel the way I do, but in time I hope that you can reciprocate. Please, don't answer just now. Think about it and allow me to see you again."

Chapter 9

It quickly turned sour in Fayetteville for the newly minted Lord Markham Latham. Cursing his luck at again being suspected of cheating, Marcel wasted no time decamping to the railroad depot. He stood in line mulling over his options. Considering an unfortunate reputation attached to both his name and his new alias, he decided it would be healthier to head for more remote climes. The idea of San Francisco, awash in the heady euphoria of newly acquired wealth from gold, silver, and shipping, appealed to him. In 1865 alone over fifty five million dollars passed through San Francisco. The idea of a city that was increasingly cosmopolitan as a result of that wealth was an added inducement. He was tired of the small southern towns that he had made home for over two years. The yearning to return to Paris was strong, but for now the "Paris of the West" would suffice. With a few thousand more he could pay off the debts he had incurred in France, those that had required his unannounced decampment to spare his hide. He was determined to amass sufficient wealth to allow him to return home and to live the lifestyle that his pedigree warranted. How he garnered it mattered not at all. The sooner he had it, and Logan Gwaltney and Cissy LaRoque were taken care, the more quickly he could resume his former life in the city of his birth.

When his turn arrived to purchase a ticket, he announced his destination in a firm voice. The agent peered over the tops of his spectacles with rheumy eyes, "You ain't from around here, are you feller?"

"I should think that immaterial. The ticket is all I require, not a conversation, nor an acquaintance."

"Ain't no need to get all puffed up." The man grumbled as he handed over the required ticket.

Had he know that the transcontinental railroad was not yet completed and segments of the travel were of necessity by overland coach, he might have considered taking a ship around Cape Horn. Even with his piecemeal travel arrangements the trip was considerably quicker than the more than three months required for a sea voyage with stops in ports along the way.

Marcel arrived in San Francisco covered in cinders and the filth of travel. En route he had gleaned what information he could from fellow travelers. Using his new found knowledge he wasted no time in locating the Occidental Hotel where he registered under his own name The Marquis de Rochefort, Marcel Lambert. The clerk, upon spying the title, quickly assigned him a suite that he assured was worthy of someone of his eminence.

Handing over the key, he commented, "You will note sir that we have the latest facilities with your own private chamber for sanitation and bathing. Should you require anything at all, we will be happy to oblige."

"A bottle of an excellent French champagne and the services of a good tailor are my priorities at the moment."

"Of course, sir. The champagne along with some complimentary dishes will be delivered to your chambers immediately. I will arrange for a tailor to arrive within the hour if that is suitable?"

"Allow me twenty minutes for a bath before sending up the champagne."

"Yes, sir. Er, your majesty, sir." The clerk bowed nearly banging his head on the desk where the registry bore that titled signature.

"Please, just keep it a simple Mr. Lambert. I prefer not to have my title touted about in this country of yours where titles have no meaning."

After another bow and a stuttered apology from the clerk who had begun to perspire heavily, Marcel strutted away. As a betting man, he figured the rumor of the their titled guest would soon be proclaimed from door to door as fast as the clerk could spread it. He counted on its usefulness in meeting men of substance in San Francisco.

Marcel stopped in the middle of his chamber and glanced around at the opulent room. His mouth twitched in a momentary smirk before he walked over to the lace-under drape of the window and lifted it to look at the scene below. Montgomery Street was filled with luxurious carriages, elegantly attired pedestrians, and a general hum of activity. Looking towards San Francisco Bay he spotted fill-work underway in the area that he would learn was called Mission Bay.

The porter entered and placed his tray on the table before he walked up beside Marcel and pointed with pride to the prosperous looking Houseworth and Company Opticians building. Just down the block another imposing office building built by Henry Halleck, he informed Marcel, housed the leading attorneys and financiers of the city along with artists and writers. It also had the distinction of being the first fireproof building in a city notorious for fires. Pointing again towards the bay he guided Marcel's eye towards Talbert Wharf in Mission Creek where the masts of ships pierced the sky.

"We have a fine city here. It sure has boomed in the last five or six years. I suspect the population is already over 130,000 people...had 108,000 in the census of '64. Some French gentlemen like yourself, the Verdier brothers, run a grand mercantile on the corner of Geary and Stockton called The City of Paris. I suspect you will want to visit them and survey the goods they carry. You also might want to visit the amusement park at Woodward Gardens, and for walking around there's Stowe Lake. We got the best restaurants in the west and some of the most beautiful mansions in the country up on Rincon Hill. I particularly like Milton Latham's house. And another one...."

More interested in non-residential establishments, Marcel interrupted, "Where might a gentleman go for a bit of entertainment?"

"We got more whorehouses here than about any place in the world I reckon. For gambling there's the El Dorado or Dennison's Exchange. If you want something a little less fancy, I'm kind of partial to Willow's Bar. There's a slew of others. Just about anything you could ever want we got right here. Fine city we got here, fine city."

More than eager for a hot bath he generous tipped the porter in order to hasten his exit and to insure ready service in future. It was a contented man that clambered from the tub, wrapped himself in his robe, and emerged into his chamber to find a perfectly chilled bottle of Veuve Clicquot champagne. Beside the wine bucket was a plate of fresh oysters, cheese, crackers, and strawberries. Next to that lay a copy of the San Francisco bulletin. Marcel sank into the cushioned depths of a club chair and poured a glass of the champagne. He sighed with pleasure. Realizing it had been hours since he had eaten, he proceeded to demolish the food as the level of champagne steadily sank in the bottle. He had just picked up the newspaper when a knock sounded at the door announcing the arrival of the tailor.

It was a happy tailor that departed Marcel's chamber clutching his sample bag and an order form detailing the sizes and quantities of items ordered. Chance Simpson was glad for having the foresight to bring the finest quality fabric samples after the desk clerk mentioned that the guest he was to visit was a nobleman. He had not been disappointed for the Frenchman had ordered the best of everything: suits, trousers, vests, shirts, and cravats. He had also taken measurements for shoes, gloves, and hats that he would deliver when he returned with the clothing. He was whistling as he walked to the Niantic Hotel on the corner of Clay and Sansome where another client awaited his services. If this order proved as lavish as the last, he would have a prosperous month indeed.

Unfortunately Logan Gwaltney was more prudent with his coins and limited himself to middle grade fabrics and only a few basic pieces. Logan's wardrobe was practically non-existent after years away at war. When he stopped by his home in New Berne prior to leaving for California, he had found only a few items that would fit his emaciated frame. As it was, he still looked like a one-legged scarecrow, as weight was slow to return. Logan chortled to himself when the tailor took one look at him and shook his head. Heaving a distressed sigh, the tailor began the process of measuring.

"You do seem to run a bit on the thin side," Chance remarked.

"Four years of war with slim vittles will do that to a man." Logan chuckled, "I suspect a few months of decent food will find me needing your services again. You might want to allow for a bit in those seams, mind you."

"I'll be happy to do that." The tailor stood to move to the rear to resume measuring. "Where you from, Mr. Gwaltney? You sound like you might be from the south."

"That I am. I come from New Berne, North Carolina. It's a port city, too, but nowhere near as bustling and populous as this one."

"People come here from all over. Lots of foreigners here, too. Come here for the money that washes through this town like a river of silver and gold. I just fitted up this Marquis fellow from France. He is the first titled gent that I have tailored for. He bought the finest of everything, and enough for three men. Yes, sir, Mr. Lambert is going to be stepping out in style."

Logan jerked involuntarily, "What did you say his name is?"

"Let me look here on this order. Ah, yes, I thought that was right. It's Marcel, Marcel Lambert...says he is the Marquis of something or other. Says he is from Paris."

Logan felt an icy wave wash over him. He could not stop a sudden shiver. Damn, that son of a bitch was supposed to be rotting in the woods on the edge of Dover Swamp where he had shot him and left him for carrion. What kind of bizarre fate had determined that Marcel be alive and end up in the same place he was? For a moment he considered going to the local sheriff and turning the man in, but then what proof did he, a stranger, have to offer beyond his word against Marcel's? If he ran across the man, he would decide then what to do. In the meantime he would just let sleeping dogs lie. But it angered him. It angered him that Lambert should be allowed to get away with kidnapping Evangeline and Cissy. If he had not happened on them when he did, Marcel would have raped Cissy.

In the week while Marcel awaited the wardrobe that would allow him to dress according to the image he wanted to project to the men of money in San Francisco, he culled the daily papers, quizzed the loquacious porter, the maid who not only provided information but also her body, and anyone else that could provided him useful knowledge. His first destination would be the high-end gambling clubs. With that decided on he drew up the list of people he would visit and cultivate, those that could provide him an entree into upper crust society. With his title, good looks, and cultivated charm he anticipated no problems. Fingering his lucky deck of cards, Marcel leaned back in his club chair and smiled with satisfaction.

He glanced down just before climaxing. The maid's lascivious movements in his lap were just one more pleasure to be afforded by San Francisco. Soon he would have less need of her services. He intended to bed someone of higher station that could further his prospects in the community. He hardly glanced up when the maid left.

The final tally of men to cultivate included George Ensin,

president of the Spring Valley Water Company. In an area with limited rainfall and a growing population, water was becoming a critical element. The prosperous Peter Donahue of the local iron works made the list along with Commodore Henry Platt of the yacht club. He added Milton Latham and the financiers in the Hallack building. Soon he had a list of twenty-five of the most prominent and affluent citizens. He did not intend to stop his merger into local life with the upper crust. He had found the naive and gullible were a ready source of revenue with far less effort. They would keep him in spending money. The pathway to real money would come from bigger fish. The idea of grubbing in the dirt for gold and silver ore did not appeal at all. He would much rather take the gold and silver from the stupid sods who had worked for it and were not smart enough to keep it.

* * * * *

Logan sat on a stool in a waterfront tavern nursing his whiskey. Beyond procuring his new wardrobe he had made little progress. He had no such detailed plans as Marcel for surviving in the rowdy city. He did not know where or how he would make a living. Having only one leg was a serious impediment that made physically demanding work impossible. Hell, Logan mused he was still learning to balance himself on one leg and the crude peg. He had to find work, and soon, as the money Harvey had sent him for the sale of his farm would not last forever. But where to begin was a puzzle he had yet to solve. Struggling against melancholy for the life he had envisioned and would never have, Logan did not at first hear the man that stood beside him at the bar.

"I said judging by the way you're favoring that stump of yours, it's a relatively new one. You in the war?"

Logan was reluctant to answer since he did not know the man's political leanings and wanted no confrontation. He hesitated until the man said, "Lost your ears, too?"

"No sir, just my leg. Lost it at after the battle at Fort Fisher in February. It still pains me."

"Reb or Yank?"

"I don't see how as it matters anymore, but I was a Rebel."

"That's alright with me. Fought for the Union but I ain't holding grudges. You boys put up one fine fight. Me, lost my leg at Antietam."

Logan glanced down and saw the one shoe that protruded beneath the man's trousers on the right side. The left side ended in a peg. "You seem to be managing a lot better with that thing than I am."

"Takes time. Gave me the devil for over two years. Now I swing along pretty well. Give it a little longer and you'll get the hang of it. Stump will heal so you don't feel it as much. Kind of toughens up, I reckon."

"I sure as hell hope so. It hurts like the devil most times."

"Know a man that makes a good peg. Knows how to cushion it and position the straps. Think he might be able to help you. Planning to have him do me a new one, too."

"I appreciate it, sir. By the way, my name's Logan Gwaltney. Yours?"

"Abel Benson. An honor, my lad." Abel grinned, "Must say meeting over whiskey is a damned sight better than meeting over a bullet."

"Damned if that ain't so." Logan shook his pro-offered hand, "Let me buy you a drink, Yank."

"Don't mind if you do, Reb."

Logan laughed for the first time in months. Abel was a gregarious man with a wicked sense of humor. After several rounds of whiskey and much good joshing, the two men were on their way to a warm friendship. Abel told Logan that he had a spread in the Sacramento Valley and was raising cattle. He nodded in recognition of the perils Logan had endured running his own family farm in North Carolina.

"Farming ain't ranching, but both depend mighty strong on the good Lord's mercy. Been lucky, it was running well before the war. Got a good foreman who ran it while I was skylarking in the war. Made me money selling beef for the army. Now I'm doing real fine for myself. Still farming?"

"Sold it and headed west."

"Running from your other leg, I reckon. Know how it made me feel. Finally figured out I was more than a damned leg. My brain, my heart, and everything else works fine. Learned to cope and not feel damned sorry for myself. You will, too."

"I hope so. Right now I need to dig myself out of the doldrums and find a way to make a living. Money from the farm won't last forever."

"You married?"

"No, you?"

"Not yet, but ain't giving up. Got me a gal that waited this whole war for me and now she's waiting for me to get my head straightened out. Feel like I have to give her the chance to find someone else with two legs. But, she refuses to look beyond me. I am beginning to feel mighty lucky. Got anyone back home waiting for you?"

Logan looked into his glass and swirled the amber liquid. His voice was soft and broken when he answered, "Not anymore."

"Well, that's a hell of a mess. Right sorry about it." Abel screwed up his mouth and sat studying Logan for several seconds before asking, "Know anything about keeping books?"

"I kept our records at home. Arithmetic and figuring were always easy for me. Why do you ask?"

"Just so happens I need an office manager at the ranch because I can't do mathematics worth a damn. You need a job; I'm hiring. What do you say? Figure two gimpy legs are better than one."

Logan grinned, "Yank, you just hired yourself a bookkeeper. When do I start?"

"Fast as we can high tail it out of here. I'm leaving in the morning. Meet me at the Saint Francis Hotel at eight o'clock and we'll head out."

Logan had paid his bill at the Niantic, stuffed himself on breakfast...which helped ease a slight hangover, and was waiting in the Saint Francis Hotel's lobby at seven thirty reading a newspaper. At seven forty five Abel walked up. "Like a man who knows how to be on time. No sense burning daylight. You ready to head east?"

"That I am. I like San Francisco pretty well but it's a little overwhelming for a boy from a small southern town. I confess to a preference for a little more country and a lot less city."

"That you are going to get. Hired hack should be waiting at the curbing. Taking the railroad to Sacramento and then on to Folsom. My man will meet us there. Ranch is about midway between Folsom and Coloma. Need any help with your baggage?"

"No, thank you. I have just my portmanteau. I think I can manage. I just don't look graceful doing it."

"Get a longer strap. I like this one that will go over my shoulder and across my chest. That way my hands are free to balance, and if need be, use my cane."

"Right now I can see the practicality in that. If you have some leather and some tools, I will see what I can do when we get to your ranch and I have some free time."

The trip to Sacramento gave Abel time to tell Logan a little about the area around his ranch. He explained that it was hot in summer with little rain. Winters were cool with occasional frost. Rain and frequent fog brought moisture to the grassy plains and low hills from fall until spring. Logan watched the countryside roll past his window and found that he liked the vast empty stretches.

"Lots of Spanish folk around here. Hell, this was a part of Mexico not that far in the past. Some folks pretend it still is. You speak any Spanish? Ain't necessary but some of the ranch hands don't have much English. Not that you will be dealing that much with them directly except payday."

"How many acres are you grazing?" Logan asked.

"Ranch has about thirty thousand acres running from the American River towards the El Dorado Hills. House is set on a high point since the river will occasionally flood things out in the low lands. Right now, I'm running about eleven thousand head of cattle. Got a contract with the government during the war and they're still buying. Just not as much. Working about twelve all total. One in the kitchen, one in the house, rest are cowboys."

Logan commented, "Your ranch makes my little farm look right puny. I had six hundred acres and thought I was doing well. By the way, what do you call it?"

"Renamed it after the war. Call it One Less. Reckon you can guess why. Makes for a simple brand."

Chuckling to himself, Logan wondered if the man ever spoke in anything but clipped sentences.

Chapter 10

Cissy sat in her father's office biting the corner of her lower lip. Her father glared at her, his face grim and uncompromising. He had returned from New Berne and the family had resettled into the home on Orange Street that was to be their permanent abode. Evangeline had accepted that her house in New Berne would be sold and that temporarily they would keep Graham's house for visits to the office there as needed. While he had been pleased with Cissy's management of the Wilmington office in his absence, he was far from pleased with her at the moment.

"I have explained to you my objections to having you move to New Berne and run the business there. It is simply no place for a woman and I absolutely do not want you living there alone. You need to meet some of the nice young ladies in town and become active in the local circle and meet available gentlemen. This determination of yours to act like a man is not one that is going to be viewed with favor by local society. Young ladies do not belong in a man's world, Cissy, at least not yet, maybe never."

"You want me to meet available gentlemen, settle down, get married, and have babies? That's all men think women can do. It's not fair. You said yourself that I did a superior job here and even increased business. Doesn't that prove I can run a business and run it well, even if I am a woman?" Cissy bit her lip again, wondering if she dared say more. Deciding to throw fat into the fire, she challenged, "So, you want me to find a husband? Maybe, I have."

"Ah, wonderful. When may we meet this young man?"

"You don't mind that he is a Union officer then?"

"Cissy, you have said quite enough for one day. I suggest you return home. I'm sure Evangeline will be glad for your company. I have more serious matters to deal with that arguing with a stubborn, insubordinate daughter." Graham rose from his desk and stormed from the office.

Snatching her bonnet from the rack, Cissy slammed it on her head and jerked the strings into the semblance of a bow. Grabbing her cloak she followed him from the office. If anything, her rage exceeded his. Zeke Smathers winced and shook his head when the second LaRoque banged the office door. He was not a betting man, but he had learned not to underestimate Cissy when she had her head set on something. Deceptively beautiful, she was smart as a whip, and as determined as Graham had ever been. If he were a betting man, he would put his money on her. Yes, it was going to be interesting around the office in the coming days. He chuckled softly. He was going to miss her when she left to run the New Berne office. He had enjoyed her wit and sparkling personality. Plus, she was far better looking than anyone else that worked around the wharves.

Cissy stomped down the Water Street seething with fury that her father would order her home after all she had done for his business. At first she did not hear her name being called. When she did, she paused and looked about in confusion before glancing back to spot Brandon emerging from Dorsey's Tavern. Turning she waited for him to catch up with her. Hiding her inner rage, she plastered a welcoming smile on her face.

"You are leaving the office earlier than your custom, I believe." Brandon could tell that the smile on her face did not reach her eyes and her face was red with emotion. Even had he not noted her angry stride, he would have known she was upset. "I trust all is well with you?"

Biting her lip, Cissy pondered the scene she had just had with her father. Before she could reply, Brandon remarked, "I can always tell when you are fretting about something because you bite your lip before you speak. Do you want to talk about it?"

"You must forgive me. I am in such a temper with my father because after all the work I did to learn the business and do well while he was gone, now he just wants me to walk away. I really want to go on doing what I was doing. If not here, since he is determined to make this his primary office, then in New Berne where he could use me. But, no, he just wants me to tat doilies and twiddle my thumbs while I wait for a husband. I simply do not understand why men think that is all women want."

"I will grant that you may not want that now, but someday you will want a husband and children. Do you really want to be a spinster dependent on a male relative to support you for the rest of your life and never have a home of your own? At least in your own home you have some say in your life, particularly if your husband is a decent sort. Many women might envy your independence, but others would resent that you can so easily feel contempt for the things they yearn for and may never have. With so many men killed in the war, far too many women will find themselves with a bleak future lived without the hope of finding someone to love and care for them. You are so fortunate. You're beautiful, intelligent, accomplished, and oh, so desirable. You can have any man you want and yet you would shun us all."

Cissy exhaled loudly. "You make me sound so dreadful."

"That is the last thing you are. Don't you know by now that I wear my heart on my sleeve where you are concerned? I realize it is far too soon for me to make such declarations, but do remember that I care for you and want you in my life for as long as you will have me."

"You are far better than I deserve." Cissy smiled, "I will let you buy me an ice cream. Perhaps that will cool my temper."

"It would be my pleasure to buy you as many dishes of ice

cream as you would like." Brandon extended his elbow and she slipped her hand through. As they walked to the ice cream shop, he kept up a witty conversation. The more she laughed at his humorous stories of life in the army the harder he searched his memory to find more such episodes.

They were both so engrossed in one such story that they did not notice her father emerging from his bank on the corner of Market Street. He saw them, however, and turned to catch up with them before reconsidering his course of action. He would deal with Cissy later when he was less angry.

Cissy left the ice cream parlor surprisingly lighthearted and could only thank Brandon for lifting her mood. She still did not want a committed courtship with the intention of marriage, but she very much enjoyed the flirtation Brandon provided. She realized his seriousness and surely after her previous remarks he knew that she was not. So, what could it harm? Besides, it might provide the spur she needed for her father to allow her to run the New Berne office. All she had to do was to convince her father that Brandon was indeed a serious suitor.

Brandon walked Cissy all the way to her door and waited until Evangeline opened it at Cissy's knock. Standing there, he could not help but fidget, as he had no way of knowing how he would be received. When Evangeline opened the door the first thing she saw was the blue uniform. Looking up from the button that resided at eye level she met his eyes.

"I don't believe that I have had the honor of an introduction." Her voice was cool but polite.

Before he could answer, Cissy piped up, "Evangeline, I would like you to meet my very good friend Colonel Brandon McLean. Brandon, this is my stepmother, Evangeline LaRoque."

"Colonel McLean." Evangeline nodded her head in acknowledgement, but did not stand aside to invite him in.

Nervous and unsure what to do next, Cissy commented,

"Brandon was kind enough to walk me home after a lovely ice cream downtown. I told him after the concert we attended at Thalian Hall that you play the harpsichord since he loves music and plays piano. Perhaps, we can have a musical evening soon and invite Brandon."

"I will check with your father to determine our schedule, however it may be sometime as the harpsichord is badly in need of tuning."

"Please, don't worry about that on my account, Mrs. LaRoque. Any opportunity to spend time with Cissy and get to know her family is fine with me."

"I see." Evangeline commented with a noticeable lack of emotion.

The moment had become decidedly awkward. Bowing to the two women, Brandon excused himself promising Cissy that he would call on her soon. Despite the lack of warmth in his reception, he was determined in his pursuit. He left her door with his shoulders squaring for battle. Neither Cissy nor Evangeline missed the subtle shift in his posture.

"Cissy, I don't need to remind you how your father feels about the occupation forces. He is going to be very unhappy when he learns that you are consorting with one of the officers. I don't want to chide you, but I fear I must. Graham has so much on him now with trying to get his business growing again. Surely you don't want to make his life more difficult?"

"Shucks! I am not trying to make it more difficult. If he wouldn't be so stubborn he would realize I am trying to help him."

"You think it helps him for a Union officer to be courting you?"

"I'm talking about business. I am good at it. I've proved it."

Exasperated, Evangeline exhaled between pursed lips. Cissy could tell She was trying very hard to keep her temper. Seeking to mollify her, Cissy soothed, "Please don't be upset. It isn't good for your baby. I'm not sure how serious I am about Brandon, however he is a very nice man and a cultured one. Yes, he is the former enemy, but that is done with now. The war is finished."

Softly Evangeline exhorted, "No, Cissy, it really isn't done with. Not as long as we are an occupied, militarily controlled city. Not as long as feeling are still so raw. Not as long as widows, mothers, fathers, and sweethearts walk around with tears of fresh grief. You are intelligent enough that I should not have to point these things out to you."

Annie walked into the foyer, and realizing they were arguing, softly backed out again to call from the hallway. "Cissy, is that ye there?"

"Yes, Annie. I'm home early."

Walking up she smiled brightly, "Wonderful. I was hoping we could go shopping for the ribbons I need to trim me bedraggled old bonnet."

Grateful for the escape option, Cissy readily agreed. Soon they were walking towards Market Street to shop. On the way Cissy vented her frustrations and her plan to escape to New Berne to work from the office there. "I definitely will not be allowed to go there and live alone. I was hoping you would go with me."

Annie beamed with glee. "Jesus, Mary, and Joseph! Me prayers are answered. Me new beau is moving to New Berne. He was there during the war and liked it so much he wants to stay there. I like him a lot and was wondering how I could be near him. He says he likes me, too. 'Twould be a pity not to see where it might lead us. If we were to go to New Berne, I could go on seeing him. Who knows what might happen then."

"Father is furious with me at the moment for wanting to keep working. I may need your help and encouragement because our coming battles are going to make the recent war look tame."

"Ah, Cissy, me girl. "Tis not the way to do it. Remember ye catch more flies with honey, so try not to provoke him too much." Annie grinned, "Let's stay low and see which way the wind blows before we stir up a storm."

While the girls shopped and talked about the handsome soldier Annie had fallen for, Graham stewed. Sitting at his desk staring out at the wharf where one of his ships bobbed on the tide, he mulled over what to do with Cissy. The very idea of a Union soldier squiring her about made him sputter with fury. The more he thought about it the more the idea of sending her to New Berne appealed. With her there, even if it were not his preference, she would no longer be able to see the man that he had seen her laughing with that afternoon. Such things needed to be nipped in the bud before they could grow. He walked home slowly that night still undecided. When Evangeline told him what had transpired at their door earlier, his mind was made up. It hurt that this gulf existed between his daughter and him. It hurt that she was so adamant about opposing him. It hurt that once again they would be separated. But it could not be helped. Cissy would be leaving immediately. He would carefully avoid mention of the Union officer. It was better that she think it was a business necessity.

That night Annie and Cissy entered the dining room with trepidation. Neither girl knew what kind of mood Graham would be in after the earlier blow-up at the office. To their surprise, after a quiet intonation of a blessing over their supper, Graham proceeded to talk about mundane affairs never alluding to the earlier events of the day. Evangeline followed suit keeping the conversation flowing along non-challenging lines. Cissy and Annie devoted their attention to Andy...slicing his meat, and helping him with his cup of milk. When the meal was finished, they left the dining room together. Annie and Cissy were preparing to go up for the night when Graham halted them.

"Cissy, I would like you to return to the office tomorrow. There are several matters you organized in my absence that we need to discuss so I know what I am dealing with in future."

"Of course, Father. I am happy to do whatever you need."

"Good. I will see you at breakfast and we'll walk to the office together."

When they reached the top of the stairs, Annie and Cissy raced to Cissy's room both eager to discuss the total lack of any expected remark of censure about Brandon. They could neither one ferret out what was going on her in father's mind, but judging from his carefully guarded expression they decided he was definitely up to something. Until they knew what it was, Cissy hesitated to put any further arguments into the mix. Both girls felt somewhat letdown as they had been bracing themselves for theatrical fireworks.

"It is just really strange. I cannot for the life of me figure out what he is up to. This is not typical. I know full well Evangeline has told him about Brandon walking me home. You know how he feels about that, so what is going on?"

"Aye, it be puzzling for certain sure. Mayhap tomorrow he will say something. In the meanwhile, I thank me lucky stars for a calm evening."

"I just hope it stays calm. But, sooner or later I am going to ask him again about New Berne."

"Aye, but mayhap ye might wait."

Graham kept her busy at the office the next few days, acting as though nothing had happened. He chuckled to himself when he saw Zeke cut his eyes at the two of them and shake his head in puzzlement that there were no slamming doors and quarrels as he had expected. Cissy resumed her work as though it had never been interrupted by her summary dismissal the day they had argued. She and Zeke both treaded warily, careful to keep out of her father's way except when necessary. Both were waiting for something. They just didn't know what.

When Graham called her to his office and shut the door, Cissy prepared for what she thought would be a lecture and battle of wills. Instead Graham walked behind his desk, seated himself, leaned forward, and smiled. "You really have done a fine job here, Cissy. I was hasty to ignore how valuable you were in my absence. Everyone that I have talked to in the office, the warehouse, the wharf, or those we do commerce with, has praised your acumen. I am proud of you, even if it isn't the role that I would like to see you in someday."

"I know, Father. I accept how you feel and realize that working in your business flies in the face of convention. I'm just proud that you appreciate the work I did while you were gone. I worked so hard to do a good job."

"You didn't just do a good job, you did a superb job. Well enough that I am reconsidering the New Berne office."

Cissy held her breath and waited. Her father continued, "Perhaps, it would be helpful to have you work there until I can find a permanent replacement that we can depend on to run it the way it needs. In the meantime, I will turn it over to you. But, I do not want you there without a companion. Beulah, Bessie, and Toby are all there to help with the house and yard, but you need someone besides servants. Do you think Annie will object to relocating with you for a time?"

Keeping it low key to match his own tone and demeanor, Cissy responded, "I will ask her. I will be busy, so at times it might be lonely for her, however, I have reason to believe she will be willing."

"Cissy, as much as it surprises me that time has flown so quickly I have to accept that you are a grown woman with a mind of your own. I only ask that you use it to safe guard your personal reputation and that of the business. I do not want to have to worry about that. I hope that is all I need to say on the subject."

"Thank you for trusting me. I will do all I can to make sure that you are happy with me." Cissy walked around the desk and leaning over, kissed her father's check. "Thank you. I love you so much, Father. I never want to hurt you and make you unhappy with me."

"I feel the same way, Cissy. I love you, too...more than you can ever know. It pains me that we are going to be so far apart, as I have missed you."

"We can visit back and forth. As soon as the railroad is fully repaired it will be easier and in the meantime we can use one of the packet boats."

"Yes. Zeke has already arranged transportation for you. We have a shipment of tools to take to New Berne. If you can be ready by tomorrow, you can go on the boat with them."

Chapter 11

Marcel could feel luck running with him. The two Frenchmen he had met at the Willow Bar were unskilled but avid card players. He had allowed them to win steadily for the last hour. With the pot in the middle of the table more and more appealing, he decided it was time to start winning.

Durand Lagrangere had come to San Francisco to start a new life with more promise than his past had provided. In his mid-forties, he had yet to do more than struggle by. The fact that cards were responsible for some of that eluded him. Louis Babin, some ten years younger sat across the table from Durand fingering his cards nervously. Louis had several habits that gave him away whenever he was bluffing. Marcel wiped his brow as though he too were nervous.

Noting the two men's body language, Durand decided his moment had come. "I am all in, messieurs."

Louis grimaced before reluctantly laying his cards face down on the table. As an accountant's clerk he did not have money to lose. "I'm out."

Marcel sat without expression several tense moments before remarking, "I will see you."

When Marcel turned over his cards and Durand saw that he had been beaten, he was shocked. He had counted cards carefully. How could Marcel have drawn the one card that would beat him? He would have sworn he remembered the card being turned up and discarded earlier. Puzzled he watched, Marcel rake in the pot that should have been his. Tossing back his drink, he stood and looked down at the others without comment. Then he turned and left, lurching slightly when he reached the door.

Louis commented, "You have rare luck, mon ami. Durand was certain he would take that hand. I know him well and I can tell when he has a winning hand. He leaves unhappy now."

"Alors, that is the way with cards, is it not? Just when you think you cannot lose, you do. I have lost many such games that way." Marcel rose from the table and shook Louis' hand, "Another time?"

"Another time," he agreed. "Perhaps my turn then, eh?"

Marcel left the saloon satisfied with his evening. His stash was growing slowly but steadily. Soon he would have the entree he needed to play with the big boys. Already he had met several and with a bit more careful cultivation they would begin to include him in their leisure hours. In the meantime he would cull what he could from the small fry. Lost in reverie, he did not see the shadow that quietly detached itself from the alley by the Willow and began to follow him.

Durand was a little drunk and a lot furious. He was certain he had been cheated. He fingered the knife in his pocket lovingly. That fancy snob was going to find out how he felt about being played for a fool. The fog that had rolled in from the bay was his friend, giving him cover in the open spaces. He was oblivious to the fact that at some point Marcel had become aware that he was being followed. Turning a corner he found himself grasped firmly from behind.

"What have we here, Durand?" Marcel snarled, "Was there something you wished to say to me? If so, no need to sneak around behind me."

"You lying, cheating, whore's son. I want my money back."

"Unfortunately, it is no longer your money. You lost it, remember?"

"You stole it, you mean. Give it back and no hard feelings." Durand fumbled for the knife but could not get it out quickly enough.

"Ah, I regret I cannot do that, my friend. I also regret that we must part company." Marcel listened to the man's last futile gasp for breath as he choked him. Durand's fingers clawed frantically but could not free the iron grip from around his throat. "Foolish man, foolish man, you lose your life over a bit of coin. You should have known better than to challenge me."

Hefting the limp body over one shoulder, Marcel walked the short distance to Mission Creek and heaved it in. It would not be the first or the last body to exit San Francisco's nightlife via the waterway. Shrugging his shoulders, Marcel walked back to the hotel. He fully intended to return nightly to the Willow until he could cultivate richer prospects at the El Dorado and Dennison's Exchange. The men there were more sophisticated and thus would require far greater finesse than such gullibles as Louis and Durand.

Morning arrived with some of the thickest fog that the city had seen in years, it was not until late afternoon that it cleared sufficiently to expose the body bobbing alongside the wharf in Mission Bay. Fished from the water by a seaman, the police quickly claimed it. Using the items in his pocket they managed to determine his identity as Durand Legrangere and his local address. The garrulous landlord was happy to sit and chat. His days had been far to dull. Durand's death brought the greatest excitement he had known in years. At the end of a rambling discourse on his own life, the police detective determined that the Willow Bar and several others were favorites of the late Frenchman. That night he was sitting at the first of the bars on the list when the night crowd began to drift in. No one proved of interest, nor did he learn anything at the next bar. Frustrated at the waste of time, he walked home fuming.

While Sullivan wasted yet another night sitting in a bar, Marcel was busy elsewhere. On November 14th, Marcel was robbing the What Cheer House. The night watchman never saw what hit him. Much to his delight, the take was far more than

Marcel had expected. He now had the money to gamble at the El Dorado and Dennison's Exchange with the high rollers of the town.

On the fourth night the detective was at the Willow. He watched each man enter and then drift to join what, he assumed, were previous acquaintances. He had almost given up on the Willow, thinking it as useless a lead as the others, when a man walked up to the bar and in accented English requested a whiskey.

"Excuse me my man. I don't believe I recognize your accent. Where from do you hail?"

"I am from Bordeaux, monsieur. I think you are new here."

"Yes. I normally go to a watering hole nearer home." The detective smiled and held out his hand, "Keith Sullivan, sir."

"Louis Babin."

"French then. I say do you happen to know a friend of mine, Durand Legrangere?"

"*Bien sur*. That is *very well*. He is my good friend. We were just playing cards together a few nights ago. I hope he will be here soon as it is unlike him to be so long away," Babin lifted his shoulders in a Gallic shrug, "But then, he lost much money. Perhaps, you join us if he comes?"

"Oh, I would not want to intrude. Is it just the two of you, or is the table full?"

"Non, Non. Was me and Durand usually, but a couple of weeks ago another Frenchman started to join us."

"Do you think they would mind if I make it a foursome?"

"Hah! The more who play, the more the money, no? So why should they mind?"

The two men sat at the bar and chatted for another hour before Louis remarked, "I think Durand is broke. He lost much money that night so maybe again he does not come tonight."

"You sly fox. So you beat your friend out of his money, did you?"

"Ah, no, not I. Marcel Lambert, he won. It was a surprise. I know Durand well enough to say he thinks he will win, not Marcel. He was very angry, I think."

Keith listened without remarking. After several more drinks, Louis left disappointed that his fellow Frenchmen had not arrived to join him. Keith followed him out promising to return. An emergency late the next day kept him tied to his office until too late to go to the Willow.

That evening, Marcel was the first to arrive. Louis came in not long after. Both men sat drinking, as Louis did not want to begin playing until Durand arrived. After two hours and still no Durand, Louis sighed, "I think you take all of our friend's money. Until he makes more, I don't think he will play with us. Another man I met last night will play. He said he will come tonight, but I have not yet seen him. He says he knows Durand."

Immediately Marcel was suspicious. "Tell me about this man. Did you learn his name?"

"Keith Sullivan. Big Irishman. He seemed nice. He asked many questions. Not like most Willow customers who don't want to know anything."

Trying to seem casual, Marcel asked, "Did you learn what he does?"

"No. We waited for Durand and you and when you did not come I left. He left when I did."

Marcel, nursed his drink for several long minutes trying to decide how best to cover his tracks. The naive and talkative Louis was a definite hazard. Eliminating him seemed to be an obvious step. *How to do it* would take some thought. Marcel bought them both drinks, careful not to drink enough to become inebriated himself. He did not intend for Louis to leave until he had determined the best method for resolving his problem. Louis chatted about first one thing and then another despite minimal response from Marcel. Marcel had lost interest in cards for the evening and Louis was reluctant to play until his friend Durand arrived. At closing both men arose to leave. Unsteady on his feet, Louis accepted Marcel's assistance. They walked along the waterfront as Marcel followed the drunken man's mumbled directions to his lodging. The evening was mild for November and for once no fog spoiled the evening. Marcel was far happier in the fog for excursions like the one that night, but it did not stop him from executing his plan. In a dark stretch between wharves, he stopped Louis.

"I hear someone following us. I would sure feel better if I had brought my gun with me. Do you have a weapon on you?"

"'S in my pocket," he slurred. Louis struggled to keep his balance as he reached into his pocket to extract the pistol. "Take it. 'Spect I'd shoot myself if I tried to use it."

"Let's step over here in the shadow of this building and wait to see who's trailing us."

Once in the darkened corner, Marcel put the pistol to Louis' temple and pulled the trigger. He then wrapped the corpse's right hand around the hilt of the gun. It would look like a suicide to the police. He congratulated himself on his superiority over men like the two who now lay dead. Such men were no threat to him. He would no longer return to the Willow Bar so the man that was asking questions was unlikely to find answers.

Considering the problem solved, Marcel strolled back to his hotel where he had told the maid to expect him. With a sizeable sum of money from the robbery in the hotel safe adding to what he had already won from gambling, and any threat removed, Marcel was ready to celebrate. At the front desk of the Occidental, Marcel paused to order a chilled bottle of champagne. By the time he had donned his robe, both a waiter with champagne and the maid arrived within moments of one another.

He did not bother to offer her champagne, just poured his

own glass, untied the sash of his robe and indicated what he expected from her. Anticipating the customary money for her services, she obliged. Besides, she liked bragging to the other girls about the French Marquis, leading them to believe that he was in love with her. As for herself, she was far too cynical for that. She smiled through gritted teeth when she pocketed her money and left. She did not even like the arrogant bastard.

Sated with sex and champagne, Marcel shucked his robe beside the bed and slid between the smooth, fresh smelling, ironed sheets. The longer he stayed in San Francisco, the better he liked it. He drifted into contented sleep certain that he was on his way to a bright future among the noted men of the town.

When the corpse arrived in the morgue, Detective Sullivan paid it a visit. Checking the body of this man who had reportedly committed suicide, he lifted the right hand. There was no residue of cordite to indicate that the man had been holding the gun when he shot himself. Out of idle curiosity he lifted the man's left hand and noted ink stains on the fingers that would have held a pen. He had been a lefty. Checking his notes he found the name he sought: Louis Babin, friend of Durand Legrangere. Interesting, he thought, two best friends both dead within days of one another. It was time to track down the other name on his list.

*****

While Marcel wedged himself into the circle of men that frequented the El Dorado, Logan was learning his job in the shadow of the El Dorado Hills. He and Abel Benson had established a natural rapport and easy working relationship. Soon he was not only a respected employee, but also a friend. The other workers on the ranch accepted his easy-going manner and quiet competency. Juana, the cook, had made it her immediate mission to fatten him up. The unaccustomed Mexican cuisine was fast becoming a favorite. She smiled with satisfaction when she noted that he had loosened his belt a notch and some of the gauntness had left his checks. The dry climate relieved some of the ache in his stump, allowing for more peaceful sleep. He and Abel had already visited the man that made artificial limbs and Logan was eagerly anticipating the completion of a wooden leg that would give him better balance and mobility. With his pants leg no longer pinned up, his handicap would be less noticeable. Juana assured him that the senoritas were going to be chasing him in no time. Despite enjoying the flattery in her remark, he resolutely closed his mind to any thought of the only woman he had ever wanted. All in all, he was as pleased with his new abode as Marcel with his not that many miles to the west.

Once a week on Friday morning he and Abel drove into Folsom to pick up the payroll for the week. Generally they would stop for dinner at one of the hotels before going to the bank. Despite both men's love of Juana's cooking, they occasionally wanted something less Mexican. Today they would forego the dinner as they wanted to pick up the new wooden leg that each man had ordered. Anticipating their new limbs the way a child waits for Christmas, neither man minded the change of routine. Abel was the first to strap his on and stand. The grin that broke across his face was enough to spur Logan to attach his own. His stump was still a little tender at odd moments, so he was wary when he put his weight on the new artificial limb.

"Well?" Abel anxiously inquired, "What do you think?"

Logan took care to stand erect getting his balance as he did so. A slow smile stretched his lips before he burst into laughter, "Oh, damn! Abel, I think I could run a race with this thing."

"Any time you're ready, say so. I'll give 'er a go." Abel walked around the small front room of the shop testing his leg. Logan watched for several minutes before he dared risk following suit for fear his newfound balance would desert him.

He began with caution, one careful step after another until he, too, could walk with relative ease.

"Well, it's not as good as the leg I lost, but it is a damned sight better than the peg I was using." Logan turned to the shop owner, "Mr. Shelby, I am mighty grateful to you, sir. You make me feel like a new man."

"Agreed, Mr. Shelby. Mighty pleased myself, sir." Abel turned to Logan, "Well, let's give these new legs a little exercise. Want to get to the bank and on home for supper. After missing dinner, be glad for some of Juana's chili."

After supper both men settled in the ranch office for a glass of whiskey. After several drinks, Abel became somber. "Talked to my gal, the other day when I rode out. Thinking about asking her to marry me."

"That's wonderful, Abel. I'm happy for you. She sounds like a fine woman from what you have told me."

"She is. Not been a very good suitor. Just hope she don't give up on me before I get a chance to ask."

"She's waited this long. I'd say the odds are in your favor."

"Think I'll meet her after church on Sunday; take her for a buggy ride and pop the question."

"So what is her name? I don't believe I ever heard you say."

When Abel replied, Logan shook his head as though to clear his ears, "Who did you say?"

"Cecily Lawrence."

Logan looked like a man who'd been pole axed. Abel watched him turn pale, "What the hell is wrong with you man? Look like you've seen a ghost."

"I'm sorry. The similarity of names is a bit uncanny. You see the girl I left behind was name Cecily. Cecily LaRoque. Everyone called her Cissy. She is the prettiest thing I ever laid eyes on. I feel in love with her when I was ten years old and never looked back. That's finished now, but I miss her like hell."

"Never took you Rebels for cowards. Write her. Tell her how you feel. Maybe she still wants you."

"No. I just can't do that. Not now for sure, probably not ever."

"Dammit. If my Cecily will have me one leg and all, what makes you think your Cissy won't have you?"

Logan's voice was barely above a whisper when he replied, "She is not for me. I know she cares for me, but she just never loved me the way I have her. I don't want her settling for me out of pity. I don't think I could live with it. The doubt would eat me alive. We both deserve better than that."

"See your point, but it's a damned shame."

Chapter 12

Cissy was happy. She and Annie had wasted no time in settling into the LaRoque house on the extension of East Front St. The three long-time servants greeted Cissy with open arms, delighted to have family back in the house. Annie quickly charmed them and had Beulah and Bessie vying to cook favorite dishes for her.

Cissy left them to the house and ensconced herself in the office at Union Point where she struggled to sort out the files and records that had been ignored during the last two years of the war. With no one in the office of whom she could ask questions, her task was even more onerous. Only Jacob in the warehouse had remained after the war; the rest had either been killed in the fighting or left the area. And Jacob did not like working for a woman. She felt as though the man was deliberately frustrating her at every turn. He gave erroneous answers that were so patently obvious she could only shake her head in exasperation and swear not to ask again. Inevitably some knotty issue would arise and she would be forced to seek him out. Little good did it do. After a month she gave up and resolved to advertise along the wharf for other employees. Jacob had friends among the men she approached and their loyalty lay with him. As a last resort she ran an ad in the local paper. Buying a dozen copies, she had the captain of the Cecily take it to Philadelphia and New York when he sailed there the following week. He also promised to ask around in the various ports of call. Along with the advertisement for employees, he carried a handbill Cissy had designed and had printed that promoted the advantages of doing business with LaRoque Shipping.

She was so preoccupied with making the New Berne port a profitable one again that she had little time for social activities. Annie was busy courting her Union friend and didn't mind Cissy's constant inattention. On several occasions, Cissy had spotted Ryan Madison walking with a woman she assumed to be his wife. It was obvious to her that the couple was very much in love. Squelching the increase in her heart rate each time she saw him, she scolded herself for carrying an impossible torch. When rumor reached her that her nemesis, the catty Lizzie Berkely, had seen Ryan for a short time towards the end of the war and was still chasing him, Cissy felt some of her attraction diminish. Learning he had courted Lizzie made her angry and jealous at the same time for he had never courted her, only flirted. She was in Wilmington at the time Ryan had squired Lizzie about but that did little to soften her animosity to the very idea of the two of them together. She did not know his wife, however, Cissy felt some sympathy for the woman with Lizzie after her husband. She knew just how bitchy and underhanded Lizzie could be.

She was busy enough that she had no time to dwell on Ryan. After another two months, she managed to hire an office manager, a replacement for Jacob, and additional men that were needed now that business was beginning to pick up. Her ploy was paying dividends bringing new shipments of sugar, rum, molasses, and coffee from the West Indies. With the war ended, naval stores, wood products, cotton and tobacco were again in demand in foreign ports. Talking with the new hire from Philadelphia, she began to form an idea for even more options for the business. Previously most of their commerce had been with the shipment of goods. *The Cecily* offered another possibility. With it's modern steam propulsion and its spacious hull, Cissy decided that with a bit of carpentry and modification, the ship would be suitable for passenger service to the northern ports. With the former Union men that had settled in the area and increased trade with these ports, it stood to reason that passenger travel would also increase. Before the war her father had carried numerous travelers to Philadelphia, Boston, New Port, and New York. While the war had brought that to an end, there was no reason why it could not resume. While most of the southern clients could no longer afford theatre, shopping, and holidays in the northern cities, new voyagers were in the offing wanting to come south from northern ports.

She pondered asking her father for permission, but rather than risk a rejection she decided to go ahead with her plan and deal with any fallout afterwards. She wasted no time putting her plan in motion for fear that her father would come for a visit and stop her. A letter from him arrived to scotch that worry. Evangeline had lost the little girl she carried when the child was born prematurely. Both her father and her stepmother were in mourning and her heart broke for them. She was sad for herself as well. Growing up an only child, she had longed for siblings. Andy had arrived when she was eighteen, and though she loved her half-brother dearly, she had always wanted a sister.

When she stood on the wharf several months later watching *The Cecily* leave with a full complement of northern bound passengers, she jumped for joy. Twirling in a circle, she was oblivious to the stares of others on the waterfront. Even a cold sleety rain was not enough to dampen her excitement. She did not see Ryan watching her.

He had walked down to Union Point to clear his head. His wife's friend and would-be suitor, Marcus Cauley, was charged with murder and it was Ryan's job to prosecute him. He hated it. Not only that, but Penny was furious with him for agreeing to do it. Ryan was standing in the rain questioning his sanity for being in the weather without an umbrella, when a peripheral movement caught his eye. Turning he watched the young lady capering like a girl as the ship departed. Noting the name of the ship, a bell rang in his head. He wondered what Cissy LaRoque was doing back in New Berne and when she had returned. He smiled at her exuberance. Some of his black mood lifted as he watched her joy. He was curious as to the reason, but shrugged and walked back to his office. She was a delight, but one that belonged in his past. Penny held his heart. Thinking of his son and his wife, he smiled. Now if he could just get his wife to see reason.

Unaware that Ryan was watching her, Cissy raced back to the office with renewed vigor. With *The Cecily* refitted and on her maiden voyage as a passenger ship, she now needed to procure another merchant vessel to handle regular shipping. Reviewing the books and trying to project profits, she arrived at a price that she could pay for another ship. Again, she decided to keep her plans from her father. As long as she sent regular reports and showed a profit, he seemed happy to leave her alone. His office in Wilmington was consuming his attention with little energy left for worrying about New Berne.

She corresponded regularly with both Graham and Evangeline in hopes that her chatty and upbeat letters would prove reassuring to them and prevent a visit. Annie's up and down courtship with her friend, Charles Wright, was an entertaining addition to the letters. She carefully avoided their allusions to the prospect of news of a romantic relationship of her own. Brandon was writing regularly, but as long as he was assigned to the occupation office in Wilmington he could not move to New Berne. With her there, a transfer was his greatest wish. Cissy was careful to avoid encouraging him despite longing for his weekly letters and answering them. Despite all of her protestations that she wanted no man in her life and no husband in her future, a part of her longed for the very things she rejected.

The Cecily was a success from the first voyage. With a regular route that was usually sold out in both directions, she was making money that she could use to pay for the ship she had ordered from the John Laird Company at Birkenhead Docks near Liverpool. Her father had bought steamers from them prior to the war so she had not hesitated to commission them to build her ship. A year later it rode the waves that lapped against the wharf at LaRoque Shipping.

Her father and Evangeline arrived for a visit while both *The Cecily* and *The Intrepid* were tied up awaiting their next departures. Graham had long been curious what Cissy had done to make the New Berne port into such a moneymaker. Business issues and Evangeline's slow recovery had kept him tied to Wilmington despite his longing for his daughter. She had proven her worth ten times over and despite his earlier misgivings, he was enormously proud of her. When he saw the two ships at the wharf, he could not hide his astonishment at what she had done on her own initiative. In that moment he realized why profits had soared in the company. Not only had she inherited some of her father's business acumen, but she also was unafraid of taking intuitive risks. As he looked over the two ships under his daughter's guidance, he could not stop the sudden rise of tears in his eyes.

"Cissy, I am so proud of you. I was so pig-headed wrong to think you could not handle the office here. Not only have you done it; but, you have exceeded anything that I could have dreamed of. I could not have done as well. Your employees are well trained and seem proud to be working for you. You were wise to remove Jacob as he would have been an impediment with his hostile attitude towards women."

Cissy could not help the subtle teasing when she remarked, "Perhaps in time I might have converted his thinking about a woman's place the way I have others."

Graham laughed, "I deserve that comeuppance. You, my pretty little daughter, can do anything you set your mind to, I do believe. Evangeline told me when we left Wilmington and discovered that you were not with us that you 'are smarter, braver, a better shot, and a better equestrian than most men.' I think we can add businesswoman to the list."

"That means a lot to me. I felt so worthless for so long, that it is good to know that I can do something like this and do it well."

"I'm sorry you felt that way, sweetheart. I don't think I ever really understood how much you suffered from your mother's rejection. I tried to make up for her lack of feeling as a mother so you wouldn't suffer."

"I don't blame you. You are the best father any child could have."

"I am glad you had Evangeline after Monique left us. She loves you like her own."

"I love her, too. She was more a mother to me than my own." Cissy paused to consider her next words. "Father, is Evangeline unwell? She is so thin and pale that I am worried about her."

"She is getting better. I feared for her after she lost our daughter. You know that she lost her first daughter Lorena to diphtheria at the age of six. Losing this baby prematurely I think

reminded her once more of the pain of losing the daughter she had by her first husband. The doctor says that physically she is recovering. I am hoping visiting here with you and the others will cheer Evangeline up. Maybe between them Bessie and Beulah can fatten her up a little. They are beside themselves with joy to have her back. If they have their way, she and Andy are going to be spoiled rotten."

"I think Beulah wants to go with you to Wilmington when you leave. She has never gotten over being separated from Evangeline. They were together for so long it just doesn't feel right to her for Evangeline to be so far away. I don't need Beulah here with Bessie to do the cooking. If things get too much for Bessie to handle, I can always hire another woman to help her."

"You know, I think you have hit on something. I'm sure Evangeline will be thrilled to have Beulah go back with us. Maybe that's what she needs to turn the corner on this melancholy."

"Let's walk down to the Gaston House and have dinner. I have missed seeing my old cronies there. It'll give me a chance to show off my daughter and new partner." Graham cut his eyes at her to see if she had caught the significance of his last statement.

It took her a moment to realize the import of what he had said. Not sure she had heard right, she asked, "I'm sorry; what did you say?"

"You heard right. I'm having John Harvey draw up the papers making you half owner. You've earned it."

Beaming, Cissy threw her arms around her father's neck and hugged him. "I love you. Let's go celebrate with a bottle of champagne."

When they walked into the hotel dining room, a number of Graham's friends rushed over to greet him and welcome him back to New Berne. Cissy stood quietly by his side glancing around the dining room. At first she missed him. Ryan was sitting alone by the window. His face seemed gaunt and he looked as though he had aged overnight. Seeing her glance, one of her father's friends commented, "That's Ryan Madison. Former Union man but a prominent citizen here now. Sad thing about his wife...she is missing and presumed dead. It's an awful shame. It's just about killed him."

"Oh, no. How terrible for him. I hear they have a little boy, too."

"Yes, poor child to grow up without a mother."

"Yes, I did as well. I know how painful it can be." Before Cissy could walk over to speak to him and offer her sympathies, her father turned and took her by the elbow to usher her to their table. She glanced at Ryan again but he did not look up. With the champagne and the news from her father, Cissy chatted happily about the plans she had for further expanding the business. One that she had toyed with was expanding trade to Brazil to take advantage of the importation of fruits and vegetables that ripened for them during their summer when New Berne, in the throes of winter, had no such items available fresh beyond cabbage and collards. Coffee was also an important export and one the South had longed for during the war.

"I have not directly done business there before. I suppose I could ask around and see who has connections there if that would help?"

"I have already checked. One of our customers said that he has a brother in Rio de Janeiro who is a broker of produce and might be interested."

"I suppose his brother moved to Brazil like many of our fellow Confederates?"

"That's what Hezekiah told me when he mentioned it. He said his brother refused to be repatriated. I wrote him that I would be interested in importing his goods and asked what they could use that we have. He wrote me back to say that he is definitely interested in cotton, tobacco, and pine pitch."

"Which ship do you plan to divert to trade with Brazil?"

"I ordered another from Laird's just for this route. I hope you don't mind. The net earnings from *The Cecily* have almost paid for it. I should have it in port in another three or four months."

"Good. Let's plan on stops in Wilmington and Nassau on the way to Rio. There's no reason why our existing ports should not take advantage of the new market as long as you have no objection. Since this is your idea, you have the right to say."

"Of course. That will only make the trade with Brazil even better."

"Good." Graham smiled, "Enough business for now. Let's go tell Evangeline about Beulah."

All though her family's visit was just a few short weeks, Cissy loved every minute and she was sorry to see them go. Having her father to talk with about her dreams for the company and having him listen with approval and excitement at her vision was a euphoric experience. As she and Annie stood on the wharf waving goodbye, she could not help but wonder how long it would be before she would see them again. Her responsibilities in New Berne and the lack of anyone capable of running the office in her absence precluded the possibility of her visiting Wilmington. For a moment Brandon's face swam before her eyes. He still wrote but his letters were becoming less frequent and not so ardent as during the first months after she moved. She could not blame him if he had found someone new to capture his heart and his attention. She accepted that her own lack of ardor was to blame if his devotion had wandered.

Cissy was jolted from her thoughts when Annie seized her elbow, "Isn't that the officer that brought food and ate dinner with us right after Wilmington was taken over by the Yankees? Not Brandon, but the other one."

"Where?"

"Over there on Union Point staring out at the water."

Cissy looked where Annie was pointing, "Oh, Ryan Madison. Yes, I think it is." Once again she thought of walking over to offer her condolences.

That idea was quickly dismissed when she saw Lizzie walk up to him and take his arm possessively. The idea that Lizzie was actively pursuing him made Cissy want to scream at him for being so stupid as to fall for the woman's scheming ways. She had no way of knowing just how much Ryan wanted to scream for the same reason. Lizzie had pretty much stalked him since Penny's disappearance and had wormed her way into his son's life as well. Despite repeating to her at every meeting that he was heartbroken and uninterested in a relationship with her or any other woman, she gave him no peace.

Ryan moved away from Lizzie, effectively breaking her hold on his arm. When he turned he saw Cissy staring at him before she quickly motioned to the woman she was with and walked off. He would have liked to speak to her and inquire if the rumors he had heard about her business enterprise were indeed true. From what he knew of the daring Miss LaRoque he could well believe that she was as aggressive and successful as a businesswoman as she had been as a spy. Some of his anger at Lizzie dissolved as he walked back to his office thinking of the times he had run into Cissy over the years. She never left him less than entertained.

Chapter 13

Marcel was uncomfortable. Something did not feel right and he had learned always to trust his gut. Several times he had felt as though someone were following him. He could never prove it but that nagging feeling was present too often lately when he was walking on the street. He kept telling himself it was just nerves over the two men he had killed and the robbery of the hotel, but he could not squelch that small frisson of fear. Despite having gained entry into the homes of the town's leaders at various social functions and being accepted in their gambling circles, he was uneasy. Despite charming the seemingly naive daughter of the wealthy Woodward family into a torrid courtship, he had to consider whether or not it was time to move on. He was loathed to do so when he only needed a few thousand more to be well set for life. Not only that, but the enamored Adelaide Woodward had dropped numerous hints that she would welcome a proposal of marriage. Her family's wealth made the LaRoque fortune that he had once hoped to achieve through marriage to Cissy look second rate. He was a gambler and he would gamble. Deciding to keep a wary eye out for any trouble, Marcel remained ensconced in his suite at the Occidental where a steady stream of invitations to various functions assured him that his title and charm were a sure draw for the class-hungry nouveau riche of San Francisco.

Ordering the ubiquitous bottle of champagne and the lascivious services of the maid, Marcel fingered the latest invitation. Engraved on heavy linen paper, it was a request for his attendance at a formal dinner at the Woodward mansion to be followed by a ball. Only the inner circle was invited to the preceding dinner. Marcel suspected that Adelaide had procured the coveted invitation in hopes that he would be inspired to offer for her. Although she was naive, he knew she was not so stupid that she did not appreciate the draw of her family's wealth and prestige. She was pretty, too...not beautiful, but more than attractive. The latest Parisian fashions and exquisite jewelry enhanced her looks and she shamelessly flaunted them before those less privileged. He could see her all but drool at the idea of marriage to a titled member of the French aristocracy. Marcel smirked at how easy it had all been. Perhaps, he would propose just before the ball so it could be announced to the upper crust of San Francisco.

Little did he know that the resourceful and methodical Detective Sullivan was building a file labeled with his name. Sullivan was no fool and had watched the shysters and crooks that descended on his city with a quiet contempt. It was his personal mission to start cleaning up the cesspool that comprised much of San Francisco. Sending east to police departments there, he was waiting for any information that would provide helpful clues to Marcel Lambert. He was smart enough to know that with the man's title and connections he had to tread with great care. He would make sure his case was fool proof before he went after the marquis. If he were the murderer Sullivan wanted, he would nail him in the end. He quietly watched the Frenchman's rise in society as he maneuvered into the ranks of the rich. He waited for any misstep that would give the man away. He was good at waiting for his prey to slip up.

With Marcel's entry into the higher echelons he had no need to associate with the ones he had previously bilked. He had no need to commit even riskier robberies. Careful to avoid any suspicion, he played a straight game of poker as he developed the trust of the men at El Dorado and Dennison's Exchange. He had time, and if he married Adelaide, no need to cheat. He snickered when he thought of self-reformation. He enjoyed cheating too much to give it up entirely.

The Woodwards' ballroom was crowded with the best of San Francisco society proudly strutting about in a wealth of jewels and elegant clothes. A large orchestra played from a raised platform against one wall, screened from the dancers by a row of lush palms. Beneath sparkling gaslight chandeliers, Adelaide twirled across the polished dance floor in Marcel's arms. Her deep green gown belled around her exposing a black lace petticoat that matched the black trim of the dress. Emerald, diamond and ebony jewelry completed the look. On arrival at the ball, he had eyed the diamond tiara in her hair and the rest of the jewelry and assessed its value. He was decided.

"Adelaide, my beautiful darling, I took the liberty of asking your father for permission to plead with you to be my wife. I hope that was not presumptive of me?"

Her eyes sparkled with joy, "Oh, Marcel. Not at all."

"Then, my dear, will you do me the honor of becoming my wife."

She all but shouted, "Yes! Come, let's stop the musicians and announce our betrothal. Oh, I am so happy. It is going to be wonderful. I just know it. I can hardly wait to marry you."

The announcement was everything that Marcel could have wished for. In one fell swoop he had assured his status even among the more reluctant of the elite. As the applause died, he turned to Adelaide and gave her a chaste kiss on her cheek. Her father and mother wasted no time in arriving at their side to offer best wishes and express delight with the match. Soon the couple was surrounded by well-wishers.

* * * * *

At One Less ranch, Abel and his new wife enjoyed a robust kiss to the hooting delight of their guests. "Deed's done, ladies and gents, now on to the barbecue. Juana's been cooking for a week, so eat hearty or her feelings'll be hurt."

Cecily chimed in, "And that band's going to be wasted unless you gentlemen get over your shyness and ask the ladies to dance. Now, let's party."

Proud of his ability to balance on his new artificial limb, Abel led his bride onto the makeshift dance floor for the first dance. When the dance was done, Logan was at Abel's elbow requesting the honor of the next dance with the bride. "You'll have to excuse me if I am a little clumsier than Abel. My stump is still a little sore, so I'm slower to get the hang of things."

Smiling sweetly, she replied, "I'll be delighted to dance with you. We'll just keep it slow and easy, no need to work up a sweat and spoil my pretty wedding gown is there?"

"Slow and easy sounds about right to me." Logan grinned at Abel. "We'll see you in the morning."

"Like hell you will. Got some plans for this girl before morning comes." Abel laughed as Cecily turned a bright red. "Soon as this dance is over, grab yourself another heifer to flirt with. Hear? Done and put my brand on this one. "

"Yes, sir, boss man."

Logan was the happiest he had been in months. He wasn't as good a dancer as he had once been, but he could still get around on the dance floor for a slow one. Hell, he admitted to himself, he had never been a great dancer. Cissy had told him more than once to stay off her toes. Now he didn't have as many feet to get in the way. He chuckled to himself. He had noted a number of pretty girls standing on the sidelines watching him. Even without a leg, he was still a handsome, well-built man. With Abel's encouragement, he would ask other girls for a dance whenever the music was slow enough to allow it.

One blond stood out from the others. Something about her reminded him of Cissy. When the music ended, Logan thanked Cecily for the dance and walked over to the girl. "I don't think I have met the prettiest girl here. I'm Logan Gwaltney."

She smiled prettily, "Thanks for the compliment, Mr. Gwaltney. My name is Rachel, Rachel Riley."

"We are going to be good friends, Rachel. So, you can call me Logan."

Looking up at him through her eyelashes, she murmured, "And why do you think we are going to be good friends, Logan?"

"Just a feeling in my bones. Would you like some punch or something? As soon as that music slows, I'm claiming you for a dance."

"I'd love some punch and that dance as well."

* * * * *

Across the country in New Berne, Lizzie Berkely was once more thwarted in her plan to marry Ryan Madison. He knew she was furious that he had scorned her despite her blatant attempts at seduction. When his wife Penny had been lost in the hurricane, all had presumed her dead. Even a monument with her name had been erected in the cemetery. But she had not died. Washed ashore, barely alive and bereft of memory, she had been nursed to health by a demented old man who thought God had returned his dead wife to him. Marcus Cauley, once he had been cleared of murder, had made it his mission to go back to the shore and look for her. Now, thanks to Marcus' initiative, Ryan was once more united with Penny. Judging by her hostility he supposed that Lizzie had accepted the futility in continuing to chase him. She was a pretty woman, and in the depth of his misery he had been tempted by her bold offer of herself. No doubt, she would find another man to chase.

When Cissy read the news of his wife's return in the New Berne Progress, she was happy for him. He had seemed so dejected the times she had seen him during the months his wife had been presumed dead, that she had mourned for him and the loss of the woman that he loved so deeply. With Penny returned to him, she was glad that she had not pursued her infatuation of him, but had respected his need to grieve. She wondered how Lizzie was reacting to being rejected yet again.

The coming months were happy ones for the Madison's as they welcomed a baby girl to their family. Ryan, Penny, their son Rye and the baby they called Carah were frequently seen in town. Ashamed that she had been so aloof, Cissy made it a point to nod politely whenever she met them in the street, although she did not stop to chat.

They were happy months for Cissy, too, despite bouts of loneliness that assailed her from time to time. She saw in the eyes of those she met confusion that she had secluded herself in the business. Using the lack of time as an excuse, she avoided invitations and social contacts except for sporadic church attendance. Most of the time she was so tired from her time at the office that she had no energy for anything but her evening meal, a hot bath, and curling up in bed.

Annie made up for Cissy's lack of sociability by meeting their neighbors on the other side of Evangeline's empty house. Caroline Framingham, an elderly widow, and the Madison's...who's property had once been part of Caroline's, soon found Annie visiting regularly. Caroline's acerbic wit and zest found an echo in the Irish girl. Having been born into a large family back in Ireland, the gregarious Annie missed children and loved playing with the Madison's two. Although she had not yet told Cissy, Annie had agreed to marry her on-again, off-again beau. The first Cissy knew of it was when Caroline Framingham sent out invitations for a ball in honor of Annie O'Neal and Charles Wright to celebrate their coming nuptials.

When Cissy picked up the invitation from the foyer table, she read it twice to make sure her eyes were not deceiving her.

Then she called for Annie at the top of her lungs, not caring that it was unladylike to holler.

"Coming," Annie answered as she hurried down the front stairs. "Saints preserve us, ye would think the house was aburning."

"Annie, I cannot believe you said nothing about this to me." Cissy waved the invitation above her head accusingly.

"Now, me girl, just tell me when ye have been around for a wee chat with me?" Annie grinned, "So, I'm going to be a bride. Now, ye need to wish me happy, not caterwaul like a banshee."

Cissy hugged her as the two girls danced in circles. "Oh Annie, you know I am happy for you. You are going to be the most beautiful bride ever. But, goodness gracious, I will miss you so much."

"Mayhap, not so much. I was meaning to ask if it be a problem were we to stay here for a bit until we can find a house of our own?"

"Of course, you can. Even better, Evangeline's house is empty since it has not yet been sold. It is a shame for it to just sit there going to ruin. Why don't you and Charles move in there? When you can afford to buy something, if that suits you, I could see if Papa and Evangeline would sell it to you. She even left a lot of furniture that didn't fit here or in Wilmington so you would have to buy very little. Please, say yes. I don't want you to move away from me. Having you right next door would be wonderful."

"I'll ask Charles, but I think he will be happy for the offer."

"Good, now let's get you a wedding dress made." Cissy was excited for Annie and threw herself into plans for the wedding and the upcoming pre-nuptial party. In the middle of their busy plans, Cissy suddenly stopped. "Oh, no. I just remembered. I have not had a new dress since before the war. Huge hoops are becoming passé. I saw in the fashion book that hoops are much narrower and flatter in front. It's a pity that we still have to wear a corset to cinch in our waists. I want a new dress, too. If we have enough time before the wedding, I will order us both something all the way from Paris. My present to you is going to be a wedding gown to die for."

"Ah, Cissy, that would be a wee bit of heaven, but Paris is too far for us to get something for me party at Caroline's. We will have to make do with something we can have made here."

"Let me check the manifest for the ship that just arrived today from New York. Some of the cargo originated in London and LeHavre. If there is any fabric on-board, we are going to see if it will suit for the party. If not, to the attic we go. My mother left tons of dresses here when she went to France to live. They are fabulous even if they are years old. The thing is, the fabrics and trim are still good. We can have them remade for us in time for the party."

"I like that idea even better. There be no need to waste good stuff. Let's go look now. I am too excited to wait."

The girls brought armloads of dresses down from the attic. One in particular had caught Cissy's eye. It was the most exquisite gown she had ever beheld. Made of heavy ivory satin and trimmed with miles of delicate lace and beadwork, she knew it had to have been her mother's wedding gown. Annie and she had both gasped in amazement when they had unwrapped it and held it up. Part of Cissy wanted to hate it, but another was so enchanted by the gown she could not resist trying it on once they reached her bedroom. With Annie's help, she pulled the dress over her head and stood while Annie fastened the buttons in back. Walking over to the cheval glass she stood transfixed.

"Jesus, Mary, and Joseph, Cissy. That be the most amazing dress I ever did see. Yer mother must have been the same size as ye. It be a perfect fit."

"It is stunning. I don't think I have ever seen a more

beautiful dress even if it is hopelessly out of date. Somehow, I don't think that matters with this gown. I wonder what my father thought when he watched her walking towards him in it. I know that at one time she enthralled him with her beauty. She must have been breathtaking in this. It is a pity she could not have been a warmer person. She made him so unhappy, and me, too. As I grow older, I think maybe she was homesick for Paris. She hated it here. Maybe that made her bitter and cold. I detested her for so long I could not even regret when the ship bringing her back here was lost at sea. I felt so mean at the time. Now, I can even feel a little pity for her."

Cissy caressed the fabric of the dress as she turned back and forth in front of the mirror. "Annie, let's remake this for you."

"No, Cissy. This dress be for yer own wedding day, not for mine. It would not suit me at all. It be perfect for ye, old fashioned or not."

"My wedding day? Since when do I have time to find a husband? At well over twenty everyone considers me a spinster. Besides, I don't have anyone I want to marry." For a fleeting moment, Ryan's face swam before her eyes. Annie saw Cissy's face turn somber.

"Ah, Cissy, love. I think someone has yer heart after all. Be it Brandon?"

"Not Brandon, and no use thinking about it. I'm just a fool for still dreaming. The man's married." Cissy shrugged as though to shake off her thoughts. "Help me out of this dress will you, Annie? I'm going to hang it in the armoire. I cannot bear to return it to the attic, even if neither of us will ever wear it."

"The Lord moves in mysterious ways me girl. Who knows what tomorrow will bring ye? Someday I hope to see ye wearing that dress on yer own wedding day."

"Pfff... Let's look at these other dresses and see what we can remake for the party at Mrs. Framingham's. I certainly don't want to wear one of my old gowns, even if I am an old maid and no one will look at me."

"Fuss and feathers. Will ye listen to ye now? Old maid ye are not."

"I assume there will be a lot of people there. I cannot believe how long it has been since I was a part of New Berne society. I think the last party I went to here was in 1862. That's over five years!"

"Caroline has invited all the neighbors and about half the town. I'm sure ye will meet lots of old friends."

Cissy was more concerned with concealing her emotions when meeting her immediate neighbors than running into former friends. It briefly annoyed her to be going to a ball without an escort. In the past she would have had her choice of willing beaux. She did not want Ryan, and those who had known her when she was the belle of the ball, to look at her with pity for her spinster status. Regardless of what Annie said, girls over twenty were considered on the shelf. Enough self-pity, she decided.

"Let's think about what to do with these dresses. You go through one pile and I'll take the other. If I find something that will go nicely with your red hair I will put it in a pile for you and you do the same for me."

For the next hour the girls alternated between squeals of delight and shrieks of merriment as they held up dresses before themselves and modeled them in the mirror. Soon they each had an assortment of gowns that they thought could be adapted. Cissy's would be an easier task as she was the same size and height as her mother when she had worn the gowns. Shorter and plumper, Annie's would require a bit more work. Cissy picked up a stunning aqua blue gown. Stripping to her chemise she slipped the silky confection over her head. Despite yards of skirt that billowed around her, the dress was perfection. She liked the way it brought out the emerald color of her eyes and golden skin tones. Nor could she hide a smile of pleasure when she saw the way it enhanced her curves.

"What do you think Annie? I think it would work if I pulled some of the skirt back and looped it behind somehow so it isn't so full looking." Cissy twisted to see her back view in the mirror.

"Let me hold it and we'll see." Picking up the fabric on either side of the gown, Annie pulled it behind to drape from the waist where it cascaded down in a ripple of soft ruffles. "I like it so much. Ye will be beautiful in this. Every woman there is going to envy ye especially with so much of that bosom of yers showing."

"I think it's perfect even if it is a little more daring than I normally wear, and it will not take a lot to alter the skirt. Help me get out of this and let's see what works for you. It has to be just as perfect."

Chapter 14

Marcel walked into the master bedroom of the stone mansion that was the wedding present of Adelaide's parents. He could not have been more pleased with the path his life was taking. The wedding had been lavish, the nuptial gifts abundant, and then the surprise of this magnificent house. This, one of the largest houses in the best neighborhood of San Francisco, announced his success to the world even if it had come to him through his bride's parents. He walked over to the damask draped table by the bay window and lifted the magnum of champagne from the epergne. Expertly popping the cork, he motioned to his bride to join him. He was pleased to note that she had changed into a lacy, semi-transparent silk peignoir that displayed her curves to advantage. He was looking forward to the coming evening. With her money secured and his entree into San Francisco accomplished, he was in an amorous mood.

"Shall we celebrate with a bit of champagne, my dear?"

Smiling archly, Adelaide accepted the glass that he held out to her. "I would love it."

By the time they had finished the bottle, Adelaide was flushed and a little tipsy. Walking closer, he slowly untied the ribbon to the peignoir and allowed it to drop from her shoulders onto the floor. Her lush nude body beckoned him. He led her to the bed and then dropped his own robe onto the floor. Smiling to himself he climbed in beside her. He had once enjoyed a reputation for being an expert lover. With the whores that he had taken for the last few years he had not bothered to concern himself with finesse. But tonight was different and he intended to show his bride just how fortunate she was. Sensing she was nervous, although she had said nothing, he went slowly and with far more consideration than he had ever used before. But then, he excused himself, he had never taken a virgin before.

Virgin Adelaide might be, but soon she was panting for him. Giving her what she begged for, he stilled while she adjusted to his penetration. When she relaxed, he consoled her with murmurs of appreciation for her beauty. Once again she responded with ardor as he began to move within her. It vaguely registered in the recesses of his mind that the penetration had met no barrier, but at that moment he paid no heed. Afterwards as they lay panting beside one another, he remembered. Jolting upright, he swore.

"*Putain*! You were no virgin."

"Neither were you, Marcel."

"That's different. I am a man and I expected my bride to be a virgin."

"Why should you be upset? You have what you wanted and so do I."

In the dim candlelight, Marcel studied her face. "You lying, conniving bitch. You and your parents were damned eager to land me. I can only wonder why. If you plan to pass a bastard off as mine, you might better rethink it. I know you wanted my title and were willing to pay for it, but what else did you think you were buying?"

"You think all women are naive and stupid, just waiting for a crumb from your table. You conceited man. I knew exactly what you saw when you looked at my parents and me. You shine with charm and sophistication, and also with greed and arrogance. If you think about it, we are both opportunists. Why not enjoy it? After the last hour, I think it's obvious we enjoy one another in bed. We both dared to go after what we want. You got what you want and so did I. What is the importance of a hymen in that equation?"

Marcel looked at the woman beside him. He looked hard. He had never really seen her before, only what she represented. Suddenly he began to laugh and did not stop until tears were rolling down his cheeks. "Ah, *cherie*, I think we are perfect for one another. But if you carry some other man's seed, you had best lose it. I draw the line at that."

"I am not pregnant, so set your mind at ease on that score. I am not so stupid that I could not have eliminated that as a reason for marrying you."

"We just may be a perfect match, my dear. You are as ruthless as I am when it comes to getting what you want."

It was a long time before Marcel could sleep. This was a turn of events that he would never have imagined. A part of him enjoyed the humor in the situation, but he also realized he would have to be far more careful with this woman in future. It would never do to underestimate her. If she thought he no longer met her goals, she might not hesitate to dump him. And she was smart enough to know that the same held true for him. He wondered just how tightly she had sown up her father's fortune. Be damned if he would be led by the apron strings begging for every dollar. He should have hired his own lawyer to go over the marriage contract. He cursed himself for being too sure of her parents and Adelaide's eagerness for marriage to question the fine details. Turning it over and over in his mind, he decided the surest way to grasp control of the vast Woodward fortune was an heir begot on the daughter and only child. His mind made up, he awakened his bride and proceeded to up the odds of meeting his objective as many times as it took to do so. She was passionate and comely enough that it was no chore.

The next few days saw neither of the Lamberts out of their bedroom. With meals brought to their opulent rooms and the latest of bathrooms en suite, they devoted the remainder of their time to enjoying the pleasures of connubial bliss. Adelaide was as eager as he, for she was not as confident of the emptiness of her womb as she had led him to believe. She had no compunction about passing off someone else's child as his. With his rampant sexuality, he would have every reason to believe he had impregnated her were that to prove to be the case. After all, a month is not a lot of time. Many children had been born prematurely...some legitimately so, some supposedly so.

When they finally emerged from their suite to breakfast downstairs in the morning room, Marcel looked at his wife over the top of his newspaper before laying it to one side. "You should know that I fully intend to return someday to France and restore my family chateau just outside Paris. That doesn't mean that we need to stay there permanently, but it does mean that we will have a second home. Mine is an old and respected family. I wish to restore the family name and fortune. I suspect you will have no objections to being a part of the aristocracy there. I also hope you have no compunction about helping me secure the funds I will need to do that, as well as enlarging our coffers to afford us the lifestyle we both desire here. With your contacts and entree into the upper echelons of San Francisco, I need you to keep your eyes and ears open for opportunities to create wealth beyond what your father so generously provides you."

Adelaide leveled her eyes on him, "Make no mistake, I fully support those goals. Between the two of us working toward those ends, there is no reason we cannot make them happen. I intend to enjoy being married to a fancy title and I intend to go on living with wealth. As long as you cause me no grief, we should deal admirably." Her eyes were as cold as glaciers when she inquired, "You do understand my meaning?"

With an equal chill, Marcel responded, "Without doubt. You do as I need and expect and we will have no problems. But, I warn you: you do not want to underestimate or cross me, wife of mine."

"Of course not, husband of mine. And lest you forget...nor me."

Marcel's jaw flexed as his lifted his cup to his mouth to sip the rich coffee and cream he favored. Biting back a retort, he forced himself to smile across the table at Adelaide. He despised being control by anyone, especially a female, but at the moment he had no choice but to tread carefully around the woman he had so misjudged. The first thing he intended to do was take the marriage contract to his own attorney. If there were anything in it that kept him with an eternal hand extended for Woodward charity, she would quickly find herself looking for another husband.

Determined to keep his cards close to his chest, he forced his voice into dulcet tones. "Adelaide, I have to run out for a short while to take care of some business, but I should be back within an hour or two. If you are free to join me for lunch in our bedroom, we can have the afternoon to ourselves. I find my appetite for you is insatiable."

Adelaide was equally pleasant when she replied, "Of course, Marcel. I will have a nice soaking bath while you are away. When you return we will see what we are hungrier for, lunch or one another."

"You, of course. However, passion requires food for energy. So lunch first and a good bottle of champagne, then making love."

Marcel stood and walked over to her. Taking her hands, he pulled her to her feet. He kissed her with feigned passion, caressing her derriere before sliding his hands up to cup her breast. Lightly pinching her nipples, he continued exploring her mouth with his tongue. His mind was already focused on the marital contract, so he found no pleasure in the seduction. Soon Adelaide was tugging at the sash of his robe.

"You are a greedy one, my dear. Patience. I must dress

now, but I will not be long. We'll continue this when I return. Perhaps, a bit of absence will make your heart grow fonder."

Adelaide shrugged her shoulder, her mouth twisted into a pout. "You will learn I don't like waiting for what I want."

"Don't be a shrew, darling. That fails to arouse me." Marcel turned on his heel and marched into his dressing room where his newly hired valet was laying out his clothes for the day.

Marcel glared at the man. Daniel Carson was much too handsome for his taste and a little too sure of himself. "Make it quick. I am in no mood to dilly dally here."

"Yes, sir. Everything is ready. Perhaps a shave first?"

Marcel rubbed his day old beard, "Yes, fine."

Once Marcel was groomed and dressed, he wasted no time fetching the contract from the desk in his office. Swinging onto his new stallion that had been saddled and waiting, he hurried to the Halleck building for the answers he needed.

Adelaide wasted no time either, ringing the service bell, she ordered her maid to send Daniel in. She was on the bed nude when he entered, locking the door behind himself. Smiling he walked over to her, "You needed something, miss?"

"You know damned well what I need, Dan." Adelaide reached for his trouser buttons and grinned. "Ready for me, I see."

"Always. I didn't think your fancy new husband was ever going to go out. I confess I was jealous."

"Don't be, darling. You know I would never leave you. Didn't I arrange for you to be hired?"

Afterwards a sated Adelaide relaxed in her tub and chuckled to herself. She had arranged everything perfectly. Yes, she liked being married to a marquis and the sophisticated polish he brought. She liked being envied for having landed the eligible bachelor that had more than one woman panting for him. She liked Marcel's lovemaking, but Daniel had been in her blood for a long time and she was not willing to give him up...at least not yet. And, she saw no reason to do so. Just because she refused to marry a man with no status beyond servant, did not mean that she could not take one for a lover and had. In the meantime, she intended to thoroughly enjoy the amorous attention of both men. Smiling at her reflection in the cheval mirror, she called out to her maid. "Sally, bring up a chilled bottle of champagne and some refreshments the moment my husband returns."

Marcel was anything but smiling as he claimed his horse for the return home. The attorney had explained in terms Marcel could understand that the marriage settlement provided him with a generous annual stipend as long as he remained married, but the bulk of the annual funds provided by Mr. Woodward went to Adelaide. In the event of children, a trust would be set up in each child's name with Adelaide as the executrix. An additional sum would be added to Marcel's income to assist with the additional expenses entailed by the baby, as well as for a nurse, to assist Adelaide in its care. Each year that he an Adelaide were married, provided there were children born of the marriage, his annual stipend would be increased by five percent in addition to the amount provided for expenses related to the children. In the event of Adelaide's death, her estate would devolve to the children with her father as executor, or in the event of her father's death, his attorney would serve in that capacity. If no children were born of the marriage he would receive no further stipend and would retain only the house that had been a gift to the marriage, along with his personal assets and property purchased jointly during the marriage. He had no choice but to assure a lengthy marriage and a procreative one if he were to attain the wealth he desired. It was also imperative that he began to acquire real estate and business interests using as much of Adelaide's wealth as he could finagle. And finagle he would.

Taking advantage of the contacts he had made through

introductions by his father-in-law, he gleaned as much information as possible about properties in desirable locations. With an aristocrat's disdain for working, he had no intention of going into business. He was merely looking for investment opportunities in areas where land would appreciate in value. With building and expansion all around him, the list soon grew to include property in San Francisco as well as nearby Sacrament where Governor Leland Stanford's house served as the state's executive offices. Almond groves and railways offered further investment opportunities. Always a gambler, Marcel intended to gamble on whatever offered sizeable prospects for big returns.

Once he had culled his list, weighed the pros and cons, he set out to convince Adelaide to invest with him in those that he had selected. First he presented her with a diamond bracelet she had admired while strolling with him on Montgomery Street, followed by an elegant champagne dinner at the St. Francis Hotel. Afterwards he made love to her until they were both exhausted. As she lay panting in his arms and more than a little drunk, he presented his case. Eager to please him, she agreed to invest in three large parcels of land in the city and an almond groove near Sacramento. The price he quoted was nearly the total amount involved, although he was careful to imply that it was half and he was covering the remainder from his own funds.

It would not have mattered to Adelaide. She wanted him pleased and obligated when she told him she was pregnant. The pregnancy she had suspected prior to her wedding had become a reality. To avoid any suspicion on Marcel's part, she had angered Daniel by withholding her favors for the last few weeks. Now she need only convince her husband that the baby's arrival was premature. Hoping it would be small at birth, and thus an early birth more believable, she already had begun curtailing her food intake. Using his pleasure at her ready acquiescence to the investment scheme, she decided the moment was opportune for delivery of the big news.

Nestling closer, she cooed, "Darling, we have wonderful news. I think I may be pregnant. I hope you don't mind becoming a father so early in our marriage?"

Marcel laughed with satisfaction. It was all coming together for him. Twins would be even better as that would mean double the money. Hell, he would welcome quadruplets. "Why do you think I would mind? I am delighted, indeed. I think this calls for a celebration. Let's have a dinner party and announce the news to your parents. No doubt they will be thrilled."

"What a wonderful idea. But, let's wait a couple of weeks or so just to be sure."

"Whatever you say, darling." Marcel was so busy calculating what his new income would be that he barely noted what she said. He would not be so pleased if he knew that the Detective Sullivan had added even more to his file after receiving responses to several of the letters he had sent east.

Chapter 15

Cissy's breath caught when she walked into Caroline Framingham's home. Annie, Caroline, and Ryan's wife Penny had worked for days decorating with fresh garlands of greenery. The result was not only beautiful, but smelled like walking into a evergreen forest. Cissy walked up to Caroline Framingham with a ready apology on her lips for having been so negligent of her neighbors. Caroline gave her no opportunity for regrets as she swept her into a warm hug.

"You are more beautiful than your mother, Cissy. I cannot believe the men in this town did not long ago chase you into marriage with one of them. I think I am going to have to revise my opinion of local manhood." Her eyes twinkled when she said it and Cissy relaxed in the warmth she exuded.

"Miss Caroline, if anything, the fact that you are still single is proof they are all lacking."

"Fiddlesticks! I am older than dirt and ornery to boot. They were just showing their smarts. Enough of this admiration. I want you to meet your neighbors. Ryan's wife tells me she has yet to meet you."

"No, I haven't met her, yet. I confess I have done nothing but work since returning from Wilmington. There was so much to do to get the business here running again I ignored anything else. I did meet her husband during the war when he and his fellow officers were occupying Evangeline's house." Cissy hoped that her voice had remained casual. She would die if anyone guessed the torch she had carried for Penny's husband.

"Lord, I cannot believe you didn't set your cap for him before someone else caught him. If I had been younger, I would have given him a merry chase. That I would have. I purely love that man! I suppose Penny and Ryan and their children now have become the family I never had. Speaking of family, how are Graham and Evangeline doing? There have children, too, I believe?"

"My half-brother, Andy. Unfortunately, the last child Evangeline was carrying was born prematurely and died."

"I am so sorry. That is a terrible loss." Caroline patted her arm. "Enough of sad talk. This is a happy occasion. We have to find you some dancing partners before the musicians wind up, and I still have to introduce you to Penny."

At that moment, Cissy heard Ryan's voice behind her. "So, who is it that Penny has to meet, Miss Caroline?"

Cissy turned to find Ryan and his wife standing near her. She was immediately struck by the happiness that radiated from the couple. Anyone could see from the way they tilted their heads towards one another that theirs was a loving relationship. For a moment jealousy and envy for that love threatened her. Shaking it off, she smiled brightly. "Colonel Madison, we meet again."

"Miss LaRoque, I must say you look lovely. Allow me to introduce you to another beautiful woman, my wife, Mrs. Penelope Madison."

Ryan spoke the truth. The auburn beauty he had married was a lovely woman.

"Mrs. Madison, I have heard nothing but good things of you. It is a pleasure to meet you at last. Please forgive me for not being more neighborly."

"There is nothing to forgive. And do call me Penny. Annie has explained to Caroline and me just how very hard you have been working to salvage your father's business here. I am just glad to at last meet you."

"I think she has done more than 'salvage,' my dear. The word around town is that what Miss LaRoque has done with LaRoque shipping is remarkable. Your father must be very proud of all that you have accomplished." Ryan could not help but notice that Cissy was more than striking in the gown that accentuated every curve of her lush body. He had tried not to look but the décolleté of the gown was hard to ignore. He chuckled. He was happily married to a woman he adored, but he was still male and far from blind.

Penny, ever attuned to her husband, heard the soft chuckle and understood the reason. Pinching his arm gently, she remarked, "She is a beauty, Ryan. If I had known such temptation was around, I might have moved to New Berne much sooner. Miss LaRoque, you must allow my husband one dance so he doesn't pine away."

"Mrs. Madison, I assure you, your husband, justifiably, only has eyes for you. I fear I was just an annoying rebel when I knew your husband during the early days of Union occupation here."

"Ah, I think you must be the little spy that he could never quite catch?"

Cissy could not resist a saucy grin. "I'm sure I don't have a clue to what you refer. Surely you mean some other?"

They soon moved to the refreshment table, leaving Cissy momentarily alone. Searching the crowd for a familiar face she spotted Annie and Charles in deep conversation. Walking over she took Annie's arm and smiled up at Charles, "Annie, I hope you have told your fiancé of my offer of Evangeline's house. I could not bear to have you too far away."

"Aye, I told the stubborn man, but he insists it be too much."

Turning to Charles, Cissy asked, "Why do you say that Charles?"

"I'll not begin our marriage by taking charity. I intend to support my bride."

"Wonderful. I totally agree. If I charge you rent would that make a difference?"

Charles hesitated before answering, "If it is affordable, I

think so. I know you girls want to be near one another and I don't want to get in the way of your friendship."

"Charles, the house is empty. To have someone living there to keep squatters away is a favor to us. Real estate is depressed at the moment as most people have little money. Those that are able to buy aren't investing because they don't know what will happen tomorrow with all of the local unrest. It would be a blessing to know the house is safe and I have neighbors I can depend on should my own home be threatened by some of the lawless gangs that are roaming around. Tell me what you can pay. If it is reasonable, I have no reason to object. You know you can have it for nothing and I would be just as happy. I also would be glad of a man nearby that would protect us. I have been really uncomfortable of late."

"I can understand your concern. It bothers me that Annie, you, and your servants have been living with no one but an elderly black man to protect you. More than one out lying home has been torched and the residents harmed. I will accept your offer and do what I can to protect both houses and all of you. I also suggest you get a gun if you don't have one. We will talk about rent later as I will not move in without paying something. Let's party now. I want to dance with my girl and the musicians are about to play another waltz. Ready, Annie?"

"Thank you, Cissy. I be glad you and Charles had a chance to talk." Laughing she turned to her fiancé, "I be ready if you will dance on the floor and not me toes."

Cissy felt conspicuous standing alone and had turned to walk into the shadows on the edge of the room when she felt a hand on her elbow. "Excuse me, I would love a waltz with you."

Cissy looked up into Ryan's dancing eyes and panicked. Just his touch on her elbow had electrified every nerve ending. How could she manage an entire dance in his arms without him guessing how she reacted to his touch? Forcing an iciness she did not feel, she responded, "I'm sorry. This dance is taken."

Watching her walk away, Ryan was puzzled at the tone of her voice and her rejection. He had meant nothing more than a friendly offer at his wife's suggestion. He could not imagine how he had caused offence, for surely he had. Walking back to Penny, he explained, "She says the dance is taken. Would you dance with me?"

"Always, darling." Penny laughed at his confusion, "You silly man. I think that woman is enamored of you? I cannot say I blame her. I am myself."

"Now you are the one being silly. I have always managed to rile the little minx."

"Oh, you rile her alright. Now, stop talking and let's dance."

"Yes, ma'am."

Cissy danced several dances that night with kindly elderly men that knew her father and wanted to talk about what she was doing with the shipping business. Even while she talked and danced, her eyes followed Ryan. She could not stop herself. For a moment, she even felt sorry for Lizzie. Was she any better than that wonton deep down inside? Lizzie wanted Ryan, too. At the moment, Cissy just wanted the evening to end. She just wanted to go home. She just wanted to climb in her lonely bed and sleep. Then in the morning, she just wanted to go to work and forget useless longings for someone she could never have. As soon as she could, she retrieved her shawl and slipped through the terrace door, determined to make her way home alone. Rather than risk the road, she would make her way along the river front to Evangeline's house and from there through the woods to her own home. She did not care if her slippers and gown would be ruined; she just needed to escape. She was frustrated in even that.

"Cissy, are you leaving? Do let us offer you a ride home. It isn't safe to walk at night." Penny's genuine concern for her shone from her eyes making Cissy feel even worse.

"I confess I have a bit of a headache and just wanted to slip away. Annie and Charles should not have to leave their engagement party to take me home."

"Assuredly not. But, since we are leaving, too, there is no reason why we cannot. Ryan has just gone to fetch the buggy, so it will only be a moment."

Cissy bit her lower lip and then not knowing what else to do, responded, "Thank you, that is more than gracious."

Cissy sat as rigid as a corpse opposite the couple, thankful that the drive was a short one. They chatted with relaxed ease oblivious to her brief and barely courteous responses. Although she chided herself for being foolish to react like a jealous idiot in front of the couple, nervous tension held her firmly in its grasp. When they pulled into the drive leading to her home, she relaxed. Soon the evening would be over and she could retire to her bed. The thought of what they would soon be doing in their bed made her blush. Firmly she pushed the thought away, and forced her voice into casual tones.

"I am so happy to have had the opportunity to meet you, Penny. Again, I do ask for your forgiveness for not having made your acquaintance sooner."

"Nonsense. There is no need to apologize." Penny leaned forward and took Cissy's frigid hand into her warm one, "I look forward to becoming good friends. I confess to a paucity of women friends since moving here, so one more would be most welcome."

"Thank you, that would be lovely." Cissy smiled at the open charm of the woman. Turning to her husband, she remarked, "Ryan, it is good to see you again. I hear that you have become well known as a lawyer and active in our local politics. I am glad that the town has been accepting of you. I know some have not always found it so."

"That is true and I consider myself fortunate. I fell in love with the town from the beginning and consider it my home. I intend to do all I can to help us transition through the difficulties of digging out from under the burdens created by the war."

"We need all the help we can get, for sure."

The buggy stopped at her front veranda where Ryan leapt down to assist her out. "We will wait here until you are safely inside. I see lamps are lit, so I assume your servants are awaiting your return."

"Yes, they are," Cissy noted with relief. "Thank you again for bringing me home."

Ryan smiled, "You're welcome. Good night now, and don't be a stranger to us."

Cissy walked into the house and called goodnight to her servants before climbing the stairs to her room. As she carefully hung her gown in the armoire, she caught a glimpse of herself in the mirror. Pausing, she studied her reflection. Did she see the beginning of wrinkles on her brow? Was the gray hair she found and carefully plucked the day before just the beginning of many more? Would she really be happy to spend her life as a spinster never having the kind of love she had seen between Ryan and Penny? She mused on the idea of marriage to Brandon. Perhaps, he was still interested? And Logan, who had professed to love her until the last tomorrow, where was he? Why had he left her with no explanation? Would she want to be engaged to him again if he returned? Ryan's face shimmered before her eyes. Resolutely she turned from the mirror. She needed to rest for tomorrow would bring another day of work as she chased the dream of making something of her life apart from being the appendage of some man.

She heard Annie come in some time later and tiptoe up the stairs. Annie paused at her door and called softly, "Cissy, are you awake?"

She did not answer and the soft footsteps continued on down the hall to Annie's own room. She was happy for Annie in her love for the man she was marrying, but she could not deal with any more talk of happy couples for that night. When she finally drifted into restless sleep, Ryan kept invading her dreams until she finally threw the covers off in exasperation and dressed by the soft glow of the embers in the fireplace. Stirring them into a blaze, she added more firewood before settling in her chair. The dancing firelight lit the room with flickering shadows as she waited for the dawn. When she heard Bessie rattling pans in the kitchen, she slipped on her dress and shoes, grabbed her pelisse and walked downstairs.

Bessie looked up in surprise when she entered, "You shore is up early this mawning, Miss Cissy. You be feeling all right, now?"

"I'm fine Bessie. I just have a lot on my mind and want to get to the office to take care of some things."

"Lawdy, chile. You done and forgot this be Sunday. Ain't you goin' to church with Miss Annie?"

"Oh, dear. It completely slipped my mind." Cissy reached for the coffee Bessie handed her and idly stirred in cream and sugar. She had hoped to lose herself in business matters, not sit through a sermon and then make small talk with others afterwards. At least the church was not such a far walk from the office. Since the weather was sunny and mild for winter, she decided she would have Toby drive Annie home and come back for her in late afternoon. Perhaps the walk to the office and some quiet time there would lift the black mood she felt. When Bessie sat breakfast on the table, she picked at it morosely not really caring if she ate or not. Laying her fork to one side, she traced the worn wood of the tabletop lightly with her fingertips feeling the raised grain of the hardwood. She wondered how many others had sat at that table over the years.

"Bessie, do you know how old this table is?"

Momentarily puzzled at the suddenness of the question, Bessie was slow to respond.

"Well, do you?"

"I just be thinkin' on it. I believe it belonged to yo' Pa's father. Seems like he told me that it was brung here all the way from France or some such. Why come you askin'?"

"No reason. I was just curious."

Bessie shot her an inquisitive look but let the subject rest. Eulalie and Annie entered before she could change her mind and probe Cissy's pensive mood with more questions. Something was for certain eating at the girl. She had known her from birth and could sense when she was unhappy. Bessie shook her head and muttered under her breath.

"You takin' to yo'self again, ole woman?" Eulalie, the woman Cissy had hired to replace Beulah and keep Bessie company, asked as she walked over to grab an apron from the peg by the stove.

"You mind yo' own b'i'ness. And mind who you callin' ole woman." Bessie grumbled goodnaturedly.

Annie sat at the table with Cissy. She chatted happily about the ball and all of the people there, what they were wearing, what they said, and the dances with Charles. Cissy said little other than an occasional uh-huh. Annie stopped and looked closely at her friend. "Do ye have a headache or something? Ye be mighty quiet. Didn't ye enjoy the ball? Ye looked beautiful in that dress. I think every woman there was eaten up with envy. Why did ye leave early? Several gentlemen were asking for ye and wanting to dance with ye."

"I was tired and had a bit of a headache is all. The ball was lovely, Annie. It was wonderful of Mrs. Framingham to do that for you and Charles. It tells me just how much she thinks of you." Cissy picked up a fork full of grits and put it in her mouth in hopes Annie would not ask her anything more while she was eating. Annie persisted anyway.

"Penny remarked on how pretty ye are. She is really a nice woman don't ye think? I hope ye will get to know her better.

Some of the ladies in town have shunned her since she is married to a Yankee. I know that Caroline would like it if both of us called on her more, as well. Since Ryan's mother died and his sister married and moved to Kinston, Caroline has only Ryan's family for company. She has friends in town but none that she is particularly close to. That Ryan sure is a charmer despite being a Yankee. Don't ye think he is a fine figure of a man? I remember how ye blushed around him in Wilmington when he came a calling on us. Are ye going to visit them now that ye have met Penny? Would ye like to go to Penny's or Miss Caroline's with me next time I visit?"

"Annie, I am working very hard just now. The Brazil venture is beginning to provide a lucrative trade, but I need to continue to find new products we can export to them and things they can send us. The renewal of contracts with companies in the north is something I am spending a lot of time on as well. I would like to be able to visit more, but my time is just so limited." Cissy recognized the lie for what it was...avoidance of Ryan and his wife for fear that her infatuation with him would be discovered. While she was busy, the business wasn't so consuming as to preclude all social life. It was her escape from facing her own insecurities and emotional issues.

Bessie and Eulalie walked over to the table, their faces serious. Bessie cleared her throat in preparation for speaking but Eulalie interrupted before she could begin, "Miss Cissy, we is worried somethin' terrible. They's talk about some trashy black folks doin' some bad stuff to white folks. Miz Roberts say her preacher over in James City tole the congregation they need to 'set a fire to white people's houses, murder them in they beds, and steal all they can from them.' We worried they be comin' here one night and with nothing but Toby to protect us women folk, we be in a heap of trouble."

"I've heard rumors but not that one. Fortunately so far nothing really bad has happened on this side of town." Cissy thought for a moment, "If it will make you feel better, I will hire a man to live in the quarters over the stable. I know Toby is tired of making so many trips to town for me."

" You bes' make sure he is young and a better shot than ole Toby then," Bessie commented wryly.

Cissy turned to Annie with a speculative look, "Do you think Charles would move into Evangeline's house early just so we have another man nearby until I can hire someone?"

"I'll ask him. I would love to have him close for a number of reasons." Annie giggled softly.

"I just bet you would." Cissy returned her grin. "You best behave and remember the wedding is not that far off."

"Aye, and I still need to get me dress made. Did the fabrics ye ordered come in yet?"

"They are supposed to be on the ship that I am expecting to arrive tomorrow from New York. As soon as it is unloaded, I will find the fabrics and we can get take them to the dressmaker so both of our dresses can be done in time."

The coming weeks were busy enough that Cissy had little time for socializing other than a little meeting and greeting after church services on Sundays. With the wedding arrangements made and the dresses ready for their final fitting, Cissy organized details and tasks with Annie and her servants for the reception she would hold for the couple following the ceremony. Fortunately spring seemed to be arriving early promising fresh tulips and other springtime blooms for decorating both the church altar and the LaRoque parlor.

Chapter 16

Rachel Riley cocked an eyebrow at Logan, "Are you proposing to me?"

"I guess I am if you'll have me. I know I have just one leg, but I'm trying to compensate as best I can. I hope that doesn't matter to you?"

"Don't be silly. That doesn't define who you are, so that isn't the issue."

"Hmm...Is there an issue?"

"Well, yes. I have yet to hear why you want to marry me." Arms akimbo, she stamped her foot, "You men! You have no idea what a woman needs to hear sometimes."

"I'm sorry, Rachel. I don't want you to think I don't care for you. I do. I know we have known each other just a few months now, but I have come to know you and to think you would make me a fine wife. I can take care of you now that I am working with Abel. I know you are friends with Cecily so we should manage just fine, don't you think?"

"No, I don't." Rachel sniffed. Rising from her chair on her father's porch, she turned to him. "Thank you for a lovely picnic. Now, you must excuse me. I am suddenly really tired."

"But, Rachel, are you telling me that you don't want to marry me? I don't understand. I thought you cared for me, too." Logan was puzzled and unsure of what to do. He did not want to leave with Rachel in a snit and not knowing how he had created it.

"I don't want to talk about it anymore today, Logan."

Logan kicked his horse into a canter as he rode home. He did not slow until he reached One Less Ranch where he had to swing down to open the wooden gate supported by large brick piers, a gate he thought as useless as tits on a boar hog. Most of the cattle roamed free on the open range to the west of the house. The pigs were secured within their own pen. Only the chickens roamed free in the area around the house and the fence was no deterrent to them anyway. He had asked Abel about the sense in a fence. Abel had chuckled and informed him that when a man reached that gate, he had to slow down and think about what was on the other side. Logan smiled at Abel Benson's gate thinking it looked like something that should open onto a large eastern estate, not a dust-cloaked, rambling ranch house in the hills of California.

Abel was sitting on the porch puffing on his pipe when he rode up. Logan tied his horse to the railing and swung down. He climbed the steps and sank into the rocking chair beside Abel. "Damned waste of time. I thought you said she was sweet on me. If she is, she sure didn't let on."

"Turned you down, huh?" Abel shook his head, "Reckon I should of been the one to propose for you. Got to sweet talk these fillies. Bet you didn't even bother...just jumped in with both feet."

"Hell, I asked her to marry me. Ain't that sweet enough?" Logan shrugged. "I thought I was over that foolishness when I came out here leaving my sweetheart behind. I don't know why I let you and Cecily talk me into going for another one."

"You been miserable, boy. See the way you look at me and Cecily. Know you want it for yourself. Rachel's a good 'un. Give her a little time, then go over there and ask again. Next time take a bunch of flowers and put some sugar in your mouth."

"Ah, the hell with that." Logan stood up, "I'd best see to my horse. I'll be into supper soon as I get her stabled."

An hour later, Logan was sitting at the table looking out the large window to the distant hills almost lost now to the purple haze of dusk. His plate was largely untouched, the food just pushed from side to side. It barely registered that Abel had said something to him. "I'm sorry, you were saying?"

"Been talking to my wife. Thinking about taking a partner. You interested?"

"What? Are you serious? You realize I don't have enough to buy into half of this ranch." Yet the very idea of it caused a soaring feeling in his chest that he could not squelch.

Cecily smiled, "You would be doing Abel a favor. He respects your business acumen. We both think it is a good idea. He brings knowledge of ranching, but you know how to run the books and how to make it profitable."

Abel leaned forward propping his elbows on the table. "Thought you could buy in over time. Take it out of your earnings. Thinking to buy the ranch that butts up to the back of this one; maybe try almond farming. Hear there is a real future in it. Need someone that knows about farming. Carve yourself out a piece for a house. You interested or not?"

"More than interested. I'm in. Just let me do my fair share, no favors. I don't know anything about almond trees, but I'll see what I can learn." Logan grinned, "You have sure put the sun back in my day."

Cecily rose from the table and walked to the sideboard where she cut three pieces of pie. Serving Abel and Logan, she walked back to the sideboard for her own plate. Once seated, she studied Logan for several minutes as he polished off his pie.

"Abel tells me Rachel is being a little difficult." Cecily gave him a sympathetic smile. "Maybe you didn't go about it just right. Did you tell her she's beautiful, that you love her, and can't imagine life without her?"

Logan blushed and looked at his plate refusing to meet their dancing eyes. Abel spared him the need to respond by ordering, "Need you to go over to Vance Riley's tomorrow and ask him for that book he was telling me about on almond farming. No point in wasting time now that we are partners.

Mayhap, you'll run into that woman of yours."

"Logan, I don't mean to pry, but Abel was telling me about the girl you left back in North Carolina. Are you over her? If you aren't, you need to wait until you are sure before you ask Rachel again."

"It has taken me a long time to see the truth of it. Cissy and I were friends since the time we were children. I have loved her since I first laid eyes on her, but deep down I have to accept she was never that in love with me. When I lost my leg, I couldn't face her. Like a coward I ran out, never giving her the chance to accept me like I am now. Looking back, I think I was wrong. She deserved an explanation for why I left the way I did. As for how I feel about her now, I think it was more a long term expectation and infatuation than anything else." Logan stopped and shook his head, "That may be a damned lie. She is a beautiful, exciting woman, headstrong and sassy. Any man would want her. However, I think I may be getting over her. The fact that I would even ask Rachel to marry me is proof of that, isn't it?"

"Maybe, and maybe not. I know this husband of mine would like to see you married and happy and I would, too. You don't need to rush into it until you are sure. I think Rachel just needs a little more courting. She is already mighty taken with you. When you know beyond a doubt that she is the woman you love, then you will find the words to convince her. Right now she may feel that your heart is not totally free."

A morose and fretful man tossed on his bed that night. The rising of the sun shot light through the dusty window over his head. Weary from lack of sleep and troubling thoughts, Logan threw back the sheet and stood up. After stretching Logan walked behind the bunkhouse and relieved himself. That done he went back to his room, sat at the table and with sober resolve pulled paper and pen in front of him. Staring at a cobweb in the corner, he nibbled at the end of the pen before beginning a letter that was many months over-due. He hoped that someday Cissy would absolve him of his cowardly behavior in having John Harvey break the news that he was setting her free. He tried, always conscious of the limitation in words when trying to express such intangible feelings and emotions, to convey to her his abiding friendship and respect and to plea for forgiveness that he had not had the courage to tell her the truth before he left. He wrote that he hoped that she had moved on with her life, as had he, and that someday they would meet again in friendship. That done he carefully addressed an envelope before wiping the pen and laying it beside the ink well. With a determined tilt to his chin he walked to the main house for breakfast. He and Abel were riding into town that morning for the weekly payroll and he would post his letter then. Afterward he would ride to the Riley ranch for the book and the opportunity to do a little sweet-talking to Rachel.

Logan wiped his feet at the back door. Cecily and Abel had just sat down when he entered the kitchen and joined them at the long pine table. The aroma of strong brewed coffee, sausage and flapjacks greeted him like a benediction. "I think I'll ask Juanita to marry me instead and make me fat with her cooking. Despite getting tired of the chili, I sure do like her breakfasts."

Abel laughed, "Let's get the blessing done and then we need to shovel this down and head on into town."

As they ate, both Abel and Cecily watched him. Looking up, he would find both sets of eyes quickly shifting to some location on the opposite wall. Finally he could stand it no more, "Did I grow another nose or something? Y'all have done nothing but stare a hole in me since I walked in here."

"No reason, just thinking you look a lot more chipper than you did when you went to bed last night. Must have done you some good to sleep on it." Abel chuckled as he winked at Cecily.

"I'm not sure you could call it sleeping." Logan remarked

with a wry quirk to his mouth. "I did a lot of thinking. This morning I wrote Cissy the letter I should have written nearly two years ago. I feel better for it, like a weight is off my back."

"That is a good thing, Logan. I know how I would have felt had I been in her shoes. Somehow, she will understand and forgive you. Abel and I want you to be happy. Since I have known you, there has always been a sad look about your eyes. This morning it's gone. Now, you will be really free of your past and free to move forward into what life holds for you here."

* * * * *

Marcel was smug with satisfaction. His wife had just delivered a robust, squalling brat that guaranteed his position with the elated Woodward grandparents. Lifting a glass of champagne, Marcel rose to his feet. "I would like to drink a toast to my son, Bernard Woodward Lambert."

The proud Bernard, lifted his own glass, "And to our daughter and her husband who have blessed us with this beautiful grandchild. May there be many more. Diana and I always wanted a big family but God saw fit to bless us with Adelaide and no others. Now, God willing, we will have a big family after all. Just think, Diana, someday our grandson will be a marquis."

Diana Woodward lifted her own glass in salute. "We are grateful to you Marcel for making our daughter a good husband. We know you will be an equally good father to your son."

"I will do my best." Marcel smiled at them both before inviting, "Let's take a glass of champagne to Adelaide and visit the baby. I know you are both eager to see them."

They followed him from the parlor and up the grand staircase to the nursery to admire the baby before entering the master bedroom. Adelaide was sitting in bed wearing a frilly bed jacket and surrounded by at least half of the fresh flowers in San Francisco. Her face was sullen. Spotting the champagne stem and the bottle Marcel carried, "I'm glad to see you remembered me. Here I have done all of the work and you three are sitting downstairs ignoring me."

"We were giving you time to rest a bit, my brave darling, so don't pout at us. We were just saying what a beautiful mother you are," Marcel soothed more for the benefit of the parents than his wife.

"Hah! At the moment, I don't feel beautiful. I will be glad when I get my figure back. I am tired of feeling like a whale."

Diana took her daughter's hand and cajoled, "Hush, sweetheart. You are still beautiful and you will soon be back to normal. It is all worth it to have a child."

Adelaide snorted before throwing back the champagne. She held her glass up for a refill not caring that her parents looked mildly disapproving. The baby in the adjoining nursery raised a healthy bellow causing both grandparents to smile. They did not see Adelaide roll her eyes. "Why doesn't the nurse stop that noise? My nerves can't take it."

Diana laughed, "That's a healthy son letting his mama know he's hungry. We'll leave you, darling, so you can see to your baby. We are just so pleased for you and happy you are both fine."

Her parents hugged her before walking out the door with Marcel. Over his shoulder he glimpsed his wife frowning at the swaddled bundle the nurse place in her arms. Somehow, he did not think his wife was cut out for motherhood. Despite his own reservations about being a father, he felt himself softening towards the wee mite he had sired. It might prove interesting to raise the next marquis and share his proud heritage now that he had the means to reclaim it.

In the foyer, Marcel smiled when Bernard turned and clapped him on the shoulder, "That's a fine boy, you have

Marcel. I intend to do right by you and our little Bernard. I will have my solicitor call on you tomorrow with some papers you will need to sign." Bernard laughed, "I suspect you will be happy to sign them."

"Thank you, sir. I appreciate all that you have done for me and my little family."

"Oh, Marcel, you are so welcome. We are just thrilled and hope that this little one will have brothers and sisters soon. Bernard and I have waited so long to have more children to love." Diana smiled at her husband. It was obvious they had a genuine love for one another. For a moment, from somewhere lost in the boy he had been, Marcel envied them the honest emotion.

He was indeed happy to sign the documents the lawyer brought the following morning. Bernard was generous in his delight with a grandson, more generous than the marital agreement provided even. Not only was the allowance for the household tripled, but Marcel also had been generously gifted with cash and the deed to a prime business property containing a handsome building standing at the intersection of Bay and Stockton Streets. The rents from the building alone were enough to cover any household expenses, no matter how lavish. His fortune was well and truly secured with these latest additions to the property that he had already purchased, plus the house, its luxurious contents, and the mounting pile of gold and cash in the Bank of California. The founders, William Ralston and Darius Mills, knew him by name and hastened to invite him to join them for various functions. Marcel was quickly becoming a respected and prosperous man in the heyday of San Francisco.

He surprised himself in the coming months at the growing affection he felt for his son. The only real thorn in his idyllic new existence was the constant carping of his never satisfied wife. She paid about as much attention to her child as the wallpaper. Had it not been for Diana and the kindly nurse who did her best to make up for the mother's neglect, baby Bernard would have had little motherly love. It did not help her disposition when less than six months later she again found herself pregnant. The diamond and ruby necklace with matching ring that her parents gave her after hearing the news only served to cheer her for a couple of days before she was complaining again. Marcel escaped the house whenever he could and was rarely at home in the evening, much preferring the company at the El Dorado.

Adelaide was terrified every time she looked at little Bernard. He seemed to look more and more like Daniel daily, much to the valet's smug satisfaction. If Daniel could see the resemblance, she wondered how long it would be before Marcel noticed. Even though she was pregnant and unsure which man had fathered this one, she again avoided Daniel sexually for fear Marcel would discover their affair. The constant worry and the misery of morning sickness did little to enhance her disposition. When she looked at her baby she felt remorse that she was not a better mother, but lost in her own turmoil and misery she had no energy to spare for anyone else.

Little did she know that Marcel was already suspicious and the sly comments his detested valet made did little to assuage his internal conflict. He did not love Adelaide, but he did love the advantages marriage to her brought. The news of another child meant only more money in his account. As soon as the child arrived and the grandparents again increased the money coming to him and his wife, he would take stock of his worth. If he had enough wealth of his own to give him the life he wanted, he would dump the miserable bitch, take his heir and move to France to continue without her. He would have to be careful though as the Woodwards were well connected and powerful. He did not want them for an enemy.

As for Daniel, Marcel had had enough. Not caring what

Adelaide might say, he called the valet into his study a week after the announcement of the new pregnancy. He watched through narrowed eyes as Daniel sauntered in and took an uninvited seat across from him. Secure under Adelaide's patronage, he sat back, crossed his legs, and cut a smug grin at Marcel. "You wanted to see me?"

Marcel snorted, "No. Actually I never want to see you again. Pack your things and get out of here. You have an hour to do it. Your pay is in that envelope there. Take it and the devil take you."

"You arrogant French son of a bitch, what's the trouble? You afraid I'm a better man than you are?" Daniel taunted, "Your wife seems to think so."

Marcel went deadly still, "That was a serious mistake."

"So what are you going to do about it, you fucking dandy?"

"Oh, I'll do something, never you fear. And in my own good time."

"Are you threatening me?" A shiver went up his spine when he looked into Marcel's cold eyes. It occurred to him that he just might have underestimated the man. Clearing his throat to settle the bile he felt rising up, Daniel stood and picked up the envelope. "I would not advise any rash action on your part. I have friends here that would not want anything nasty to happen to me."

"I promise you, I am never rash." Marcel's slow smile and deadly soft voice made Daniel more than uneasy. It crossed his mind that the sooner he left San Francisco the better it would be for his health.

Daniel could feel Marcel's cold eyes drilling his back as he walked from the room. He wasted no time packing what he could carry and giving the housekeeper orders to hold the rest until he could check into a hotel and send for it. A few more days and he would have his mind focused and move on. First he needed to settle a couple of bills with some unforgiving acquaintances. Before he left the house, he walked up the servants' stairs and slipped into Adelaide's room locking the door behind him.

She looked up in surprise from the book she was reading. Rising from the lounge chair she studied him for several long minutes. "What's wrong?"

"Wrong? That asshole husband of yours just fired me."

"But, why? I have been so careful. You didn't give us away did you?"

"He's not stupid, Adelaide. I suspect he is also far more dangerous to cross than either one of us know. Be careful. I intend to be."

"Don't be ridiculous. He is much too happy with his life right now to bother with you and I'm not afraid of him."

"We had both better hope you are right." Daniel grinned, "Care to give me a proper send off?"

Daniel was chuckling when he picked up his valise and left her room an hour later. He would miss the horny bitch, but then the world had lots of ready women. Unfortunately not all were as wealthy as Adelaide. He had enjoyed the luxury his position afforded. Perhaps, he would find another man with a willing wife to valet for in Sacramento or some other town.

Several hours later, an inebriated Marcel stormed into Adelaide's room in a towering rage. Adelaide was frightened but refused to let him see it. Squaring her shoulders, she lifted her chin and demanded, "What seems to be your problem?"

Marcel didn't bother to answer. She never saw the blow coming. For a moment the room spun before she regained her equilibrium. "If you ever hit me again, Marcel, I will kill you."

Chapter 17

Cissy pocketed the letter from California. She recognized Logan's distinctive handwriting and wondered why he would be writing after years of silence. She decided she would read it in the privacy of her office where she would be alone to deal with whatever it contained. When she arrived at the office, where she had been driven by Dugald...the recent hire who still spoke with a strong Scottish brogue, She was met with the newly arrived *Intrepid* to log in and register the cargo. She had no sooner finished with that when *The Cecily* off-loaded passengers and yet more cargo that needed checking against the manifest. It was not until late afternoon that she finally relaxed at her desk. The letter in her pocket rustled against her skirt reminding her that she had not yet read it. With a weary sigh and a good deal of uncertainty about how she felt about even receiving it, she pulled it out. Reaching for the letter opener, she slit the envelope and removed the single sheet of paper. She read it through twice before she leaned against the back of her chair and closed her eyes. While she understood now what Logan had done, she could not help regretting that he had not even trusted in their years of friendship to come to her and tell her face to face, rather than running and leaving her with nothing but silence and a broken engagement.

Night fell and she still sat in quiet contemplation. It was not until Dugald knocked on the door that she realized it was time to go home. She needed to write her father and Evangeline to tell them where Logan was and why, but first she needed to let it settle in her own mind. She walked into the kitchen where she and Annie preferred to take their meals when it was just the two of them. Annie, Bessie, and Eulalie were in the midst of a heated argument about the best cake for the wedding. When they all three turned to her to arbitrate she held up her hand, "Don't even think it. There is no way I am getting into this one."

"Well, as the bride, I be thinking I should decide. I don't know why you old women think ye know it all."

"Well, Missy, mayhap you should think about how many cakes you done and cooked afore you start telling me how and what to do." Bessie glared at her, arms akimbo.

Eulalie piped up, "We done and told you we cain't go cooking no fruitcake that be worth eatin' no more time than we got. You gotta age 'em and pour brandy on 'em once a week for over a month or they ain't fit to eat. We ain't got but two weeks, so, you ain't gettin' no fruitcake outta us'uns."

Once again all three turned to Cissy. "Fine, I'll tell you what I think. Annie, you love a pound cake with pecans and icing. That is something that doesn't take a lot of time and it always seems to be a hit with everyone. Is that an acceptable alternative for you?"

"That be fine. I don't want to worry with this anymore." Annie rolled her eyes. "At least there be no objection to the rest of the menu."

Cissy shook her head and sat at the table. Shifting her fork to one side and then back, she looked up. "Do you think we could have supper now? I'm starving. I had no time to eat dinner. I had two ships come in today and all kinds of problems to deal with all day long. I am worn to a frazzle and don't want to do anything but have some food, a long hot bath, and go to bed."

"I done and got some water on the stove, Miss Cissy. Soon as you finished here, we gonna fill that tub of yourn up so you can git in it."

"Thank you, Eulalie. That would be a blessing."

Annie and Cissy had consumed most of the meal in silence

before Annie asked, "What in the world be eating at ye? Ye scare said two words since we sat down here."

Cissy worried her lip, not sure she wanted to open up the subject and answer inevitable questions. Finally she said, "Logan wrote me."

"Joseph, Mary, and Jesus! What?"

"He said he lost a leg because of a wound at the battle of Fort Fisher and he just couldn't face me as less than he had been. He's living in California and says he is happy there and doesn't plan on ever coming back. Apparently he has met a girl he really likes and wants me to wish him happy."

"Do ye?"

"You know, Annie, I really do. I never wanted to marry Logan. He just wore me down. Plus father was promoting us marrying. I'm happy he is alive and doing well. I'm just sad he didn't trust me enough to tell me to begin with. It would have saved a lot of worry for Father, Evangeline, and me, too. They love Logan, and so do I. I just never did love him like more than a friend or a brother. I tried, but it never felt right."

"Tis glad I be ye are not sad. He never was for ye. I could see that."

Listening intently to the conversation, Bessie nodded in agreement, "Miss Annie, is right, Miss Cissy. He is a good boy, jes' not the one for you."

"Ye going to be writing to him?"

"I am. I plan to answer his letter tomorrow and write Father to tell him what Logan wrote. It will be a relief to them to know he's doing well." Cissy put her fork on her plate and rose, "Eulalie, if you will take the water upstairs, I would like my bath now."

"Yes'am. I git right on it."

Annie began to rise as though to join her upstairs. Holding her hand out to stay her, Cissy pled, "No more talk tonight, Annie. I am just too tired."

Cissy soaked in her bath until the water grew chilled before climbing out to towel off and put on an old nightgown, her favorite worn thin by years of use. Brushing her hair, she quickly braided it. Her bed with its soft eiderdown bedding beckoned her. Despite the thoughts that continued to swirl in her head she was soon lost to sleep. Sometime during the night a sound that did not belong to the deep stillness roused her. Vaguely the sound of gunshots registered. Springing from her bed in alarm, Cissy grabbed her pistol and ran into the hall where Annie was already standing, eyes wide with fright.

"What do ye think it be, Cissy?"

"I have no idea. Run to Papa's room and get the rifle there. It's loaded and if you can hold it and point it, you shoot at anything that doesn't belong here. Now, hurry."

Annie spun on her heel and went racing down the hall. Calling over her shoulder she cried, "Where should I go?"

"You take the front door and I'll take the back. Whatever you do, don't open the door unless you recognize who's on the other side. Hopefully Charles has heard the racket and will be here shortly to help Dugald and Toby."

Several more shots sounded before the night grew quiet again. Using her pistol, Cissy cautiously pushed the drape aside to peek out the window into the back yard. Off to one side she could see Toby and Dugald standing over a dark shape on the ground. Before she could open the door to join them, she heard pounding on the front door.

"Annie, Cissy! Are you girls safe?"

Throwing the door wide, Annie fell into Charles arms sobbing. While he consoled her with soft murmurs, Cissy said, "I think it's over. It looks as though my men shot someone in the yard back by the stable. I'm going to go see what happened."

"No, you girls stay inside with the door locked until I get back."

Reluctantly Cissy nodded. "I need to check on Bessie and Eulalie. I am sure they are scared stiff. They warned us there is unrest in the area."

Annie closed the door behind Charles, and she and Cissy walked to the kitchen where they found the two women crouched in a corner. "I think it's fine now. Toby and Dugald seem to have it under control. Charles just got here and has gone to check on things."

Bessie slowly stood up, "I be a sight too ole for this. I 'spect I need to put some coffee on for the men folk soon as they git finished out there they'll be coming in."

"Mercy, it is five o'clock already anyway. Eulalie, Bessie I suspect it would be a good idea to get some breakfast going along with that coffee. With our nerves rattled, I doubt anyone is in the mood to go back to bed."

With breakfast underway, Annie and Cissy sat at the table and waited for the men to come in and report what had happened. They had only taken a few sips of the freshly brewed coffee when Charles knocked on the door and called for them to unlock it.

Seeing no sense in formality, Cissy motioned all three men to the table. If Dugald was surprised to see both white and black sitting down together, he did not show it. "Y'all sit down and join us. Coffee is ready and breakfast will be shortly. Annie and I are dying to know what happened. Bessie and Eulalie, y'all sit, too."

Charles sat at the table and toyed with a spoon lying there. Looking up he smiled reassuringly at Annie, "This was just a couple of starving men looking to take what they could. One of them is hurt. Toby is going to take him into town to the doctor. The other one got away. Dugald, Toby, and I are going to take turns tonight patrolling both here and Evangeline's house. The problem is so many are without the means to earn a living. So many have no home for their families and no way to feed them.

It is a serious issue. Stephen Moore, superintendent of the eastern district of the Freedman's Bureau told me the poor house and the jail are both filled to capacity and they have to turn folks away. The leaders here have appealed to the North for financial assistance to help care for these people. Local resources are overwhelmed by the large numbers of both poor whites and blacks that gravitated here while under Union control during the war. I just don't see it getting better anytime soon."

"Nor do I, Charles. I for one was feeling pretty hopeless until Miss Cissy hired me on to help out here. I confess I even toyed with returning to Scotland even though I have nothing there to go back to or for. Most of these folks have nowhere to go and are to poor to do much more than sit down and starve. The streets are full of them. Some of the black folks are surly and angry at the situation they find themselves in when they thought freedom was going to mean a better day...not this kind of suffering. Their behavior influences the way the local citizens feel toward all of them and not just the trouble makers that deserve censure."

Toby rose wearily from the table, "I bes' git on into town with that feller. I got him tied up pretty good, but I shore don't want him to git loose afore I git him to the sheriff and a doctor."

Cissy rose, "Let me make you something to take with you for breakfast. We will have you a better breakfast when you get back, Toby."

With breakfast done, Cissy went to her room to dress for the day. She would see what was in the warehouse that she could take to the poorhouse to feed the people there. Before she left the kitchen, she asked Annie to go to the attic and find extra blankets and some of her old clothes that she could donate. Although she had given at church the previous Sunday, she had not realized just how dire the situation was and how great was the plight of so many former slaves. The whites that had been burned out and lost everything were almost as desperate. She was determined to do more. And it was not just altruism. She realized that with so many struggling just to stay alive by any means necessary, they were all threatened. She felt a momentary guilt that she had left the auxiliary led by Sophia Moore and not done more to support their fund raising efforts to help those in need. The portion raised for a memorial mausoleum for fallen Confederates had been ill received by the controlling military causing some loss of energy in the group. However, she could have remained a member and done more to steer them into practical service of the communities needs. It hurt to see her once prosperous city bankrupted by overwhelming demand on its resources. She could not solve the problem alone, but she could and would do better.

With summer almost upon them, she hoped the situation would ease. However a relentless drought that devastated crops sent the town reeling into despair. As though God were setting the ancient plagues into their midst, the warmer months brought pestilence. The poor and weak were the first to sicken and die, but soon others were suffering from Yellow Fever, and cholera, that scourge of poor sanitation. Cissy joined the newly married Annie, Miss Caroline, and Penny in helping neighbors that were stricken with fever. Penny worked tirelessly compounding herbal medicines from plants gathered from her garden and that of Caroline Framingham. Cissy grew to admire her quiet competency and cheerful manner in dealing with the sick. Soon she saw Penny as a friend. While she still had an occasional wistful thought about Ryan, she shrugged it off. She was too overwhelmed by nursing and running her office to think of anything beyond the moment. Penny sensed Cissy's greater ease around her, and soon the two women were laughing and talking like lifelong acquaintances. By August, the worse of the fever had passed.

Determined to celebrate, Annie persuaded Cissy and Penny

to host a masquerade ball in the Masonic building theater. For once, Cissy turned over some of the office responsibilities to her staff and concentrated on the joy of planning a party. Penny excitedly told her about the 1867 New Year's Day celebration featuring a medieval pageant with twenty-two knights representing not only New Berne, but also the surrounding towns of Kinston, Goldsborough, and Wilson. A celebration ball attended by over two hundred people followed the tournament.

"What would you think about doing another with a medieval theme?"

"I suppose we could, Penny. With the weather so hot just now, we could just make it a King Arthur and the Knights of the Round table feast without doing the tournament."

"I don't know. I think every woman in town will show up dressed like Guineviere and the men like Lancelot."

Cissy laughed, "You're right; I had already thought of dressing like her. Let's do something different. What about circus performers like the ones that came with Barnum and Van Amburgh's Menagerie last year? The ladies could be equestrians or tamers or something and the men could be clowns or even dress up like some of the animals. Or we could do something like a Night at the Forum theme with Roman senators, gladiators, and ladies dressed in classical robes."

"I like the forum idea and the costumes won't be as difficult as trying to make animal ones. Besides, the ladies are going to love wearing the roman style gowns after years of hoops, corsets, and crinolines."

"I suppose some will be scandalized?"

"Absolutely. But, not most of the men! Let's do it." Penny grabbed her hands and they twirled in a circle laughing.

While she had no escort for the grand evening, Cissy had such fun she did not even care. She danced with most of the single men at the ball and several of the married men including Ryan. When he asked her to dance, she blushed remembering her refusal to do so the last time he had asked. She gave him her hand and allowed him to lead her onto the dance floor for a waltz.

"I think you and Penny have pulled off a great success. Everyone is raving about the decorations, the costumes, food, and the music."

"I think it is just wonderful." Cissy bit her lower lip and concentrated on the steps for a moment, before she softly said, "I have grown to like and admire your wife. She is a really fine woman."

"I'm glad you two are friends. Penny has needed a good friend near her own age. I know she likes you very much. I think she liked you even more, little Rebel that she is, after I told her about your spying activities."

"I was no spy. I just couldn't help it if I learned interesting things and passed them along, could I?"

Ryan laughed, "Now that is a whole new way of describing spying. I will have to think about it."

"You never did catch me." Cissy grinned up at him.

Ryan grinned back, "I never did *want* to."

Chapter 18

Daniel was worried. Twice when he had gone out from his hotel he had felt as though someone followed him. Thinking back to the final confrontation with Marcel Lambert, he shivered as though icy fingers were walking down his spine. He didn't like nor did he trust the man. Some premonition cause him to write a short note to put in his pocket saying that if something were to happen to him, to seek Marcel Lambert for the murder. While he worked for the man he had sensed there was dark and sinister side to Lambert that was kept hidden under that careful aura of aristocratic hauteur. With his final business done, Daniel threw his things in his portmanteau and settled his bill. Although nearly night, he thought he probably had enough daylight left to make it to the harbor where he intended to catch a boat to the Yukon. Once he was away from San Francisco and lost in Alaska, he would rest a lot easier.

So intent was he on scurrying to the wharf that he did not hear the soft steps of the dark clad man that followed him always hugging the shadows. With the boat he sought in sight, Daniel breathed a deep sigh of relief. It was his last breath. He never felt the practiced plunge of a long dagger into his back, under the ribcage and up into his heart. His body lay for hours on the dark street. Rats scampered over him before returning to gnaw at exposed flesh. When morning came, Adelaide would not have recognized her handsome lover.

Marcel had just climbed from his bath and was anticipating a trip to the bank to arrange purchase of another property when the butler knocked on his dressing room door. Oscar, the elderly new valet opened the door to admit the man. Annoyed at the interruption to his toilette, Marcel snarled, "What do you want, Regis? Can't you see I am readying to go out for the day?"

The butler stammered, "I'm sorry, sir. There is an insistent man in the foyer that demands to see you."

"And just who is this insistent fellow?"

"He says he is Inspector Sullivan, sir. I think he is a policeman, sir."

Marcel felt cold sweat break out on his body. For a moment he said nothing as he marshaled his composure. "I have an important meeting this morning. Please inform the inspector to call on me day after tomorrow as I am out of town until tomorrow night."

"Very good, sir."

Marcel let Oscar finish dressing him, before sending for Regis. The minute the butler appeared, he demanded, "Did you deliver my message?"

"Of course, sir. Just as you said."

"And he left?"

"He was none too happy, but he left. Said he would be here tomorrow night waiting for you to get back."

Marcel dismissed both his valet and the butler. For several long minutes he stood looking out the window. The view suddenly held no appeal. He needed to leave and fast to let things cool down. He had been careful when he killed Daniel to be sure the streets were empty. It puzzled him that a policeman should be calling at his home so quickly. Perhaps, the inspector wanted a mere interview with the former employer, but did he dare take a chance that was all? With two more dead men and a robbery for which he had successfully eluded detection, he damned well did not intend to get trapped for killing his wife's greasy lover.

He walked into the hall and called for his valet, ordering him to pack his traveling trunk. From there he marched into his wife's bedroom where she was still lolling in bed. "Get up. Call your maid and pack your trunks, the baby's things, too. Also the nurse, your maid, and my valet, tell them all to pack. We are going to Paris and then to my family chateau. I am needed there on urgent business."

With the first smile she had shown in a week, Adelaide sat up quickly, "Oh, wonderful. When do we leave?"

"Tomorrow morning." He wheeled around and was gone leaving her staring in amazement at the spot where he had just stood.

Marcel raced from the house to his bank where he arranged for transfer of his liquid assets to the bank he frequented in Paris and the sale of three properties that had appreciated considerably in a short time. That done he hurried to the booking agency to arrange tickets on the first ship out of San Francisco the next morning. When he returned to the house he had come to love, he paused just inside the foyer and looked around. When things quieted down, he would be back. He watched the servants scurrying about before walking to his library. Opening his safe he withdrew the sizeable stack of bills, along with Adelaide's jewelry, and place them in a small lockable box. He sat it on his desk and then pulled the cord for his butler. When Regis walked in, Marcel motioned him to a chair in front of his desk.

"I am preparing a letter for you to deliver to Mrs. Lambert's parents. Also, the bank has a household account that I have arranged for you to draw on to keep the house running in my absence. The housekeeper, the cook, and a maid to maintain things is all you will need until we return, let the others go. My wife's maid, the nanny, and my valet will be going with us."

The butler's eyes widened with shock. He gasped, "Ye-yes, sir. Do you know how long you will be away?"

"No. In the meantime, if there are any problems while we are away, Mr. Woodward can assist you."

Regis ducked his head for a moment, "What shall I say to the police inspector, sir?"

"Please express my regrets and say that I was called away unexpectedly due to a death in the family."

"I'm so sorry, sir. Yes, sir; very good, sir." If Regis doubted Marcel's story the stoic expression on his face divulged nothing.

Marcel entered his wife's bedroom that night. For the first time in over a week, he claimed his marital rights unconcerned if she enjoyed the event or not. When he was finished, he left her bed and sought his own in the adjacent bedroom. Adelaide didn't really care. She was just happy to be going to France where her new aristocrat title should guarantee her the kind of acclaim she craved. She turned over in her bed pondering the sudden decision of her husband to decamp with undue haste to Paris. He had never really mentioned relatives, living or otherwise, nor any business concerns. The underlying nervous tension she sensed in Marcel when he told her about the trip did not quite fit with his story. But then, she decided, what did it matter? She was bored with San Francisco, sexually frustrated without Daniel, angry with Marcel for his treatment of her, and tired of motherhood. Paris was a welcome diversion.

Marcel smiled as he watched the shoreline of California recede. Once again he had outsmarted his opponent. He laughed aloud when he thought of the surprise awaiting the inspector when he came for his evening interview.

Adelaide looked up at her husband from the corner of her eye, "What's so amusing?"

"Oh, nothing really. Perhaps the exhilaration of the sea, or returning to my home, or just the sudden freedom I feel." Marcel turned to offer his elbow, "Would you care for a stroll around the deck?"

Pleased by this new solicitousness, she wasted no time complying. Perhaps, she thought, the voyage will be good for our marriage as there is little other company to enjoy in such restricted quarters as a ship.

* * * * *

As the boat left the harbor, Keith Sullivan was busy marshalling his evidence to present to the judge. While the two previous murders of the Frenchmen might implicate Lambert, he hoped the murder of Lambert's valet would help seal the case against the man. Without a witness and considering the importance of the man and his in-laws, Sullivan was careful to tread with caution. The letters from law enforcement offices in the east were a part of the documentation that he took with him for the judge to consider. He intended to be awaiting Lambert with an arrest warrant when he returned that evening. Before he left his office to go to the judge, he dispatched an officer to keep watch on the house until he could arrive to await Lambert.

Judge Hardison looked up at Sullivan and raised his eyebrows. "Do you realize what a mess this will be if you are wrong? Not only is he married into the Woodward family, but the man also is a titled aristocrat and a French citizen. I just don't know. Most of this is circumstantial. I'll grant you the note is pretty damning but that could just be a grudge of some kind...far-fetched maybe, but still, it doesn't prove that Lambert killed him."

"Your honor, the man is crafty. The folks back east have suspected him for sometime..."

"Yes, and they did nothing because they can prove nothing either," the judge snapped as he studied the papers arrayed on the shiny top of his mahogany desk. Slapping his hands on top of the pile, he said, "I think you need to back off until you have something more to go on. I can't give you an arrest warrant without something to cover our asses on this one. If it were some common dockworker it would be different. But, that is not what we are talking about here. Why don't you continue your investigation? If he is as nasty a fellow as you say, sooner or later he will slip up. In the meantime, I don't want

Woodward and his fancy lawyers after us on behalf of the man's son-in-law."

Inspector Sullivan walked from the Hardison's office in a foul mood. He was so sure the judge would see it his way that he had not stopped to consider the political implications. Hardison would soon be running for office again and he wanted nothing that might be a hinderance to getting re-elected. Stopping in the street he barely looked up in time to dodge a carriage that was hurrying towards him. He looked down in disgust. The carriage had splashed mud on his trousers as it drove past. He decided his day was turning out to be a pisser. Cursing under his breath, he walked up the street to the Lambert mansion. Nobody could stop him from questioning the man.

After dismissing the policeman that had been stationed at the house since noon, Keith Sullivan stood at the door of the mansion admiring the lines of the house. It was an impressive one to say the least and announced to the world the prosperity and importance of the owner. But, even wealthy men could murder and go to jail, he reminded himself. And this particular one he was determined to nail. Even though he had never met the man he didn't like him. The butler opened the door as he raised his hand to lift the knocker again.

"Yes, may I assist you, sir?"

"Has your employer returned? If so, I would like to see him, if not, perhaps I could wait in the parlor?"

I regret, sir, but he was called from town on a personal matter of some urgency. He left with his family this morning."

It was all he could do not to curse when he grimly replied, "I see. When do you expect him back?"

"I'm sorry, I couldn't say."

"Do you know where he was going?"

"Returning to his home in France, I believe, sir."

Sullivan turned on his heel and marched up the street

furious that the wily Frenchman had bolted. "Dammit," he cursed. Lambert still had his big mansion and servants so surely he would return. When he did, he planned to be waiting for him. He had spent far too much time chasing the man, and deep in his gut was too certain of his guilt to just give up.

* * * * *

Cissy sat onshore watching *The Cecily* bob gently up and down at the wharf. After several minutes she stood and stretched, too restless to sit any longer. Walking to Union Point, she stared out over the water not really seeing it. At her back the trees along East Front Street were loosening the moorings of their leaves and sending them flying on the wind like colorful kites. A few swirled to a halt at her feet before lifting off again in their sporadic flight. She pulled her shawl a little closer although she was not really chilled and tucked her head down.

The day after the ball she had called on Penny to find her worried that Carah seemed to have developed a fever. The baby was crying fretfully.

"I am so terrified, Cissy. Pray to God that she has not developed Yellow Fever." Penny's eyes were stricken as she stared at Cissy over the baby's head.

"It's probably nothing more than the normal childhood thing. Try not to worry over much. If there is anything at all I can do, you know I will."

Penny shook her head, "I've sent for the doctor but he hasn't arrived yet. Perhaps, you are right and it's nothing serious."

Penny brushed her hand across her brow and stilled with surprise. At the expression on the woman's face, Cissy had leaned over and put her own hand on Penny. "My goodness, you are burning with fever yourself."

Silent tears began to roll unnoticed down her cheeks. The loss of Penny's daughter Carah and then Penny herself when all thought the fever epidemic had passed was a stunning blow.

Cissy had come to love the woman and would miss her dearly.

In the last days of her life, she had sat hours by her bedside trying to ease the woman's suffering.

With the loss of her child, before the next day faded into night Penny was dead, too. It was as though all fight had gone from her after the death of her daughter. Cissy had called Ryan from a nap when it was obvious the end was near. Leaning over to kiss Penny's forehead a final goodbye, she left the room so her husband could spend the last moments of life with her. She had not seen him since the funeral when his grief seemed to have added ages to his face overnight. Their son, Rye, had sat mutely staring at the men throwing dirt on his mother's grave. At last he realized she was truly gone from him. It was then Rye began to cry inconsolably. Caroline, who was also devastated by grief, took him by the hand and led him to Ryan's carriage. She held Penny's son to her chest and sobbed with him for the woman who had been like a daughter to her, a childless widow.

Cissy registered the soft footfalls that stopped nearby but paid no notice until a hoarse voice, in so low a tone she was not even sure she heard it, commented, "Bleak winter is announcing its arrival not long from now. It always makes me sad to see the leaves fall. Maybe, this year more so, as it puts a final end to the warm summer of my life."

Cissy wiped her tears and turned to the man, "Ryan, I don't know how to tell you how very sorry I am for your loss...a loss for all of us. I loved Penny as a dear friend even though it was for such a short time. It is a double blow for you to lose not only your precious wife, but your sweet little girl as well. It seems so unfair after Penny saved so many from the fever. I thought when we had the ball it was a celebration of the end of the disease. Little did we know Carah and she would fall ill within the same week."

"It is selfish of me but I wish to God she had stayed home

and let someone else tend to the stricken. I would still have Penny and our daughter. I resent the ones she saved when no one could save them. She wouldn't want me to feel this way, but I can't help it."

Cissy nodded her head in mute understanding. They stood side by side, saying nothing for half an hour or more before both, silently turned back to their offices. When she reached hers, she touched Ryan's arm and gave a soft smile goodbye before opening the door to LaRoque

Shipping. The quiet period of mutual mourning there by the water had been surprisingly comforting to her. Walking to her desk, she settled into her seat and began to go through the details of the last manifest. Realizing her mind was only half on the details, she shrugged. It was time to go home anyway.

After her supper, Cissy wandered into the parlor and picked up a novel that she had laid aside a month before. It didn't interest her. With Annie no longer in the house, she was suddenly conscious of the quiet. For the first time since moving back to New Berne, Cissy was lonely. She no longer needed to spend hours studying books or researching shipping concerns as the business was running smoothly and growing at a rapid rate. Her new employees were doing a good job and relieving her of much of the tedium. Not knowing what else to do, she walked to the library and sat at her father's desk to write a letter to him and Evangeline. When that was done she looked at the clock on the mantle and sighed. It was too early to go to bed. She thought of writing Logan to congratulate him on his marriage, but did not have the motivation to do it. What could she say anyway that she had not already written when he had sent her a letter telling her about the event? She was happy for Logan, and while she envied him and Annie for having found someone to love, she was melancholy for herself.

Shaking her head to dispel the gloom, Cissy stood gazing out the window into the night. She had set her life on its present course and rejected suitors in order to prove her worth not only to herself but others. Now, she wondered what life would have been like had she chosen another course. Would she have been happy married to Logan, or perhaps Brandon? Now she would never know, as Logan had married another and she had heard nothing from Brandon in months. She suspected he had moved on with his life and she could not blame him. It never occurred to her to think that Ryan was now free. He was so deeply hurt she did not think he would ever be the same man again.

Chapter 19

Adelaide swirled across the polished dance floor with giddy delight. The gilded world of aristocratic Paris was everything that she could have imagined. Marcel tightened his grip about her waist as they finished the final waltz of the evening and pressed a kiss at her temple. She admired their reflection in one of the many mirrors that lined the ballroom of the grand mansion. Her new gown was the most flattering she had ever owned and cut in the latest French style. She liked the bustle so much better than the ante-bellum hoops. Marcel was equally elegant in his new evening clothes. More than one head bent their way in whispered consultation and conjecture. Smiling as the tune drew to a close, Adelaide looked up at her husband, "I love it. This is all that I dreamed of and more. I cannot image what inspired you to leave Paris for the States. We have nothing to compare to the beauty and magnificence of this city."

Marcel merely smiled and offered no comment. She did not need to know that he had spent a day mollifying his debtors with repayment and calling on his father's cousin in humble atonement for his past history. He was rightful heir to the large manor to the southeast of Paris in Melun, however his cousin was the trustee and reluctant to turn the house over to the family reprobate. It had taken considerable effort and a recounting of his financial particulars and those of his new wife, before cousin Bertrand was sufficiently relieved of his misgivings. Why Bertrand was so averse to handing the property over to him he could not imagine. He knew from his previous visit several years past, the property suffered from decades of neglect and would take no small sum to renovate and refurbish. It didn't matter to him the cost. That estate represented the cachet of his old and illustrious family name. Now that he had money, he intended to reclaim that heritage.

As they claimed their wraps, Marcel asked, "I would like to shop tomorrow for some of the furnishings we will need for our estate in Melun if you feel up to it? With another baby on the way, I do not want you to become overly tired."

"I want to come. Of course, I'm not too tired. I feel fabulous. I so love Parisian shops and all of the fabulous things they have. I would be desolate not to be included. Besides as chatelaine, I should be the one with some say in the furnishings."

"Good, as I fear we shall have to wire for some of your funds for the refurbishment. Mine are temporarily depleted due to the suddenness of our trip. I was only able to procure limited cash at the last minute." He did not mind lying.

"You should have told me sooner. We must wire immediately to my bank and have them send as much as you think will be needed. I do want it done well."

"Yes, it would be a pity not to restore the estate to the former grandeur." Marcel smiled at her, "Did I tell you how ravishing you look tonight?"

"So ravish me, darling." Adelaide batted her lashes at him while smiling coyly. She recognized she was being played but didn't care. She wanted the manor to be every bit as grand as money could make it. If she had to spend some of her own money, so be it. That house and the title were now the heritage of her son. That Daniel's child would one day be a Marquis secretly amused her. Marcel was the means to procuring a status and prestige that money alone could not buy. She meant to have it not only for her son, but for herself as well. He owed her that and she intended to make the best of the situation. She had brought him the wealth he needed to regain his place in French society and her family money was an ongoing gift to him. Yes, he played her, but she could play him just as easily. He looked down his nose at her, at all women, thinking that they were no match for his intelligence. She resented his supercilious attitude and the surface charm that hid who he really was. She had not forgiven him for hitting her either. She never would. Smiling to herself, she turned into his arms. She might as well enjoy his passion. In that way, they were alike.

Marcel rolled off his wife and lay panting at her side. They had been insatiable after arriving home from the ball. He chuckled softly. She did not need to know that two things alone were responsible for his ardor: the spending of her money on his home and the saucy widow he had danced with several times that evening. When he learned that Comtesse Denice Clareaux made a permanent home near his own in Melun, he was intrigued. Perhaps, a dalliance would enliven the rural scene.

"What's so amusing?" Adelaide murmured.

"I'm just happy, darling. It is so good to be home and to reclaim my heritage." That, he decided, was about as truthful as he had ever been.

"Hmm, I thought maybe the last few hours were responsible."

"Of course, that, too." With her protruding belly, she was the last reason for his sexual energy.

As if in denial of his thoughts, Adelaide reached over and placed his hands on her belly. "Do you feel our son kicking?"

"Perhaps, he protests the nudging," Marcel laughed, before turning serious. "If this one is a boy and he is mine, it will pose a dilemma."

"What do you mean?"

"Surely you do not think I will allow your bastard to inherit my family title?"

"You don't seem to mind the income from my father that my suppose 'bastard' brought you, now do you? Besides, who is to say that you are not the father? After all, we were married months before his premature arrival."

"You bitch! You know he isn't mine so stop the pretense." Marcel snapped.

"Oh, but he is legally."

"I swear to you that boy will never be my heir." Marcel left the bed and stormed into the parlor of their suite where he wasted no time pouring a large glass of brandy. If she bore a son this time, Daniel's child would be history. It did not matter to him what he had to do to guarantee that his own child would be his heir. He was fond of the Bertrand, but he would do whatever he had to do to protect his bloodline. He settled onto the sofa with the brandy bottle on the floor beside him. He had had enough of his wife for one night. Maybe, the boy wouldn't be the only one that needed removal.

Adelaide glared at the ceiling. How she could ever have fallen for him she could not fathom. His title had impressed her. His looks had captivated her. His Parisian style and charm had enticed her. But, how could she have been so stupid as not to see the selfish bastard he was? She decided she could be just as selfish and determined. He would not conquer her. The first order of business would be to write her father to assure that any funds were doled out sparingly and infrequently. She was not stupid enough to allow Marcel free rein with her fortune. With expenditures already committed to for the renovations and furnishings, he would have to find the money in his own pocket. Future expenditures would go by her, one way or another, before she allowed a cent of her money or her father's to be turned over to her husband including those of the morrow's excursion.

Adelaide walked from the hotel on her husband's arm the following morning. Furnishings were a priority if the condition of the house was even close to that Marcel described. Not only that, but she intended to buy a new ball gown for the soiree the coming evening, one that would hide her growing girth. She had seen Marcel ogle other women and then look sneeringly at her. He had especially focused on the Clareaux woman who had made it a point to give him a clear view down the deeply cut front of her gown. Adelaide snorted. She would see to it that the cut of her own dress gave him something to focus on.

She encouraged her husband as he indulged in an orgy of buying luxurious furnishings for the house. It was not until time to settle the bill at the prestigious auction house Drouot-Richelieu that Adelaide realized the enormity of what he had spent. No doubt the pressure he would exert on her for more funds would be equally enormous. She wanted the purchases, too, and if necessary she was willing to toss in some of her own money, but he would have to pay the bulk. Discreet inquiries over the last months in San Francisco had given her a fairly good idea of the amount of wealth the man had managed to amass. She did not know that a sizeable sum had already been used to pay off the debts that had forced Marcel to flee to the States to escape his creditors years before.

Following an aperitif at a sidewalk cafe, Adelaide was determined to peruse the shops along the Rue Faubourg for a dress. She was relieved when Marcel begged off, despite suspecting that he only did it to avoid paying. For the next several hours she looked for the perfect dress and waited patiently, glass of champagne in hand, while they altered it to fit her expanded waistline. Despite being the most shockingly revealing dress she had ever owned, the deep emerald of the gown was perfect for her coloring and with the jewels she had brought from home would be dazzling. She also intended to meet this countess and let her know that she was onto the game. If Marcel took objection, too bad.

She did not emerging from her dressing room that night until her evening cloak was securely fastened, hiding the dress from view. She intended for Marcel to be surprised when they entered the mansion and the butler took her wrap. Stepping from the coach they ascended the steps of the palatial house. Her husband was visibly puffed up with pride for receiving the much coveted invitation which acclaimed his return to, and acceptance by, the haut ton that had previously shunned him as a worthless reprobate. Holding her arm solicitously, he guided her up the steps and into the large marble vestibule where mirrors reflected their image under the light of sparkling chandeliers.

"Lovely," she whispered as she surveyed the glittering space. Removing her wrap and handing it to the waiting attendant, she turned to face her husband..

"Mon Dieu, Adelaide. You do look stunning." Marcel stood with mouth agape. She looked the most dazzling he had ever seen her. The immodest cut of her dress left him temporarily disconcerted. When she raised her eyebrows in inquiry, he shrugged. "My compliments, darling. You do justice to the dress, to say the least."

He lead her into the ballroom, aware that every eye turned their way and more than one fan was raised to hide whispered comments. His wife was definitely turning into a Parisian sensation and since that would add to his own panache, he was pleased. When he left to fetch a glass of champagne, he returned to find Adelaide surrounded by an admiring throng of young and titled Frenchmen. Chuckling to himself, he seized the opportunity to search for the Comtesse Clareaux. He spotted her by the doors to the terrace and immediately made his way through the chattering throngs.

"You look lovely, my dear Comtesse. I confess I had hopes of seeing you here tonight," he murmured as he bowed low over an extended hand.

"And why is that?" she queried archly.

"How could I not be charmed by such beauty, Comtesse? You have me in your thrall."

"I notice your wife has more than a few admirers of her own. I am surprised that you are not with her assuring that none become too amorous."

Marcel sneered, "I think that unlikely considering her current circumstance."

"Yes, I did notice the other night that she is *enciente*. However, the dress this evening is quite concealing of her condition."

"Precisely. *Concealing* is indeed the operative word."

"That is rather uncharitable of you since you are responsible for the 'circumstance,' one would assume?"

"Yes, one would assume."

Denice gave him a sharp glance, reading much into his grim face. Ah, perhaps this one would be fine for a bit of bed play. Currently she was without a lover as the Duke of Nemours had left her to pursue another interest. Perhaps this Lambert fellow would assuage her wounded pride and provide a lively romp or two before she tired of him. She did not particularly care for the darkness she sensed in him, but he was handsome enough, sexually alluring, and seemingly available. She glanced invitingly at the open terrace door.

Marcel quirked a brow, "Would you care to take some air? It is rather warm in here."

"Thank you. Perhaps it will prove far warmer outside...but, more stimulating."

Marcel glanced around the room and saw that Adelaide was on the far side and looking in the other direction. A sibilant murmur in Denice's ear assured her, "That would be my preference, my dear."

Offering his arm, he escorted her onto the terrace and then down the wide stone steps to a garden dotted with numerous topiaries and shaded bowers. Leading her into the dark shadowy recesses near the perimeter wall, he turned her to him. There was no subtlety about the seduction that occurred, as it was more an expression of lust for both of them. When they were finished, Denice pulled her bodice up so that it just barely covered the nipples, more a result of the cut of the gown than an attempt at further allure. She rose from the bench, brushing off her clothing and pushing errant pins back into her coiffure while Marcel adjusted his own attire. They re-entered the ballroom by separate doors, but Adelaide was not fooled. She could discern by the slight derangement of their attire and the flush on their faces what had happened in the garden; nor was she surprised.

She deliberately turned her back on them and continued an animated conversation with the smitten young man who had attached himself to her. She was ready to leave Paris. The sooner she reached the manor in Melun and left the Clareaux woman behind the happier she would be. She saw Marcel too clearly to love him, but she would use him to rise in French society and to have a more cultured and diverse life than that afforded in the rough and tumble city of San Francisco. It piqued her vanity that he was unfaithful, however she could ill afford to hoist him on that particular petard.

The house in Melun was like a small Versailles with a coffered gallery on the rear where large floor to ceiling doors flooded the room with light in daytime and a myriad of twinkling chandeliers continued the dance of light into the evening. With refurbished upholstery, freshly lined walls, and cut flowers from the abundant flower beds, it would not be long before it would be suitable for entertaining. Adelaide spent the coming days in a flurry of activity. If Marcel disappeared for hours on end with no explanation, she did not care as it left her free to deal with the tradesmen that came to the house with wares needed for the refurbishment. Thinking that money from her coffers would arrive soon to restore his own diminishing funds, Marcel was liberal with expenditures and did not question her purchases when he saw that her taste and judgment were superior to his own.

The coming weeks saw the house turning into the vision that Adelaide had foreseen. The only snag was Marcel's increasingly sharp questions as to the delay in the arrival of funds from her account. She merely shrugged her shoulders with implied ignorance of the cause while inwardly smiling. Without her money to tap, he was forced to continue spending his own. Wanting the house completed and impressive as much as his wife, he had no choice.

For the next month his dalliance with Denice kept him out of the house and thus made life with Adelaide easier, as whenever they were together they continued to argue about the lack of money from the account established by her father and now under his control in their absence. As Adelaide's time drew near, she was forced to curtail much of what she was doing to ready the house and began to depend more and more on the servants to carry out her wishes. Demanding and exacting, she was meticulous in watching every change to assure it was done to her specification as she wandered from room to room. The main reception areas were completed, as were the master bedrooms, dressing rooms, adjoining sitting room and nursery.

That was fortunate as Adelaide went into labor a couple of weeks early and despite being ahead of schedule the delivery was an easy one. When the midwife exited the room to announce the birth of another son, Marcel wasted no time hurrying to his wife's bedside. Taking the infant in his arms, he folded back the blanket carefully studied him from head to toe. On the right buttock was the roughly star shaped birthmark that had long been a talisman of Lambert males. This was the son of his loins and he would damned well be the heir to his title and property.

He nodded his head at the baby before addressing Adelaide, "Congratulations on delivery me an heir of my own making."

"He is not your first born son according to law."

"To hell with law," Marcel snarled. "Marcel Frederique is my son, not your bastard. I told you that boy would never be my heir. The sooner you accept that the better."

"Better for whom?"

Marcel turned on his heel and stormed from the room without bothering to answer. Celebrating alone in the study with a bottle of champagne, he made a sudden decision to visit Denise. More and more he found his thoughts centered on the woman. He felt like a man bewitched...a feeling that was new to him. Within minutes he had called for his horse and was cantering down the tree lined alleé that led to the Comtesse's manse. He decided on the way over to liquidate all of his assets in San Francisco after the delivery of the expected bonus for the new baby from his father-in-law. In a few months he would find a way to be free of both Adelaide and the bastard Bernard. Then he would marry the widow who would bring even more financial benefits into the marriage than anything Adelaide still held. It helped that Denice seemed to be as eager for him as he was for her. Slowly he would begin to plant the seed of a future for them.

Adelaide heard him galloping down the lane knowing his destination. She shivered. For the first time she truly worried for her safety and that of Bernard. Although she had been happy at the birth of her second child, she now feared that his arrival posed unknown difficulties for her first born.

Chapter 20

It was a beautiful Sunday afternoon, mild for the middle of December. Most of the color on the trees had gone, leaving branches silhouetted against the deep blue of the sky. Kicking through the leaves on the ground, Cissy made her way to the riverbank behind her house. From there she turned right and walked along the bank behind Evangeline's old home. She started to walk through the yard and visit with Annie but she was morose and not good company even to herself. Continuing on she walked to a grassy tuft beside the water and sat looking out at the river as it flowed past on its way to the sound and then the ocean beyond. By the water, the wind was cooler causing her to pull her shawl up around her shoulders. Heaving a sigh, she watched the sunlight glinting on the tops of small waves. From time to time, a heron would swoop down and rise back up with dinner secured in his beak. The squawk of gulls added a note of cacophony to the peaceful lapping of the river and the soughing wind in the pines along the verge.

She was lost in quiet contemplation when a sharp rustling in the leaves startled her. Attempting to gain her footing and see what it was, she slipped and plunged headfirst into the muddy edge of the water. Lifting up with water and tidal debris clinging to her face and hair and down the front of her bodice and skirt, she could not stop the curse that escaped. "Damn! What a mess."

A soft chuckle at her back made her freeze.

"Do you typically go for a swim in your full attire?"

"Oh, for Heaven's sake! You scared me. Don't you know better than to creep up on people?" Embarrassment at having Ryan see her in such dishabille made her voice sharp.

"Come on up to the house and lets see if we can get you dried off. That wet dress and hair are going to have you chilly in no time."

Cissy hesitated, her vanity wounded by her predicament. But it was a long walk home. She had not realized that she had come so far.

Sensing the problem, Ryan laughed, "I think you are lovely even doused with river water. Now, be sensible and lets get you dry. Gave me your hand so you don't tumble back into the drink."

"I might as well," Cissy answered grudgingly as she extended her hand to him. The minute he took it she felt a jolt along her nerve endings. Feeling her face turn red at her reaction, she studiously watched her feet as they walked.

"Stand still a minute."

Cissy stopped and looked up to see Ryan smiling at her in bemusement, "Let me at least pull the debris out of your hair, then maybe you can look up."

"Oh." Her hands flew up and started brushing at her hair. Catching them, Ryan slowly pulled each piece of trash and tossed it away, his gaze never leaving hers.

"It is a lovely day for a walk. I was having one myself when I saw you sitting by the river. I am sorry I made you throw yourself in. I was just hoping for a bit of company. I'm tired of sitting in the house feeling sorry for myself. Surely a lovely girl like you can spare a few minutes of her company for a lonely old widower?"

The twinkle in his blue eyes reminded her of the sparks of light on the river. "I was lonely and feeling sorry for me, too."

Perceptive of her mood, he stated, "No doubt you miss Annie now that she is married and living with her husband. Annie must have been fun company for you."

"I do miss Annie. But..." Catching herself she stopped before blurting that she regretted spurning opportunities to have a man in her life.

"But...?"

"Oh, nothing."

Ryan decided not to press her to finish her statement. Once they were in the house he suggested that she retire to Penny's dressing room where she would find towels and a dressing gown until they could dry her own clothes for her return home. He could see the reluctance on her face at the impropriety of not only being alone in his house but also wearing intimate apparel when they were both unmarried people. Were it known, her reputation would be ruined.

"It's alright, Cissy. None will know that you are in dishabille. We will hang your clothes by the fire to dry and as soon as they are, you may leave. My servants are off this afternoon...visiting, I suppose...and won't be home for some time."

"I see. Thank you for understanding."

Ryan took the ewer of water from his washstand and gave it to Cissy to freshen up and remove the mud. Cissy waited for him to leave before removing her gown and washing up, then she donned the dressing gown that he had draped across the chair by the dressing table. Using Penny's brush, she cleaned and rearranged her hair as best she could and re-pinned it. Just as she finished her ablutions, from down the hall she heard Rye's heartbroken sobs. She waited for a moment to see if Ryan would go to him, but apparently he had not heard. Rushing to the child's bedside, she gathered him in her arms and murmured soothingly in his ear. Soon his cries were mere whimpers. Easing the sleeping child from her arms, she pulled the covers up and kissed him on the forehead. Rye sighed in his sleep. Cissy turned from the bedside to find Ryan in the doorway.

"Thank you, Cissy. I seem to be unable to comfort him. He misses his mother and sister so much. I guess having a woman hold and comfort him is better sometimes than me."

"I doubt that. He loves you. I just happened to be nearby."

"It's more than that. I think he blames me for not saving them."

"Ryan, he is confused and mourning just as you are. In time, he will realize that you love and miss them, too, and would have done anything in your power to save Penny and Carah."

Tears welled in his eyes. Swallowing hard, he cleared his throat and said, "Let's get those clothes of yours from the dressing room and put them by the fire to dry. They won't be pristine, but at least they will get you home without catching a chill."

As they waited by the fire in the parlor to dry her garments, Ryan offered, "Let me pour you a brandy to warm up?"

Cissy hesitated. Shrugging her shoulders, she said, "Why not? I think it would be welcome at the moment. Thank you."

She had never tasted brandy and was unprepared for the breath-snatching sting of it when she took a large swallow. She felt the warming liquid hit her stomach and spread outward. Sputtering, she gasped for air. "Good Heavens. I had no idea."

"I am so sorry. Had I known, I would have warned you to go easy." Ryan studied her reddened face before asking, "Are you sure you are alright?"

"I'm fine, just surprised at the taste of it."

He chuckled, "It's made to be sipped slowly, not gulped."

"I think that is what is referred to as a belated warning." Cissy laughed, "Now I know why the Indians call liquor 'fire water.' It certainly is warming."

They watched the flames in companionable silence as they sipped their brandy. Cissy secretly rejoiced that he had found her even though she would have preferred not to have dived into the mud. A jolt skittered along her nerve endings when she caught him studying her. Their gazes locked as they assessed one another. Cissy was the first to look away.

"My clothes must be dry by now and I really should be getting home. Rye is probably ready to awaken, too."

"He didn't rest well last night or he would not have slept so long this afternoon. Thank you again for calming him. He needed this sleep." Ryan watched as she picked up her things.

He suspected they were still damp, but she did not comment other than to say, "I will be down in a moment."

Their time together had helped to assuage his loneliness for the moment. He remembered all of the times her spunk and quick wit had made him laugh. Even now in the midst of mourning, she eased the darkness just by being near. Although he was reluctant for her to leave, he knew she had stayed far longer than propriety allowed under any circumstances. And while he was drawn to her, his heartache was still too raw. It would not be fair to lead her on when he did not feel as though he could ever love again. He accepted the attraction between them. It had always been there, even before he had met Penny and lost his heart to her. He wondered why Cissy had never married. Well into her twenties, the townspeople considered her a spinster who preferred the world of commerce to home and hearth. It was a pity that a woman of her beauty and vivacity should remain alone, and judging by her melancholy when he happened upon her by the river, she was not the happy woman that she pretended to be.

When she returned, he was standing with his arm on the mantel leaning over to look at the flaming log he had just stirred with the fire poker. Turning he saw her holding Rye by the hand.

"Look who found me while I was dressing."

"I did not realize he was that precocious. I think my son is overdue for a man-talk." Ryan laughed as he motioned his son over.

Rye ran to his father and stood tucked by his side. "Can Miss Cissy stay and have supper with us, Daddy?"

"I am sorry, Rye, but I really want to get a bath and into some clean clothes. But thank you for asking me. I'm honored."

Rye shook his head, "Ladies shouldn't play in the mud, Miss Cissy. You do look awfully messy."

Ryan and Cissy both laughed at the quizzical look on the boy's face as he studied her.

After they saw Cissy out, Ryan and his son returned to stand by the fire. Rye looked up at his father, his face suddenly serious. "Daddy, may I ask you something?"

"Of course, son."

"I've been thinking about it. We're lonely and I think we need a new mama, a nice one like Miss Cissy. She's real pretty, too. I know 'cause I saw her in just her underwear. Do you think she would like to be a new mama for us?"

"She is pretty, Rye. But it's for certain, we do need to have a man-talk soon." Ryan chuckled before he continued, "Son, if you broke your leg could you run on it right away?"

"Why are we talking about a leg when I am talking about a mama?"

"I'm trying to explain, son. When you break your leg you have to wait for it to heal before you can run on it again. It's that way with hearts. Ours have been broken and we need to wait until the hurt isn't so bad before we think about a new mama."

Rye nodded sagely, "I understand, but we better not wait too long. I'm telling you Miss Cissy is mighty pretty and somebody else might want her for a mama, too."

Ryan shook his head, "You are one smart little boy."

"I think I am, Daddy. If you don't want to marry her, I think I should just as soon as I grow a little more."

"After you grow a little more, we'll see."

"I sure hope I grow fast 'cause I don't want her to get away."

"You are growing plenty fast enough, my boy. Now,

enough of this! Let's go see what cook has made for our supper. I'm hungry."

"Yep, I need to eat to grow up fast."

"Come on, Rye. You will grow up in all good time."

"Now is a good time."

Ryan laughed at his son and tussled his hair. "I don't know about you but I'm ready for something to eat. I'm the hungriest I've been...," He stopped himself before saying since your mother died, and continued, "...in ages."

While they were eating a cold dinner, Cissy was bathing and shampooing her hair. She could only hope her dress was salvageable despite Eulalie's warning it would never come clean. It was not one of her favorites but still she was conservative enough she hated to see it wasted. If it were not too badly damaged, she could always add it to her collection for the needy. She arose from her bath and tied a warm robe snugly at her waist before sitting by the fire to comb and dry her hair. She chuckled to herself, at last able to see the humor in the sight she must have made. The walk and visit with Ryan had lifted her spirits. It suddenly dawned on her that Ryan was now free, but she did not know how to let him know she was interested; nor did she know when he might be healed enough to court. It was provoking that Caroline Framingham had told her that Lizzie was already chasing him again. Lizzie was wasting no time. She and Caroline had both expressed the hope that Ryan was too smart to be taken in by the woman. Knowing from past experience how shamelessly determined Lizzie could be, she wasn't so sure. She just knew she could not be another Lizzie.

Despite Monday arriving with blustery winds and dropping temperatures, Cissy went to her office in an upbeat mood. A letter from her father arrived midmorning telling her that Evangeline was once again pregnant. He seemed so happy to have another child on the way. Cissy said a quick prayer that this time all would go well for her. With the end of her childbearing years so near, Evangeline would have no more chances. Considering her stepmother's age, Cissy was surprised that they would even want more children. Andy had made her father feel young again. But after losing the second baby prematurely, she could not help but worry a little for them. Suddenly she missed her parents and her half-brother. Looking at her calendar she wondered if she might be able to squeeze in a visit to Wilmington. With everything running smoothly and *The Cecily* not due back for a month, she decided why not. As though it was meant to be, *The Intrepid* was leaving the next day for a run to Brazil with a stop in Wilmington to pick up rice that her father was shipping to their factor there. It was the perfect opportunity to leave for a visit. She would either catch a ship of her father's that was headed north or take the train for her return. She wasted no time in instructing Dugald what needed to be done in her absence.

After leaving work for the day Cissy stopped by Annie's and Miss Caroline's to let them know that she would be gone for a couple of weeks to visit her parents in Wilmington and to ask if there was anything she could pick up for them in the larger city. Then she hurried home to pack a valise for the trip. With an early departure scheduled she would have no time to tarry come morning. She had issued strict orders early on that all ships would depart on schedule and she did not intend to amend that for her convenience. Wanting to surprise her family with the unexpected visit, she did not telegraph them of her arrival.

Steaming up the Cape Fear, Cissy stood on deck straining to catch a glimpse of the city. Captain Radford Marshall joined her briefly to point out changes wrought by war. The ruins of Fort Anderson on the left bank were followed by the former sites of the Meares, Campbell, Lee, and Davis Batteries on the right bank several miles up river. On reaching the last of the battery sites Captain Marshall left her to take the helm for the final approach to her father's wharf in Wilmington harbor. Sea gulls circled in squawking swoops above the din of the bustling wharves. Cissy had to stop herself from jumping up and down like a child when she spied the spot near the central group of wharves that jutted out from her father's warehouses and offices. Judging by the pile of goods waiting at quayside, the cargo for *The Intrepid* was ready for loading. Her father had early on taught her the importance of maintaining schedules and he was obviously still practicing the regimen.

As the ship maneuvered into its berth, Cissy spotted the tall figure of her father as he strode out to greet the captain. He had not yet seen her on deck. Ducking below she quickly arranged for her baggage to be off loaded before hastening to the lowering gangplank. She saw her father's face beam with delighted surprise before she was wrapped in a warm embrace, his laughter ringing in her ears.

"You never cease to amaze me, daughter of mine. Just this morning I was telling Evangeline how much I miss you. And just look. Now you are here. She is going to be as pleased as I am."

"How is she, father?"

"She seems to be doing well at the moment, despite the doctor's worries for her. But, lets not dwell on that. I want to hear all about what is happening in New Berne before we get home and Andy claims all of your attention. You will not believe what a big boy he is getting to be." Cissy smiled at the pride on her father's face. She was not jealous of her stepbrother. Her father loved her just as much, and she knew he was beyond proud of the job she was doing in New Berne.

"I need to talk to the captain and get my men started on loading the goods. Would you like to wait inside or walk along the quay?"

"It is so refreshing out, I think I will just walk a bit. Do you think you will be long?"

"Perhaps thirty minutes or so."

"No worry, father. I will be fine and I will see you back here then."

Cissy ambled off down the wharf towards Market Street savoring the bustle of the harbor that seemed to have only grown larger since the war. She was so enraptured by all of the activity that at first she did not hear the voice calling to her.

"Cissy! Wait up!"

Turning at the persistent shout, she saw Brandon hurrying her way. She was surprised that he had not long since departed the south to go back to his home in Philadelphia.

"Brandon! I cannot believe you are still here."

He grabbed both of her hands in his, "My God, Cissy. You are a feast for my eyes. I didn't think to ever see you again. Tell me you are here to stay."

"I am sorry, Brandon, but I only came for a short visit with my family. New Berne is my home now that I am running that branch of my father's business." Cissy smiled, "It is good to see you. I confess I have missed you."

"Ah, I can only hope you mean to rectify that for good!" Brandon stood back to look at her, "You look as lovely as ever. Do say you will allow me to see you while you are here. We have much to talk about."

"That would be nice." Cissy could but wonder what her father would think if Brandon should knock on their door. Was he still as intransigent about a Yankee suitor for his daughter?

As though Brandon heard her thoughts, he commented, "I have made it a point to get to know your father through business. I think he will not find me so objectionable a suitor as previously. At least I hope that is the case, as I have never stopped thinking about and wanting his daughter for me."

"And how did you do that, Brandon?"

"I used my inheritance to buy shares in The Bank of North

Carolina and am now Vice President. I did a good bit of business with Alexander MacRae who died recently. He was a good friend of your father's. Did you know he lived near your father at 420 Orange Street? We all dined together on several occasions. He nicely coerced both your father and me into making sizeable donations to Thalian Hall."

"You have been busy. I'm not surprised that you contributed to Thalian as I remember how much you enjoyed the performance we attended there." Cissy paused, "I have no letter from you in so long, I confess I thought you had long since forgotten all about me."

"That, Miss LaRoque, is far harder to do than I ever thought possible. And, yes, I did ever more try. By immersing myself in business and seeing other ladies, I hoped to forget about you. Sad to say, it has been to no avail. There is just not another Cissy out there, and not another woman for me."

"You flatter me, Brandon."

"No, Cissy. As usual I bare my heart to you. I hope you will give me another chance to win your hand." Brandon lifted the hand he still held to his lips and kissed it. "I am so happy you are here."

"So am I. I never thought I would miss Wilmington, but I have. I missed my family and yes, I have missed you, as well. New Berne has been very lonely at times."

"That I shall do my best to remedy."

Chapter 21

Denice's eyes narrowed in thoughtful conjecture as she stood at her bedroom window watching Marcel leave her chateau. While she enjoyed him for a lover, she suspected for once she had taken on a far bigger problem than ever before. She could see through his suave veneer to the ruthless man beneath and while she would regret losing his skillful services as a lover, it might be time to cut him loose. Unless she was mistaken in the interpretation of his calculated comments, he fully intended to rid himself of his wife and the child that he claimed was a bastard. His proclamations of love did not persuade her. Marcel loved the thought of her purse far more than the pleasures of her body she, suspected. He had tried hard to hide the roving eye he cast around her sumptuous abode. But she had caught his assessing appraisal on more than one occasion. She chuckled. He wasn't the first lothario to come her way as a result of her wealth. She was vain enough to consider herself more than attractive despite being past the first blush of youth and she was skilled at pleasing a man, but too often of late she suspected those were not her first attributes.

It would take some careful planning to disengage herself without arousing his hostility. If Marcel thought he would embroil her in his nefarious scheme to kill his wife and child, he was sadly mistaken. She surmised he could become a danger to her, as well, now that he had hinted to her about his plans for the future if he suspected her of telling his wife of his plans.

Denice walked to her desk and picked up her pen. Chewing the tip, she thought for long moments before beginning to write a letter. That done she called her maid and gave specific instructions for it delivery. God forbid it should be intercepted by any but the addressee.

Adelaide was sitting in the garden enjoying a cup of tea and the springtime color of newly blooming flowers. Her sons were on a blanket at her feet reveling in the warm sun. The soft breeze rustled the new spring leaves overhead and filled her with a sense of peace. She treasured the fleeting sense of well-being. All to often of late, her husband had made her uneasy. It was nothing that he had said but rather the way he studied her. Once she had asked him about it, only to be shrugged off. Recently she had experienced several falls, always when he was near. She suspected he was leaving things where he knew she walked and would trip on them. The last near miss had been when she tripped on a glass ball laying at the top of the marble staircase, but she managed to catch her balance before pitching forward. The first time there had been grease on the top step. Had she not caught herself on the banister as she fell, it would have been fatal. As it was, she suffered from bruises and soreness for days afterward. The servants all swore that the steps had been newly cleaned and could not explain the grease nor the small glass ball. Whatever he was up to, her husband left her more and more alone. She could only assume that the countess was occupying his time and assuaging his passions. Lost in reverie she did not at first hear the quiet footsteps that sounded by the gate that opened into a wooded verge.

She startled when a soft voice, inquired, "Are you Madame Lambert?"

Twisting around she looked up at a seamed face now wrinkled with nervous apprehension. "Yes, I am. May I help you?"

"My lady asked me to give you this letter with her best wishes. She says it is very important and very private."

"And who is your employer, please?"

"I would rather not say, Madame." The woman bobbed a brief curtsey before scurrying back the way she had come leaving a puzzled Adelaide to stare after her.

Hearing Marcel walk her way, she quickly slipped the letter into her pocket to read later. She could only surmise that whoever had sent it did not mean for her to share the contents with her husband. As she watched him come near, she felt a shudder run through her. She wondered when she had come to fear her husband.

"Enjoying the weather, I see." His smile was cold when he remarked, "I thought the nurse could watch the children while we go for a ride. The countryside is particularly lovely this time of year."

She did not understand why he kept hounding her to go riding with him. He knew full well that she was unsure of herself on horseback, particularly after the last excursion when someone had placed a sharp metal spike under her saddle. As they were riding, with Marcel well in advance, the horse had reared and thrown her to the ground. She had rolled to the side just in time to avoid the horse's murderous hooves. Again, no one could explain why the spur had been there. A chill tremor went down her spine as she wondered what he might have planned this time. She struggled to keep her face impassive as she replied, "I am sure it is, but I have correspondence from home to reply to this afternoon. Perhaps, tomorrow."

Marcel gritted his teeth before forcing himself to relax. What would another day matter after all? Sooner or later the bitch would meet her end. If not an accident today, something could always be arrange for tomorrow. After that the boy would meet his own tragic demise. "Well then, I shall not detain you further. Do enjoy your day."

"Will you be here for dinner? I have enjoyed your company most rarely of late."

Marcel paused to consider his reply. It was better to lull her into thinking he was happy with her than to arouse other emotions. "I do apologize, my dear. Yes, I'll make it a point to return by then. Have the cook make us something lovely."

"Of course. Have a pleasant ride."

Marcel turned to leave, before whirling back to add, "If you are writing your father you might inquire as to why we have been forwarded no funds since our arrival. My bank assures me there should have been no problem with transmittal. The money I wired here is running dangerously low."

"I'm sorry. I will remind him that we need a wire immediately."

"See that you stress that." He mused as he walked towards the stable to fetch his horse. It was just as well he had left her to write that letter. Once she was gone, her father might prove more difficult to squeeze for funds.

Adelaide waited another ten minutes after he left before pulling the strange missive from her pocket. Unsealing the envelope she extracted a single sheet of fine quality linen stationery. She glanced up at a squeal from the baby and assured that he was fine, she unfolded the paper. When she did so, a small packet sealed with wax fell into her lap. Setting it aside, she began to read:

"As another woman I can understand the fears you might feel when confronted with someone who would be happier were he freed of the encumbrance of a wife. Such a man is capable of much evil. Perhaps, I am unduly pessimistic. If so, please forgive my intrusion into your personal affairs and I beg you to destroy this letter immediately in any event, for both your protection and mine. I have been remiss in welcoming you to our community and as a token of my esteem for you I have enclosed the seeds of the Monkshood plant that is noted for its lovely dark blue spikes of flowers. You must exercise great care when handling the seeds, as they are highly poisonous. Indeed as a poison in past times they were ground up and put into food. Death for those who consumed it was certain and fast. Even taking note of this fact, you might find them advantageous for your garden. I would suggest planting immediately as it might well prove

too late should you wait."

Adelaide held the letter at arms-length contemplating it as though some secret motive would emerge. She then picked up the packet of seeds with great care, not daring to open it for fear she would be poisoned on contact. Putting the seeds down, she began to read the letter again. The implications of what she was reading caused shivers to run up and down her spine. Again she read the letter pausing over each sentence. Even though it was unsigned, only one woman could have written this with any sure knowledge of the state of her marriage. Marcel must have told her of his plans for the future, a future without his current wife. Adelaide picked up the packet of seeds. She wondered if she dared use them. But, with her life and that of her first born hanging in the balance, did she have any real choice?

She called the nanny to help her gather things and get the children back to the nursery for naptime. As she returned to the house, she touched the pocket that held the dangerous seeds. If she was interpreting the letter correctly, she had no time to lose. Squaring her shoulders with her mouth set in a grim line, she instructed the nanny to take the children. She would see them later. First, she was going to bake Marcel's favorite cake.

The cook looked up in surprise when Adelaide entered the kitchen. Using her limited French she explained that she wished to make her husband's evening dessert. Marie shrugged her shoulders with unconcern and directed Adelaide to the various things she needed before continuing with her own preparations. The two women worked in companionable silence each focused on their own tasks. Carefully Adelaide mixed the small cake that Marcel had come to love in San Francisco. For once she was grateful that her mother had insisted she learn to cook. When Marie went to the larder to procure needed ingredients for her own preparations, Adelaide shoved the letter into the stove before taking the mortar and pestle from the cupboard. Dumping in the seeds, she carefully ground them into a powder. That done, she added it to the batter and then thoroughly washed the mortar and pestle before returning them. Soon the cake was baking in the oven.

While she waited for it to be done, Adelaide joined Marie for a cup of tea and an attempt at conversation. She decided at that moment that she would become fluent in French. In the future she would make her home on two continents. One son would be the heir to an illustrious old French title, and the other would inherit New World wealth. As for herself, she was disillusioned of men. She wasn't sure that she ever wanted another husband. Lovers she had had before marriage and could have again. With her wealth and Marcel's family titles and property, she would secure a station for herself and her sons. For a moment she felt sad that she would be the cause of another's death. However, when she considered that her own life and Bernard's would end if his did not, she put her trepidation aside.

When the cake was done, she carefully put it on a plate and announce that she would take it up to the dining room for serving after dinner asking only that Marie provide a small bowl of berries and whipped cream to serve alongside. Marie, busy with her own chores, merely nodded and waved Adelaide on her way.

As Adelaide placed the cake on the sideboard in the dining room, Marcel was storming about the courtyard in Denice's chateau. He was furious that she had instructed the butler to tell him she was away. The bitch should have waited on him before going out since she knew he tried to come around this time each day. Slapping his riding crop against his thigh, he was so irate he barely noticed the sting. Since he had made his plans for a future with her known, surely she would not suddenly spurn him? She had already told him how much she enjoyed their lovemaking. He was vain enough to think she was enamored of him and for once he had lowered his own guard and feared that he was in love with her. Of course, her wealth helped. Her beauty helped. But, Adelaide had both beauty and wealth and he had never loved her. There was some illusive quality in Denice that had drawn him in like a moth to a candle. Remounting his horse, he resolved to canter into the village. Perhaps he would run into her there. Suddenly he was desperate to see her.

Denice looked down from her window as he galloped off, peering from behind the drapery in case he looked back. She wondered what the evening would bring. Had her letter, despite the veiled nature of it, set things in motion? She could only hope that Adelaide had the presence of mind to destroy it. Neither woman could afford for it to be found had the import been perceived. And, had it not, it might well be a death warrant for her were Marcel to find it.

Marcel arrived home in a foul mood. After not finding Denise at home, he had galloped up and down the streets of the village to no avail before trying once more at her home, only to be told that she was still out. He rode home like someone with the devil on his tail. At the stable behind his mansion, he tossed the reins of his horse to the stable lad and stormed into the house. Tossing back a second brandy as he sat brooding in his library, he did not at first notice Adelaide in the doorway.

"I hope I'm not interrupting, Marcel. Supper is ready and I would like you to join me."

Marcel glanced up at his wife and snarled, "Couldn't you find a dress that fits you. I swear you are as big as a cow after having this second brat."

"I am still trying to lose the weight I gained. It just takes time to return to my former figure." Adelaide kept her voice even. She was furious with him but could not afford for him to suspect anything. She had deliberately chosen the dress as it had always been a tight fit, and after childbirth, noticeably so. She now had the excuse she needed not to indulge in dessert.

"The children have had their supper in the nursery. I thought we might enjoy a nice dinner with champagne. The cook has gone to a lot of trouble to make your favorites, including your favorite gateau."

"Wonderful." Marcel forced a smile. He might as well sweeten up the bitch, as he was still sexually frustrated from the afternoon. He had no compunction about having sex with her tonight and murdering her tomorrow. After all, she was just another female body. "Shall we?"

Adelaide took his proffered arm. In the dining room she noted that the flowers on the table had been freshly arranged, an epergne holding champagne waited at Marcel's place, and dinner was steaming on the sideboard. Oscar who had been elevated to butler hurriedly assisted her into her chair and then Marcel. At Marcel's nod, he served the dinner, poured two glasses of champagne and excused himself. Marcel lifted the champagne glass and said, "To a bright future filled with all of the things I have dreamed of."

"I can drink to that, "to a bright future filled with all of the things that *I have dreamed of.*"

"Touché."

The coq au vin was cooked to perfection and the freshly baked bread delicious with it. Marcel relished his meal. When he was finished he signaled Oscar who was waiting discreetly in the background. "The gateau, please."

"None for me, Oscar; just some berries. As you noted, Marcel, I do need to watch my diet until I lose a little weight. After all, I would not want my figure to be displeasing to you."

"As you wish." Marcel dug into the large piece of cake with gusto. He sighed with pleasure, "This is delicious. It has a slightly different taste from the usual, but I like it."

"I am so glad. I actually made it for you as I know how much you love it."

"Thank you. That was thoughtful of you."

"Yes, I thought quite a long time about what to serve you tonight." Adelaide replied cryptically. She had also added honey and extra sugar and more cinnamon in order to hide whatever the taste of the seeds might be. At least he liked the gateau enough that he was quickly finishing the last of it so she would not have to worry about hiding the remainder so no one else could eat it. Pushing his dessert plate away, he ordered coffee for the two of them.

Adelaide watched his face closely, not sure what she was looking for as she had no idea how the poison worked. Carefully she stirred sugar into her coffee and waited. He had not taken more than two sips of his own beverage, when he shook his head as though to clear it. "I must have overeaten."

He pushed the coffee away and leaned back in his chair. "I don't feel well. My heart is palpitating and I feel strange.... I don't know."

"Shall I summon a doctor, Marcel?"

"We'll see. Hopefully it will pass. Perhaps I should go up to bed."

Adelaide hastened to his chair and helped him rise. "Let's get you upstairs." She shook her head at the butler who stood anxiously by in case his assistance was needed. "I'm sure you will be fine in the morning. You probably just ate too much of the cake."

Adelaide helped Marcel shed his clothes and climb into bed. Tucking the covers around him, she inquired, "Is there anything more I can get you?"

"A basin. I feel as though I'm going to be sick. I really should not have had that second slice of cake.

"No, doubt." Adelaide fetched the basin from his bureau and then pulled a chair to his beside. "I'll sit here with you for a minute or so just in case."

Marcel groaned and clutched his belly, "My God, I hurt." When the spasm passed, he fell back against his pillow. He worked his mouth as though he was having trouble speaking. Adelaide watched intently to see what would happen next. Continuous spasms gripped his intestines causing him to heave into the basin several times. After an hour, it was obvious that he could no longer form words. He was groaning almost continuously and writhing in pain.

For a moment she felt great remorse, certain that she would suffer in hell for the grievous sin she had committed. Then she remembered what had brought her to this point. Looking him in the eye, she could see that he was still somewhat lucid. Slowly she began to speak. "I know you wanted me and Bernard dead. I know that had I waited we would be. Remember on our wedding night you warned me never to underestimate you? I replied that you should never underestimate me either. You should have listened, Marcel. You really should have. You were too arrogant and sure of yourself to think that someone else would see through you and thwart your evil intentions. I never underestimated you as you did me. And that, husband, was your undoing."

Marcel's eyes went wide with fear. Struggling he tried to sit up and call for help, but could not. Frantically he clawed at the covers. Adelaide shook her head, "It's too late. There is no help for you here."

She disposed of the contents of the basin in the water closet, cleaned up the room and arranged his clothes neatly. Looking around, she was satisfied that it would look as normal as any other night. She left his room and crossed into the adjoining dressing room, donned her nightclothes and climbed into her own bed. Morning would bring a different era into her life and hopefully a brighter one. Looking back she regretted the shallowness in her character that had led her to choose someone like Marcel. She regretted the duplicity inherent in her marriage and she regretted that it had come to this kind of an end. The only thing that she rejoiced in was her children despite having arrived late to an appreciation of motherhood. It was a sad and introspective woman that finally fell into fitful sleep.

Adelaide slept late. It was not until she heard a discreet knock at the door that she sat up and gave permission for entry. She looked up as Sally entered, careful to keep her features relaxed. "Forgive me ma'am, for intruding, but Oscar asked me to tell you that he thinks the mister is unwell."

"Really," Adelaide feigned surprise. "He seemed fine at bedtime once he rid himself of an excess of dessert." Tossing back the covers, she strolled over to her wardrobe to select a dress.

"I don't mean to rush you ma'am, but Oscar said you should hurry. Perhaps, you could just put on your dressing gown."

"My goodness, Sally. Now you alarm me." Grabbing her robe, she hurriedly tied the sash and slid her feet in her slippers. Following Sally through the dressing room, she reached Marcel's bedside. Oscar was bending over him and feeling for a pulse.

"What's seems to be the trouble, Oscar? Is my husband not well?"

"Ma'am, I'm sorry to tell you this but I think Mr. Lambert is dead."

"No! That's impossible. When I left him he said he was fine. He thought he had eaten too much, but once he vomited that eased him."

"Perhaps it was his heart," Oscar offered. "I heard him say in the dining room that it felt funny."

"Oh, I had forgotten that. Poor, poor darling. I should have called the doctor. I blame myself that I did not."

"These things can't be helped ma'am." Oscar shook his head, "I don't know what the procedure is here. Should we send for the doctor or the police?"

Looking at Marcel's still face, she felt overwhelming sadness. Tears welled in her eyes. Her voice barely audible, she said, "I don't know either. We must summons both, I think."

Adelaide returned to her room and selected the dullest dress she possessed and even it was unsuitable for mourning. "Sally, you must send for the modiste immediately. I'm going to need mourning clothes, and if she has something suitable ready-made, a dress for the funeral."

"Yes, ma'am. I just want to say I'm real sorry. It ain't easy to lose a husband. And with us foreigners here, I just don't know what is to become of us."

"Sally, nothing has changed. This is my home as well as the one in San Francisco. I will hire someone to help me with legalities and sorting things out. We are going to carry on as normal. To do otherwise will only make this more painful for us all. Fortunately, the babies are too young to understand what has happened. Furthermore, I have no intentions of abandoning this house, rather I shall make my home now in both worlds."

The rest of the day went by in a fog. The doctor and police inspector had come and gone, ruling the death a heart attack. The undertaker had removed the body to prepare for burial. The priest had consulted with her and together they had walked in the cemetery to stand by his parents' crypt. They decided Marcel would lie next to his father. She had agreed for the priest to hire professional mourners...something that she had never confronted before. She had telegraphed the cousin whose name she found in Marcel's office to notify him of the death and funeral. Her modiste had hastily modified a dress to fit her, along with a hat draped with yards of black tulle. The local gazette had interviewed her for an obituary, which they supplemented with information compiled on his family through the years. By evening, she was exhausted.

After a light supper and a hot soak in her tub, the new widow kissed her babies goodnight and crawled into bed. Tomorrow she would welcome his cousin, Pierre Lambert, as overnight guest, and entertain the few mourners at a meal following the graveside service. Then she would take time to determine her immediate future. She had already written her parents to tell them of Marcel's death and to ask that funds be sent immediately until she could gain access to his accounts in Melun. The family attorney would need to finalize Marcel's estate in San Francisco and place those funds in her account and arrange for management of any properties that it was prudent to hold onto for future increase in value. Until she could hire a local man of affairs to finalize Marcel's French properties, there was little she could do with her limited French and ignorance of French laws regarding inheritance. Somehow she would find a way to ensure that the younger boy and the true heir would be able to inherit the title and estate in France. Bertrand would be more than wealthy through her father's estate at his demise. In a way, it was her atonement to Marcel for what she had done. Perhaps, it would earn her some small measure of peace that she had done the right thing for the new Marquis de Rochefort.

Bertrand was an elegant man bearing a marked resemblance to her late husband. There the likenesses ended, as he was genial and charming with a welcome openness of character. Adelaide took an immediate liking to him and the two chatted as she walked him to his room to change clothes, now dusty from the road, prior to the early afternoon funeral service. He descended an hour later looking much refreshed.

They settled in the parlor for a few moments together. She could not help noticing the appreciative glances he cast her way. Before they left for the service, Pierre offered to settle the estate for her and procure a prompt transfer of funds at the bank into an account in her name allaying a major portion of her immediate worries. Thinking long and hard during the night, she had devised a ruse that she hoped the servants would not inadvertently reveal. She would simply switch the names of the two children when she introduced them insuring that the title would go to the correct son. Once Pierre had it on paper she would no longer worry. As babies with only a year between them, it would not be long before they were of a similar size, particularly since Marcel Frederique gave every indication of being a taller and larger framed child than Bernard. She would return to San Francisco for a few months once Pierre had everything sorted out. In the meantime, she would keep the children out of the public eye.

Following the funeral service, Adelaide was turning to leave when she noticed a heavily veiled, black clad figure standing some distance from the small group around Marcel's crypt.

Adelaide walked over and squeezed the woman's hand, "Comtesse, I would be honored to have you join us for a repast and to introduce you to Marcel's cousin Pierre. Under the circumstances, it seems only fitting that you join us."

"I do not mean to intrude. I wished only to pay my respects and ascertain your well-being."

"Nonsense. It's no intrusion. I fear I have not been a good neighbor and hope that we can remedy that."

"I have not always been your friend, but I would like to be. We have much in common, I suspect."

"No doubt. Let's pretend we have only just met and agree that the past is laid to rest."

Denice murmured softly so no one else could hear, "So to speak."

The co-conspirators smiled as they walked arm in arm to the small group of family and local dignitaries.

As Pierre was leaving the following day, he took her hand in his and squeezing it gently, said, "I look forward to getting to know you far better, Adelaide. I will need to visit from time to time as I conduct the necessary transactions."

Adelaide returned his smile. "That will be lovely, Pierre. And of course, you must stay here."

She stood watching him drive away in his coach, the

beautifully renovated mansion an elegant backdrop for her figure. At the end of the estate, the coach came to a halt. She was surprised to see him step from the coach and wave goodbye to her before climbing back in and signaling the coachman to continue. She could not help but hug herself with delight. This genuinely charming Frenchman held unexpected possibilities for her life.

Chapter 22

Sitting on the porch with Evangeline, Cissy enjoyed looking out at the moss draped live oak trees that shaded the backyard. A pleasant breeze wafted stray ends of her hair as they rocked in wicker chairs turned to catch the rays of sun. It felt good after winter to see the tender new leaves and brave flower buds unfurling in the light. Andy was sitting in her lap enjoying a cuddle as much as she was enjoying giving it. Graham had gone to work at the office and she had promised to go in later to catch up with what was happening in the Wilmington branch of the business and tell her father about the New Berne office. The previous evening had been devoted to local happenings and the sharing of details of personal events. Today they were just enjoying the quiet morning, but Cissy was not as relaxed as she appeared. She wanted to broach the idea of having Brandon call on her but hesitated to raise a subject that might still garner her father's ire and upset Evangeline.

Glancing at her stepmother, she coached her voice to calm indifference when she inquired, "Has my father softened his views on the Yankees that have begun to work their way into local businesses?"

"The less than flattering term is carpetbaggers. The Union sympathizing scallywags are almost as reviled." Evangeline shrugged, "There's still a lot of frustration as a result of the war and occupation. At this point, due to the influx from the countryside, the colored population of the city is almost eight thousand while whites number less than six thousand. Far too many of the blacks are unemployed which creates great poverty and greater problems. Most of them are crowded into the area south of here, the one called Dry Pond. Even though we were never slave owners, we cannot help but feel that the freed slaves are ill prepared for their freedom. The Freedmen's Bureau and the Republican Party are pretty much controlling things and trying to help them. You may have heard of the mulatto, James Sampson, the free black who became wealthy through his carpentry business. His children were all educated up north and one son is now working with the Bureau. The northerners are promoting political activity by blacks that they seek to control. We are fortunate that we are in the second military district under control of Major General Daniel Sickles. He was a New York attorney noted prior to the war for defending the rights of southern states to secede. He is more sympathetic to the southern plight than many, so Graham suspects he will not last much longer as Washington politics are pretty much against us."

"Things are pretty much in the same fix in New Berne except the city is recovering much more slowly. Fortunately for us, shipping has never been better." Cissy paused to prepare her words, "I ran into the Union officer I met before I left to go to New Berne. He tells me he has done some business with father and is part owner of a bank here."

Andy wriggled from Cissy's lap. He was bored with their conversation and looking for more interesting diversions. Smiling, Cissy watched him walk to the edge of the piazza and jump onto the grassy area beneath.

"Yes, I think I recall Graham mentioning him a time or two." Evangeline cut her eyes at Cissy, "Are you thinking of seeing him socially, then?"

Cissy bit her lip telling Evangeline all she needed to know. "I suggest you tread lightly on that subject around your father as I am unsure what his reaction will be. He has softened as a result of commercial interaction, but I don't know how much. I know he invested in the Wilmington and Manchester Railroad along with your officer friend. Graham thinks it is a great advantage to have interest in a railroad to move the goods he imports inland. The line runs all the way to Camden, SC, and allows us to compete with the port in Charleston."

"I wish I had rail access other than the Atlantic and North Carolina Railroad to Goldsboro and Beaufort. It was badly damaged during the war and still is not fully repaired. I suspect it is on the verge of bankruptcy. Has father thought about buying shares in it and getting it repaired and extended? I think I may talk to him about it."

"He has pretty much left things there up to you, hasn't he? So, I have not heard him mention it. Lately he has been working pretty much exclusively on developing a market for our local rice in Brazil for the ship you have working that route."

"That's wonderful. If we can develop more goods to trade there, I think we will soon have enough to justify buying another ship for the Brazilian trade. Papa and I are going to walk back to the office together after dinner so I will mention it to him then."

Evangeline chuckled, "You are a wonder, you know? Your father was shocked at first that you were doing so well. Now he is so proud and so amazed. I'm happy, too. I'm proud of you, but I am also relieved that you can take some of the burden from Graham."

"Andy! Stop that. That's a nasty bug you're holding."

"But, Cissy. I think it's funny."

"Your brother doesn't seem to have our squeamishness about insects and such. I cannot tell you all of the little surprises he has brought me." Evangeline glanced fondly at her son, "Run inside and wash your hands, Andy. Your father should be here any minute for dinner."

Cissy followed Evangeline and her brother into the house. When Andy dashed off to clean up, Cissy said, "Evangeline, is my father not doing well? When you said that you are relieved to have me take on some of the burden, I wasn't sure if you were implying that he might be ailing."

"Oh goodness me. I am so sorry if I gave that impression. He's not as young as he thinks he is, but he's in fine health."

"And what about you? I have no personal knowledge, of course, but carrying a child must not be so easy." She caught herself before adding at your age.

"I'm fine. I just tire more easily now. It's good to have you here to entertain Andy. Sometimes his exuberant energy is more than I can handle. I suppose we are a tad long in the tooth to be beginning a family, but we both feel as though we have a new chance at life. After losing my first husband and child, I never dared hope to have a family again and one that I love so much. Sometimes it seems like a dream and I will wake up to find that I am alone once more."

"Never. You have us now and we all love you so much. You are, in truth, the only real mother I have ever known."

"I remember the first time I ever saw you. You were the saddest, most mature little girl, and so very charming. I think I loved you from that first moment."

"I was only seven but I remember. I was glad when my mother left to live in France and I could spend as much time with you as I liked. I especially recall the fun we had painting together. Do you still paint?"

"I confess I have not had the time or energy lately, but your father has promised to fix the spare room up so I will have a studio. Perhaps, after this new little one is born, I will have the time again in a year or so."

"I love your paintings too much to want you to stop. I just wish I were half as good. I think you should find a good nurse to relieve you of the constant daily care of two children. It would give you time to paint and it would not be such a continuous drain on your energy."

"I hate to give my babies over to someone else, but you may

be right. I know Graham is constantly after me about it. He worries over me like an old clucking hen."

"I think he would rather be compared to a rooster." Both women were laughing when Graham came into the house.

"Now, that is what I like to come home to: a happy family." Graham took each by the arm and led them into the dining room. They arrived at the table just as Andy came tearing into the room. "Goodness, son. The food is not going to vanish before you get a chance at it, so slow down."

Andy hung his head, "Yes, sir."

"No moping now, I've got a surprise for you."

"You do?" Andy's eyes grew as big as saucers.

"I do." Graham waved them all to their seats without offering edification. He took his own seat and then carefully spread his napkin in his lap. Andy followed suit but was fidgeting for all he was worth.

"But, papa, you didn't tell me my surprise."

"I didn't? Oh well, it will keep until after dinner."

Evangeline glanced at her crestfallen son and took pity. "We are all curious now, Graham. You mustn't keep us in suspense any longer or we won't be able to eat a thing."

Graham grinned at his son, "Very well, I see you cannot wait until after a hungry man has eaten. You, my boy, are going with me on a train ride all the way to Camden in South Carolina."

"When, Papa? Can we go today?"

"Not today, but tomorrow. Would you ladies care to ride along? It will be an overnight stay. I will be somewhat occupied as I must call on some of the gentlemen I am trying to persuade to use our port rather than the Charleston port."

Evangeline reached over and laid her hand on her husband's, "Thank you for the offer but I will defer until another time. Cissy, what about you? Will you go since you also are interested in the railroad venture?"

"I think I would prefer to stay with you so you will not be here alone."

"That's settled then, though I must confess I will miss having my favorite ladies along." Graham winked at Andy, "I guess we men will just have to fend for ourselves."

When Cissy and her father arrived at the warehouse after their midday meal another ship had just arrived and *The Intrepid* was readying for departure, leaving no time for discussions of his feelings about her seeing a former Union officer. Even her interest in the business buying into the railroad serving New Berne was touched on only briefly.

Graham and Andy left the house long before she arose the following morning. When both she and Evangeline were dressed and had breakfasted, Cissy suggested a shopping excursion. Her wardrobe had not been replenished since well before the war and she was tired of cutting down her mother's old clothes to resemble something currently in fashion. Excited at the prospect of a day with Cissy, Evangeline was happy to go along. They spent the morning wandering among the shops where Cissy was able to buy new camisoles, shoes, a parasol, a reticule, and several bolts of fabric with ribbons and lace to match. A particularly fetching bonnet caught their eyes just as they were preparing to leave the last shop.

"You must have that, Cissy. The color is perfect for your eyes and will go beautifully with the emerald silk you just bought."

"It is lovely, but I fear I have spent far too much already. I want another ship and an interest in the railroad far more than any bonnet."

"Good Lord, Cissy. That is a sacrilege. Don't let a soul hear you say something like that or they will all think you have deserted the ranks of proud womanhood." Evangeline laughed at the look on Cissy's face. "Don't worry, I will buy it for you. I have been wanting to buy you something special so this is it."

"Please, you don't need to do that. I have other bonnets."

"I know I don't need to; I want to."

Cissy hugged her stepmother, "I love it. I do want it so very much. And you are right. It is perfect with the fabric."

Dividing the parcels between them, the two women emerged onto Water Street blinking in the bright midday sun that reflected dancing ripples on the facades of the shops lining the water. Encumbered by the packages, Cissy could not see where she was walking and tripped on one of the cobbles in the street, dropping several of the boxes as she caught herself. Both women were so busy picking them up, that they did not notice the man that had walked up to them until they straightened. Evangeline was the first to speak.

"Colonel Madison. How wonderful to see you again. I have always wanted the opportunity to thank you for all you did for us before the war. Not only sending the food we so desperately needed, but making sure my home was unharmed after your troops occupied it."

Ryan smiled, "I am always at the service of beautiful ladies and it looks as though you could use a bit of help right now. Let me have some of those packages. And Cissy, close your mouth before the flies make a home."

Cissy's mouth snapped shut in irritation at his observation. "If it's open it is because I'm just surprised to see you here. I had not idea you were planning a trip to Wilmington."

Ryan's face immediately sobered, "I commissioned a special memorial sculpture for my wife and daughter's tombs. I came to pay for it and take it back to New Berne. I only learned yesterday that it is finished."

Evangeline grasped his hand in both of hers, "Oh, Colonel Madison, my most heartfelt sympathies in your loss. I lost my first husband and child many years ago, but it still hurts despite having moved on with my life. I truly do share your pain."

Ryan's eyes were damp with unshed tears. Not trusting his

voice, he merely nodded.

"We were just thinking of having a meal at the hotel. My husband and son are away at the moment, so we allowed the cook to take some time off. Won't you please join us?"

"Cissy?" Ryan raised his eyebrows in query.

"Of course, please do."

Cissy blushed and was flustered for having done so. The last thing she wanted was for Evangeline to think she was chasing the new widower. And with rumors rampant that Lizzie was once again doing her utmost to rope him in, she had no desire to pursue him despite the flutter he caused every time he was near. That did not mean that her yearning for him had lessened, only that she refused to compete with a woman that she held in deep contempt. If he wanted Lizzie, he was not a man that she wanted. She was happy to listen as Evangeline talked to Ryan. Her stepmother's gratitude was so great for all he had done for her during the war, that her warmth created a corresponding and apparent appreciation in Ryan.

Cissy studied him under her lowered lids. He had aged in the recent months and it showed in the harsher lines around his mouth and across his brow. Silver threads were sprinkled throughout his hair. It made her sad to see the evidence of his suffering. Looking up she caught him watching her as well.

Cissy wasted no time diverting her gaze to Evangeline, but Ryan was not to be deflected. "You look lovely today, Cissy. That color is very becoming to you."

"Thank you. This is one of my mother's Parisian dresses from years ago that I had made over for me. I confess I like it, too."

"Oh, Cissy, I had no idea that you had some of your mother's dresses. That must be of some comfort to you," Evangeline exclaimed.

Cissy cast Evangeline a wry look, "Considering the situation with my mother, I have to admit that there is nothing sentimental about using her dresses that were left behind. It was a matter of pragmatism and the unavailability of any quality goods for such a long time that my wardrobe was either worn out, faded out, or I was jaded out from wearing everything too often. Annie and I were churning in the attic and discovered a trunk full of clothes. One dress we cut down for Annie's wedding gown and it was perfect for her."

"It's good that lovely things do not go to waste and ruin from years of neglect. I'm glad you found them and used them."

Ryan wanted to ask about her mother, but gathering from Cissy's tone of voice and expression when she had first commented on the dress, he decided to leave it alone for the time being. However, he would ask Caroline when he returned to New Berne. He suspected there was a story there that would give him insight into Cissy's character.

Hoping to lighten the conversation, he commented to Evangeline, "My son Rye is smitten with Cissy. He is eating all of his vegetables at the moment as I managed to convince him he would grow up quicker and be able to propose once he is a little bigger. I'm not sure what I will do once he figures out that the growing is a little slow for his liking." Ryan laughed, "He is threatening to march over to your house, Cissy, and propose right away for fear someone else beats him to it."

Evangeline laughed. Teasingly she said, "I wish he would. I have been telling her it's time she married."

Ryan chortled, "I think half of New Berne speculates on that."

"Both of you stop teasing me. I am far too busy at the moment to consider a beau, much less a proposal." Cissy carefully plopped a sautéed shrimp into her mouth and chewed appreciatively. The whole conversation was making her more than a little uncomfortable. "The food here is surprisingly good, Evangeline. It makes me glad the cook took some time off."

"Reesie has her moments, but admittedly her fare is not gourmet." Evangeline turned to Ryan. "Will you be in town long?"

"Another day or two at the most. I want to consult with the military commander here about the applicability of North Carolina law to a new case of mine and I still have to arrange delivery of the monument."

"I know Graham would like to meet you and thank you for helping us during the war. I fear I might well have lost Andy were it not for the nourishment you provided and the doctor you sent to treat me. Our son is growing like a weed and thinks himself all grown up. If you are still in town, please join us for supper."

"I would be delighted."

"Wonderful. Let me give you the address and we will see you at seven."

Ryan chuckled and with tongue in cheek, commented, "That won't be necessary. I know the house. It is quite remarkable for the linens decorating the exterior from time to time."

Evangeline looked puzzled. "I'm sorry. I don't think I follow you?"

Remembering the sheet left dangling from the window the day she had run into Ryan, Cissy could not stop the giggle that erupted. "Don't worry. I will explain later."

Ryan was laughing when he saw a fellow soldier approaching. Standing he reached out to shake hands. "Brandon, it is good to see you again. Allow me to introduce you to my lovely dining companions."

Despite struggling to hide the expression on his face, Ryan could see Brandon's jealousy. The timbre of his voice when he replied clued Ryan into the fact that the man resented that he was the one dining with Cissy. Ryan could not quell the rising antagonism he felt at the idea of someone seriously courting her. He didn't want to even explore why, but it was enough to make him bristle in return.

"I have had the pleasure, thank you. Ladies, it is good to see you both. Please excuse my intrusion." Brandon bowed stiffly and quickly walked away.

Evangeline shook her head, "Another disappointed beau I fear."

"Nonsense. He just an acquaintance that merely kept us from starving those last weeks before you and father returned from Nassau. Like Colonel Madison, not all Yankees are devils."

"Thank you for that. I recall a time or two when I distinctively thought you saw hooves and horns when you looked at me." Ryan smiled when she blushed at his words.

Wrinkling her nose, she exclaimed, "Well, I never mistook you for a saint either."

"Cissy, mind your manners. Colonel Madison, I do apologize."

"No offense taken. Miss Cissy and I have met on numerous occasions over the years and they have never failed to entertain me."

Chapter 23

The supper with her family went far better than Cissy had feared. Ryan was at his most charming and soon had her father laughing with delight at some of the stories of cases he had represented in court. The fact that during the war the man had helped those that he loved most played no small part in Graham's reception of the former Union officer. After Andy was bundled off to bed, Graham poured port for the two men and sherry for the ladies, while Evangeline played the pianoforte. Cissy looked up in stunned surprise when Ryan, standing behind Evangeline, joined her in singing. His rich baritone was a marvel. Soon she and her father were standing arm in arm listening to the two of them perform. When the song was finished both clapped heartily.

"What marvelous entertainment. This woman of mine never ceases to amaze me. And you, Colonel Madison, have a professional quality voice." Graham clapped Ryan on the back as he said it.

"Thank you, sir. The compliment is appreciated but much too generous." Ryan smiled, "Now, I fear I must take my leave. Thank you so much for your hospitality and the nicest evening I have had in months. I confess I was much in need of such conviviality. If you should find yourselves in New Berne, please allow me to reciprocate."

"With a little one soon to arrive, my wife and I are pretty much tied to home at the moment. When the baby is old enough that we can travel, I am sure we will be coming your way. I want to see what wonders Cissy has accomplished since my last visit." Graham turned to Cissy, "That reminds me. We need to talk. As much as we would all love a prolonged visit, I suspect that regrettably you may need to return to New Berne fairly soon."

Puzzled, Cissy glanced at her father, "Of course."

"Perhaps you would like to take the train with me day after tomorrow. It is much better that you travel with someone than alone, and I confess I would love the company." Ryan looked at her expectantly as he awaited her reply.

Cissy blushed as she answered, "Thank you for the offer. I will talk with my father and let you know. Would that be agreeable?"

"Yes, indeed. Until then I will bid you all a goodnight and my thanks again for such a pleasant evening." Brandon's jealous face flashed across his mind causing him to turn to Cissy, "Perhaps, you would walk a short way with me?"

"Father?"

"That's fine. Just don't go far. I don't want you walking back alone for any distance."

Cissy grabbed a shawl from the coat tree in the foyer and tossed it around her shoulders. It was still a bit cool at night and with a breeze blowing from the river, she was glad for its warmth once they left the shelter of the house.

The streetlamps cast shadows from the trees that lined the quiet street. A full moon could be seen through the leafy canopy. From the nearby harbor, they could hear the soft clinking of ships riding at anchor. Cissy admired the elegant houses that lined the street, lamps glowing from lace draped windows. "It's a lovely night, isn't it?"

Ryan looked down at her, as she walked by his side, "Not as lovely as you are… I can understand why my son is so smitten."

Cissy laughed nervously, unsure of how to respond and how serious the implication of his words. "No doubt Rye will soon find another to admire."

"Since he saw you in a state of undress that he found most pleasant, I fear he has an indelible image that he is unlikely to forget for some time."

"Oh, my Lord." Cissy was shocked into silence.

Suddenly Ryan laughed and pulled her to face him, "It's time you turned back. I'll watch you until you reach home."

Without waiting for a response and before he could reconsider his actions, he wrapped his arms around her and settled his lips on hers in a gentle kiss that quickly became more demanding as she responded. Ryan was shocked at the intensity of feelings that assailed him in that moment. He would never stop loving Penny but something about Cissy made him reconsider whether or not he could love another. He had always been attracted to her, even before he met Penny, but she had been too young then. She was no longer the immature girl she had been when he first met her, but the spark he had felt then was now a blaze in his blood. Her reaction told him that she was not immune to him either. Part of him wanted to caress and take as much as she would give, but the saner portion of his anatomy cautioned him to take his time. Cissy would take cultivating and he needed to consider just how ready he was for another marriage so soon after losing his wife. For his son's sake, he wanted the boy to grow up with a loving woman to care for him, however, he knew himself too well to think he would ever marry for that reason alone. When he pulled back from the kiss, they were both rattled.

"I must say I have never been kissed like that before!" Cissy stammered. "I'm sorry. It's just that I am a bit surprised."

"So am I. Now you turn around and march home before I kiss you again and forget to stop." Ryan put his finger on her nose before gently turning her back towards her home. Softly he pleaded, "Ride home with me on the train, Cissy. I think we need to talk."

Ever sassy, she tossed over her shoulder as she turned to leave, "I must say you seem to say more without words than you do with them."

Ryan laughed, "Go home."

When she reached the door to her house, she turned to see him still standing under the streetlamp watching her. The light spread an aura about him that made him seem almost spectral. Bemused, she lifted her hand and waved goodbye. He waved in return before turning and walking into the shadows under the trees as he made his way back to his hotel. Cissy stood on the porch until he was long out of sight. She was reluctant to enter the house with that passionate kiss still on her lips and her face flushed with desire. She did not want to face her father for fear of what he might say. Although her father had been warm and hospitable to Ryan, he was still a Union officer. Since he rejected Brandon out of hand for his past affiliation, would he not do the same for Ryan despite the good he had done them during the war?

Riding beside Ryan two days later, Cissy watched the endless expanse of pine forests slide past the window of the train. While she was grateful for the pine products that formed a chunk of her export business, she could not help but be bored with the sameness of the landscape. As though he read her thoughts, Ryan commented, "It really is rather boring to see nothing but pine tree after pine tree."

"I was just thinking the same thing!"

"I am delighted you could come along and relieve the tedium." Ryan paused, "I hope it is not some emergency that caused your father to send you back so quickly?"

"Oh no, not at all. He is negotiating a deal to buy into a railroad for the Wilmington terminal that reaches to inland South Carolina so we can siphon off some of the trade that is now going into Charleston. I mentioned that it would help New Berne to have greater rail access as well, particularly to the north. He wants me to research that and if it's feasible, we'll line up partners to go in with us. I need to hire someone to survey possible routes to avoid as much swamp as possible and

I need to meet with our New Berne bankers. A couple of his investors in the railroad to Camden indicated they might be interested also."

"It's obvious your father has great respect for your business sense. While I don't know that much about the business you run in New Berne, everyone I have run into gives you accolades. Some of them a bit grudgingly as they cannot reconcile your female status with a success at business."

"Do I ever know that! My first manager made life so miserable I finally had to let him go. The people working for me now are all that I could wish for and they make it so much easier to do the things that I must do."

"I have some funds to spare, if you decide to go ahead with the railroad out of New Berne and need a partner."

"Wonderful. I will keep that in mind and let father know of your interest."

"Good."

They both fell silent, lost in their own thoughts. The rhythmic click clack as the train ran over junctures in the rails filled the silence. After perhaps fifteen minutes, Ryan reached for Cissy's hand. "I don't regret kissing you. I hope you don't either. It is early for me to get involved with a woman. I don't even know if I am capable. I just know I have always been attracted to you. I don't think you are indifferent to me either. If your family has been willing to accept Brandon as a potential suitor, do you think they would object to me?"

Cissy bit her lip while she pondered how to answer. Finally she blurted, "If you are messing around with Lizzie I am not interested."

Ryan was momentarily taken aback. "I'm not sure where you got that idea, but I assure you she is the very last woman I would ever want. So, please don't worry about that."

"I'm sorry. It's just that she has been spreading the word that you are hers.'

"I never have been and never will be. During the war, I flirted with her briefly but it never amounted to anything. After Penny was lost at sea, she tried again to entice me, but I wanted nothing to do with her. Thank God, since Penny was found not long after. She is a malicious, desperate woman who will stop at little to get her way." Ryan could not help remembering the night he had found her naked in his bed. While he had been tempted by the idea of momentary comfort, he could not go through with it. Lizzie had been furious with him that her seduction had failed and the vicious tirade that followed convinced him that rejecting her was one of the brighter things he had ever done.

"That still doesn't answer my question. I remember how furious Penny's father was when she married me. He eventually came around which is a good thing as Penny's brother went on to marry my sister. He's got a double dose of Yankee in-laws. I don't know how your father feels, but I'm sure that matters to you as it did Penny. Of course, if you are not interested in me, that's another matter."

"When you kissed me, I was thrilled and remember I kissed back. I think that answers the question as to whether or not I am attracted to you. I don't think Evangeline will be a problem as she is so grateful to you. Father is grateful, too, but not as willing to overlook past allegiances, I fear. He seemed to really like you at supper, so who knows." Ryan sensed her uncertainty when again Cissy bit her lip, "I confess I have always been attracted to you even when you aggravated me."

"I may still aggravate you from time to time, but I'll try to watch it." Ryan smiled and squeezed her hand, "I need to go slow, but I agree with my boy. If we don't toss our hats into the ring, someone else is going to snap you up."

"I haven't been very *snap-able* for a long time, so you don't have much to worry about." Cissy pulled a wry face when she said it.

"What about Brandon Sullivan? He seemed to think he had some claim to your affection. He was more than a little jealous when he saw we were together that day at dinner. A blind man could have felt him bristling."

"I like him and I was attracted to him. There was a time I encouraged his attention and considered him as a possible suitor. When I was in Wilmington, I ran into him by accident. He would still like to pursue me and I was considering it. Mainly, I suppose it was because I couldn't have---the one I really wanted." Had she had almost said 'you' he wondered.

"I hope you are over this man, then." Ryan grimaced, "I suppose you are referring to your fiancé?"

"Logan? No, sad to say he was always like a brother to me. I suspect he finally realized I could not return his love the way he wanted. We grew up together and he was my best friend for years. Logan is a good man and I still treasure him as a friend. He's living in California now and married to a woman he loves. The last letter I received from Logan said they are expecting their first child. I'm truly happy for him."

"So not Logan? Hmm. Could it be me?" Ryan teased. He wanted it to be true and secretly feared it might. His arms still ached for the wife he would never hold again and the daughter he had lost. He wasn't sure he could love this woman the way she deserved...and knowing Cissy, the way she would demand. Her head was down so he could not read her face. Silently he awaited her reply and dared to hope that there might be a new life for him someday.

Cissy looked up at him, her eyes dancing, "We'll have to see, won't we?"

Ryan chuckled, "You are the coy one. But, yes, we will see."

Ryan was lost in thought for the next few miles before he said, "You have made a life in the world of business despite societal expectations that you would have long ago married and confined yourself to the pleasures of marital life and motherhood. That doesn't mean that someday you cannot have both."

"How many men would tolerate that do you suppose? I certainly haven't met many. That was one of the reasons I did not become more involved with Brandon several years ago. He could not understand why I would want to work in a man's world."

Ryan met her eyes. His voice was soft when he asked, "What was it that made you so determined to defy society's expectations of you?"

"That's a long story."

"We have a long ride."

At first he did not think she would respond. He watched her fidget: fingering the lace on her dress, adjusting her bonnet, and shifting away from him in the seat. With a heavy sigh she turned back to face him.

When Cissy had finished describing her childhood, Ryan was careful to disguise his shock. Hearing her mother had rejected her gave him needed insight into why she had chosen to spy and then run her father's business. Even more than her feelings of unworthiness engendered by an unloving mother, he suspected much of her determination to succeed was due to her own intelligence and independent personality. "Thank you for sharing, Cissy. I just hope you now realize your mother's inadequacies had nothing to do with you, only her. Everyone that I know greatly admires you for who you are as a person above and beyond your father's success and your own."

"It means a lot to me to hear you say that." Cissy looked out the window as the train passed over a trestle. Speaking of her childhood had resurrected old ghost and old hurts that she obviously disliked remembering. They were in the Dover Swamp and would be in New Berne before too much longer and there was still something about her that nagged at him. Before they left the train he planned to satisfy that lingering question.

Lost in thought, Ryan and she road on for another thirty

minutes. Breaking the silence, Ryan carefully inquired if the abduction by Marcel Lambert had affected the way she felt about men. He strongly suspected the man had raped her before Logan Gwaltney tracked them down and shot him. Perhaps that would help explain why she had not allowed a man into her life.

Cissy was surprised that he had asked and wondered how much he knew about that awful time. She chewed her lip for a moment before answering. "Fortunately Logan arrived in time to prevent him violating me. Lambert was evil through and through. I'm just glad Logan shot him and left him to roast in hell. I am not so foolish as to judge all men by him." She felt better for telling him, but she did not want to dwell on the old pain any longer. As though he sensed how she felt, Ryan was at his most amusing for the remainder of the trip. The pulled into the station laughing and a little disappointed the time together had ended.

*****

In San Francisco, a doggedly determined detective was sewing up his case. The break had come when a filing clerk bustled into his office waving a piece of paper.

"I just found this, Mr. Sullivan. Someone stuck it in the wrong file. I found it purely by accident and thought you ought to have a look. It is about that Lambert fellow you were investigating and the body we found. Seems this dead fellow was the man's valet and said he feared for his life. Seems he was poking Mrs. Lambert and her husband found out."

Impatient at the clerk's gloating, Sullivan snapped, "Hand it here and stop yammering about something I need to read for myself."

The man beat a hasty retreat while Sullivan sat fingering the note. He read it twice before digging out Lambert's folder. He added the valet's note to the sworn statement of a man who had at last come forward. The witness testified he had seen Marcel Lambert stumble out of the bar with the Frenchman who had turned up dead the next morning. He now had the final evidence needed to reopen the case. He left his office determined to arrest Marcel Lambert. At the Lambert house, the valet was quick to say that the family was still in France. Not knowing where else to turn, he walked to the Woodward mansion. Surely Mrs. Lambert's family would have some idea of when they would be returning. There he found the entry draped in mourning. A somber butler opened the door to his persistent hammering of the ornate silver knocker.

"Please, sir. Mr. Woodward is out finalizing some business and Mrs. Woodward is resting. They have had a terrible shock."

"My apologies. I noticed the black draped at the door. Did someone in the family die?"

"Their daughter's husband had a heart attack. They just received a telegram telling them the news of his death."

Sullivan stood stunned in the open doorway, oblivious to the man's desire to close it. He shook his head and smiled at the man, "They say the Lord moves in mysterious ways."

It was the butler's turn to look stunned, "What was that, sir?"

"Never mind." Sullivan just shook his head.

"Should I say who was calling, sir?"

"No need. I don't think that will be necessary now."

"Very good, sir." The man watched the detective walk away, puzzled as to why he had come and then left without stating his business. Shrugging, he quietly close the door and headed back into the dark and silent house. He and the other servants had never liked the arrogant Frenchman and were not mourning his death. He was going to the basement and for another glass of wine with the rest of the staff. While it might not be an open celebration, it was far from a wake. He was whistling as he went down the steps.

Chapter 24

It was an achingly beautiful spring morning, the kind that made Cissy twirl with giddy delight in her bedroom. Flowers were blooming, Cardinals darted among the tender new leaves on the trees, and the breeze from her window blew softly against her batiste nightgown. Walking to her wardrobe, she withdrew one of her more attractive dresses, a floral sprigged muslin trimmed with yards of dainty lace. Tossing things willy-nilly she unearthed the matching parasol from the bottom of the armoire. Cissy dressed with greater care than usual and paused for a final inspection before the full-length mirror. Satisfied that she looked pretty and fresh, she grabbed her bonnet and descended to the kitchen. While her breakfast was prepared, she had the two women working to produce a savory picnic luncheon. As they packed the basket, Cissy explored the wine that her father had left in the house.

After weeks of desultory courtship on Ryan's part, Cissy had decided to take matters into her own hands. They had not talked of anything intimate since the return from Wilmington nor had he done more than take her hand. There had been none of the kisses that turned her to molten desire, no smoldering looks, nothing to suggest the conversation on the train had taken place. Twisting her mouth to one side she pondered if part of the blame could be hers. She had been aloof, waiting for him to take the lead. Certainly, he had not left her for more than a day or two without a visit. Often he came at lunch and they would walk to the Gaston House hotel for a midday meal. Today she would take the initiative by walking to his office with a picnic. A few blocks walk would bring them to the gardens that still bloomed around the ruins of the colonial palace built by the British governor, Tryon. It was perfect for the tryst that she envisioned. Closing her eyes she could picture the shade from the trees dappling the blanket with sunlight and shadows while around them flowers perfumed the air. If that did not inspire a little romance, she didn't know what would.

Smiling her thanks to the servants, Cissy bustled out the door with her basket. She did not see the knowing smiles the women sent her way. She did not hear their chuckles. At the office, it was all she could do to concentrate on business while the hands of the clock on the wall slowly crawled their way towards noon. At a quarter of twelve, she tied on her bonnet, grabbed her parasol, and draped the basket over her arm. She was going to surprise Ryan at his office.

Swinging the door open she backed out to carefully maneuver her open parasol through the door. Turning around she bumped into Ryan who was grinning at her with a foolish expression on his face. On his arm was a basket similar to the one she carried. "Well, Cissy, it seems the siren song of springtime has lured your thoughts into a similar vein to my own. I think with whatever you have in that basket and what I have in this one, we should have quite enough to satisfy our appetites."

Cissy laughed, "Speak for yourself. I feel very hungry."

"My appetite is improving by the minute. So, where are we off to then?"

"The old palace grounds are lovely this time of the year even if a bit overgrown. I thought it would be nice to walk there."

"Hand me your basket so you can keep that parasol in place."

Ryan grunted when she handed it over. "Good grief, this thing is heavy."

"It's the wine. I couldn't decide what to bring so I brought two."

"There goes any work this afternoon." Ryan bowed, "Lead the way, my dear."

They found a shaded bower among Camellias that had a few late blooms clinging to the branches. With a view of the river where birds wheeled above the ripples waiting for their next meal swimming in the sparkling depths, Ryan and Cissy opened the blanket and then began to spread their respective feasts. Long before they had finished they were laughing at the bounty provided by their housekeepers. Cissy shook her head in amazement.

Looking at the spread, Ryan laughed, "With your two bottles of wine and the One I brought, we are in danger of becoming so heavy with food and dulled by wine, we will have to spend the rest of the day here before we will be able to stagger away."

"What a terrible fate," Cissy teased.

"I can think of worst fates than spending a day with you in a beautiful spot." Ryan leaned over and kissed her gently on the lips. "Now before I am more drunk by your beauty than wine, let's enjoy the rest of this picnic before the ants find us."

For the first time in years, Cissy felt a total peace overwhelm her. She had worked so hard for so long that she had forgotten what it felt like to simply give herself over to the pleasure of the moment. She watched Ryan tearing into a piece of fried chicken, obviously relishing every bite. His face was the most relaxed that she had seen in the months since Penny's death. As they talked and ate, he frequently reached over to touch her hand and shoulder. The lingering caresses had her hungry for more than the picnic food. She knew she was indulging in far more wine than she should, but she did not care. The day was too perfect to allow past inhibitions and insecurities to rule her. She realized with perfect clarity that this was the man she had always wanted and waited for, never allowing anyone else to breech the wall she had surrounded herself with. Her decision made, she leaned across the items spread between them and took his face between her hands.

"I want you to love me, here and now, Ryan. I want to know what it is like to be with a man that I desire and hopefully desires me."

Ryan took her hands in his and slowly lowered them from his face to his chest, never letting them leave his grasp. "Cissy, I think I have wanted you from the first minute I laid eyes on your sassy, beautiful face. I want you now so much that I tremble from restraining myself. I want you in every way a man can want a woman. I want to make you mine, body and soul, and I want to know when I do that we are both free of the ghosts of the past. I cannot take you here in this little paradise and spoil a moment that should be sanctioned by all that is holy and good in both of us. When I make love to you for the first time, it will be with love and the promise of a lifetime in my arms and in my heart."

Cissy looked down at the blanket now scattered with crumbs from their feast. Embarrassed by her blatant offer and his rejection, she could not look up. She did not see him silently rise and walk around to her. Pulling her to her feet, he drew her into the circle of his arms. "Look at me, Cissy."

Slowly she raised her chin and looked into the blue of his eyes, thinking she had never seen anything more compelling. He continued staring into her eyes as he slowly tightened his arms around her and pulled her closer. His lips met hers and she could feel his hunger for her, his desire obvious even through the layers of their clothing. She was panting with need when he released her lips. He too struggled to regain his wits. She could see in that moment he needed and wanted her with a desperation that might even exceed her own.

"My own sweet girl. You are a treasure and I am so grateful you are in my life. Be patient with me. I still have a few demons to banish before I can offer you all you deserve." Ryan grimaced, "I am a fool not to seduce you this very moment when I want you so badly."

"It's alright, Ryan. Just know when you are ready, I will be waiting." Cissy smoothed her hair into place and pulled her bonnet on her head, quickly tying the ribbons.

Recognizing the clues, Ryan began returning items to the baskets. Together they gathered the blanket and folded it. Ryan pushed it into his basket on top of the residue of the picnic. He stopped her when she leaned over to pick up her basket and pulled her into his arms. Gazing into her eyes, he slowly claimed her lips in a gentle kiss. "I suppose we should return to work before it's time to close up and go home. Despite the fact I would much rather linger here with you, I have an appointment with a client at four o'clock."

"I need to go as well. I have a manifest to review before I leave tonight."

As they walked neither felt very conversational. Whatever they wanted to say was too weighty to bring up in the time remaining and the timing was wrong for both of them. Ryan glanced up Metcalf Street at the intersection with Pollock. Not far from the corner he saw Lizzie sauntering along toward Pollock. Taking Cissy by the elbow, he increased his pace to prevent the pesky woman from catching up to them. They stopped at his office and conscious of proprieties, squeezed hands goodbye rather than the kiss they would have liked.

Lizzie, watching the way they leaned towards one another, seethed with anger. She had waited far too long for Ryan Madison to allow that spoiled and privileged woman to have him. Pausing to look into a shop window, in the reflection she saw Ryan entering his office door as Cissy walked away. Smirking, she stalked after her. She would take care of that bitch.

Cissy had just seated herself at her desk and picked up a manifest when the office door banged against the wall. Lizzie barged in followed by an anxious Dugald.

"I apologize, Miss LaRoque, but she stormed past me."

"It's not a problem, Dugald. I will deal with Miss Berkeley. Please close the door." Cissy turned to Lizzie and nodded at the seat in front of her desk. "Sit down Lizzie and tell me why you have barged in here uninvited."

"You think you are so grand with your fine airs. If your daddy had not been rich you would be a nobody." Lizzie flounced over and sat in the indicated chair.

"Shall we cast aside the aspersions for the moment and hear why you think it necessary to call on me so precipitously?"

"Hoity-toity aren't we?" Lizzie smirked. "You are nothing but an old maid who knows nothing about pleasing a man."

"And that's why you are here---to instruct me?" Cissy scoffed. "As for being an old maid, I would be careful not to paint me with that brush, Lizzie. After all, we are the same age and you are just as much a spinster as I."

"That's where you are wrong. I may not have married, but I know what a man wants and how to keep him happy."

"So why should I care?"

"Miss 'High and Mighty' LaRoque do you really think Ryan Madison is going to fall for you? I have been his mistress for years. We were together before he married Penny and he never stopped seeing me. He likes what I give him and it's me he is going to marry."

"Lizzie you are so pathetically transparent. You must have seen us together and you are here out of jealousy and spite. Ryan would never stoop to consort with the likes of you. Now, if you have finished with what you came here to accomplish, get out before I have you thrown out."

Lizzie jumped up and whirled around. Grabbing the doorknob, she cast one parting shot, "Leave him alone. He's mine."

Cissy winced as the door slammed with a bang. Dugald poked his head in shortly after, "Are you alright?"

"I'm fine, but if she comes here again, stop her and I don't care how you do it. Just throw her out on her vulgar derriere."

"Now that I will do with pleasure." Dugald shook his head, "It amazes me how one woman can be so nasty. She's a fine looking woman and some man should have tamed her by now."

"Dugald, if you are that courageous and that foolish, please do."

"Whoa, Missy. I'm not about to take on that set of problems."

Cissy stood and put her hands on the desk, "I need to simmer down. I think I'm going to take a walk. Would you mind going over this last manifest for me before we leave?"

"Sure, not to worry about a thing, Miss."

Cissy walked to Union Point and sat on a bench staring out at the distant shore. She hated to admit it even to herself, but Lizzie had rattled her. In truth, she didn't know what to do to please a man. Most women her age were long married and mothers many times over. Yet the only world she knew was a man's world, shipping and commerce. She wondered how long it had been since she had flirted and sought men's eyes. Even Ryan had rejected her obvious overtures, no matter how nicely. Her old insecurities threatened at the edge of her consciousness. Firmly she pushed them away and shrugged her shoulders. Dugald should be finished and waiting by now. Stiffening her spine, she walked to the waiting carriage.

She said little on the ride home. Sensing her mood, Dugald left her alone after a few abortive attempts at conversation. When she climbed from the carriage, he handed her the picnic basket.

"Thank you, Dugald. And please, forgive my moodiness."

"If there is anything I can do, you tell me. You know we would all fight bears for you."

Cissy smiled, "I know. I appreciate it, too."

It wasn't so much that she credited Lizzie's tall tales with any credence as it was her own trepidations that caused her to be out of the office at the time that Ryan usually stopped by. After a week of avoiding him, Cissy despised her own cowardliness, still she was unwilling to face him remembering his rejection of her overtures and Lizzie's gloating.

Tired of calling at her office only to find her gone, Ryan refused to be put off any longer. He had stopped in at noon to see if she would have dinner with him at the Gaston House only to be told that she was not in the office. This had gone on for far too long and he could only surmise that she was avoiding him. A certain amount of panic accompanied that realization. She meant far too much for him to allow her to continue to elude his company. Ryan fretted all afternoon in his office. Pondering why he was so distressed, he walked over to his office window and stared out at the street. He had accomplished nothing all afternoon. He could not go on this way. His law practice was suffering for his inattention, and the cold sweat on his brow when he thought of losing Cissy was telling him more. He had fallen in love with her far beyond the initial attraction and the enjoyment of her personality. He realized that he wanted her, not just for her beauty, but for the zest she added to his life. She was like the sun and without her there were only dark shadows and gloom. Penny would always be a beautiful memory of the love, children, and pain they had shared. His wife would have wanted him to find love again and to find a mother for their son. But, it wasn't for that reason alone that he wanted Cissy. He wanted her because he accepted that he needed her like oxygen to breathe. He truly loved her. Glancing at the clock on the far wall, he noted that he had just enough time for a critical errand.

Ryan dashed from his office. His staff would lock up for him and he had no time to linger. Almost running, he reached his destination and procured what he needed. Claiming his horse and buggy, he drove home where his son was eagerly awaiting his return after a day spent with Caroline Framingham who was doing her best to make up for the mother he still missed. Leaving his buggy with orders that it be left out, he swung Rye into his arms and gave him a hug.

"Son, despite your tender years, you may be the smartest man in the world and I am taking your advice. As soon as we finish supper I am going calling on Miss Cissy and if she will have me, I intend to marry her."

"It's about time. I had planned to go see her tomorrow and ask her myself, as I had about given up on you." Rye shook his head, "I hope she says yes to you. If she doesn't, would you mind if I court her myself."

Ryan laughed, "That's a deal, son."

He tasted nothing of his meal so intent was he on the hours ahead. Kissing his son on the forehead, he promised, "I'll be back soon."

Cissy had just finished her own supper when she heard the knock at her front door. Not expecting anyone to call, she smoothed her hair into place and walked to the front foyer. Through the frosted glass of the door she could discern the shadowed form of a man. Aware of continued problems in the area, she was momentarily shaken.

"Who is it?" she called.

"It's me, Cissy. Ryan. May I come in?"

A tremulous smile crossed her face. It was unlike him to call at her home at night due to their mutual awareness of the proprieties. But such niceties be damned, she was thrilled he had come. She had missed him to the point of desperation, even if the absence had been her own doing.

Forcing herself to a dispassionate expression and a calmness she did not feel, she opened the door to him. "Come in, Ryan."

Ryan stepped into the foyer and swept her into his arms. When the kiss ended, he dropped to one knee and took her hand in his. Looking down, Cissy saw that he held a ring in his other hand and she began to tremble.

"I love you. I beg you to do me the honor of becoming my wife. I cannot go on without you."

Pulling Ryan to his feet, Cissy hugged him. "Oh, Ryan. I love you, too. I have for so long. Yes, I will marry you."

"Does that mean you will stop avoiding me, too?" Ryan asked with a twinkle in his eye.

"I guess I will have to when we are married." Cissy laughed, "Now kiss me again, please."

About the Author

Betty J. Vaughn, former department chair and art teacher at Enloe Magnet High School in Raleigh, NC, launched a career as an author after leaving the classroom. She is the 2013 winner of the award for historical fiction from the North Carolina Society of Historians for her book ***Run, Cissy, Run***. Previously her books ***The Man in the Chimney*** and ***Turbulent Waters*** won the awards for 2011 and 2012 respectively. ***The Intrepid Miss LaRoque*** is the fourth book in the series. The novel ***Yesterday's Magnolia*** is not part of the historical fiction series.

In honoring her books, in a unanimous decision, the judges commented: "It is gratifying to find an astute historian whose skills far exceed that realm; someone who can take facts and weave them together with fiction and end up with a story that actually could have happened...[It is] a wonderful story full of emotion, unexpected twists and turns, close calls and tragic moments...Mrs. Vaughn can consider herself a seasoned novelist...[Her books] are fast paced, action packed, and full of adventure...Her work simply isn't just a flurry of words, dry, and boring...She is a master of literary technique as she weaves together her tapestry of words."

A prize winning visual artist with paintings in collections worldwide, Mrs. Vaughn designed the magnet art program at Enloe where her students consistently won top honors. The recipient of a three year Federal Grant to the Wake County School System, she led Enloe Enterprises, Inc. in operating an art gallery, a summer arts camp, and an Emmy award winning television production company. As a result of the Enterprises Enloe was selected as one of the ten best art schools in the nation by Business Week Magazine. She wrote and published a monthly newsletter for the Enterprises and is the author of numerous professional articles.

She loves to travel and led study tours of Europe for many years. History, art, and books are a lifelong passion. Both as a teacher of advanced placement art history and as a writer, Mrs. Vaughn brings the story of the past alive through the people who lived it.

"Vaughn's first book, MUDDY WATERS, was reviewed by our panel and selected as an award-winner in 2011. We reunited with memorable characters and were introduced to new ones as the saga continues in TURBULENT WATERS. The characters in this novel become real to the reader. We became swept up in the novel and didn't want to put it down until we had finished reading it. Vaughn captured the essence of the difficult reconstruction period. So smoothly did she work 'history' into the story, that we were taken aback at times when we realized the book was a series of 19th century life's lessons.

Vaughn can consider herself a seasoned novelist! Her work simply isn't just a flurry of words, dry and boring. She is a master of literary technique as she weaves together her tapestry of words to develop a picture that is complete, yet can be added to in the future. Each volume is self-sufficient but leaves the reader wanting more, hoping for more...and this volume is no different from the first in that respect.

This novel earns the 2012 Historical Fiction Award due to the unanimous decision of our panel."

--The North Carolina Society of Historians

Other Titles by Betty j. Vaughn

Title: *Yesterday's Magnolia*
- Paperback: 350 pages
- Language: English
- Hard Cover Book ISBN: 9781590955543
- Paper Back Book ISBN: 9781590955550
- eBook / ePub: ISBN: 9781590955567

Jo envies Margo and Maurice for their ready charm, looks, wealth, glamour, and exciting lives never realizing that it is she who is envied for a life that contains the things that they themselves long for and have not attained.

"It's a shame to have so damned much and yet so little." An eastern North Carolina farmer's daughter, Margot, streaks like a comet into the life style of the rich and famous. Her beauty and exuberant, zestful personality gain her entrance to boardrooms, the White House, a corporate jet stocked with Cristal champagne and caviar, a villa in Italy, and marriage to one of the world's most powerful men. Maurice, the spurned suitor, seeks friendship and comfort from Margot's sister, Jo, a quiet, bookish art history teacher. Jo envies them both for their ready charm, looks, wealth, glamour, and exciting lives never realizing that it is she who is envied for a life that contains the things that they themselves have not attained. Like the comets they so resemble both Margot and Maurice are consumed by the friction of life, leaving Jo to remember the magic moments they brought to a more conventional path.

Title: *Run Cissy Run*
- Paperback: 304 pages
- Language: English
- Hard Cover Book ISBN: 9781590956748
- Paper Back Book ISBN: 9781590956755
- eBook / ePub: ISBN: 9781590956762

You would think Cecilia LaRoque has it all: a loving father, wealth, beauty, social position and a devoted suitor. She doesn't. Crushed by a cold and critical mother who soon absconds to live with a dissolute lover, 'Cissy' struggles to prove herself worthy of love and respect. She could not have foreseen in her teenage years that the genteel and privileged life she had led would come to a crashing halt with the outbreak of Civil War, a bitter struggle that would tear her world apart. Despite the hardships and inherent danger, she seizes the opportunity to forge an unorthodox role for herself as a spy.

Title: *Turbulent Waters*
- Paperback: 328 pages
- Language: English
- Hard Cover Book ISBN: 9781590951743
- Paper Back Book ISBN: 9781590951750
- eBook / ePub: ISBN: 9781590951767

LOVE IS PERSONAL, WAR IS NOT, especially in North Carolina, 1865-1867, during the reconstruction. With a love they are certain will transcend all else, southern belle Penny Kennedy marries Union Officer and attorney, Ryan Madison, despite the condemnation of those around them. The initial days of wedded bliss end abruptly when Marcus, the man who courted Penny for years in anticipation that she would marry him, is arrested for murder, and Ryan is assigned to prosecute him. As hard as this development is to tolerate for Penny, she will discover worse things await her before Ryan and she can attain the life they desire.

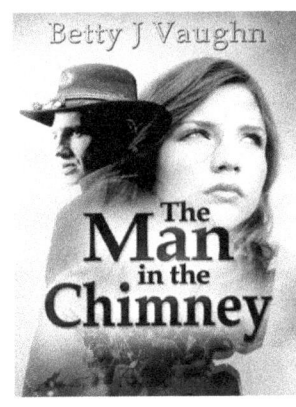

Title: *The Man In The Chimney*
- Paperback: 352 pages
- Language: English
- Hard Cover Book ISBN: 9781590956021
- Paper Back Book ISBN: 9781590956038
- eBook / ePub: ISBN: 9781590956045

The War Between the States has come to eastern North Carolina, bringing hardships, pillaging, and fear to the local residents. For those left at home, the struggle to procure the needs of daily life is all-consuming; for those serving in the armies of both North and South, death is a daily companion. Against this backdrop, an unlikely and forbidden love affair between a local woman and a Union officer leads to difficult choices for them both—choices that will tear them apart and force them to deal with the abandonment of their dream of a life together.

Despite broken hearts, misunderstandings, and missed chances, Penny and Ryan strive to survive the dangers and ravages of war and make the best of their separate futures. With the surrender of the South at Appomattox, Penny realizes she has one last chance to either find the man she loves or settle for a life alone.

Lightning Source UK Ltd.
Milton Keynes UK
UKHW042115180620
365226UK00003B/209/J